A Separate Reality

A SEPARATE REALITY

Robert Marshall

CARROLL & GRAF PUBLISHERS
NEW YORK

A SEPARATE REALITY

Carroll & Graf Publishers
An Imprint of Avalon Publishing Group, Inc.
245 West 17th Street, 11th floor
New York, NY 10011

AVALON
publishing group incorporated

Library of Congress Cataloging-in-Publication Data is available.

ISBN-13: 978-0-78671-715-6
ISBN-10: 0-7867-1715-7

9 8 7 6 5 4 3 2 1

Interior design by Maria Elias
Printed in the United States of America
Distributed by Publishers Group West

To my parents

"One can't exaggerate the significance of what Castaneda has done . . ."

I
A Separate Reality

I woke not long ago to find myself on a mattress in the East Village next to a boy who was probably much too young for me. Uncertain how long I'd been asleep, I began to lick his neck, knowing I might never see him again. Still, he had lovely skin. While my tongue traveled slowly down his side, he began to tell me about himself. I always like this Arabian Nights part. Through the open window, traffic and shouting from the summer street. He'd grown up on Long Island; he was going to study fashion in the fall. He believed, he said, in reincarnation. My tongue circled his nipple. Wondering if we had anything in common, I touched his wrist; I knew the affection I felt might be temporary and could vanish, easily, in the next day's light. I licked and took in the candlelit room. Clothes on the floor, an empty birdcage, some fashion magazines. A mirror. A bookshelf. I looked, curious to see who I was with: *The Art of Happiness. The Barbie Chronicles. The Complete Poems of Cavafy.* I can't tell much from this, I thought—the usual odd combination. Then I noticed, on the top shelf, by itself: *A Separate Reality.*

Weird, someone his age reading Carlos Castaneda. The don Juan books: I'd thought they were a seventies thing.

Castaneda, an anthropologist from UCLA (supposedly), wandered through the desert in Mexico with his mentor don Juan, an old Yaqui Indian who, in their endless conversations, taught Carlos all sorts of mysterious stuff. They had talked to coyotes and flown over canyons, and Carlos had learned how to *see*.

"Have you read it?" I asked, pointing to *A Separate Reality*.

"Castaneda?" he replied. "I only found that recently. He's really interesting."

Although it had been twenty years since I'd read the don Juan books, they still made me a little uneasy. Intrigued, I looked some more: *The Secret of the Golden Flower*. In seventh grade, my teacher, Anna Voigt, had told me I wasn't yet ready to read it. Maybe I would be in several years.

Another lost world, I thought, looking at the boy, his pale back's curve. He'd raised himself on his elbows and his face had come alive; he was beginning to find me interesting.

". . . A transformation of consciousness to this other level," he was saying earnestly. "Where you give up the idea of the individual self. Which isn't real anyway. That's transcendence."

I thought of Anna standing in the sunlight under the white archway of Loloma School.

"You know what I mean?" he asked.

"I think I do," I said, trying to sound affectionate, hiding my disappointment.

"So you've read those books?" he continued.

The candles flickered. Waves of light crossed the wall. Maybe, I thought, I should try to explain about Castaneda. But he'll never understand. That's because I don't. And maybe those books didn't have that much to do with what had happened, for a while, to my mind.

I ran my hand through his dark hair. Bird wrists, pale skin, coal eyes. He looks *sensitive*, I told myself, wishing I lived in a world of perfect surfaces. The Buddha smiled from a postcard on the wall. I could almost smell the mown grass of Loloma School and the dry Phoenix air. Smells remain, I thought, but what about ideas?

"No," I said. "I haven't read Castaneda."

"You should," he said emphatically, and then added, in a more considerate voice, "when you're *ready* to. Things come into your life when you're ready."

"Yeah," I said, annoyed at his condescension—and my own. Why, I wondered, do I lie about unimportant things? "Maybe," I added, "I'm not ready."

I walked home at four A.M. A dog barked; I could smell the ailanthus. On Ninth Street an old woman looked through the trash. My mind wandered. Don Juan was a sorcerer, Carlos, his apprentice. He taught him the secrets of the invisible world, I explained to someone in my head. He taught him *not-doing;* a sort of spiritual mélange. At first he was taken seriously. How odd, I thought, that I remember this. The stores were shuttered. Pieces of a bottle glimmered in the streetlight—shattered bits of stained glass. Beautiful. Red and yellow lights. A woman stumbled past, disappearing like a phantom. I won't care about the boy tomorrow, I told myself. The dark, orange, starless sky; the warm night air. The feel of the air the same in different places; the feel of the mind the same. Can't get away from it. I stopped to buy the paper. Melons shone in the Korean deli's light.

Almost dawn.

The next day I wished I'd slept. At the flea market I thought about the boy—and don Juan. In the evening I considered calling. But he'll probably blow me off, I told myself, while I made tea. I'm not really interested in him and he was bored with me. I blew on the tea and picked up a novel I thought I ought to read. I soon put it down. Years ago I'd been able to get through anything. No longer. I still bought books but rarely finished them. What had happened to my mind? Putting the tea down on the book, I took *Hejira* out of the CD player and put in Sarah Vaughan.

I looked for a moment at the lights of Seventh Avenue and then sat back down. I didn't know what to do with myself: an old feeling. I decided to call my friend Eric; he was the kind of person who would know about Castaneda.

"What I remember," he remarked, "is those books never had any author photos. Which I guess is because Castaneda didn't exist."

"Oh no," I responded, confident of the expertise I'd acquired when I was twelve, "it's don Juan who was supposed to not exist." But then I started to wonder about the possibility of this greater fiction.

A few days later I went into a bookstore and briefly pretended to look through a display of new memoirs. I want to go into the past, too, I thought. But it doesn't exist; it's not a place one can *go*. No shit, Sherlock; you'll never get it right.

I came to the children's section. They were doing inventory. I saw, down one of the well-lit aisles, sitting on the floor, surrounded by a picnic of books, a mother and son. The boy knelt engrossed in *The Wizard of Oz*. His mother's hair was turning white. Passing them, and then *The Tales of King Arthur*, I remembered how my father had read this book to us, in his low, sonorous voice, so often, in the evening, before bed. I wasn't sure why I was on this quest; maybe, I thought, I should just go home. Walking by the religion section, I remembered Eric's comment and imagined the possibly nonexistent jacket photos of Castaneda. Carlos in the driveway of his LA home. Carlos, still youthful, a student at UCLA. Carlos and don Juan in the Sonoran Desert. I continued toward Occult, knowing he'd probably been exiled, years ago, from Anthropology. Maybe they wouldn't have Castaneda at all.

But there, in the corner, he was. I'd vaguely recollected that he'd written some books after *Tales of Power*. He'd written a lot after *Tales of Power:* an entire shelf. He hadn't disappeared; he'd been as prolific as L. Frank Baum. *The Eagle's Gift. The Second Ring of Power. The Power of Silence. Power* and *silence.* Those two words, again and again.

Eric had been right: no jacket photos. But there were blurbs. When I'd first read Castaneda, it had been enough for me that he was classified as nonfiction. But today's new reader had more: *The New York Times, Psychology Today,* the *Saturday Review.* "His sanity lends to even his most lurid experiences the force of data," wrote the reviewer for *Life.* "Castaneda's meeting with don Juan," Robert Hughes commented in *Time,* "now seems one of the most fortunate literary encounters since Boswell was introduced to Dr. Johnson." What would these blurb authors think if they came upon their endorsements now? I thought of a sofa commercial I'd seen on TV in which a couch's lasting appeal was contrasted with various fashion debacles from the seventies. The announcer promised, as each travesty appeared, that if you bought a Huffman Koos sofa, you would never have to ask yourself, as *Time's* reviewer might, "What was I thinking?"

What was I thinking? And how had I come across those books in the first place? Maybe through Anna—she had given me so many books. Or perhaps I had found them myself; after all, I wanted to read everything. My grandmother, Nanna, had often sent me books; when I visited her farm in Connecticut she'd read to me at night, in front of the fire, from the poems of Robert Burns and William Blake. And I always sent the poems I wrote to her. One time, the year before she died, I took down a copy of *To the Lighthouse*. Nanna told me I was too young to read it; I wouldn't be ready until high school or college. I was disappointed; this seemed a long time to wait and I didn't quite believe her. I sat down and started to read, soon realizing she was probably right.

Sometimes my father worried I spent too much time in my room with my books. He encouraged reading but thought that if I spent more time outdoors I'd have more friends. At school, some people were impressed by how many books I'd read. Others told me I thought too much.

But there was a lot of time to think. A vastness of time in which to think. I picture myself in seventh grade on the soccer field at Loloma School. The crinkly grass beneath my sneakers was worn threadbare, reminding me of the ancient rugs Anna had shown me when we went on the field trip to the Heard Museum. The Hohokams always left an error in them, she explained, something missing and incomplete so they wouldn't be in competition with the gods. Eventually their civilization just disappeared.

I would rather look at the sun than at Douggy Dale, the other fullback. I'd known him since my first morning at Loloma. We were the two far ends of the body's bell curve, me skinny, him fat, the last two chosen.

"Crush, kill, destroy," said Douggy lethargically from his side of the field.

He didn't hate me; he was on automatic. Maybe he resented that I had, that afternoon, been picked before him. There was nothing I could do about Douggy. Even Anna, who was able to bring something out of almost any kid, couldn't get far with him. She encouraged Douggy to draw different robots, but he just kept doing the same one.

Douggy wasn't my worst problem. Tim Ratter was. He hated me. He called me toothpick. Smaller than me, he had a silver tooth, stringy hair, and no friends. Now and then, Ratter would pants me, throwing my shorts in the weeds at the edge of the soccer field.

To my left, the field was lined with a row of pale palo verdes through which "American Pie" could be heard from a senior's car parked on Montecito. Behind me, the goalposts' double white crucifix. Beyond them, if I turned my head, I could see the power lines leading past South Mountain to the desert. Power lines, *lines of power,* the lines of the world. Don Juan said you could feel them in your hand, these imperceptible white fluorescent fibers crisscrossing the air. Sometimes, standing on the dead-grass field, in the heat and the afternoon glare, I felt I could.

It was, I guessed, a hundred miles to Mexico. I could follow the power lines, I could turn and start walking. I imagined the TV movie they would make, the point in the afternoon when someone would notice. I wouldn't get to see the movie, I'd die in the heat. Even don Juan's friend, don Genaro, couldn't find Ixtlan on a map.

A ball came whizzing toward me. A cloud of boys rushed in pursuit. I tried to stop it but didn't have "the gait of power." I ran like a girl.

"Get it, big guy," Dan Baltz, the blond-haired center, shouted. An affectionate sort of joke: "big guy." Dan was popular and he was nice to me—or at least decent. It was, I knew, part of the personality he'd chosen. But sometimes I wished he would ignore me the way most boys did. His "you-can-do-it" made it worse when, in a gawky display, I missed.

Douggy missed, too. Their team scored. John Friedman, who used to hide under the bleachers with me in fifth grade, rushed by without looking in my direction. John, who was not much bigger than me, had gone out for football the year before. He'd transformed himself. I hadn't. Sometimes John was still friendly—because of our parents. Dan Baltz was always friendly: no risk to him. Dan, trotting past, slapped me on the shoulder. The game again became a far-off thing.

Anna had said that in a few years Dan would be breaking hearts. She'd said that someday I, too, would break hearts, but not until I was older; she said it would happen when I was thirty—a distant, unimaginable time.

Anna was full of predictions. Some were based on revelations from her dreams. Others were intuitive, like the one about how attractive I would be when I was thirty.

After PE, I walked up to Anna's room but she wasn't there. On the way to my locker I passed the teachers' parking lot and saw her truck. She must be in a faculty meeting, I thought. Anna always complained about those faculty meetings.

Her light-green pickup. I planned to drive a pickup too, someday. I couldn't imagine what other car I would drive. I wanted to be able to think of some other car besides one just like hers, I wanted to be a *little* different, but I couldn't think of another car that would have the same magic.

The other cars, Mr. Lewis's Buick, Mrs. Binder's Ford, were just cars.

Anna's pickup had a bumper sticker: "Think Trout." Her boyfriend, Karl, a sculptor, liked to go fishing near Grand Junction. I knew my parents would never have a sticker that said "Think Trout." Ours were for the UJA and the Sierra Club, and my brother Jason had put on one for the Suns.

———

Dr. Kurtz leaned back, a bemused expression on his salt-and-pepper bearded face. On his desk, three kachina dolls, a large black notebook, a box of Kleenex, an ashtray. Above him, diplomas from Indiana University and the Menninger Institute. He and Dad were in the Charros. He was one of the best doctors in town.

We'd been sitting silently for a while. The smoke from his Marlboro curled toward the ceiling. "Maybe you should try to cut down gradually," I suggested.

"You're worried about me?" he inquired.

I nodded.

"I'm wondering why you changed the subject," he remarked.

"I thought we were *done* with that." We'd been talking about my problems with my peers. *Peers:* we'd circled like crows around the meaning of that word. Peers in what sense? I didn't want to say I was better than anyone else, but I kept getting cornered into it. Dr. Kurtz had suggested that sometimes, when I was trying to make friends, I assumed it wouldn't work in advance. The topic was complicated. I didn't think he was giving me credit for all the progress I'd made. Maybe I *had* changed the topic because I was angry at him. I didn't know what I felt.

I sat on the floor in front of the desk, worried that when the session ended I'd feel worse than when I'd come in.

I'd been seeing Dr. Kurtz for years. I'd known him longer than anyone at school; I could hardly imagine life without him. As long as I went to Dr. Kurtz there would be someone to talk to. I missed being able to talk to Nanna; she had died the year before. I still needed to talk about her. I could often depend on my mother for this, and now I could talk to Anna (about some things) but still it seemed good to have a backup. Sometimes I thought that, perhaps, I no longer needed these sessions. But I was used to them. They were easy, like putting on a seat belt.

I did worry about how much money my father spent on Dr. Kurtz—forty dollars a week—but Dad said I shouldn't worry about the money. My mother said that if I felt ready, I could quit; if not, I could go as long as I needed. I'd been making some progress on stuff with Dad. And I liked the time I got to spend alone with Mom on the way to my appointments.

I had first been sent in second grade. I kept getting in the girls' line at lunch; I told everyone that when I grew up I was going to be a girl. During recess I played troll dolls with my friend Bonnie. The teacher called my parents.

On my first afternoon at his office in the medical complex on Civic Center, Dr. Kurtz had taken me to a room at the far end of a hallway. A playroom. It was filled with dolls and toys and paper and crayons to draw with. Dr. Kurtz and a tall, younger colleague (who would disappear after the first few weeks) explained there was nothing wrong with me. I should just play. I did. They would occasionally ask what I was drawing on the large pad of paper, and I would explain the crayon family's crayon house. But mostly they sat quietly and watched.

Dr. Kurtz reminded me of Burl Ives, whose song about the old gray goose would always make me cry. His voice was comforting and deep—like Ives's.

For a few weeks we went to the room with the dolls. One afternoon a woman came and took me to a conference room; we sat at a wooden table and she showed me pictures. Dark black blots.

"It's an angel."

"It's a tree."

"It's a witch."

It was interesting. She nodded at my answers. I liked her— and tests.

Later we went to Dr. Kurtz's real office at the other end of the hall. I would sometimes wonder, years later, when I left his office, about the playroom—whether it was still used, whether it still had the dolls. One time I asked him. He suggested we have our session in there. I nodded. We walked down the hallway past his receptionist's watchful eyes. The room was just as it had been.

Dr. Kurtz always wanted me to be comfortable during our sessions. He would get down on the orange-carpeted floor, in order to be closer to me. He agreed not to smoke when he was on the floor. He'd lie there, his stomach an oversized white pillow, his bolo tie catching the atrium light.

He sat now, ruddy faced from the effort of getting up, behind his desk.

"I wasn't changing the topic," I said.

He smiled. We sat silently another minute.

"By the way," he asked, "what are you reading?"

I showed him the book. On the cover, a large moth hovered above a mountain range.

He nodded knowingly and looked at his watch.

"Time?" I asked.

"Time."

———

"You're too weak," he said. "You hurry when you should wait but you wait when you should hurry."

"How lovely are thy tabernacles, O Lord of Hosts."

"You think too much. Now you think that there is no time to waste."

"What can I do, don Juan? I'm very impatient."

"I had rather stand at the threshold of the house of God than to dwell in the tents of wickedness."

"Live like a warrior! You failed with the guardian because of your thoughts."

Mom looked and saw I wasn't reading the Union Prayer Book. She might have thought this clever. Once, when we'd belonged to our old congregation, Temple Micah, I had read *Newsweek* during one of Rabbi Horowitz's sermons. Everyone had laughed about it afterwards. My parents hated Rabbi Horowitz. He'd ruined everything Temple Micah stood for. When his contract was renewed, my parents and some other members quit; they'd started Beth Shalom and hired Rabbi Berger out of retirement. Beth Shalom hadn't taken off the way they'd hoped; I knew they felt guilty for having lured poor Rabbi Berger all the way from Fort Lauderdale to a temple that still met only every other week. Now, I thought, Mom thinks I've been disrespectful to him. Even though I was certain he couldn't have seen the book, I felt ashamed. I put Carlos on the floor under the folding chair and returned to the responsive reading.

After the service, during the Oneg Shabbat, I stood next to my parents while they talked with the Nachmanns.

"What did you think of that editorial, Nat?" Mr. Nachmann asked. He was bald and a foot taller than my father. Sometimes they played tennis together. Mr. Nachmann usually won.

"Disappointing," Dad said, taking out his pipe. "All for right to life, but what about the already born?"

I'd heard this all before; Dad liked to complain about the editorials in the *Valley Journal-Observer*. I walked over to join my sister Sharon, who was talking seriously with Dr. Wagner. My younger brother Jason stood next to them, eating sugar cubes from the silver bowl by the coffee machine. I took one and put it in my mouth. Once, at Bob's Big Boy, some tourists had been given LSD that way. They hadn't known what was happening so they'd had a bad trip.

Dr. Wagner turned to me. "How're you doing, Mark?"

"Oh, fine."

He didn't have anything to ask and I didn't have anything to say. I was arguing with myself: had I done something wrong by reading during services? I knew it didn't matter; still, it had been dumb; I'd been trying to prove something. The sugar dissolved in my mouth. Dr. Wagner asked Jason about Little League. Jason, looking down, answered quietly. I slipped out the glass doors into the dark.

———

Outside I could see the lights glimmering from the houses the other side of Lincoln Drive. Wandering away from the church that Beth Shalom rented from the Unitarians, I thought about Sharon's ideas about God. She *really* believes in the Jewish teachings. Although I like some parts of the Bible—Ecclesiastes, Micah, the Song of Songs—I don't know why the God of the Jews means so much to her. Maybe, I thought, kicking a twig down the sidewalk, she'd seen something in Youth Group. I'd tried to make him powerful in my head, the way don Juan was: it hadn't worked. I walked toward the darkness and the creosote smell. To Sharon he was wondrous. To me he'd always seemed like someone I'd grown up with, a friend of the family, an uncle perhaps. He did say some interesting things. And he had a mysterious side. But so does Mr. Nachmann. So does Dr. Wagner.

Squishing tiny skyblack fruit into the concrete, I walked slowly down a path lined with olive trees, tracing my fingers along the cool, dusty surfaces of the cars. I headed toward the empty, unpaved section of the parking lot. The light and noise of the building grew distant and the dark seemed to grow more full and alive. I felt alert in the blackness; I decided to see if I could find my place of power. At first I couldn't feel anything: my head was still too filled with thoughts. Then I began to feel something, or I thought I did, but it was as subtle as the breeze rustling the leaves of the olive trees. Still, I paid attention to it. Something led me to an acacia tree next to a chain-link fence at the desert-facing edge of the lot.

———

In the car on the way home Mom and Dad discussed how Beth Shalom could get new members.

14

"Why is Temple Micah so terrible?" Jason asked.

Jason was three years younger than me and the quietest. He liked to read *Sports Illustrated* and play in his room with his Hot Wheels, listening to Three Dog Night. He liked Simon & Garfunkel; so did I. At least, I thought, we've got one thing in common. Sometimes Mom worried he was being overshadowed, but this didn't bother me.

Why, I wondered, is he asking this? We all knew what Dad would say: because Jason was the youngest, he didn't remember how Rabbi Horowitz had taken over Temple Micah. A lot of people no one had ever seen before had shown up the night of the contract-renewal vote. He didn't remember how upset everyone had been by Rabbi Horowitz's weekends of couples counseling up in the mountains near Payson. Rabbi Horowitz had been rude and evasive when Dad and Mr. Nachmann had questioned him *very politely* about getting the board's authorization to use the van. Dad had never seen why a temple needed a van in the first place.

"Temple Micah isn't terrible," Dad said calmly (not in my head, but from the front seat). "Horowitz, on the other hand . . ."

"Is a schmuck," said Mom.

"And happens to think he's some kind of prophet," Dad added.

"Rabbis played many roles in the Talmud," Sharon replied patiently, seeming, I thought, reluctant to get into an argument. But eager, too. She'd been as upset as my parents by the Temple Micah takeover—she'd gone with them to the contract-renewal meeting—but three years had passed and she was now best friends with Beth Fineman. Every now and then Sharon went with Beth to the Temple Micah Youth Group meetings; Beth's

parents were big Horowitz supporters. It was troubling to think
everyone had their opinions just because their parents had them.
I wanted to think that if Mom and Dad weren't Democrats, I'd
still be one.

"That may have been so in the Talmud, but we're not
living in the Talmud," Dad commented.

"She wasn't saying we were," Mom said, a bit impatiently.

"I'm joking," Dad said, frustrated. I felt a little bad for
him.

"We know, honey," Mom said, backtracking.

Sharon sighed with half-reluctant drama.

"Anyway, Jason," he continued, "to answer your question,
as I was going to do *before* I was interrupted, he did things he
wasn't authorized to do. A rabbi is a teacher. But a teacher of
psychology? And if he's going to teach psychology, why gestalt?
Why not Freud or something that's been proven?"

Sharon sighed again.

"The point is, Jason, a rabbi works for the community.
That's what the van business was about. He should have gotten
our permission. Otherwise, what's the purpose of a board?"

The question hung in the car as it moved down Forty-
fourth, past the Frontier Bank's lit fountain, past the school,
past Texaco. Above, the stars were chromosomes of light. I
pressed my face against the window, trying to get back the
feeling I'd had in the parking lot. I could, somewhat.

———

*"I see both ways. When I want to look at the world I see it the way
you do. Then when I want to see it, I look at it the way I know."*
"Would I feel differently if I could see?"

"Once a man learns to see he finds himself alone in the world."

He paused for a moment and looked at me as if he wanted to judge the effect of his words.

"I am going to tell you about something that is very simple but very difficult to perform; I am going to talk to you about not-doing, in spite of the fact that there is no way to talk about it, because it is the body that does it."

I closed my notebook, but to my amazement he insisted that I should keep on writing.

"That rock over there is a rock because of doing," he said.

I felt that I was landing in a world vast beyond anything I had ever conceived.

———

It was a busy week at school. Anna told me about a dream she'd had of a river overflowing its banks. She had started to write about it. During home room, Schaeffer, the dark-haired star of the rugby team, talked about his party; he'd gotten to third base with Cheryl McCrae. We studied Mesopotamia. I kicked the ball the wrong way during soccer, helping the other team score, and felt ashamed all day. I tried to discuss this with Dr. Kurtz but we didn't get very far. He told me everyone had probably already forgotten about it. I didn't think so. Tim Ratter left me alone. My grandfather, Posha, wrote me a letter critiquing several of my poems. Some of his points were useful. Each night, before going to sleep, I read Castaneda.

"After all these years of learning you should know better. Yesterday you stopped the world and you might have even seen. A magical

being told you something and your body was capable of under-
standing it because the world had collapsed."

"What was the thing that stopped in me?"

"What stopped inside you yesterday was what people have been
telling you the world is like."

I heard Sparky barking; a car had pulled up. I had almost
finished *A Separate Reality*. My sister rapped on my door:
dinner. Although I was eager to read about Carlos's vision, I
folded the corner of the page and put it back on the shelf next
to *The Chronicles of Narnia*.

Thinking how inadequate my existence was compared with
don Juan's or Anna's, I took my mouse Lilly out of her cage.
Carlos, too, often felt inadequate. I began to apply Lilly's
medicine; she'd been sick for a while. My father had gotten
some ointment from Dr. Ziegler and shown me how to rub it
on with my finger. Dad thought Lilly looked better now. I
heard my parents open the front door and greet Mrs. Weinberg. I put Lilly back in her cage. She got on her little wheel,
and I wondered how my room looked from her point of view.
Her vision of the room was an equally valid version of reality.
Maybe more valid. She is more at the *center*, I thought, hoping
I'd remember the thought so that later I could write it down.
Remembering your best thoughts was a problem. But I had to
go to dinner.

Everyone was seated in the dining room. I greeted Mrs.
Weinberg. She'd known my parents years ago in New York; she'd
been a friend of their friends, the Epsteins. Then she'd gotten
married and moved to Indianapolis, where she'd lived until her
divorce. Now she'd come to Phoenix. Mom and Dad were
hoping she'd join Beth Shalom. Mom thought she must be

lonely living by herself; she'd been meaning to have her over for a while, but Dad kept putting it off.

I sat down next to my mother. Her dress was the same color as the sky above Squaw Peak. Dad blessed the wine and us; I felt the warmth flow from his palm. While shadows grew complete and claimed the lawn, Mrs. Weinberg updated my parents: Epstein Brothers' Construction was thriving; Andy had been accepted to Williams. They reminisced about the summer they'd met. Mom had come to New York from Madison where, at the University of Wisconsin, she'd met Dad. Mrs. Weinberg recalled how much the Epsteins had immediately liked Mom, how they'd encouraged the romance. Dad had met Dick Epstein in the army, and then they'd traveled across the country together. When they came back to New York, Dick had introduced Dad to Jack Weinberg, his old childhood friend. They'd all been so happy, Mrs. Weinberg remembered, when Dad had, at last, proposed to Mom in the cabana out at the beach club on Long Island.

I'd heard all this a million times.

"That really was an exciting year," Mrs. Weinberg remarked. "Do you remember, Nat, that time you took us to that little out-of-the-way jazz club in the Village?"

Dad nodded patiently.

"Ever pick up the saxophone anymore?" Mrs. Weinberg continued.

No, Dad said, he'd sold it years ago. He explained that there wasn't much jazz in Phoenix. But they went to the symphony once a month; Phoenix actually had a pretty good symphony. Mrs. Weinberg said they had a good one in Indianapolis, too. Dad said the one here used to be just all right, but now, with the new conductor, it stood a chance of becoming one of the best in the country.

I hadn't been to the symphony in a while. I used to go regularly. I would sit next to my parents in my blue blazer, wondering, while listening to the music, how I'd respond when, during the intermission, Dad asked which piece I'd liked most. Sometimes this was hard; I'd respond equally to different parts of the program. The distinctions weren't as clear as in rock. Often, in spite of my best efforts, I drifted into my thoughts. But even if I hadn't been listening, when Dad asked I'd reply, "I liked the Liszt, but I wasn't sure about the Mahler."

The candles flickered; I put some olives on my plate. One time, Mrs. Weinberg remarked, she'd gone to hear Vladimir Horowitz with the Epsteins. He'd been to Phoenix, too, Dad pointed out. He'd been fantastic. They'd gone backstage—they had an introduction through Posha.

Jason and Sharon and I sat silently. I ate all the olives in my salad, wondering how I might bring the conversation around to something that had more to do with me.

My mother asked Mrs. Weinberg what she'd thought about the services at Beth Shalom. Mrs. Weinberg thought Rabbi Berger had made a very interesting point about Watergate being mentioned in the Bible: Habakkuk had gone down to the water gate.

"Quite a coincidence isn't it?"

Mom and Dad agreed. I thought it was kind of dumb. Dad said he thought Nixon had two major weaknesses: Martha Mitchell and John Dean. Mrs. Weinberg thought Nixon had done one good thing: opening up China. Dad knew a lot about Mao's Long March. My boredom gave way to an older feeling; I liked the way our family seemed when we had guests; it seemed the way my father wanted it to be—and the way it really sometimes was.

Sharon said the communists had improved the lives of the peasants. Mom said she didn't think her legs would have held up too well on the Long March. I looked at her and at the centerpiece of garden flowers she'd arranged in a ceramic bowl from the House of the Spirits gallery. Outside, the olive trees and the palm fronds gestured in the wind that came to us from somewhere past the houses, from past Bell Road, from past the Gunderson Ranch, from the darkness of the silent and near and distant desert.

"So Judy, what did you think of B'nai Israel?" I heard my father asking Mrs. Weinberg. B'nai Israel, the conservative synagogue out on Thunderbird. One of the temples she'd visited.

"I must say I thought Rabbi Wagner was a very intelligent man," she replied, "but the congregation did seem rather old."

"I don't think that sort of conservatism appeals to young people today," Dad commented.

I wasn't sure if he meant to needle Sharon, or if Sharon thought he did, or if she minded. She shook her dark curls in disapproval.

"It certainly wasn't too appealing to *me*," said Mrs. Weinberg. I could tell she wanted my parents to like her.

"A lot of young people *are* embracing conservatism," Sharon commented with poise, containing her irritation. A Star of David dangled from her neck.

"I've read about that," Mrs. Weinberg said, sounding interested.

Dad raised an eyebrow. "Would you really say *a lot*?"

"I've read that, too," Mom said firmly, sounding a little tired.

Outside it was completely dark except for the stars and our patio lights. My parents, I thought, don't believe in God. They never say this directly. Instead: "Jews are more concerned with

21

what can be accomplished here and now on this earth." Dad thinks the Red Sea parting is a metaphor. I know this sometimes really bothers Sharon. And me, too. How do you know which parts of the Bible are metaphors? If you don't believe in the six days, why the one God?

Sparky barked at a passing car or the wind. Maybe it's unfair of me to think Mom and Dad are hypocritical. If they don't believe in God, it's just because they're more comfortable that way. But there were moments, I knew, when I'd sensed something else. Once we'd gone to Wickenburg and stayed at a dude ranch; Mom and I both got up early and went walking in the chaparral; light woke the desert, and I knew she felt the same thing I did, something that could not be put into words.

"And so you do think there *is* a return to more traditional values?" Mrs. Weinberg asked Sharon.

"It isn't just young people," Sharon answered in her most sincere and mature voice. She smiled, her braces glinting in the candlelight. "It's across the whole society—a need for the spiritual."

"And what do *you* think about this whole issue?" my father asked me.

A year ago I would have been eager to contribute. I still wanted to be a part of things, but I didn't know how to fit in what I had to say.

"I think there is *some* kind of spiritual need," I said carefully, "but I don't know that it's always traditional." I tried to imagine what Carlos would do if he were sitting here, the floral centerpiece and the white tablecloth in front of him, the Ben Shahn print behind.

"What about the people I love?" I asked don Juan. "What would happen to them?"

"They would all be left behind," he said.

"Could I rescue them and take them with me?"

"No. . . . Spinning with your ally will change your idea of the world," don Juan said. "That idea is everything; and when that changes, the world itself changes."

"That's interesting," Mrs. Weinberg said to me.

"I think . . ." Sharon began to respond.

"Instead of debating," my father suggested, "why don't you help your mother in the kitchen?"

Mom had made her famous *boeuf* carbonnade. Although I was, like Anna, a vegetarian, I knew how hard my mother had worked on this dish. Remembering that don Juan had taught Carlos to respect any being he ate, I thanked not God, but the cow, and dug in.

"Delicious," Mrs. Weinberg said, and it was. I sopped up the juice with my challah.

After Mrs. Weinberg left, my mother and I did the dishes. I liked having my hands in the warm water with hers. She wore her yellow plastic gloves.

"That was a good dinner," I told her, with emphasis. "The carrots turned out . . . mwah," I kissed the air and gestured as I thought a French chef would. She'd tried out a new carrot dish from one of the Sunset books.

"I'd like to have more *small* dinner parties," she remarked. "We don't do enough of that."

"It's hard with your new schedule," I said, sympathetically.

Mom had taken on more duties with Jewish Family and Children's Services.

"I don't know," she said, "maybe I could get Connie to come and help. I'll talk to her. She might want the money."

I wished I hadn't spoken; I didn't want Connie to be in the house more than she already was. Connie had been our maid for five years. She was originally from Los Angeles and lived on Alvarado, a ten-minute drive from us. She and her husband Lloyd, who worked as a guard at First Federal Savings, were, Mom said, the only black couple in their condominium complex. "I wonder what that's like for her," Mom would sometimes say. The maids we'd had before Connie had lived in South Phoenix. Mom liked Connie much more than any of them. "She's bright," Mom would say. "I think she's someone who would be capable of doing a lot if she had a chance."

So why, I wondered, did she have to vacuum while Sharon and I did our homework in the living room? Sometimes I tried to talk to her. It was odd to be in a room with a person and not talk to her. I knew Connie belonged to the Desert Calvary Baptist Church and had a sister in Los Angeles and cousins in Chicago. I knew she'd been to Hawaii twice. She didn't know how to swim, she'd once wanted to be a nurse, and she owned a terrier named Captain. It didn't take long to run out of questions on these topics. And I wasn't sure how much she wanted to talk to me. She seemed content to have the same few conversations.

Connie often brought books to read during lunch. One afternoon I noticed her reading *I'm OK—You're OK;* I wanted to talk to her about it but didn't. Once, not long after she'd started working for us, Connie had come across me in the backyard while I was reading *Uncle Tom's Cabin;* years later I still felt embarrassed. I knew Sharon was as uncomfortable as I was around Connie; we didn't talk about it with Mom and Dad. I couldn't imagine saying, "I'm uncomfortable with Connie because she's black." And if either Sharon or I made a face when Dad suggested Mom get Connie to come in for more hours, he'd say we were selfish; Mom needed the help and Connie needed the money.

I took a towel and started drying the dishes. Growing up in Omaha, Mom had said, she'd never imagined having a maid. I knew I couldn't talk to her about any of this.

"I think we did a good deed having Judy over," Mom continued. "She really is a *nice* person. It must be hard to move out here without knowing many people."

For a long time, Sharon had been the one Mom confided in most. But that was changing—because of Sharon's problems with Dad. She was always a daddy's girl, I imagined explaining to an imagined someone (who seemed to hover near the ceiling). The situation between them is really *complex*, I continued. They'd always argued; Dad had enjoyed arguing with her; he thought she was a good debater. She could, like him, become a lawyer. She could join McGrath and Greene if she decided not to be a marine biologist—if, he'd add, she *ever* got over her obsession with Jacques Cousteau. Which, I thought, she has, although Dad doesn't realize this. It bugs her when Dad teases her about that— and other things. When they argue now, they are really arguing. Then, sometimes, Mom gets in the middle. And the more that happens, I thought happily, the more I take Sharon's place.

I tried to remember the thought I'd had before dinner. What had happened to the words to the thought? In the living room Jason turned on the TV.

"So how's the magazine coming?" Mom asked. "Are you having another meeting?"

I had thought that I wanted her to ask me about the *Amethyst*.

"Oh, pretty well," I mumbled. "Maybe next weekend." I sensed she sensed I didn't want to discuss it; she seemed to know that I wanted to share—but that, at the same time, I, too, preferred safer topics: the family, the temple. I took a casserole dish from her. I knew where her body was, and where mine was, next to each other in front of the sink, under the kitchen's fluorescent light, beneath the wandering Jew that hung from the ceiling, but I didn't know about other, less certain boundaries—where the words were supposed to start and end.

Sparky yelped; Mom looked at me. My job to feed her. I went to get the Purina Chow and then carried the plastic bowl outdoors.

Sparky leapt all over me. The day before, I'd been in the car with Mom. We were driving past a long row of dying ash trees. "You know," she'd said, "sometimes I look at trees like that, and I know they're not supposed to be beautiful, but *I* think they are."

"Yes, I think they're beautiful too," I'd said.

I put Sparky's bowl down. In the darkness all the backyard trees had merged into one large mass. I'd often heard that all the different religions were expressions of one essential truth, but now I could only pretend to believe this. I looked in the sky for Cassiopeia and saw the lights of a plane heading toward Sky Harbor. The concept of *not-doing*, which don Juan tried to teach Carlos, was the same as the Tao. But to even think in this way was *doing*. What was real lay in the silence, in the darkness, somewhere behind the trees. I found Orion's belt and went indoors.

In the living room Jason lay curled in front of the football game. Richard Stansfield had mentioned a show that was on that night, *"Video Visionaries,"* which was like being on acid. Someday I was going to do acid and I wanted to know what it would be like. I thought of asking Jason how long he'd be watching, but I didn't want to get into a fight.

"A man is only the sum of his personal power, and that sum determines how he lives and how he dies."

"What is personal power?"

"Personal power is a feeling," he said. *"Or one may call it a mood. I have already told you that a warrior is a hunter of power. . . . "*

———

I sat in Anna's office, beneath a poster for the Hayden's Ferry Crafts Fair, across from a shelf filled with City Lights books. Anna's office was next to the art room. I spent a lot of time there; so did Richard Stansfield and Ian van Liere, who sat next to me on the couch. We were all on the staff of the *Amethyst,* Loloma's literary magazine. I wanted to think of them as my friends even though they were in the eleventh grade. I knew Dr. Kurtz would say they weren't my peers.

I held one of the pillows Anna's friend Nicola had made and looked out the window. On the patio, Anna was talking with Mr. Ramsay, the librarian. Richard and Ian were talking about Richard's girlfriend, Lisa. She'd graduated the year before and was living in Los Angeles. He wrote a lot of poems about her.

"God, I've gotta get a letter from her *soon,*" Richard moaned.

I fidgeted, uncomfortable with their conversation. Looking out the window, I saw Mr. Ramsay was leaving; I went outside.

Anna was sitting by the pottery wheel. A warm October day; leaves from the mulberry tree were scattered on the patio.

"What were you three cooking up in there?" she asked. I shook my head, making a humorous face.

"Look at these," she said, pointing to some drawings pinned to the wall. "Aren't they amazing?"

"They are," I said respectfully. I was a little jealous of other kids' work.

"We did them out in the wash." The desert wash, behind Loloma, where kids went to smoke and make out.

Suzy Jones, a fifth-grader, came and listened. Anna took out a cigarette.

"First they did landscapes. Then they put on blindfolds and did another. See how intuitive it is."

"They're not so right-brain," Suzy said, sincerely.

She was no longer the bratty daughter of Sharon's orthodontist. She seemed to reflect some kind of light from Anna and became someone new.

Anna's Camel smoke circled toward the sky. She brushed back her long, copper-blonde hair.

"Look," she said, pointing toward a flock of crows. "I know it's not random, the way they fly. I wish I could read it. . . ."

II
TALES OF POWER

1

Force is followed by loss of strength
This is not the way of the Tao.
That which goes against the Tao
Comes to an early end.

—Tao Te Ching

I had first met Anna a year earlier when she'd just arrived at the school. I was in her sixth-grade art class but did not stand out. I sat next to John Friedman and quietly drew my dreams.

One afternoon I overheard Allison Brown, a girl a year ahead of me, talking to Anna about a story she'd written. I had an envelope filled with poetry that I kept in my desk drawer. I'd continued to write since Nanna's death but no longer had anyone to show the poems to. Posha had asked me to send them to him. Although he tried, he didn't quite understand things the way Nanna had.

I brought a few carefully selected poems to class. That afternoon, Anna showed them to Richard, announcing excitedly that she'd discovered a poet.

"Shit," he said jestingly as he sat on Anna's couch, "we've got a prodigy." I stood in the doorway, pleased and embarrassed. After Richard left, Anna and I discussed the poems. I thought my best was "Another Time," but Anna wasn't sure. She explained different people liked different things. Sometimes, she said, artists don't know their best work. She didn't realize "Another Time" was my poem about Nanna.

One day just before the end of school, Anna joined me while I sat by myself in the cafeteria. We talked about the food. Anna had taught for one year in a public school. She said the food there was actually better. I told her my secret: I was a vegetarian. She said she was, too. We discussed our reasons. I told her (as I had often told my grandmother) that I didn't want the animals to die. Even if they weren't like us, they had feelings. They might not be as smart as we were, but that wasn't a good reason to kill them. They should be allowed to live out their natural lives. Anna told me she was a vegetarian because it felt good.

This was a new idea: that people did things because they felt good. I was used to thinking you did things because they *were* good. I was certain the sadness of the last year was about to end. An image of dawn occurred to me. I thought I might use it in a poem for Anna.

The school year ended. There wasn't too much to do during the summer (Mom always worried about this). Dad and Jason went to Indian Guides. Sharon, as usual, was the busiest; she went to debate camp at Phoenix College, she and Beth Fineman did volunteer work with senior citizens at the Jewish community center, and she also did some filing in Dad's office.

I read and worked on my poems. Sometimes I played gin rummy with Sharon or Hot Wheels with Jason.

In August we visited Posha at the farm in Connecticut. It was the first time I'd been there since Nanna's death. When we arrived, I went to look at all the familiar things that would prove I was at last in the place I had thought about so much. The parsley bed, the rusted pump by the lilac bush, the leaning fence, the hill I'd once rolled down. In the evenings we played cards in front of the fire in the living room where Nanna used to read to me. *"Tyger, Tyger, burning bright."* I remembered how Posha would listen, smoking his pipe, smiling, while she explained all the symbols. Past the lace curtains, outside on the porch, fireflies went on and off, and the garden and the fields and the woods grew dark.

During the day, Posha led us on hikes and we had long talks. Jason found Dad's old Lionel trains; he played with them, by himself, in the attic. Our cousins visited; there was a baseball game. I thought of pretending to be sick so I wouldn't have to play but decided not to. Early one evening, walking past Nanna's garden, on the road down toward the brook, my mother, noticing my wet eyes, held me. Sharon came up and touched my hand.

In the fall I started seventh grade, secretly glad to be back in school. One day, early in September, I sat with Anna by the pottery wheel on the patio. The air smelled of dust and mown grass; the leaves of a mulberry tree glazed the concrete with their shadows. Anna asked what my first impression of her had been.

"I thought you were a witch," I said. I had in mind Glinda, the good witch from the south of Oz.

She clasped her hands in delight. "Oh," she said, "you *knew.*"

She sometimes repeated that story to other people, or had me repeat it. "Tell Mr. Lewis your first impression of me. . . ."

Anna lived with Karl in a house on the West Side. They

weren't married legally, but there had been a ceremony in the desert. Everyone they knew had come. Karl was on the road a lot, but Anna rarely seemed to be alone. Friends from LA and Santa Fe came to visit, and sometimes older kids having trouble with their families stayed a few nights. Nicola, her former roommate, came over all the time.

Sometimes Anna got exhausted. She would have to drink a lot of coffee with nondairy creamer from the earthen-colored mug she'd glazed and fired in the school's kiln. I wasn't good at the wheel. I wasn't like Leslie Papadakis, a junior, whose bowls always turned out perfectly; she gave each one a dark glaze. Mine had weird shapes, but Anna still liked them. Perhaps, I thought, if I became more centered, I'd become a potter and move to Colorado.

One night toward the end of September, Anna and Karl had me over to their house by myself. Karl took me in back to the garage where he worked on his sculptures. A small corner of the garage was Anna's studio; her circular, all-white paintings hung on nails from the wall. After a few minutes I noticed they *weren't* all white. They had silhouettes of mountains—mountains she'd seen in her dreams.

"I wish I was as productive as he is," Anna laughed, pointing at Karl's welding. We went back in the house. Anna had made fish. "I hope you'll be able to eat this," she asked, remembering I was a vegetarian.

"Oh, I'll eat anything," I answered, thrilled to be in their small white house.

"We've got some woolly mammoth in the freezer," Karl joked. Anna served the fish. While we ate, Anna told me she'd been talking to Richard about starting a literary magazine for the school. Would I want to work on it?

"Oh, yes," I said, attempting to contain my excitement.

That night, before I left, I looked at their bookshelves. There weren't as many books as at our house, but each one, I sensed, was special and rare. Among them I noticed the *Tao Te Ching*. A few days later at Briscoe's I bought a copy, and the next week I borrowed *The Way of Chuang Tzu* from Anna.

For more than a year I'd thought of myself as "sort of a Baha'i." I'd discussed this with Nanna the last time I'd seen her. Sitting at the foot of her bed, while she ate breakfast from a tray, I explained that I liked their idea of bringing all the religions together. The light came in through the window of the Desert Palm Inn. I said I wasn't sure the Baha'is had enough followers. Nanna thought bringing all the religions together was a good idea; it would stop war. She didn't really follow the Jewish traditions anymore; instead she went to Quaker meeting—Quakers were more for peace, she said. Nanna was still in her nightgown; she always stayed in bed late. When she did get up, we walked to the goldfish pond. Pink and yellow snapdragons were planted around the inn's adobe buildings. I told her they were my favorite flower. The air was cool and dry; the week before Christmas. We talked about the Baha'is, the Quakers, inner light, and peace. I shared my idea: the universe was God's body. We looked at our reflections in the pond and tried to count the fish. Now, a year later, reading about Taoism, I felt I had come across a more meaningful philosophy and wished I could share it with her. Taoism had stood the test of time; it wasn't something someone had made up recently. Learn to yield—I never refused to help anyone cheat.

But when I announced to Sharon, one evening during Oneg Shabbat, that I was now a Taoist, my sister, who knew a lot about world religions, declared, "You are not a Taoist. You are *way* too contentious." Also, Sharon pointed out, while we stood eating sugar cubes, I'd mispronounced Taoism.

"It's Daoism."

"No, it's not."

She was right: I was contentious. I certainly argued with her and Dad. Sometimes I argued in class, where the teacher could protect me. And often with myself.

———

"I see," said Yen Hui, "what was standing in my way was my own self awareness. If I can begin this fasting of the heart, self-aware-ness will vanish."

"Yes," said Confucius, "that's it. If you can do this, you will be able to go among men in their world without upsetting them. You will not enter into conflict with them. If they will listen, sing them a song. If not, keep silent. . . . Just be among them, because there is nothing else for you to be but one of them."

———

Wearing my blue "Hang Ten" T-shirt, I stood holding my tray, after going through the lunch line, thinking about the states McGovern could carry. I had to decide where to sit. Baltz, Schaeffer, and Hoffman were together, Douggy alone. I hesi-tated. Schaeffer gestured to me. Surprised, I headed toward their table and put my tray down.

"I didn't mean *you*," Schaeffer said. I'd made a ridiculous mistake. John Friedman, who'd been behind me, joined us. "See Notre Dame yesterday?" Schaeffer asked. He looked like Jim Morrison—sort of.

"Yeah," said Friedman, "man, they kicked their ass."

I pretended to follow what they were saying. Then they started talking about the weekend; they'd gone tubing down the Salt River; they'd partied. What did *partying* mean? You drank and smoked pot and made out. Making out was kissing but more. I hadn't ever tubed down the Salt. Or kissed. I didn't want anyone to know. If I ever did, would I know how? Some people weren't good kissers. If someone asked whether I'd kissed, I wasn't sure what I'd say. I kissed my mother every night: that was different, but what *was* the difference? *Kissing:* the *word* was the same. There was kissing, making out, and finally fucking. Mercury, Venus, Pluto. Sometimes people fucked at parties; they always made out.

"Yeah," Baltz said, "we were frenching."

My silence, I thought, is so conspicuous. I wondered if moving to another table would make my mistake worse. I sat quietly, eating my soggy string beans. Why do I worry how I appear to them? Dr. Kurtz says not to but I do. Always with me, this worry, like my heartbeat. Sometimes I'm so aware of my heart beating. Maybe I'm having a heart attack. Mr. Rosenberg from Temple Micah had one and I thought he was going to die, but he didn't. He wasn't related to the Rosenbergs Nanna had worked for. When I was younger I thought he might be. Nanna had started the National Committee to Secure Justice for the Rosenbergs; she'd organized their rally in Union Square. She'd written a fact sheet that said one of the reasons they were convicted was because of anti-Semitism. The Jewish leaders said this wasn't true. That was when she joined the Quakers. Even though there was evidence that proved they were innocent, the Rosenbergs had still been executed. I'm not going to die now, I told myself. I'm too young to be having a heart attack.

I ate my Jell-O. They had used a Jell-O box to convict the Rosenbergs. They had a section of a box that matched the section the spy Harry Gold had. This was supposed to prove they were spies. But anyone could have part of a Jell-O box.

"Man, I'd like to get inside her pants," said Baltz.

"Yeah," said Schaeffer, adjusting his sunglasses.

I shouldn't be at this table, I thought. I wondered what I would say if someone asked why I left early on Fridays. No one ever did anymore, but they might. Dr. Kurtz had told me I didn't have to tell anyone—I could say it was personal. But I couldn't imagine that. I thought about lies I could use. Maybe I could say I was getting special tutoring. But that would seem weird, too.

I couldn't wait for the weekend. I was going to work on my poem "Sunset Symphony." The idea had come while I was taking the garbage down; I'd seen the orange and purple clouds above the olive trees—the feeling was overwhelming. You can try to capture beauty, I thought. You can come close. But you can't ever quite get it. *The Tao that can be named is not the eternal Tao.* The more you talk about it, the more you miss the point. I can sense the Tao within me. I must try to listen to it. Its emptiness will guide me if I can learn to be quiet enough. But even thinking about it is naming it.

Baltz turned toward me. "What'd ya think about that pop quiz in history?"

"It sucked," I said.

It might be OK, I told myself, to be at their table. I'd learned long ago not to push: that, I thought, is why I'm accepted. I don't argue or act too smart; I pretend to hate the day grades are given out as much as everyone else; I didn't respond when Hoffman (the most muscular kid in the class, although not the most athletic) told Mr. Lewis that poetry was for sissies. Even before learning about the Taoists, I'd been one. If I don't make too much of myself I'll survive.

I'm not sure my parents or Dr. Kurtz understand that I *am* surviving. I was right to be hesitant about sitting with Schaeffer and Baltz. My not-pushing-too-hard policy is realistic.

Schaeffer held up some sloppy joe on a fork. "It's not nice to fool Mother Nature," he said, and Baltz laughed. They were best friends. Schaeffer, I thought, used to like me more than he does now; he'd become less friendly as he got older. He was very popular, but not quite as popular as Baltz. He just wasn't as smooth. They both went to the Ocotillo Cotillion and played on the football team; Schaeffer played rugby, too. Baltz didn't, but they were both in honors band—Baltz trumpet; Schaeffer, trombone. Schaeffer's dad was a cardiologist and very right-wing. In fifth grade Schaeffer had tried to explain to me the dangers of the Trilateral Commission and the fluoridation of water.

Tim O'Donnell and John Friedman and I had argued with him. Tim's Dad was a chemist so Tim knew Schaeffer was wrong. Tim had only been at Loloma a year and a half. At his house he had all the Hardy Boys books, plus Nancy Drew. Unlike John he didn't always want to argue—and he hated PE as much as I did. We'd gone to see *Planet of the Apes* together; afterward, he imitated Cornelius. At the end of fifth grade Tim moved to Wisconsin. He sent me one postcard and I wrote back but after that I hadn't heard from him.

Schaeffer and Baltz were talking, now, about the Indy 500. Schaeffer said tensely, drumming his fingers on the table, that Mario Andretti was the best; Baltz liked Al Unser. I said nothing and remembered what Mom had said about dinner parties: "If you're silent," she'd confided, "people think you're smart." I wasn't sure this worked at school.

Baltz and Schaeffer and Friedman started comparing muscles. Strong people *should* run the world, I thought. It would be natural. The weak are getting away with something; teachers and laws protect us, but sooner or later the strong will catch on. They'll rule. As in school. That's why, I thought, some kids like the Nazis: under them, the strong were in charge.

"Come on, Grosfeld," Baltz said, "why don't you make a muscle?"

I hesitated.

"Oh, come on," he insisted.

I bent my arm. Nothing was visible. *The Tao that can be named is not the eternal Tao.*

"Wow," Baltz said. "That's amazing. You have *no* muscle." He seemed, in a way, impressed. The bell rang; everyone took their trays up. I don't care, I thought, about being strong. I finished my milk. Lunch hadn't gone that badly.

Later, sitting on the white concrete ledge by the parking lot, waiting for Mom to pick me up to go to Dr. Kurtz, my feeling that things were OK disappeared. Why, I wondered, can't I have friends? People say things will be better in the future. But happiness in the future is like happiness on another planet. It might be better there, but that doesn't help *here*. Maybe in the future I'll forget what it's like now.

I promised myself not to.

Past the school, phone poles and flat-roofed houses quivered; a car was parked in the empty lot beneath the manzanita. My head hurt from the heat: ninety-five degrees. Maybe it *is* my fault I don't have friends. The failure feeling: the worst part of loneliness—the cloud's dark center. I could, I told myself, learn the difference between Al Unser and Mario

Andretti. But I don't want to know about sports. For a moment I had a strong feeling of Nanna's presence. Then I realized she had been in my dream the night before. She had seemed so real in the dream. Perhaps she had come to me. In the distance kids laughed.

I tried to picture the willow by the brook on the farm. Willows were my favorite trees, beagles my favorite dogs, brown my favorite color. Nanna's room was pink; from her window you could see the cherry trees. No cherry trees in Phoenix—ocotillos. I was always excited when we turned off the main road onto the tree-covered lane to Nanna's house. I wanted to describe how beautiful it was. A leafy tunnel; the light came through the top of the tunnel; the leaves were like stained glass, sort of. I slept in the room next to Nanna's. In the morning I would knock on her door and get in her bed and she would read to me. *"Little lamb, who made thee?"* Bits of paper blew past. A plastic straw lay in the grass.

———

"Why don't we try something," Dr. Kurtz suggested. "You don't have to . . ."

"I'll try anything once," I replied. I'd heard Richard say this. I wanted to impress Dr. Kurtz with my humor.

"Think of someone you want to be better friends with."

"OK." I thought of Dan Baltz and John Friedman. I didn't know who I was supposed to think of. Dr. Kurtz didn't take me seriously when I said I was becoming friends with Richard and Anna. "What about the boys in your grade?" he would persist. Why did being in the same grade matter?

"Imagine some activity you might ask them to do."

"OK."

"Have you imagined something?"

"Yes."

"What would it be?"

"Go bowling."

"So now can you picture asking this person to . . ."

"I don't think it would work."

"Why?"

"It would just make things worse."

"How?"

On the floor, I twisted myself into one of my *odd positions*. "It would be like . . . it could be humiliating."

Baltz would never go bowling with me. And it would be a major mistake to ask him. I wished I hadn't started the conversation. I'd said I sometimes felt there must be some technique everyone else knew for making friends. If I just knew what I was doing wrong! But that had just been a feeling. I was supposed to be able to talk about my feelings. Dr. Kurtz was taking it *literally*.

"Mark, I wonder whether you sometimes make things complicated as a way of defeating yourself. You're always able to come up with reasons to not do things."

"I am not," I whispered, pulling into myself, wondering if he was right.

He hesitated a moment, then continued. "How would it be humiliating?"

I thought about Anna's friends. A woman she knew was building her own house in New Mexico. Why couldn't I have friends like that? Why did I have to be friends with people I had *nothing* in common with?

Dr. Kurtz and I were silent. He took out a Marlboro. I

remembered something I'd been thinking about in the waiting room, which now seemed urgent.

"Can I talk about something else?"

"It's your time," he replied, resigned.

"Maybe the thing is you should try things when you're in the right state of mind. That's what I don't know. Should you try anyway? Even if you're not in the right state of mind—or should you wait . . . should you wait until you're ready?"

"Try *what*, Mark?" he asked, trying to sound patient.

Why couldn't he follow what I was saying? It was such a basic question. I felt even more alone.

"I mean when . . . you're trying to reach out to people . . . should you follow your intuition?"

"That's what I thought you meant."

"So why did you ask me?"

"I just wanted to check. You know, Mark," he said, "you can be a little hard to follow." Leaning back, he added, "I mean that as a compliment."

—

Anna and Richard were going ahead with the *Amethyst;* he would be the editor; she, the adviser. I'd be on the staff with Ian, Drew Henley, and Leslie Papadakis. We began to meet at Anna's house. We read our work and Richard and Anna shared their discoveries: Allen Ginsberg, Robert Creeley, George Oppen.

At the second meeting, early in October, while Anna made tea in the kitchen, Richard opened his knapsack and took out a joint. He lit it, sucked in the smoke, handed it to Leslie. The room smelled sweet. I was excited—my first marijuana! There were some people in my class who hadn't smoked pot; I was moving ahead of them. Allen Ginsberg smoked it; so did James Taylor. We'd sung about Puff the Magic Dragon at one of the creative seders my father had organized, years ago, for Temple Micah. There were lots of different words for marijuana: grass, pot, dope. Dope sometimes also meant heroin; I wouldn't do dope. I had promised my mother I wouldn't take drugs, but since then I'd read an article in *Ramparts* that proved marijuana wasn't nearly as bad as cigarettes.

I thought of the couple who had eaten the sugar cubes. They just hadn't been prepared.

Drew looked at me inquiringly, not sure what to do with the joint. I reached out and took it. Richard smiled approvingly. I held it carefully, breathed in, and choked. Richard laughed. Leslie asked if I felt anything.

"Yeah, sort of," I said. I wanted to but wasn't sure I did. I glanced at Leslie in her Mexican poncho. She looked like Carole King.

"Like he's gonna get anything from *that*," Ian commented.

"Takes a few times," Richard said gently, scratching his beard. "You have to build up some THC."

———

Walking from science to the cafeteria, I saw Tim Ratter at the edge of the field.

"Hey Grosfeld, come over here," he said loudly.

I pretended not to hear, changing direction slightly so I could walk farther away from him without it appearing *on purpose*.

His stringy hair was the same color as the dead grass. "Answer me! I'm talking to you, toothpick. What's your fucking problem?"

Should I ignore him? Would that make it worse?

"Are you deaf?"

"I am not deaf," I answered quietly. I hate you, I thought. Be a Taoist, I thought, quivering like a doorstop as I continued walking.

"Then what is your problem? Get over here. I just want to ask you something."

I knew the question he'd ask once he had me in a headlock. "Are you a *fag*?" I wanted him to call me toothpick, or skeleton, or weakling. *Weakling* hurt but wasn't *fag*, the word I feared most. I only knew vaguely what it meant—it had a force, a gravity, beyond definition.

I kept walking.

"I'm not going to hurt you," he said. "Just come over here. Oh fuck you, you little coward. Wait. After school I'm gonna kick your pussy ass."

I headed for the cafeteria. Ratter disappeared.

———

"It's going to be a really great trip," Sharon said to Mom. We were in the dining room setting the table. Sharon was telling Mom about the upcoming youth group trip to Rocky Point.

"A lot of the kids aren't going to be from Temple Micah. I don't think Horowitz is even going to be there."

"You do make it sound like a lot of fun," Mom said cautiously. "Let's talk to your father about it. I've got to wash up. You two finish in here."

I arranged some zinnias in the slightly tarnished silver bowl Mom had inherited from her Aunt Sylvia in Omaha. "Nice centerpiece," Sharon commented. Dad entered from the living room, where he'd been looking through papers and listening to *Camelot*.

"Mark," he said, "maybe next weekend we can get down to the art museum."

"That'd be great," I said, pleased. Paolo Soleri, the visionary architect, was showing models of the cities he would build in the future. A student of Frank Lloyd Wright, he'd rebelled and gone to the desert, where he was building his own city, Arcosanti, north of Cordes Junction. He was financing it by selling wind chimes. The gift shop was already complete. The son of a friend of the Nachmanns had gone to volunteer.

"So who's going to tell me how beautiful I look?" Mom prompted us, coming into the dining room.

"You look beautiful," Sharon and I answered simultaneously.

"Gorgeous," Dad added.

"Thank you."

"So what tales of woe did Trevor have?" Dad asked. Trevor, Mom's hairdresser, had been through lots of tragedies.

"Apparently Tom is back in school," Mom said. Trevor's son had been at Apache Mountain Psychiatric Hospital.

Dad shook his head regretfully. "He's really had a hard time. I bet he appreciates you. I'm sure not everyone is as willing to listen as you are."

"I think he tells everyone most everything," Mom said wryly, sitting down.

"I doubt he tells them so *much*," Dad said. Mom didn't seem to take this as a correction the way Sharon or I might. "You know he was in the audience at the council meeting," Dad continued. "It would be a much better world if more people were that concerned."

My father had spoken at the city council meeting about the Gunderson Ranch. Old Mrs. Gunderson had wanted part of her land preserved as a nature sanctuary. Birds stopped at her pond on their way to Mexico. Once, Dad had taken Jason and me there. Jason had wandered off to play by himself while Mrs. Gunderson, sitting with an oxygen tank, had told Dad and me the names of the birds. I tried to remember what it had felt like to sit with her and Dad in the dry air by the pond. Now that she was dead, several council members and Tom Albertson, her nephew, were trying to get around the provisions of her will. "The good is oft interred," Dad had said to the council, speaking of Mrs. Gunderson. It was such a moving speech! But the other side was evil and the vote would be close. There was a lot of money to be made developing the land, which stretched all the way to Watson Road.

This wasn't Dad's first battle for the environment. Most of his time during his first ten years at McGrath and Greene had gone into Valley Technologies' lawsuit against Lockheed. Lockheed had stolen an invention from the Phoenix firm; Dad had taken their case all the way to the court of appeals. During this period, Dad had started ACEL, the Arizona Center for Environmental Law. They'd stopped the Cactus Canyon power plant. With Mrs. Hanson from the teacher's union, he'd developed an ecological awareness program for the schools. For several years, she, Dad, and State Senator DelBlanco had been trying to get the legislature to adopt the program. They always came up a few votes short. Dad's opponents said the program was too left-wing, even though it was actually very moderate. One of the legislators called Dad an eastern gadfly, which amused him. When he was interviewed on KPAK's *Phoenix Tonight*—he and the host were friends from Charros and Dad was a regular guest—he'd joked that he'd gone home after hearing that remark and tried to find the Eastern Gadfly in his field guide. This wasn't true but it made a good story.

Whenever Dad was on the radio, we would all gather around the stereo in the living room. The signal didn't always come through clearly: KPAK was in Mesa. Sometimes, in the middle of one of Dad's responses, KROK would interfere, and we'd hear Creedence Clearwater Revival or the Monkees. *Phoenix Tonight* was on from nine to eleven and sometimes Dad didn't come on until the end of the program. Jason and I would change quickly into our pajamas during the commercials so we could go to bed as soon as the show was over.

Mom was glad when the Valley Technologies lawsuit was finally settled. Dad still did some work for them, but he no longer had to fly off to Seattle, New York, or San Francisco at a moment's notice. Because of his work on the lawsuit, he became a partner after only a few years, which, Mom said, was almost unheard-of. Phil McGrath gave him an office on the twelfth floor. McGrath had come to the meeting about the Gunderson Ranch. Almost everyone we knew had been there. Dad spoke eloquently; when he was done the council chamber was silent. Then, resounding applause.

It was now growing dark outside. Dad sat down; Mom lit the Sabbath candles. It was one of the Fridays when the temple didn't meet. Sharon had suggested we have creative services at home on these evenings. She'd gone first, reading from Anne Frank. I wasn't sure what I should choose. I'd thought of one of the poems in my grandmother's book. Unlike Posha, who had written several volumes about political theory and international law, Nanna had only written one book. It was long—she'd worked on it for fifteen years. She'd wanted to get every word right. She'd explained to me that when she was writing, the poem already existed. You found the words for a poem, which, although unwritten, was already there. It took a long time; sometimes it took Nanna years. Then one day the word would be there. She would be in the kitchen, she'd be walking past the planter with the radishes and the parsley, and all of a sudden she would know the right word. Sometimes I'd had experiences like that. If you found the right word, if you discovered the invisible poem, then you created something eternal. Through it you would live forever.

Nanna's poems, I realized, probably wouldn't live forever. Not for eternity. You couldn't expect that. The poems I now most wanted to read were the ones that, although I wasn't sure, I thought referred to me. I found her poem about the goldfish pond. I thought about it all afternoon but then decided that reading it no longer felt right. I was listening to the Tao. *Better to stop short than fill to the brim*. I didn't know if I wanted to read anything. But this might seem hostile. After some consideration, I chose Chuang-tzu, Lao-tzu's disciple. This, I thought, showed my subtlety; it wasn't as obvious as picking Lao-tzu.

I read a parable:

> *"If a man is crossing a river*
> *And an empty boat collides with his own skiff*
> *Even though he be a bad-tempered man*
> *He will not become very angry.*
> *But if he sees a man in the boat,*
> *He will shout at him to steer clear.*

If the shout is not heard, he will shout again,
And yet again, and begin cursing.
And all because there is somebody in the boat.
Yet if the boat were empty,
He would not be shouting, and not angry."

Certain I had proven something, I closed the book. The candles flickered. Sharon looked at me strangely.

"I don't know. I might get ticked off if someone blocked *my* boat," Mom said.

"The traffic has been getting really horrendous on Indian School," Dad remarked. "And they keep building."

No one had understood. I put some olives on my plate.

"You'd think," my father continued, "*perhaps* they'd figure it out. It's going to be just like Los Angeles before you know it. They're going to kill the proverbial goose that laid the proverbial golden egg."

Anna had told me that when she lived in Los Angeles they'd have smog alerts and everyone had to stay inside; soon it would be like that here. But somehow, now, I didn't want to mention this; I wanted to keep Anna's world separate.

"You know in Los Angeles they have days you can't go outside because of smog alerts," I said.

"Is that so?" Mom asked.

"I'm pretty famished," Dad cut in as I was about to respond. He didn't seem too interested in the Los Angeles smog alerts. "And I think," he continued, teasingly, "yon Marcus has a lean and hungry look."

Outside, through the diaphanous curtains, in the cool darkness, Sparky barked at a passing car.

———

That night I lay in bed, holding my teddy bear. John Friedman had made fun of me for still having one. That had been the last time he'd been over to our house—more than a year ago. But I still hadn't gotten rid of Franklin.

———

We had another *Amethyst* meeting. Richard and Ian came and picked me up. Richard lit a joint as we drove, at dusk, down Thomas, to Anna's, where, in the parked car, Ian took the last toke. Anna opened the door before Richard could ring the bell. Drew was busy with a school play and couldn't make it. Karl sat in for a while but then left to teach his life-drawing class at the community college. Nicola came; I wondered whether she was going to read from her novel about the South. Anna had told us Nicola was sometimes a little secretive, so I wasn't surprised when, instead, she read a poem by Dylan Thomas.

> *"Because their words had forked no lightning they*
> *Do not go gentle into that good night."*

Nicola read in a sort of Welsh voice. The poem was beautiful, a little frightening, and hard to follow. I swore I wouldn't go gently into that good night. Darkness fell outside on Flower Lane and my mind wandered: Anna had said Nicola had once been visited by a UFO, but she was careful who she told— people tended not to take her seriously after they found out she'd been on acid. "That's narrow-minded," I'd said, hoping this sounded right.

Richard had never been visited by a UFO, but he'd had a telepathic experience, sort of. Actually his sister Caroline had it.

Caroline had E.S.P., because one time, standing in the driveway, she'd said to Richard, "This car is going to be in a collision." She'd just said it out of nowhere. Then the next day their father had been hit from behind when he pulled out of a gas station on Encanto.

I couldn't think of anything like that happening in our family. Once Sharon said she wished someone would shoot George Wallace, and a few days later someone did, and she'd felt guilty and freaked out, but I couldn't mention this. It wasn't a vision.

Basho, Anna's cat, rubbed against my leg, purred, and then moved on to Leslie. In my grandmother's long poem, "The Bridge on the Housatonic," she'd used the word *vision*. The poem was difficult; I'd read it many times to understand its meaning. I was sure that in her poem *vision* meant more than regular sight. Something had come to her when she looked out from the old bridge at the valley's changing leaves. Anna said people often had visions later in life. This was why, in Hopi culture, old people were respected. I wished I'd had a chance to talk about "The Bridge on the Housatonic" with Nanna. I hadn't, it was a very late poem, but I'd discussed it with Posha; he didn't agree with my interpretation, but said some people saw it that way.

Richard poured some of the wine he'd brought. I thought about what had happened when Mr. Nillson, the junior English teacher, had come to a meeting. After he left, we criticized his work. He was too analytical, too self-conscious, too eastern. "And not the kind of Eastern we like," Ian joked. He meant he was from New York, not Japan. Maybe, I thought, my grandmother's poems were also too eastern. But they weren't like Mr. Nillson's; she didn't write about Dostoyevsky in the subway. I decided it didn't matter if her poetry *was* a little eastern. Anna was broad-minded; she wouldn't disapprove.

———

Dad and I passed some kids on skateboards as we drove to the museum. His bolo tie glinted in the sun. Dr. Kurtz thought Dad and I were making progress on becoming friends; I'd told him what had happened the first week of school when Hoffman had brought his boa constrictor to science. Mrs. Binder let him keep it there; for a few days kids brought mice in for its lunch. I'd come home in tears; Dad had called the school. Hoffman had to take his snake home; his father, who worked for the department of corrections, called our house; he and Dad had argued on the phone. Still, I was worried Dad would ask (as he always did when we were alone) whether I was making friends. Sometimes, I thought, he makes it sound as if I purposely don't want to have friends. But it wasn't my fault that Tim O'Donell left Loloma. Or that John Friedman avoided me. I wished I could talk to him about Anna, Richard, and the *Amethyst,* but I didn't think I could. Why, I argued to myself, do I have to be friends with other kids when I like adults more?

We passed the white brick wall in front of the optometrist's. The boys on the skateboards disappeared in the distance.

"Seems like that berm is holding up," Dad commented.

One night a few weeks before, Sparky had dug under the gate. Dad and I drove around the neighborhood for hours in the darkness looking for her. We stopped every few blocks and I would yell, "Sparky! Come here, Sparky."

"Come on, girl!" Dad shouted. I waved the flashlight around but we didn't find her. Finally Dad persuaded me we had to go home; Sparky would come back in the morning, he said. She didn't, but a woman called us; Sparky had made it all the way to west Phoenix. Dad and I went to pick her up. The next day we'd put cement along the bottom of the gate.

"God, I hope so," I said.

"What worries me, Mark," Dad commented, as we passed a Nixon billboard, "is that McGovern's going to bring the whole party down with him. We could lose the Congress. I don't need to tell you what a disaster *that* would be."

I felt relieved he hadn't asked about friends, but then I thought about how bad a Nixon landslide would be for the farmworkers. When Dad was president of Temple Micah, he'd put together a committee of churches and synagogues to support the grape boycott. He and Reverend Stephens organized a rally at the Capitol. The farmworkers had no protection; they worked eighteen hours a day in the heat and went to the bathroom in the field. Once Mr. Martinez from the UFW brought César Chavez to our house, but I didn't get to meet him; I'd already gone to bed. Mr. Nachmann, who was, Dad said, the best criminal lawyer in the state, had also become involved. Dad felt some of the farmworkers' supporters were too idealistic; they wanted all or nothing. Dad and Mr. Nachmann thought it would be smarter to pass a few reforms rather than to try to do everything at once. That was why he hadn't wanted McGovern to get the nomination. Muskie or Scoop Jackson could have won, Dad thought, but not McGovern.

Sharon and I had disagreed. A lot of things had gone wrong in McGovern's campaign, but they weren't all his fault. Sometimes you *did* have bad luck.

"I just hope it's close so Nixon doesn't get too powerful," I said. A lot of people were worried Nixon wanted to be dictator. During four square Baltz had chanted, "Don't change partners in the middle of the screw! Vote for Dick in '72!"

In front of the Desert Cove apartments a woman stood on the sidewalk, hitchhiking; she could be murdered. Some palm-tree husks lay on the grass. Sprinklers sent a slow, light rain back and forth across them, like a windshield wiper.

Nanna had met McGovern in the early sixties. Together they wrote an article for *The New York Times* about nuclear testing. Nanna didn't enjoy politics the way Posha did, but she forced herself to become involved in order to stop the war. A lot of her old friends didn't agree, but Nanna thought sometimes you had to work within the system. After 1968, she had set up the Quakers' draft counseling program; once she spent a night in jail after a draft-card-burning demonstration.

Posha hadn't approved. He, too, was against the war, but said that you needed to change laws rather than break them. They were like trees. You might cut one down because you didn't believe in it. But if everyone did that there soon wouldn't be any forest. Sometimes, when we visited Posha and Nanna in Connecticut, they would stay up late into the night, in front of the fire, arguing about civil disobedience and the best way to beat Nixon. Nanna's Quaker friends would come over, and the judges and politicians Posha knew came, too.

I hated it when I was sent to bed; I would shake hands with the guests, kiss my grandparents and parents, and head up the carpeted stairs. I'd leave the bedroom door open a crack, hoping to hear a little of the conversation continuing in the living room. Sometimes I could make out a few phrases. "He's a madman," my grandmother might say. "That's going a little far," my grandfather would respond, and I'd hear the clinking of glasses, and my father laughing, and comments I couldn't make out, which I knew were interesting and important, but which were drowned by the sound, outside the window, of the pear tree being shaken by the wind.

We were in Phoenix on the night, almost a year after Nanna's death, when McGovern made his speech accepting the nomination. Dad let Sharon and me stay up. It was a great speech. If he hadn't made it after midnight, when most people were asleep, he might not be so far behind. Eagleton should have told him about the shock treatments. Therapy was private, but *still* he should have told. There had just been too many things that had gone wrong.

During our class discussion, Schaeffer had said, "Anyone who's for McGovern is either stupid or a commie homo."

"That is *not true*," I'd argued. But even John Friedman, whose dad was a Democrat, wasn't willing to support him.

"I'm worried about his position on drugs," John said. I thought his position on drugs was good; he wanted to make them legal. When I pointed this out, Baltz said that was cool, and for a moment I thought I might win him over. But then Schaeffer said McGovern wanted to surrender to communism. Baltz couldn't go along with that. I tried hard to persuade John, but he abstained during the class vote. He's a coward, I thought. Only Martha Wallace and I had gone for McGovern.

At the museum, Dad asked which artist I liked most. Monet, I said; I'd talked about him with Anna. Dad liked him, too. He said most people in Phoenix didn't appreciate real art; they just liked the cowboy stuff. We entered the room with the Italian paintings and admired their dark, deep reds. Titian red, Dad explained. A color the artist Titian had invented himself. It would be a great accomplishment to discover a whole new color. It was possible that in outer space there were colors we didn't know about.

Different colors, I knew, had different auras, different feelings. The feeling, walking through the museum, of *father and son* was different from *mother and son*. Because of something between Dad and me—or something larger? There were songs about fathers and sons—we'd listen, sometimes, to Peter, Paul & Mary, who sang, *Tell me why you're crying my son*. I would hear this and imagine the same moment between Dad and me. I knew that when Dad heard this song he imagined it, too. I thought about other fathers and sons: Peter or Paul and their sons, Abraham and Isaac, *My Three Sons*. How, I wondered, did we compare to the fathers and sons on TV, in the songs, in the museum with us, in the parking lot, in cars and pickup trucks, in Phoenix—everywhere?

Monet's pictures, Anna had explained, didn't have outlines: he just *saw*. In a closet at home, Dad kept the dark, semiabstract paintings he'd done years ago in New York. He'd set up a room in his apartment as a studio; for inspiration, he'd listen to jazz and drink Cointreau. He'd seemed very happy when I'd shown him the drawings I'd done for Anna's class.

I'd been learning over the past few years that he didn't know everything. Two years before, in fifth grade, I'd been puzzling over "The Lady of Shalott," a poem about a woman who lived by herself in the time of Camelot. She spent a lot of time looking in her mirror, in which she saw the whole world. At the end of the poem there was a line I didn't understand. Dad, I knew, was an expert on King Arthur; he was sitting in his favorite chair, in the living room, looking through papers about Valley Tech.

"Dad," I'd asked, "can you help me with something?"

"Sure, Mark," he'd said.

I placed the book in front of him. "I've been trying to figure out what this means: *'The mirror cracked from side to side.'* I don't know what the mirror is supposed to stand for."

"Mark," he'd said, impatiently, "you can't expect me to know everything."

I'd slinked away, feeling stupid: why had I interrupted him with something so unimportant?

We came to a room with the painting that was everyone's favorite on class field trips. A gladiator in the Roman Coliseum was pinned on the ground, a sword pointed at his heart. The empress gave the thumbs-down sign: he would die. Dad said it was sensationalistic, but a shiver went down my spine.

Tell me why you're crying my son. How Dad had shone at the council meeting. Calling Mrs. Gunderson's nephew "perfidious Albertson"—*that* had probably gone over most people's heads; Councilman Bentley told Dad people didn't get the reference to the Bard. But Dad explained it on the way home while we drove through the silent orange groves. It came from *Julius Caesar.*

We passed the Corot, which Dad said was probably a fake. We entered the gallery next to the atrium where the arcology exhibit was on view. Soleri's hivelike models shimmered in the low-lit room. I read the cards in front of them. Soleri thought that if everyone lived in his compact cities, nature could be pre-served. This was arcology—the combination of architecture and ecology. Dad said the models were interesting as art but weren't practical and would never be built. I wondered whether Anna would want to live in Arcosanti. She'd have to give up the house on Flower Lane.

On the way home we talked about the pictures we'd liked. Dad had once thought about becoming an architect. He knew Mrs.

Frank Lloyd Wright, the architect's widow. Sometimes he ran into Soleri at the grocery store.

We passed the Valley Bank's palm tree–lined glass building and turned onto Osborne. There were pink and white houses. The people in them probably think the museum is a weird place, I thought. Maybe it's wrong of me to think this. But no one in my class would want to visit it, I thought, and it seems odd that it can exist in the open, among the houses. Odd that people tolerate it. It ought to be hidden behind oleanders, like Dr. Kurtz's office. We merged into the traffic; no one knew where we'd come from. To the north, the Coronado Building. Twelve stories high. The top five floors, McGrath and Greene; Dad's office was on the twelfth. It had a plush, gray carpet, leather chairs, and a framed drawing of Clarence Darrow. There were photographs of Mom, Sharon, Jason, and me. The bookcase was filled with leather-bound volumes: *The Arizona Revised Statutes.*

"By the way," Dad said, "I was talking to Jack deSoto yesterday. Remember him?" Jack deSoto, Dad's secretary's brother. He'd done some work around our house.

I nodded.

"He got laid off from the security company. Turns out he'd be willing to come over a couple times a week to give you a little extra help with some outdoor stuff."

I looked down.

"It would be relaxed. Nothing too tough. *I* find he's a pretty easygoing guy. And he's helped some other boys with PE."

"Oh, great," I muttered.

"Mark," Dad said softly, "it's important to stay open-minded. I know how you're feeling. When I was a boy, Posha hired a German tutor, Mr. Fink. I know I wasn't too enthusiastic about *him* at first. But in the long run he helped. I've talked to some of the people deSoto's worked for and he's gotten very good recommendations."

He's been *planning* this, I thought. But getting angry won't do any good. I pictured Chuang-tzu's boat, adrift on a misty Chinese stream, colliding with me.

"How long is he coming for?" I asked carefully.

"It'll just be on a trial basis," he answered. "We'll give it a shot through Christmas. If you don't object *too* strenuously."

Dad had once tried to teach me to play football. But no matter how many times he said, "You're coming along," I wasn't. We'd already tried tennis and golf lessons. And in second grade Dad had taken me every Saturday to Dick's Gym on Cactus Road; I hit a punching bag; it hurt. I didn't know how to make a fist. The gym smelled of men. Then, after awhile, we didn't go to Dick's anymore, but tossed the football in the yard. Finally, a year ago, after Nanna died, he'd given up. Things had been better since then; we'd been working hard on getting along.

One gains by losing and loses by gaining. I don't want to feel sorry for myself.

"I wish you'd asked me or something before you talked to him."

"Listen, I'm really doing this more for his sake than yours. I want to give the guy a break. I didn't mention—his wife has left him again. But if you're *irrevocably* opposed . . ."

"I didn't *say* that."

"I know you didn't."

We drove quietly.

"Mark," Dad said, "I hope you can at least *try* and have a positive attitude about it." He paused. "You know, I've been noticing you've really grown a lot more self-confident lately. I think this will just help you a little more in that department."

You *always* say that, I thought. I wanted Dad to understand. There isn't anything *wrong* with saying I'm self-confident, I told him carefully in my head. It's just that you *always* say it. And it never has anything to do with what's been happening. When you keep repeating it, I just feel *less* confident.

"So I guess we better get used to the idea of four more years," Dad said, trying to make peace. If I started talking about politics, I'd be agreeing everything was OK about Mr. deSoto. But if I stayed silent, I would be holding on to my anger. Stewing: a Taoist shouldn't stew.

Four more years. The war would continue. Mrs. Sklar had said she might leave the country.

"Do you remember when we met Nixon?" Dad asked.

"Sure." You know I do, I thought. San Diego in 1968: that summer we rented a condo on Mission Beach next to the Goldmans'. San Diego was so beautiful. Bright pink flowers grew by the white stucco walls. Nixon was staying nearby, resting while the Democrats had their convention. One afternoon Dad took Jason and me on a walk down the beach to his hotel. We shook his hand. My molecules have touched his molecules, I thought. When we got back to the condo I said, "I'm not going to wash my hand. I've touched someone famous."

"Oh, I think you can go ahead and wash it," Dad replied.

Six years ago. I wondered if I still had any of the same atoms.

That summer, in San Diego, we'd buried Dad in the sand. We screamed when he rose, beating his sandy arms on his sandy chest. He would run down to the surf to wash off. Then he'd jog down the beach, carrying us on his shoulders one by one, although he couldn't get too far with Sharon. He explained about King Canute, who tried to order the tide to go back. It hadn't, and this led to the Magna Carta. Dad chartered a deep-sea fishing boat that summer; I got sick on the boat. The summer before third grade. Dad made seaweed soup, Sharon played with Felicia Goldman. One night we all went out at midnight to hunt grunions.

On another night, while I listened to the waves crashing outside and Jason, in the bunk above me, breathing softly, I decided that, after all, I wouldn't be a girl. It wasn't that I wanted to be a boy. It just seemed easier. The decision wasn't hard; it was like choosing between Quisp and Quake.

———

At home I got the mail; Posha had written to me. I eagerly opened his letter.

Dear Mark,

Thank you for sending your new poem. You do so well so often. Some parts are stunning. I liked the first stanza better than the second. For a more detailed discussion I will need to read it a third time. However, I suspect the second part needs some further revision.

Write and tell me more about your school and friends. And are there any sports you like just a little?

Later that night, Sharon knocked on my door: "Mom and Dad want to go get ice cream. They want to know if you want to come?" I put down *A Separate Reality*. I didn't want to be left out.

"Someone's been playing with the radio," Dad said, in the car, turning it back to the classical station. I brooded silently about Mr. deSoto as we drove down Indian School, in the darkness, past the palm trees and Taco Bells.

Jason had stayed home building a city of blocks. But Sharon and I have given in, I thought, taking the chance we'll be seen in public with Mom and Dad. We're weak; we always compromise. I used to love getting ice cream with my family; Mom and Dad think I still do.

"Look at that," Dad said, as we drove by a new McDonald's. "Another one. These fast-food places are sure taking over. I just wonder: what is everyone in such a hurry for?"

"Aw, Dad," Sharon said teasingly.

"People don't appreciate real food anymore," he said, sounding, like Posha.

"Have you tried it?" Mom asked, teasing too.

"Yes, I've tried it," he responded, in a mock-persecuted voice. "Tasted like cardboard."

Something in my back felt clogged and jammed—like the traffic on Indian School. I'd made the mistake I always made by coming: fooling myself into thinking things could be the way they'd been before.

"Haydn," Dad said, identifying the music.

"I don't know how you do that," Mom said, impressed.

"I'm not sure," he replied. "Maybe I was Haydn in another life. I hear this music and . . . I just know what the next note is going to be."

"Uncanny," Mom said supportively, as if to her brightest child.

I can't tell how serious he is, I thought, frustrated. Sort of a joke, name-dropping across time, but maybe not entirely—maybe he believes in reincarnation just a little. Maybe when someone dies they reappear in your life as another person; not reincarnation exactly but a version—Leslie Papadakis said she'd gone back to a past life on one of the Easter Islands. Anna's been back, too, although she's reluctant to talk about it—something to do with the secret name she'd once confided to me: Dhisana.

We pulled up in front of the Vanity Flair Cleaners. The parking lot was dark and silent. We walked past the cigar-store Indian in front of the Olde Arizona Trading Post and entered the busy Baskin-Robbins.

Jeff Cooper, one of the stars of the tenth grade, was working. Beth Rawley and Dan Baltz's brother Ted were waiting for him to get off. Dan, Schaeffer, and Heather sat in the back with some other seventh-graders, beneath a mural of cows, laughing. Heather had a chocolate smear on her pink shirt; Baltz kept trying to wipe it off. They didn't seem to notice me. Later, I guessed, they'd go to a boondocker. On Monday I would overhear who had fucked and who'd gotten so fucked up they had to be carried home. If I'd stayed in my room and read, while Lilly went round in her wheel, Dan and Schaeffer wouldn't have seen me with my parents. No one cares, I said to myself. But I didn't believe this. Time could not move quickly enough. I wondered why Sharon, who, before switching to Pueblo High (because Beth Fineman went there) had been in Jeff Cooper's class, didn't seem bothered. She and Mom discussed their volunteer work and calmly chose sherbets.

"Going to get one of your *wild* combos?" Dad asked.

"No," I grumbled, "just Rocky Road."

Jeff was busy with Beth Rawley, but Dad was ready to be served. He tapped the countertop. Dad didn't know how

important the boy in the orange-and-brown-striped shirt was.
Jeff, I thought, turned toward him with scorn.

> *That which fails*
> *Must first be strong*
> *This is called perception of the nature of things.*
> *Soft and weak overcome hard and strong.*
> *Fish cannot leave deep waters,*
> *And a country's weapons should not be displayed.*

———

I spent as much time with Anna as I could. We would talk in
her office, on her patio, or at one of the stone tables near the
wash. Alone, we were able to have deeper talks than when
Richard and Ian were around. Sometimes we discussed the
Amethyst. We'd agreed to concentrate on developing our
writing; the magazine would come later. At last, I thought,
this was how I'd make friends—not by trying to be someone I
wasn't, but by being myself. They might be older, but then, in
so many ways, I was old for my age. Things would work out for
me, not because I listened to Dad or Dr. Kurtz, but because I
listened to myself. I didn't have to be lonely.

I would tell Anna about different unfair things that
happened in class, about the laps we had to run in PE, about
cage ball—but I didn't want to talk too much about this
stuff. Anna saw me as something more than another seventh-
grader; no one else at Loloma did. I didn't want to waste my
time talking about school problems, although when they did
come up Anna listened, curiously, attentively, careful not to
press if she sensed reluctance, her attention as subtle as her

hands when they held the damp clay bowls she threw on the wheel.

Anna, too, had her problems at school; she shared them with me and I was thrilled. Her troubles were much more interesting than mine. The new principal, Mrs. Heller, wasn't as liberal as the one who'd hired Anna. She made the teachers do lots of paperwork; they had to submit teaching plans for the whole year. "Then we have to be on these 'evaluating committees.' Which I don't believe in in the least." Anna laughed. "But I'm *pretending* to believe in them."

"Oh, God," I said, "how dumb."

"It is. She doesn't understand she's setting up an atmosphere of *fear*. Everyone's afraid to say what they think."

I tried to imagine Anna at a faculty meeting: how she acted, how she spoke. I knew the upper-schoolers were mad at Mrs. Heller, too; she'd decided they couldn't have iced tea at lunch.

"But I'm not worried," Anna said. "I don't think the parents will let it go too far."

One day, while we sat on the grass in the shade of the mulberry, discussing the *Amethyst,* Anna explained that the abstract expressionists believed process, not product, was important. What went on internally mattered, not what ended up on a piece of paper. The object had power if it reflected something real inside. Process is like the Tao, I thought as she continued talking.

Anna told me stories about her years in Los Angeles. She'd grown up on a lemon farm near San Bernardino. When she was sixteen she'd left home and moved to Los Angeles. "My hippie days," she would say with a laugh, and I would wonder sadly whether her hippie days were over. She'd been a waitress, she'd typed in an office, she'd worked as a gofer for a B-movie studio.

I thought of asking what B movies were but decided not to. She'd even been in a film once. She'd played a woman in a car lot. All the time she was writing poetry and drawing; she would hardly ever show her work to anyone. When she did, people didn't understand it. One day in a Laundromat she met a man named Pierce. He was a little older than Anna, he taught at the university, he liked her drawings, and they were married. Every year the Rose Parade passed right in front of their house. Anna never knew which teams were playing. With Pierce's help, Anna was able to get into UCLA—even though she hadn't graduated from high school.

She majored in art and film. "They were all so serious," Anna said. One time she was in a class that was making a film called *Trash Heap*. "It was supposed to be a takeoff on Warhol," Anna explained. "They just wanted to shoot footage of this dump. But a tramp was living there and he kept singing."

"What was he singing?"

" '*I did it my way.*' Every time he finished, I applauded and shouted, 'Do it again.' And he did. Drove them crazy. They thought it was ruining the film."

"When it was making it better," I said. I thought of a comparison: it was like the way accidents improved paintings, but then I thought about the singing tramp and realized I was probably missing the point. I pictured Anna shouting, and the dump, and the tramp, and the circling seagulls, and I thought of Suzanne, who served tea and oranges amid the garbage in one of Richard's favorite songs. For a moment I could smell salt in the air, but I knew we were a thousand miles from the ocean.

"That's right!" Anna said. "You get it. They didn't."

In spite of almost failing that class, she had graduated. One of her teachers encouraged Anna to show her work to some galleries. Anna didn't think she was ready, but she put together a portfolio of abstract drawings and made a list of galleries in the phone book. At the first one the owner looked carefully through her portfolio. "These are really good," he told her, "but this probably isn't the place for you. Did you look around?" Anna looked up. All the pictures were of people having sex. "I'd been so nervous," Anna told me, "I hadn't noticed."

"Then did you go to other places?" I asked, hopefully.

"No," Anna said. "I knew that was a sign I wasn't ready. It was a *billboard* I wasn't ready."

But maybe she'd gone to the wrong place first, I thought. Maybe it was accidental. Anna had told me about some of her run-ins with galleries in Phoenix; they were only concerned about money. If she became a part of that scene it would affect her work. She'd seen it happen with Karl—even if he hadn't.

A paper bag skipped in the half-hearted breeze through the dry air; pollution covered the mountains. "Now I'm glad that happened; I learned from it. When I look back on that work I'm embarrassed. Abstract drawings. I think I was trying to hide in them." Then she added quickly, "Not that there's anything wrong with abstraction."

"If that's what you're into," I said. I wanted to like abstraction more than I did.

"Do you know what the new movement is in New York?" Anna asked, and answered her own question: "The return to realism."

"Like Warhol and Wyeth?"

"That's right. And other people."

Once, while waiting in Dr. Kurtz's office, I'd read in *Newsweek* that Warhol and Andrew Wyeth's son were doing each other's portraits. Even though Warhol was more experimental, they were friends. It was a small world. Anna had told me Warhol had said that in the future you'd be able to record shows on television and watch them any time you wanted. Looking out at the shredded wheat–colored field, I thought about the Wyeth book Anna had shown me. The paintings were beautiful. The weathered barn and the lace-curtained rooms reminded me of Nanna's farm.

Around the time Anna had graduated from UCLA, her father sold his farm and her parents moved to Phoenix. She began to realize her marriage with Pierce wouldn't work—he was brilliant but insane. The state of California gave him legal status as mentally ill; he got a check every month. She couldn't live with him, but they would always be friends—he had even come to her ceremony with Karl in the desert. Anna had gone to live with Nicola in San Francisco after leaving Pierce. San Francisco was grand, she said, but soon her mother got sick and Anna decided she needed to be with her. She got a scholarship to go to graduate school at ASU. When she was done, she'd started to teach school.

At ASU Anna had become more interested in writing. And in the ways art and writing interacted. She'd studied the Black Mountain School; I wished I could go there, but it no longer existed. Maybe, I thought, I was in a place that would turn out to be just as important. I was meant to be here. I'd often felt that I was being watched over, somehow. A few birds came and pecked in the dry grass while we talked. Gray shapes on the ochre field—how did we appear to them? I looked out toward the goalposts while Anna told me how Stieglitz had discovered

Georgia O'Keeffe. Like Anna, O'Keeffe had been a school-teacher. "At last," Stieglitz had declared, "a woman artist." O'Keeffe eventually moved west where she did her important work. She had to get away from the male critics, whom she disdained. I thought about Nanna, and Anna, and my theory of reincarnation in this life, and heard, in the distance, shouts from the soccer field.

Sometimes I found Anna hard to follow—when she talked about the Hopi creation myth, the mystic poems of William Blake, or Zukofsky's early objectivist work. There were so many things I still didn't understand. I wanted to contribute more, but what did I have to tell her? What I planned to get Sharon for her birthday? My troubles with Douggy Dale?

One afternoon I decided to tell her about Mr. deSoto. "I guess that's a cross you have to bear," she commented. Then I told her about Dr. Kurtz. "Does it help, do you think?" she asked, carefully.

"I'm not sure."

"I've thought about going to one myself," she said. "I knew some people in LA who went. It can help, I think."

Sometimes I'd bring in poems to discuss. We would stay late after school and go over them in the front seat of her pickup. She would point out improvements I could make: ways to make them clearer, words I could leave out. She wanted to know how I decided where to place the lines on the page.

"I sort of just feel it, I guess."

"That's amazing," she said. "I struggle so hard with that." A poet she knew in San Francisco had told her she should use breathing to figure it out. "But *you* just do it intuitively." She shook her head. She pointed out a line she wasn't sure about in "The Monument": *The lithic titan never moved.*

"Lithic," she said. "You looked in the thesaurus, didn't you?"

I nodded guiltily.

"You know, Mark," she said, "don't worry about what I say or what anyone says. You *know*. Listen to yourself. What you have isn't anything anyone can give you."

Achieve results, but never glory in them: the Tao. Anna's words embarrassed me, but made me happy. We're similar souls, I thought—meant to come together. Jigsaw-puzzle shadows moved slowly across the school, onto the soccer field. Anna had told me I was one of the few people who understood her. I knew it wasn't a coincidence that I'd met her just after Nanna's death.

One October afternoon on the patio, I'd talked to her about Nanna.

"This must have been a sad year for you," she said.

I nodded.

She got up and gave me a hug. "What a special person she must have been," Anna said. "And you're so much like her." A thousand yellow lines arced from the sun, a blue-white circle above Anna's hair.

At night, Mom, Sharon, and I would watch TV. Our favorite show was *Marcus Welby, MD*. His patients always got better in the end. Sometimes Jason joined us. Dad usually worked in his study, the doors closed. Every now and then he would come out and stand on the top of the steps to the living room.

"What are you all up to?" he'd ask.

"We're watching a *great* show," Mom would say. "Why don't you come join us?"

He'd hesitate (as if the living room were a place he wasn't allowed to enter). Then he would come and sit for a few minutes. Then he'd go back into his study, shutting the door. A lot of the time it turned out the patient had a hidden psychological problem, but Dr. Welby would usually still have to operate. Then Dad would reappear.

"Interesting show?"

"Yes, dear," Mom would say, sometimes, I thought, with frustration.

When I didn't feel like watching TV I would go into my room. I'd shut the door and read or listen to music. It was important, I knew, to pick the *right* music for your mood. My favorite James Taylor songs were "Blossom" and "Sunny Skies." Sunny Skies didn't have any friends.

I guess he just has to cry from time to time.

It was comforting to know James Taylor, too, was lonely.

Each day I read the paper and worried about McGovern. I'd hoped for a miracle during the last week. The paper said McGovern's crowds were becoming bigger and more enthusiastic, and that might, I thought, be a sign. Nobody talked about the election at school. November came, and Dad took me with him when he voted. That night, instead of working in his study, Dad joined the rest of us in front of the TV. Mom and Jason went to bed when Cronkite announced Nixon had won. Dad, Sharon, and I stayed up until the map had turned, except for Massachusetts, completely blue.

Sharon, her eyes red, left too.

"I think you were a little better prepared than your sister," Dad commented.

"You've got to be realistic," I said.

"Too bad about McGovern," John Friedman whispered in home-room. Most people were happy although I knew they didn't really care. "Arrest all the Democrats," Douggy said during lunch, grabbing my arm, "that's what they told me down at head-quarters." He pulled me, struggling, out toward the soccer field.

—

2
My Grandfather's New Deal

In 1929, the United States was in the midst of an era of unpar-
alleled prosperity: the Jazz Age! No one could anticipate the dark-
ness ahead. In October of that dismal year, the good times were to
end. One dark Monday, the stock market crashed. Like an enor-
mous, billowing cloud, a dark time descended. Farms across the
nation failed. In 1930 alone, more than 1,300 banks closed! By
the end of 1931, twelve million were unemployed. Many thought
there would be a revolution! But, like Marie Antoinette, Herbert
Hoover, the Republican, did nothing.

A mess, I thought. I should begin with an anecdote about my
grandfather. My family-history report was, after all, supposed to
be about him.

I wanted to put it away and work on my poem, "The Sun
Library," but we were about to have company; the McCarthys
were coming to swim. I wasn't looking forward to it.

In 1932 Franklin Delano Roosevelt, the newly elected President,
asked my grandfather to come to Washington. He was part of the
Brain Trust, which wrote speeches for Roosevelt. . . .

Brain Trust. Try saying *that* in front of class. Everyone will
think I'm being conceited. So unfair of Mr. Lewis to decide at
the last minute that we had to present oral reports. I wondered, for a moment, if I should put in what Dad had told us:
there were a *lot* of things people thought FDR had said that
Posha had actually written. No, that would definitely sound
conceited.

One of the first projects he worked on was the Emergency Railroad Transportation Act. Then Roosevelt sent my grandfather to England for the London Economic Conference, which was very important because almost every country was in shambles. My grandfather greatly enjoyed living in London.

Posha knew so many people! He said it was important not to travel as a tourist. Tourists only saw the superficial side.

Not long after the conference, my grandfather met the Sultan of Morocco. Years later, when he was promoted to king, my grandfather went to visit him. They went to the Sahara.

I'm being evasive; I haven't mentioned Cordell Hull. He and Posha had had a big disagreement in London. Posha hadn't wanted to be specific about the details when I'd interviewed him. Because of their dispute, Posha couldn't work for Roosevelt anymore. I wasn't sure how it would sound if I put that in. Plus, I'd have to explain who Cordell Hull was.

And there was still more I ought to include. I wasn't sure how my report should end. After the war, he helped plan the meeting at Dunbarton Oaks that led to the U.N. When I was little, my mother had read me *The Animals' Parliament*. All the animals had gotten together so there would be world peace. I'd pictured Posha, in a room with dark red curtains, talking to a lion. I smiled, remembering that, watching the dust motes, hearing my parents in the kitchen.

Although I'd planned to end with Dunbarton Oaks, I wondered if I should put in a paragraph about my grandfather's time on the Court of Appeals. Thinking about this, my mind felt as weary as my legs would sometimes be after hiking with

Posha. While we made our way through the woods behind the farm, he would tell me about cases he was working on. After retiring from the court, he'd kept an office with a New York law firm. They let him do whatever he liked, Dad said; they just wanted to use his name. Pushing aside the brambles, he would tell me about Roosevelt and the '32 campaign. I'd tell him about the Baha'is and he would urge me to read Martin Buber. He would explain his lawsuit to protect the Squawhill River; someday he hoped to take me hiking there. I'd ask him about the different wildernesses he'd been to. Which were the most beautiful? He would tell me about my namesake, Marcus Grosfeld, his uncle. He'd been a famous lawyer who'd loved the woods a lot. When we came back to the house (usually just in time for dinner) we would take off our muddy boots in the hallway, hang up our jackets and the red hats we wore so the hunters wouldn't shoot us, and Nanna would make sure, before we sat down to eat, that I washed, very thoroughly, with the special brown soap that prevented poison ivy.

Maybe, I thought, sitting in the beanbag chair, I should include an epilogue about Posha's life now. "After Retirement: 1963–1972." No, I thought, it's already too long. No Taoist would write like this. It's just *wrong,* somehow. But it isn't my fault, I thought, that Posha had done so many things. Still, I haven't given a real picture: the smell of cigar smoke, the hats he wears, his suspenders. The way it felt when we hiked through the muddy woods, or went out in the early morning to get fresh eggs for breakfast. Our serious talks, his comments on my poems.

"We have to do an oral presentation," I'd complained at dinner one night when Dad asked what was new and interesting at school.

"Why *don't* you want to do that?" he replied. Everyone, he

said, would probably be very impressed if I told them about my family's accomplishments.

"I'm not so sure," I said.

"You don't know," he countered. "Personally, I'm very proud to come from a family that's done so much for the world. I just hope I can live up to that tradition."

I didn't want to look at the report anymore. The McCarthys would arrive soon. But they were late—maybe they weren't coming. I could hear Sparky yelping at a bird.

I guessed Dad had invited Jack McCarthy over to talk about the Gunderson Ranch. McCarthy was the editorial-page editor of the *Valley Journal-Observer*. When Mom and Dad had first moved to Phoenix, they'd been friends. They'd played tennis together. Dad had briefly been one of the *Journal-Observer's* lawyers. Because he was Catholic, McCarthy opposed the death penalty; he and Dad had helped to get a man off death row. The man owned an Italian restaurant; we all went to dinner there after his release—they had really good blue-cheese dressing. Another time, Dad and Mr. McCarthy were on the same flight from Boston; they bought some clams at the airport and when they got home had a clambake in the McCarthys' yard. But over the years McCarthy had grown more conservative.

"He's compromised," Dad would say.

"I still think they're *basically* good people," Mom would reply.

"Basically good," Dad would say. "But *ambitious*." We hadn't seen them for years.

I decided to see what was happening. I walked to the kitchen and stood in the doorway in my trunks and sandals.

"Are the McCarthys still coming?"

"I don't know," Dad said. "They're fifteen minutes late already and they didn't call."

"Now, hon," Mom said, with affection and a little warning.

"Done with your report?" he asked. I could smell the breakfast bacon.

"Not quite."

"You know, Mark, I think you're going to be surprised. I think you're worrying needlessly."

Why, I thought, is this so important to you?

"I'll bet," he continued, "people are going to be a lot more interested than you think."

You don't understand embarrassment: a gas that *you* can't smell. Standing in the doorway, I remembered, how, in second grade, on the days when he'd take me to school, he would pull up to the front of the driveway, and I'd have to say good-bye to him there. I wanted him to let me out at the edge of the parking lot but he wouldn't. I shouldn't be embarrassed, he'd insisted.

"I'm not *worried* about it," I mumbled.

"Good," Dad said, firmly.

I left and brooded down the hall, past the Chagall posters. Just leave me alone. Don't try to control my thoughts. Maybe he doesn't care whether I'm outside when the McCarthys come. I'm always so *aware* of where everyone is in the house. Maybe that's normal but it's weird that it's normal.

Next to the *World Book Encyclopedias* in the back hallway lay a Goodwill bag filled with clothes. The dark blue wall was covered with photos. Posha in a raincoat at Campobello with Clark Clifford. Marcus Grosfeld leaning against a wooden railing in Maine. Woodrow Wilson had *almost* made him attorney general. He'd wanted to but couldn't because he was Jewish. Still, he'd been runner-up. But nobody cared about that. Some TV shows, like the Smothers Brothers', didn't get good ratings because they were on at the wrong time—if they'd had the right slot they'd have been a big hit, but the networks didn't realize this and canceled the show. Our family was sort of like that: a lot of people had come close to being famous, but they hadn't quite made it.

But, I told myself, they were a *little* famous. Some people knew about them. Marcus Grosfeld had a long entry in the *Jewish Encyclopedia*. Most books about FDR mentioned Posha; Dad said a new New Deal book was going to come out that would give Posha the credit he was due—and would be quite critical of Hull.

I liked seeing my relatives' names in books. I'd read the passages over and over, wishing they were longer. When someone from our family was mentioned in an article, Posha would send a copy to Dad, and Dad would tell everybody. Sometimes it seemed weird *who* he'd tell. It wasn't so weird to tell Mrs. Sklar or the Nachmanns, but it did seem odd to discuss it with Bob the barber or Connie's husband Lloyd.

If you thought something was weird, I thought, you should be able to explain *why* you thought it was weird, but I couldn't.

Nanna and Posha in Italy. Posha on safari. Nanna sitting on a camel, laughing, her hair caught in the wind. Dad during high school, at an American Youth for Democracy rally. Dad at Fort Benning. And with Dick Epstein, in Tallahassee, on their trip across country. Mom in Omaha, pregnant with Sharon. Dad with Jason, fishing.

Hanging farther down the hall, Dad's ancestors. Isaac Grosfeld sat expressionless in a rocking chair. Nanna's mother wore white and drank tea. Was Anna drinking tea now? I looked at Nanna's grandfather, Arthur Bloom, who had come from Germany and built a millinery firm. Nanna's father had sold the company and bought a lot of land; people had called it Bloom's Folly, Dad said, but he'd been smart—later his land became part of Queens.

The hallway's end: a little light seeped in from Sharon's room. I looked at the pictures of Mom's family and her father's hardware store in Omaha. There she was, walking through the snow, a little girl. She spent her time in the library and went to the Joslyn Art Museum. She took piano lessons with an old Polish woman who lived near them in Benson. Benson was the neighborhood where the people weren't as rich. As rich as in Dundee. Her parents had had more money, Mom had said, when she was young. She thought her mother had been happy then. Grandma Vogel—I wonder what she was like?, I said to myself, looking at a picture of a woman in a mink coat who'd died before I was born. She'd liked to make duck dinners. She spent a lot of time in her room. Grandpa Vogel was more social; he played Scott Joplin on the piano and played cards; he made investments, he'd had to sell the store—to Grandma Vogel's brother. That caused a lot of problems. Even though she'd been the valedictorian at Benson High, Mom thought she wouldn't be able to go to college. Aunt Sylvia gave her the money so she could go to the University of Wisconsin.

Where she'd met Dad.

There was only one picture from that time: they both stood holding canoe paddles; I knew that on the trip down the Mecan River, which they'd gone on after the picture was taken, Mom had tipped them over.

I looked again at the little girl, walking though the snow.

There were dark trees. She had dark hair. Her uncle lived in a big house. In Dundee. You couldn't tell from the pictures that her eyes were green. Jean Vogel. Her parents had wanted a boy: Eugene. I thought of the ways her name had changed. I tried to connect the girl in the snow with the voice I heard now from the kitchen.

I sat next to Jim and Rob McCarthy, our feet dangling in the water. They had muscles and tan skin. Mom and Dad had swum briefly and now sat with their guests; I wanted to listen to them discuss the Gunderson Ranch. The boys kicked the water. Why, I wondered, should I have to be friends with them when Dad wasn't friends with their father? I was supposed to have something in common with them because we were the same age. Dad said the same thing about Billy Smith next door. I shouldn't expect world peace unless I was able to learn to get along with my neighbors.

The bright path seems dim; Going forward seems like a retreat; The easy way seems hard.

Trees and clouds and sky turned, in the water, into bits of moving color; a mosaic, a bottle broken, then rearranged. On the patio, Dad said, "Agnew." The house and the trees dissolved in the light. Beauty can't be captured, I thought, any more than the Tao can be named. I studied our reflections, shifting and dividing in the water, wondering if I could use the image in "The Sun Library."

"Like go-kart racing?" Jim asked.

"I haven't done it *much*," I replied. A mistake: what if he asked about the times I had done it? I wasn't even sure what go-karts were.

"Does your school give a lot of homework?" I asked, hoping to keep him from asking more about go-karts.

"Not too much," he answered. He was bored with me, which was OK.

"Wanna do some dives?" he asked his brother, who nodded, getting up.

"Wanna do some dives?" he asked me, sort of politely, as if I were the guest.

"I'm gonna do some *laps*," I said. I got in the pool and started to swim, staying near the shallow end. They dove: flips and jackknifes, off the board, again and again. I tried to see how long I could stay under water; it felt sort of like being stoned. I came up; the sun a yellow smear across the sky. I swam and my arms made hundreds of pearls. Light eliminated things. There were some leaves and twigs in the pool; I hadn't cleaned it well.

After a while, my eyes stinging with chlorine, I got out. I watched the swimming boys and thought about "The Sun Library." Lines of light, wiggling across the pool. *Ripple in still water, when there is no pebble tossed, nor wind to blow.* The Grateful Dead meant sometimes things happened without a cause. The movement came from stillness, the Tao. The Grateful Dead took acid with Ken Kesey and drove across the country in a bus. I would do something like that. I wanted the afternoon to end. I went over to my parents and pulled up a patio chair. The aluminum legs scraped the concrete.

"Tire yourself out?" Dad asked.

"No," I said, irritated. Maybe he's trying to make sure they don't think it's his fault I'm not athletic. But I made an effort. I did go swimming and *tried* to be friendly. He's trying to prove to them that we're normal, I thought, shivering for a second. They returned to their conversation. They seemed to be enjoying themselves, talking about the first time they'd met, at a dinner the British consul had held, years ago, for Princess Margaret.

Mom ran her hand through Dad's hair as she got up. "Do you want another Miller?" she asked Mr. McCarthy. He nodded, and then listened, smiling, while Dad told him how Roosevelt had once suggested Posha run for governor. "Mark's been working on a report about that . . . he's the expert."

Mr. McCarthy looked at me.

"Oh, I haven't gotten very far," I said, in the tone I used at school to pretend I wasn't ready for a test for which I'd studied hard.

Dad shrugged, letting me off the hook.

I looked at Mr. McCarthy. He's humoring us, I thought; he's smirking . . . but in the brightness it was hard to tell. Salt-and-pepper hair spread across his chest like creosote covering the desert. I thought about the man he'd saved from the gas chamber. I tried to picture what it would be like to be part of their family. They were physical, went waterskiing; we didn't . . . we sat and talked about the past. Their family is real, I thought. Ours isn't. They're athletic. We're shadows.

". . . with Felix Frankfurter . . ."

Maybe, I thought, a family has to tell stories about itself. To keep them going. Otherwise, we're just bodies on the patio beneath the sky. If we don't talk about the past it disappears. Where is Roosevelt if we don't talk about him? I looked at the sky. No clouds like Campobello.

Mom came back with the beer. Why, I wondered, hugging my knees, was a story different when Posha told it (while we tramped through the muddy woods), than when Dad told it, here on the patio? It shouldn't matter who said something, but it did. A story wasn't the same when Dad told it, and it was even worse when I did, I thought, thinking of my *stupid* report. Maybe, I said to myself, memories aren't stories. People think they're the same but they aren't. They're like two people who always go everywhere together—so you get them confused. No one would know, from a story, what it had felt like that day when I'd come back with Posha from hiking, and Nanna had washed me with the brown soap, in the bathroom with the George Washington wallpaper and the wood floors on which the water from the old-fashioned tub had spilled, making lakes. The towels with the monogrammed G. The pear trees, the light through the window—no one will know what that afternoon felt like.

The boys shouted. The boys dove.

"And at Dunbarton Oaks," my father said.

Family stories could be boring and comforting at the same time, like watching reruns on our black-and-white TV. Posha and the U.N., also in black-and-white. I like a lot of lemon in my iced tea, I thought, squeezing, squinting. A billboard on Bell Road, at the edge of Phoenix, said: U.S. out of U.N. It worked the other way too: U.N. out of U.S. It didn't work that way with Salem. You couldn't take the country out of it. Mr. McCarthy put a cigarette out in the dusty-green ashtray. I remembered the time Posha had taken me to the U.N. dining room. Flowers on the tables and large glass windows and light on the river. Posha had been to seventy-five countries; he loved to travel; Nanna's friends, Mom had said, were fellow travelers. A lot of the countries Posha had visited didn't exist anymore. When I was younger I'd made up imaginary nations, putting all the best cities in one country. Favorite cities, like favorite numbers: I had a certain feeling about them.

Sparky rested on the patio; Dad drank a beer. I stirred sugar into my iced tea; it went round like the snow in one of the plastic domed toys I liked to collect. When you shook them it snowed in Paris, London, or New York. The sky isn't a plastic dome. We're not anywhere else. I squeezed a lemon wedge into the tea and picked out the seeds with my fingers, dropping them in the ashtray. The boys got out of the pool. Sparky ran up and licked them while they dried off. They joined us on the patio. Jim was on the student council; he asked Dad about law schools.

"They seemed like they've grown into very nice boys," Mom said after they left.

"Yes," Dad agreed.

———

It was time for our reports; Martha Wallace went first. She talked about the Wallace family horse farms in Virginia. When she was done, Schaeffer asked, drumming his fingers on his desk, "So when did the first Walrus come to America?"

"What did you just say?" Mr. Lewis demanded.

"I just asked," Schaeffer repeated, grinning, "when did the first Walrus set foot on our fair shores?"

Martha covered her eyes, mumbled something, and sat down. After a call from her dad, Mr. Lewis canceled the rest of the oral reports; we turned in the written versions. "Very impressive use of vocabulary!" Mr. Lewis wrote on mine. "And you certainly changed my opinion of Cordell Hull!"

———

A week later Mrs. Sklar dropped by. Most people called ahead; she just showed up. Sometimes this annoyed Dad (or perhaps he just pretended that it did.) *Dropping by* seemed theatrical to me—like someone walking on in a soap opera.

Dad and I had been about to clean the air-conditioning filters; instead we sat down around the glass table on the patio. Mrs. Sklar wanted to talk about the election. Dad asked, teasingly, whether she was still planning to leave the country. She said she wasn't ruling it out; she had a nephew who'd gone to Canada. She knew about Nanna's involvement with the peace movement; she'd read the tribute in *The Nation*. Dad began to tell her about the time Nanna and Dr. Spock had been arrested together. I felt embarrassed; he's telling stories again, I thought. But it was different when they were about Nanna; I always wanted to hear about her.

"You know," Dad added, "Mark was especially close to her."

It was a weird and awkward public balm. It felt vicariously boastful. A grapefruit lay squashed on the cement, surrounded by ants. I looked at Jason and Sharon, unable to tell if they were jealous. I felt grateful to Mom and Dad for keeping the story of Nanna and me alive.

"He's a writer, just like his grandmother," Dad said.

"Is that right?" she asked. "What kind of writing do you do?"

"Poetry," I said, uncomfortable.

"That's wonderful!" exclaimed Mrs. Sklar. "I wish I had that talent."

Beyond the phone poles rising through the citrus trees, coppery clouds wandered in from the west. Mrs. Sklar and my parents began to talk about Beth Shalom's membership problems; I felt relieved but also regretted that we weren't talking about Nanna anymore. A flock of birds settled on the phone lines; long shadows settled on the patio, and Mrs. Sklar asked Dad what he thought would happen with the Gunderson Ranch. He wasn't sure.

"You're really keeping up your father's tradition," Mrs. Sklar said to Dad. "And you," she said, turning to me. "You must be proud to be from a family that has done so much."

Smiling, sort of, I said nothing.

After Mrs. Sklar left I went to my room and tried to work on "The Sun Library." I made some changes but wasn't sure about them. Weird: a word could seem right one day but wrong the next. What shifted? You had to listen carefully and be in the right state of mind.

I got up and went into the bathroom. In fifty years my face would be wrinkled like Posha's, like my fingers when I swam. Once I had flown to New York by myself and Posha had met me; he'd stood at the end of the carpeted corridor at Kennedy in his gray overcoat and felt hat, holding his pipe, grinning. I tried to imagine looking into a mirror in the future.

Mrs. Sklar had told Mom I was good-looking but, I thought, people my age don't think so. A zit: a red island above my eyebrow's coastline. Imagining Baltz looking in a mirror, I smiled at my reflection and tried different expressions. Sometimes I imitated people's expressions or gestures in front of them and they didn't even notice. I had been using Richard's laugh for weeks. People think it's mine, I thought. Probably other people do the same thing and I don't notice. Dad sometimes imitates Posha, but he probably doesn't even know he's doing it. Maybe eventually I'd forget who I was imitating.

Even though I didn't need to, I sat down to pee. Long ago Dad had shown me how to go to the bathroom:

No matter how much you jiggle
and how much you dance
the last drop always ends up in your pants.

I'd never liked this rhyme. I sat on the porcelain, looking at the fluffy towels. When you sat, less problem with the last drop.

I tried to poo. When I was little, Nanna had worried about my bowel movements. I'd been unsure what the *movements* were that she asked about; Mom called it taking a poo. Eventually I'd understood that she was just using the old-fashioned term. She was concerned about my bowel movements, the peace movement, whether my mother was giving me enough to eat (I looked so thin), and about my ideas on religion, poetry, and the problems of the world. Once she'd asked what I thought the biggest one was; I'd told her I was worried about the water shortage, and she had assured me the scientists were making progress cleaning up the oceans. I had not been worried about pollution. I was worried that if people kept using water the world would eventually run out. Planets died of thirst on *Lost in Space*. People misunderstand each other all the time.

I could, I thought, sometimes still hear Nanna's voice, but then I wasn't sure. Perhaps I only remembered a memory of her voice, not her voice itself. But I remembered the feeling of her.

Nanna singing:

Baby bye, there's a fly
Can you catch him you and I?

I thought, while I sat, of the talks my mother and I sometimes had about Nanna and my feelings about her. Although Mom and I weren't ever able to have enough time with each other, during the last year we'd had more. She wanted to have time alone with me; she wanted to make sure, she said, that it didn't get lost in the shuffle. We would have lunch, just by ourselves, at the Sugar Bowl. Over Biltmore's, sandwiches made with turkey, avocado, and blue-cheese dressing, we would talk about many things, including Nanna. I would tell her my feelings about love, how important I thought it was. She would explain to me that there were different kinds of love. The love between a man and wife, our love for each other, the love that Nanna had had for me, the love I had for Dad and Sharon and Jason, the love I would one day have for someone else. Of course there was also the love that you had for the things you loved and for special places. I felt all these different kinds of love overlapped. I wasn't sure they really were that different. They didn't feel different. We discussed this. Our disagreements were sincere. The restaurant had nineteen different kinds of sundaes. The Pinnacle Peak. The Camelback Mountain. The Sonoran. The names made them sound very different, and they were, somewhat, although in the end they were all ice cream.

———

Tim Ratter, a headband in his stringy hair, came up to me in the corridor. He whispered in my ear. "Hey toothpick. Haven't forgotten about you. Just wait." He shoved me and went on.

Later, walking home along the canal through the eucalyptus shade, I imagined the revenge I would take, some day, when I was governor and Ratter was on death row. "You don't remember, do you? Loloma School? Seventh grade?" I would shake my head regretfully, denying clemency.

The house was quiet. Mr. deSoto was coming at four. I poured a glass of apple juice and spread peanut butter on some Ritz crackers. Connie came into the kitchen, wearing turquoise slacks and a white shirt. I hadn't known she was in the house.

"Oh, hi," I said. "I didn't see your car."

"It broke down," she said. "Lloyd dropped me off."

"That's too bad. Do you think they can fix it?"

"Lloyd's brother's going to work on it. . . . How's school?"

"Not bad." I hesitated. "Is Lloyd feeling better?"

"Oh, that cold," she said, "he's over it." She took a cloth and started wiping the counter, where I'd left crumbs. I wished I had wiped them up before she came in; I was *going to,* I said to myself, but wasn't sure this was so. I wasn't sure what else to ask. Maybe something about her church—but what? Sometimes Mom would talk to Connie about Chicago, where Connie went each Christmas to visit her cousins. Mom had relatives there, too, but hers lived in the suburbs and Connie's were on the South Side, which I knew, from Jim Croce, was the bad part of town. They both knew they weren't really talking about the same city—but pretended they were.

Maybe I could ask about her dog Captain. Captain was a terrier, not a junkyard dog. Should there be words in the room? She finished wiping the counter, the air conditioner went on, and I wondered if I was supposed to act as if she weren't there. I wanted to be friends with her; I wanted her to disappear.

"I hope you don't mind me being in here," she said.

"Oh, no," I answered. I tried to eat my snack slowly so she wouldn't think I was uncomfortable. I watched the light drift across Squaw Peak. When I was done I took my plate over to the sink.

"I'll get that," Connie said.

"No, that's OK," I said, rinsing the glass.

"Don't you worry about that," she half-insisted.

"It's OK," I said, drying the glass but leaving the plate in the sink for her.

I went to my room. Twenty minutes to deSoto. I took out "Another Time." In poetry, Anna said, you had to discover your voice. But what if there were different voices? I had decided I would change "Sunset Symphony" to "Sunset."

> *The flutes play softly*
>   *a sad melody*
> *and the Universe's drum*
>   *can barely be heard.*

I heard the back gate clang. Mr. deSoto.

We stood in the backyard. He was drenched with perspiration. I concentrated. It's a matter, I thought, of not thinking. This was still a thought. *Yield and overcome.* The football flew toward me, knocking leaves off a grapefruit tree. I caught it. Why do I have to do this? The ball wobbled perilously. I tried not to focus on my anger but kept returning to it.

"Keep your eye on the ball."

I kept returning to it again and again.

"Keep your eye on the ball."

If only I could turn away from my anger. Why couldn't I?

"Send it back, champ." My throw was wildly off; the ball landed in the pool. Then we tossed it in silence, back and forth, back and forth. *Empty yourself of everything.* Let the mind rest at peace.

I heard Mom's car. She opened the back gate, holding a bag of groceries.

"How are you fellows doing?" she asked.

"He's coming along," deSoto said. His tone was different with Mom than with me. She'll never know this, I thought. I'll never know what he really thinks of me, of my family; he won't ever call me a weakling, but, I thought, that's what he thinks. What would he be doing if he weren't here?

Another car pulled into the driveway. Lloyd. Connie came out the kitchen door. She talked quietly with Mom and then went out the back gate. Lloyd waved at me and I waved at him; Mom waved at both of us and went inside.

Maybe if I talk to her she'll talk to Dad and deSoto won't have to come. She went into the kitchen: I could see her, through the window, putting groceries away. All I want is to be with her.

Soft and weak overcome hard and strong.

Let the mind rest at peace. Ripples in the clouds: sand at the beach. I fished the ball out of the ivy and threw it back. Nothing to say to each other. Once I started to miss I couldn't seem to stop. I thought about what Anna had told me about "negative capability," the English version of *yield and overcome*.

DeSoto had to be there another hour. He's trying to think of stuff to say, I thought.

"What do you think of the Suns' lineup?' he asked.

"I guess they're OK."

Tao abides in nonaction, yet nothing is left undone.

I thought about "Another Time" and Ratter. I missed and went to get the ball.

"You know that Heather Morel?" deSoto asked. "She in your class?"

I wondered how he knew her. I nodded.

"Whoa boy—what knockers!"

"Come on," he resumed. "Stomach in. Chest out. Send it back." Cumulus shapes in the orange trees. I could smell the blossoms. Some of them lay—bits of white confetti—on the lawn, in the light.

——

Anna got a lot of mail. One day she showed me a book printed on handmade paper that had been sent from England. She corresponded with Robert Duncan, a poet who lived in San Francisco. Most of my letters came from Posha. I hoped that eventually I'd be able to bring Anna and him together. Posha would come with me to school and sit on the couch in Anna's office on one of Nicola's pillows. I imagined their conversation, how well they'd get along.

Besides my letters from Posha, I also received *Poetry* magazine. Posha had given me a subscription; sometimes I'd bring it in and discuss the poems with Anna. And she sometimes gave me poems she liked. They were different from the ones Nanna had shared with me; Nanna hadn't known about the Beats.

One day I brought in a poem I'd been trying to figure out. We sat on the patio; Anna was working on a small clay sculpture of two figures embracing. It was called *Solving the Cold War Crisis*. We went over the stanzas again and again. Finally she told me some things went beyond interpretation. I was frustrated; Nanna had always been able to explain what the symbols meant. But Anna read poems differently. Maybe, she suggested, the meaning of an image was the image itself. "No ideas but in things," William Carlos Williams said. He'd known

Allen Ginsberg; they'd both lived in New Jersey. Williams was a doctor as well as a poet. Maybe he'd been Allen Ginsberg's doctor when Allen was a little boy. That could have been how they met. A mulberry leaf fell on the patio. A plum tasting good—that was all the meaning you needed. The plum wasn't a symbol; it was a plum. This made sense. The purpose of poetry: to keep moments alive. I showed Anna the new version of "Sunset." She liked the changes.

One afternoon, while we were sitting near the wash, Anna told me about her favorite poet, Ezra Pound. He had said you should make it new. "Show not tell." In the distance, boys shouted on the basketball court. A motorcycle revved. T. S. Eliot, Anna told me, had called Pound *"il miglior fabbro"*: the better craftsman. If I wrote a book, I thought, I would dedicate it to Anna, or to someone I didn't yet know, or to that person and Anna, and I would call Anna *"il miglior fabbro."* I would also dedicate the book to my mother. The book would be in memory of Nanna. In the book, all my important memories would be preserved. I would get the images just right; they would be alive. I would write about Nanna, my mother, Anna, and everyone I loved. Then they would live forever.

That evening I tried reading "The Waste Land." It was hard to understand all the symbols. I liked the part about the blind seer Tiresias, who changed from a man into a woman and then back again. He said it was better to be a woman. People got really mad at him for this. The preface explained that Eliot had been influenced by the philosopher F. H. Bradley, who believed everything in the world had a symbolic meaning. The world was a language: flowers, saguaros, stones, and clouds.

One day Anna was very excited. Karl had gotten a commission from the city of Tempe for one of his welded sculptures. He was becoming successful. She told me she was thinking of building a house in the desert. She could buy some land. She wanted to figure out a way to quit the school. With the new principal, the situation was going to get worse before it got better; everyone was becoming so uptight.

"Do you ever think of going back to California?" I asked, hoping she would say no, and thinking that somehow by asking I would make sure this wouldn't happen.

"Karl wouldn't want to," she said. And also, she added, she wasn't sure she did either. It was important for her to be in the desert. And there was her father. Anna's mother had died not long after her parents moved to Phoenix. She'd had her second heart attack a month after they arrived and she'd had to go into a nursing home. Anna would drive out to see her. "She was happier that last year of her life than she'd ever been. She saw everything so clearly; she talked about the brightness. One day she said, 'Anna, you know, I'd like to go on a trip.' The next day she died."

Now Anna's father was alone. He lived in a rooming house on Van Buren; two of his neighbors were prostitutes and he'd become friends with them. He did some odd jobs but had time on his hands and spent it at Anna's. Sometimes he brought the prostitutes over; they got on Karl's nerves, but Anna liked them.

She was thinking of writing a book about her father. The book would include interviews and poems and drawings. It would tell his story. He'd left home when he was fifteen; he'd been a hobo and ridden the rails, and then he'd had the lemon farm. I imagined what it would be like when Anna's book came out, probably from New Directions. Would it come out before mine? I want mine to be first, I thought. What if *The Collected*

Poems of Anna Voigt is published and it turns out she's the more important writer? You're an egotist, I told myself. You should want good things for Anna.

"What I really want," Anna would say, "is to get up every morning and drive out to the desert and watch the sunrise." Someday, I hoped, I could do this with her; I knew Richard had.

One time she and Karl had gone to the Captain Beefheart concert at Memorial Coliseum. They'd danced in the aisles. I imagined myself dancing in the aisles with Anna someday.

Anna wasn't too interested in music. She had only two records, Telemann and Frank Zappa, which she kept on the window ledge in the art room. Drew had a Billie Holiday album there, too, but it never got played. Almost all the records were Richard's. He sometimes played guitar; several years earlier, before I'd known him, he'd played some antiwar songs at an assembly. He'd been a little fat then; he'd worn a flower in his long, brown hair. Lisa, his girlfriend in Los Angeles, played clarinet. They'd both been in the same Catholic youth group and dropped out together. Anna had confided to me that she thought Richard was talented in too many ways. Eventually he'd have to make choices. He was, she said, a physics genius. When the school bought a computer, Mr. Sanger, the head of the upper school math department, chose Richard to be the first student to use it. Mr. Sanger told Anna a lot of colleges would pay to have Richard, which was important because his father taught at the university and didn't have much money. Richard was at Loloma on a scholarship. His dad didn't know he wasn't planning on being a scientist anymore; now he wanted to be a poet—or, maybe, a songwriter.

I wanted to like the music Richard liked; usually I did. Paul Simon, The Fairport Convention, and Joni Mitchell. I'd dis-

covered Joni on my own. The summer we went to Vail, I had
copied the lyrics to "For Free" and sent them to my grandmother. The song was about a musician who played on a street
corner. Because he wasn't famous nobody listened. They
couldn't hear how beautiful his music was. Because she was ill,
Nanna hadn't been able to respond, but Posha wrote to say
they both liked the new writer I'd discovered.

I could listen to *Ladies of the Canyon* again and again. I
tried not to listen to it *too* much. When I put it on, I would
imagine myself living in the canyon, baking bread and weaving.
In the sunshine I would draw and gather flowers. I wondered
where the canyon was. "The Conversation" seemed to be
about Anna and me.

> *He comes for conversation*
> *I comfort him sometimes*

Anna was like Joni; I was sure Richard thought so, too. Both
had long blonde hair. Joni's daring high notes reminded me of
a quality of Anna's that put her, somehow, on another level
than the other hip teachers. She didn't call attention to herself,
and so maybe people didn't notice the ways in which she was
more advanced. It was like the difference between Joni and
Judy Collins. Joni was original; Judy was nice—but not original. Mom liked her version of "Both Sides Now," which
wasn't, I thought, half as good as Joni's. It made me uncomfortable to think I had better taste than my mother.

Anna had no interest in Joni. This seemed odd; maybe, I
thought, Anna was too sophisticated. Or maybe she didn't like
Joni's music because the two of them were so similar. A
paradox; wisdom came through paradoxes.

Ian's tastes were different from Richard's. He listened to the Grateful Dead and Jethro Tull. I wasn't sure what Ian thought of me. Once, when he asked if I liked Jethro Tull, I answered, "Yeah, I think he's good." Ian laughed. I hadn't realized Jethro Tull wasn't a person. Ian Anderson was the person. Jethro Tull was probably someone from history, maybe medieval England. Soon after, Richard suggested I go with them to the Grateful Dead concert at the stadium in December. Ian didn't seem thrilled. I was; I knew they were talking about doing hash or maybe acid; I might have a vision.

I was uncomfortable when I was alone with Ian. But usually Richard was with us. Sometimes after a reading at Anna's the three of us would drive to Richard's house, where we'd smoke some joints in the desert behind his home. In the car Richard would turn the music all the way up, blasting the Grateful Dead or Little Feat into the darkness.

Sometimes I would be brought along even when there wasn't anything going on at Anna's. Richard, I thought, wanted to be my mentor; I always tried to keep up with his humor, which I understood more than Ian's. Richard liked *The Rocky and Bullwinkle Show* and the Son of God comics in *National Lampoon*. We would sit in the overgrown, moonlit backyard drinking Jim Beam and Richard would tell jokes that always ended with "watch me pull a rabbit out of a hat." Sometimes I tried the same punch line, but I never got the delivery right. Now and then I said things Richard thought were great, but I couldn't predict which these would be. I never tried to imitate Ian; he was too incomprehensible. Ian had done drugs before Richard; he had a subscription to *High Times*. His mother came from a *very* rich family; she was married to her fourth husband. During one of her marriages Ian had been sent to a boarding school in New Mexico; Anna said he had an intense relationship with his mother; it was like Kerouac and his mom; they fought but were close.

When we smoked I would, sometimes, begin to feel that I was probably stoned. I noticed the way the wooden bird feeder slowly kept rising. It stayed in the same place, but still it was moving. I've built up enough THC, I told myself. There were boxes and old bikes on the patio; they seemed to move, too. Maybe things were always moving but you only saw this when you were stoned. The moon, above the neighbor's TV antenna, kept going up and up. I knew I wasn't as stoned as Richard and Ian; what were they laughing at? A jackrabbit ran through the yard.

I wished we'd talk about poetry when we got stoned, but we didn't. They talked about drugs and girls and Drew Henley, who'd driven Ian crazy when they'd both been in the drama club. Ian had dropped out; he'd dropped out of everything except the *Amethyst.* "Here is my poem about Maria Callas," Ian would announce pretentiously, imitating Drew. Then he'd get up, choking from laughter and whiskey and, in his quiet voice, start to describe ways to drive Drew into quitting the *Amethyst.*

I would sit silently in the darkness, feeling its mystery, urgently wanting the course of the conversation to change, wondering who Maria Callas was, repeating to myself, *empty yourself of everything, empty yourself of everything,* hoping my silence would not become too loud. If it did I would just say, "Oh, God, I'm really buzzed," and then Richard would joke about how they were corrupting me.

It was easier to be with Anna. I was her student, her favorite. I didn't tell her all my problems, but I didn't need to: she understood. She told me things she didn't tell the others. Dreams they didn't know about. Which contained revelations. They might, she said, think she was crazy.

Anna used to say the school gave out too much homework. She said the kids in my class were wild. *Really* wild. They were growing up fast. She said the boys were big, if not mature. I would feel jealous—did she mean she thought they were attractive?

She would tell me, often, that I had an old soul.

———

Running around the desert track, way ahead of Douggy Dale. A pain in my side. I stopped, my mouth full of dust. Tim Ratter, coming from behind, shoved me. "Grosfeld, know something? I could knock all your teeth out and get away with it. I'm not going to do it now. But if I want to, I can."

When I got home I took out "Another Time."

> *Gentle raindrops*
> *like delicate lace*
> *a view of the garden we must leave*
> *rain, like teardrops*
> *feeds life*
> *though we do not want them*
> *they will come*
> *(and I must hope this is not a final poem)*

Both Posha and Anna said I didn't need the last line. They were probably right, I told myself, but I wasn't sure whether the poem had enough meaning without it.

———

Dad came to talk to me.

"Mark, your mother says you're really unhappy about deSoto?"

"Yeah."

"I just want to make sure, Mark, that you know our getting deSoto doesn't mean we don't think you're anything but great."

I nodded.

"So are you *really* unhappy?"

I felt cornered; I didn't want to say I was *really* unhappy. He might think I was exaggerating.

"Well . . ."

"Listen, if you *really* can't stand it, he doesn't have to come. But I want you to give it a chance for a few weeks. See how you feel then. I just don't want you to give up *too* easily. Deal?"

"Sure," I said. Only through Christmas. I can survive that.

"I'm glad you're being so reasonable, Mark. It would be awfully awkward to tell deSoto not to come at this point." He paused and then confided, "Not that I really care about him, but Linda's been with the firm a long time."

I nodded.

"I realize, Mark," he continued awkwardly, almost wistful, "that being out of doors isn't your *favorite* thing in the world, but it is a tradition in our family. You know when your mother was a girl she stayed inside—they weren't outdoor people."

Dad sometimes made fun of Mom because she wasn't coordinated. Once, when they'd first met, in Wisconsin, he'd taken her on a bike ride. Swerving to avoid a rabbit, she'd run into a tree. Everyone thought it was a funny story. But they wouldn't, I thought, if it were about me.

"Now," Dad continued, "she's got varicose veins. I'm sure you don't want varicose veins."

"I like being out of doors," I said impatiently, wishing he'd drop the topic. I've already *agreed,* I thought, and then added, after a moment, "I like to walk and hike."

He sort of laughed, as if I'd said something cute, absurd. But why does being outdoors mean having to throw a ball?, I thought. Posha likes to hike; so do Richard and Anna. *He* doesn't spend much time out of doors; he plays tennis now and then with Mr. Nachmann, but mostly he works.

"I'm sure if you're open-minded you'll start to enjoy it. And it might help you overcome some of your shyness."

I'm not shy, I thought, wishing I could explain.

"Oh, and by the way, your point about Jason *is* well taken." I'd told Mom that it was unfair Jason didn't have to have deSoto just because he was in Little League. *The world is ruled by letting things take their course. It cannot be ruled by interfering.*

———

"Another fine mess you've gotten me into," Jason whispered, as deSoto watched us do push-ups on the lawn.

3

"Careful," Dad said to Sharon.

"What?"

"You don't need to slam it."

"I didn't *slam* it," she said, frustrated.

"Let's just say you closed it very hard."

"You don't have to talk to me in that way," Sharon said, half to herself.

"What *way*?" Dad asked.

"You know what *way*," Sharon replied, the same way.

"Can we just drop it?" Mom asked. We walked from the parking lot toward Le Chemin, Mom and Dad's favorite restaurant. Small green lamps, planted in the ground like cacti, lit the walkway; the scents of sage and orange blossoms wandered in the air. I stayed a few steps behind. When we got to the door Dad opened it for Mom but Sharon wouldn't let him hold it.

"You're so chauvinist," she said, not moving.

"I'm just *trying* to be chivalrous," Dad said, continuing to hold the door. Jason and I entered. Sharon gave up and followed us and Dad followed her, shaking his head, looking hurt, even though, I thought, he'd won.

"I don't mind a little chivalry," Mom said comfortingly—and a bit tensely. I wondered if she was annoyed at Sharon.

Henri, the owner, greeted us. "I have saved your usual table for you. Some other people wanted it, but I said, 'No, no.'"

We have no right to be here, I thought. Children in South Phoenix will starve while we eat. I can't do anything about it. But that's not taking responsibility. Blaming it on Mom and Dad but eating the food—which I don't even like that much. If I had any principles I would fast, like Gandhi.

"That's all right, Henri," Dad said, "you didn't need to."

Henri smiled doubtfully and led us through the still mostly empty restaurant to our corner table. We are, I thought, on stage. "You are looking particularly beautiful tonight, may I say, Mrs. Grosfeld," Henri remarked, holding out Mom's chair.

"You may," Mom said, seeming to enjoy her role.

Sharon made a face.

"Henri certainly goes out of his way to please," Dad remarked.

Mom agreed.

Le Chemin sat in a small grove of grapefruit trees across the street from a hardware store. The sun was going down and I could already make out the chalky moon. At the table next to us a man in a tan suit dined alone, occasionally glancing at a magazine. He's brave, I thought, to eat by himself, pretending that it's normal, that he doesn't care what other people think of him. The waiter pretended it was normal, too.

I buttered a roll; some crumbs fell on the floor. I don't want to end up like him, I thought. He'll go home alone tonight. To one of the condominiums on Osborne.

I was always lonely at school. I wanted my family to understand what it was like at school and to save me from it, although I knew they couldn't. And then I felt lonely at home because I couldn't talk about my school loneliness. I didn't know what to say about it: there's no story when you're lonely, I thought. You're just ashamed. You don't have a story; everyone else does; that's how it spreads, the loneliness, like water on a patio. . . .

"I have a question," my mother said.

"I have an answer," Dad replied.

"What kind of a fish is turbot?"

"It's a fishy fish."

"What's *that* mean?" Jason asked. "How can a fish not be fishy?"

"It just means it's got a more distinctively fish sort of taste," Dad said.

"Sounds fishy," I said, restless.

"Ha-ha," Dad replied.

Invisible fibers crisscross the air: tense tangled lines. Everyone feels them, I thought.

"How about cow-y cow?" Jason asked.

"Did you say cow eat cow?" Dad enquired, trying to trump Jason's joke.

"Cows don't eat cows," I replied.

"How now brown cow?" Sharon interjected.

"HOW COW NOW BROWN COW NOW COW," Jason continued.

"All right, now," Dad said. "We're in a nice restaurant."

Although it wasn't dark, the waiters lit candles. The tables were white islands, the napkins white mountains. Our waiter came.

"Le plat de légumes," I pronounced carefully. Nanna had wanted to take us to France, to Paris and Provence. Sharon and I discussed it with her while we walked through the meadow one summer morning on her farm. Sharon called me *"petit pois":* she was studying French. She said we *had* to go to Mont Saint-Michel. We'd walked from the willow tree to the barn, discussing all the other places we would go.

Sometimes places felt more real in memory than when you'd been there. The old barn, the willow tree, Mrs. Gunderson's bird pond, and other places, too—this was what poetry captured. I was sitting in Le Chemin, but what was real was another place. Maybe in the future the memory of this restaurant would be powerful. But now the experience didn't seem very real. In the future I would remember the candles, the orchard, the bread, and the feeling of being with my family, but not the memories of other moments that were filling this one. The willow tree near Nanna's house, the road past the Bennett farm. The dark brown bowls on the tablecloth in the dining room with the oval rug. The light coming in through the lace-curtained windows from the garden where, in the summer morning heat, among the lilies, insects buzzed. It was strange that moments became more real later, and that you knew this was going to happen while you were still in the moment. Was this true, I wondered, for everyone?

A grapefruit hung a few feet from me on the other side of the window in the darkening orchard. A scumbly painting of the Sacre Coeur hung on the wall above Sharon's frizzy hair. It looked sort of like a Utrillo. Anna had told me about the impressionists' rebellion against materialism.

"But what do you mean by materialism?" I'd asked.

"The belief that *things* are important," Anna answered.

That had been what I thought. But I didn't quite understand: things *were* important: rocks, birds, and trees.

"No ideas but in things," I reminded her. She explained that the materialists believed refrigerators and dishwashers were important. Still, I wondered, why some things, not others? Why not refrigerators? Their humming whiteness had a sort of power.

I drank my ginger ale and watched the table shadows dance. The waiters went into the kitchen, balancing their round, brown trays. I wondered how they talked in the kitchen. I'll never know, I thought; it's like the refrigerator light when the door is closed. I tried to remember the joke Richard had once made about that when we were getting stoned. The waiters acted like waiters when they came back through the swinging doors. The restaurant began to fill. There weren't any other families; most people didn't bring children here. Our waiter brought the soup. Mom let Sharon and me sip her daiquiri; I felt, for a moment, like a member of a special club.

This vichyssoise, I thought, disappointed, isn't as delicious as the vichyssoise of the past. I expect too much, I thought, thinking of how, sometimes, I would lie on a lawn chair in the backyard on a beautiful day, alongside my mother, a bowl of jellied madrilene on the glass table next to me, trying to enjoy *luxury*. Mom's better at this—these moments never seem as pleasurable as they're supposed to be. You only get to be a child once and I'm not doing a good job of enjoying it. You're spoiled, Mark. Later you're going to look back at this time, wishing you'd enjoyed it more; by then it'll be too late.

Thinking about the future, I felt a sort of pre-sadness; we wouldn't be together anymore. The clouds in the east Phoenix sky, beyond the orchard, reflected the sun in the west. They caught so much light that it seemed the sun was setting there.

"It doesn't accomplish *anything* to bomb civilians," Sharon said. "The cycle just . . ."

"It's *unfortunate* the terrorists hide in those camps," Dad interrupted. "But Jews have to protect themselves. I'd like to be idealistic, too. But when your survival is at stake you have to defend yourself."

They'd been arguing about this forever. Usually I took Sharon's side but sometimes, to be unpredictable, I supported Dad.

Self-defense. Would Ratter really knock my teeth out? Maybe I should have said something back to him. *One gains by losing and loses by gaining.* Dad had shown me how to make a fist. When I was young he'd boxed with me: Posha had boxed with him. Dad's wedding ring hurt. I *hate* boys, I thought, practicing my fist beneath the table, trying to remember where my thumb should go.

The vegetable plate came: grilled tomatoes, asparagus, mushrooms, potatoes. Gandhi, Nanna's hero, had planned to live to one hundred and twenty-five. I did, too; it was an achievable age. There would be a lot of advances in science during my lifetime. I looked at Mom and Dad eating their fish. I hoped the advances happened soon enough to help them. I had once thought that it was possible I might be the first person in history who didn't die. Some people thought it would be terrible to live forever: you'd get super bored, you'd be so old you couldn't do anything; this would be very lonely, but still—better than dying. I imagined being a thousand years old and looking back on this dinner. I might not even be able to remember my family. I traced the infinity sign on the tablecloth. I'd realized I probably couldn't live forever, but one hundred and twenty-five was close enough. How terrible if all the Jews died. Which could happen. Five thousand years, then gone. What a waste. How lonely and awful to be the last Jew on earth—like the last of the Mohicans.

Nanna liked the quiet of the Quakers; she had taken me to the Friends' meetinghouse on Stonebridge Road; an old maple cast its shadow on the white building. The Quakers, Nanna said, spoke when they were moved to speak. God was an inner light. Some people disapproved of Nanna becoming Quaker; they said the Jews didn't need defectors. When Nanna and Posha visited us over the holidays, she would get a Christmas tree for their room at the Desert Palm. We helped decorate it. She brought ornaments from New York, sparkling crimson and gold balls and Russian eggshell princesses.

Mr. Nachmann said it was shameful to have a Christmas tree.

Why would you ever be grateful to be dead? In a month I would go with Richard and Ian to their concert. We would get high in the stadium and my consciousness would be transformed. I could barely make out the shapes of the trees in the now-dark orchard. The moon was white, the potatoes warm.

"What about the human rights of the Jews in Syria?" Dad asked, knowing he was scoring a point. "Don't *they* have human rights?"

"You're the one who always says two wrongs don't make a right," Sharon replied.

She likes being angry, I thought, wondering if she was wondering how she'd sound in a book. We're all always thinking how we'd sound in the book about our family. *The Forsyte Saga. War and Peace.* A twelve-part movie on PBS. *The Fall of the House of Grosfeld.*

She hears her words as she speaks them—an echo, always.

"I don't see what *that* has to do with anything," Dad said.

I remembered our dinners with Nanna and Posha, how they would argue about Muskie and McGovern. Nanna didn't trust Muskie because he hadn't criticized Humphrey for allowing the police to beat up the kids in Chicago. Nanna had left her hotel room and walked through the riots; she would never forgive Humphrey for what she'd seen that night. Posha thought McGovern was a good man, he'd spent the night with them in Connecticut once, but he didn't think he could win. Nanna disagreed, and when she took a position, Posha had told me, she wouldn't budge. "She was the most determined woman I've ever known," he'd said. "Quiet, but determined." Maybe this was also true of me.

Nanna and Posha always asked Sharon and me our opinions. When Dad was a boy he would be allowed to stay up late when important people came over. "I've never heard such interesting, intellectual discussions," Dad would say. Felix Frankfurter would sometimes come up from Washington; he'd been Posha's professor once; later they'd become friends. Nanna felt that if he'd wanted to he could have saved the Rosenbergs. Eventually he came around to her position, but it was too late by then. And there was Nanna's friend Hans Wirtz, the scientist who'd worked with her on the campaign to stop nuclear testing. "I think it was rather intimidating to your mother when she married me," Dad would tell us, "coming from Omaha."

"I guess I was a little intimidated," Mom would say. "They could be intimidating."

I looked at the man eating by himself.

"Israel has to have higher ethical standards," Sharon answered Dad.

"And get pushed into the sea," he replied.

I pictured the Jews being pushed into the sea, their yarmulkes floating on the surf. Mom put lemon on her fish. Our debates are just imitations of Nanna's and Posha's. They had interesting intellectual discussions—we pretend to. There's only room for one winner. Who everyone will love. We pretend to be at *a nice restaurant* but we're at war; invisible soldiers, invisible planes. No one ever gives up. We don't know why it's like this; we're caught in it, like a blinding dust storm.

Jason, looking bored, played with his mashed potatoes, as

if they were a sand castle, the sauce the sea. I looked at Mom, eating her fish. I wondered what she was thinking. She was sitting out the argument. Maybe her mind was somewhere else. Maybe, I thought, she just wants to enjoy being at Le Chemin.

The waiter filled our glasses.

"I think we should change the subject," I said. Once, when Dad was a boy, Posha had taken him to meet Roosevelt, who'd said he was a "young diplomat." Everyone had called him that for a long time.

Sharon started to speak; Dad and I looked at her.

"I think your brother has a good point," Dad said.

Sharon and I are both upset with Dad, I thought, but for different reasons. And we're both trying not to be, wanting peace as well as victory.

"What do you think's going to happen when the council votes?" Mom asked.

"I talked to Bentley," Dad answered. "He's confident." The Gunderson Ranch would be saved. The pond, the birds, the old mesquite, the hills of creosote.

My father's speech. The school superintendent had slapped him on the back afterward. The reporter from KPAK had come up to shake his hand.

Sharon looked annoyed, about to speak.

"How is Mrs. Goldman?" I asked my mother, cutting her off.

"Not well, I'm afraid," Mom said.

Mrs. Goldman's husband had left her for a younger woman. He was a lawyer, and sometimes Dad saw him at meetings, but he hadn't been to our house, or Beth Shalom, since the divorce. Mrs. Goldman hardly ever went out. One time, at Goldwater's department store, she walked into a plate-glass window, but luckily wasn't badly hurt. Mom worried she was having a breakdown. She called at strange hours. They'd had lunch that afternoon.

"She kept repeating herself and she hardly touched her food. Apparently," Mom continued, in a whisper, "Felicia is into group sex."

I remembered Felicia, the Goldmans' daughter, from San Diego. Once, she and Sharon had taken me for a walk around Mission Bay; Mom and Dad had thought we were lost. "We had to send the Coast Guard after them," Mom would say, telling the story. The Coast Guard: Dad and Mr. Nachmann in Mr. Nachmann's boat. The house we'd rented had white stucco walls. White stucco walls and bright pink flowers. You could smell the ocean. I concentrated. Once I had the picture, once I could remember the scent, once I could remember the exact way the light fell on the walls and the flowers, and the shadows—then a feeling came through the image; the feeling was inside of it, its essence. That was what mattered. I could be somewhere else without leaving the table.

"That must be distressing to her," Dad said. "She really needs to get help."

I drank my ice water.

"Unfortunately, there's a lot of prejudice against psychiatry," he continued, "especially out here. But I say if you need it, get it." He was speaking to all of us, but I felt the words were for me. "A lot of people think it's shameful. When I first went *I* probably thought it was. But it really helped. I realized how angry I was at your grandfather," he said, sounding almost amused, embracing me with this intimate confidence. "I had a real Oedipal complex."

The man who sat alone asked for his check. I sliced a grilled tomato and tried again to remember the house in San Diego. I could sort of get it, some of the scent of it.

Nixon had signed the peace treaty. He'd bombed Haiphong Harbor; Sharon had been upset, but force had worked. Peace through strength. Nixon was now more powerful than ever.

In my desk I kept a letter from McGovern my grandmother had sent. I cut up an asparagus stalk while the tall, blond waiter filled our water glasses. I wondered what he looked like when he wasn't a waiter. Did he go to ASU? In a month I would go to the Dead concert. I wondered if he had a motorcycle and what he thought of us.

In the car, after dinner, Sharon said, "Thanks, Dad." She's trying, I thought, to make up for the stuff during dinner.

"You're welcome."

"It was really a great meal," Mom said.

"Yeah," I added, "thanks."

"I hope your vegetable plate was satisfactory."

"It was pretty good."

"Thanks, Dad," Jason said dutifully.

"You're both welcome."

We say the same thing every time, I thought. *Thank you* means nothing; so easy to say. Dad knows; we know he knows. He'd spent more than a hundred dollars on the meal. Even if we are grateful, I thought, he won't believe us; he'll know we've thanked him because we have to. Poor Dad; we take him for granted. Or he thinks we do. We criticize him while we eat his food.

We drove past the Ultissima Salon. We've sold out, I thought, for *a gourmet dinner*. We turned onto Fortieth Street. Behind us, the Papago Buttes and the radio towers. I remembered the time we'd gone to the moratorium march at the university. A girl sang, "I ain't a-marchin' anymore." We'd all sung, in the dark, beneath the moon and the olive trees.

I thought of my mother's song: *"I see the moon and the moon sees me. Please let the moon that shines on me shine on the one I love."* Funny, I thought, the way it really does seem to follow us in the car. Shining on us. We're lucky; nothing terrible has ever happened to us. There are accidents, people paralyzed; in Wisconsin, a whole town was poisoned. We're blessed but for no reason, it's frightening, the blessing could wear off at any moment. We drove past darkened houses; I felt but wasn't sure we all felt the same way. Mom and Dad talked about McGrath and Greene, Jewish Family and Children's Services, Mom's volunteer work.

There wasn't much traffic. Sharon, Jason, and I were silent. It didn't take long to get home.

I lay in bed, sad. Learn to let your feelings go, I told myself, hugging my pillow. Then I got up and went to my dresser, where I kept Nanna's letters. I opened the top drawer. Beneath my socks, my stamp album, and my poems: the envelope. I took it out. I didn't want to open it *too* often. The letters might lose their power.

Dearest Mark,

How are you, darling? I miss you. Has school started? Are you feeling well? You were sick, but I hope you are better.

What are you reading? I am reading Damien *by Herman Hesse. This afternoon we took a walk through the fields. We went down to the bridge. Do you remember when you were here, and we saw the deer?*

I read to the end; I knew the letter well. I thought of finding the one in which she told me how special I was, but I decided to save it. I put the envelope back carefully, on top of the wax paper sheet with the dried leaves she'd once sent me.

Resting my head on the pillow, I closed my eyes and remembered our trip home from Vail a year and a half before. We'd stopped in Moab; although the rest of us were hesitant, Dad said he wanted to look into a raft trip. Anna had later spoken of Moab, how powerful the canyons were. She had been there; she had taken pictures and was going to do gouaches from them. But I hadn't seen the canyons, just the Best Western. I lay in my bed, trying to remember what the Best Western had felt like. The ice machines. The painting of a bullfighter. Jason and I jumping up and down on the bed, Sharon reading a mystery. In my parents' room, the phone ringing. Why would someone call us there? My uncle from New York, where Nanna was in the hospital. The doctors said there wasn't any hope. My father drove all night so he could catch the morning flight to Kennedy. We played car games for a while. We tried "Twenty Questions" and license-plate bingo, but then that gave way to silence as the afternoon turned into evening, and the stars appeared in the sky, and we drove into Arizona.

We passed Monument Valley. Somewhere there were Navajo villages but we couldn't see them. There were gas-station lights; we saw them for a moment, then they were gone. We drove through the vast, cold darkness, but it was warm in the car.

Mom urged Dad to stop when we got near Flagstaff, but he still had half a thermos of coffee from the Best Western, and he drove on. The number of billboards increased and we entered Phoenix near dawn.

Nanna rallied after that; there was hope. Dad came back from New York and I began sixth grade. One afternoon my mother picked us up at school. I told her about the new art teacher who had us draw our dreams. Mom said she sounded like a good teacher. We were low on ice cream so we stopped at Baskin-Robbins. Baltz and Schaeffer were there. As a special treat, Mom bought us cones. My grandmother had died the night before, she told us when we got home.

I lay in the darkness, clutching my bear, allowing myself a little silent grief. It grew stronger, a river moving seaward. It came from some void and traveled to my throat, heading toward the sockets behind my eyes. It filled the empty spaces, the system of caverns that went on and on.

Lilly went round in her wheel. Rose, the mouse I'd had before her, was buried in the pet cemetery, beyond a patch of weeds beyond the pool. She'd died a few months before my grandmother. I'd placed her in the freezer to preserve her for the future. Sharon screamed when she found the box next to the frozen peas. My father then tried to explain death and acceptance. We went into his study, where he had explained so many things. A copy of the Declaration of Independence and a letter from Woodrow Wilson to Marcus Grosfeld hung on the beige wall. There were maps from Dad's collection and the fencing medal he'd won in high school. A photograph with Dick Epstein from their trip across the country. He smoked his pipe and talked; I sat on the floor. But what if there was a chance, I'd argued, while the light sneaked through the curtains; I'd read about cryonics in *Life*. How could you give up so easily? I knew I was fighting a losing battle. I wanted to tell him not to smoke but didn't want to bug him; I'd already gone too far by putting Rose in the freezer.

I wanted him to comfort me. He did.

After Nanna's death, I didn't mention cryonics. Dad explained people lived on in the memories of those they loved, through their actions, and through their effect on people. Nanna lived on through her poetry, through me. And because she had made the world better. This was, Dad said, the Jewish idea of immortality. I wanted it to be useful, but I couldn't convince myself that, in this philosophy, it was really the person who lived on.

———

As I walked Anna toward her room, she explained Pound's idea about using metaphors. It was like writing a check: you shouldn't unless there was money in the bank. Pound had gotten this from Chinese poetry. Of course, Anna admitted, she had written a lot of checks when her bank account was empty.

I thought about all the mail Dad got from banks in New York. Sometimes banks sent two copies of the same statement. "I've told them not to," Dad said, "but they don't listen. It's pretty irritating. They don't seem to care too much about trees."

I didn't want to get that kind of mail. I wanted to get letters with poems enclosed, like the ones Anna got from Robert Duncan. I heard Carlos, the custodian, mowing the grass; the buzzing grew loud, for a moment, in the warm air, then fainter. I turned toward Anna. "Did I tell you I'm reading *A Separate Reality?*"

"That's an amazing book," she said quietly. "Karl and I went right through it . . ." Her voice trailed off.

Mr. Ramsay, hurrying toward the administration building, waved at us. I wondered whether he and the other teachers thought it was weird that Anna and I were together so much.

We passed some fifth-graders; they, too, waved at Anna. I knew kids looked at me differently now because I was always with her, and because they knew I hung out with Richard and Ian. Richard was respected because he sometimes got people drugs. The week before, while I knelt in front of my locker, Baltz had come up to me and put his trumpet case down. "Heard you've been getting stoned," he said, approvingly. My life *was* better, but I still had to deal with Douggy and Ratter; I still wasn't invited to parties. We passed Hoffman's brother, a third-grader; he seemed lost in thought.

"I always wonder what they're thinking about," Anna said. "He could be thinking about the universe, or time, or the planets, or God, or who knows?"

I hadn't thought he might be thinking these things.

"Do you see that?" Anna asked, pointing toward a flock of crows. I looked up but didn't know what she meant. "You don't usually see them flying like that," she explained. The birds, in their strange formation, quickly turned into dots and disappeared.

—

4

I wish your soul could fathom mine
and I might catch a glimpse of you
and I think
Love cannot become routine
and I am filled with subtle fear.

Mom and I walked through Norwich's department store. During high school, Mom and her best friend Evelyn had worked at Brandeis's in Omaha—Mom in Gloves, Evelyn in Hats. Evelyn had been a better salesgirl, Mom told me; she'd always tell the customers how great they looked—something Mom couldn't do. When she moved to New York, before she married Dad, she'd worked at Macy's for six months, in Cookware; she'd been better at that.

Mom and I were alone, I thought, so rarely; now that we were, we could talk about things we could only discuss when no one else was there. Our theories of love, our plans for the future—and Nanna. Sometimes she would ask how my writing was coming along. I'd shown her a few poems; she'd been concerned: they were so sad. She told me she'd read Housman when she was young and liked him very much. I'd read his *Collected Poems;* they *were* all sad. I'd thought of them while working on *my* love poems (which I hadn't yet shown Mom). Sometimes she'd ask how things were going with Dr. Kurtz. And she'd confide her problems at Jewish Family and Children's Services. Even though she wasn't supposed to, she'd tell about the couples she counseled. Things weren't going well with the Schwartzes. He'd stopped paying the phone bill. Mrs. Schwartz spent all her time talking to other people; he just wanted her to spend more time with him. Sometimes she'd tell me that she was worried Dad was working too hard.

"I just wish he could learn to take a break. I'd *hoped* things would settle down now that that damn Valley Tech suit is over. But they haven't. He gets so caught up in other people's expectations," she said, frustrated. "Maybe it's a male ego thing," she added tentatively. "Always needing to prove yourself. I think he *has* proven himself." Then she continued, her tone lifting slightly, "He really does want to spend more time with all of you."

He spends a lot of time with us, I thought. We passed Watches, then Jewelry. Jewelry doesn't have anything to do with Jewry, I explained to an imagined inquisitor—they just sound the same; it's not because the Jews are rich.

"So do you think Dad will let Sharon get her ears pierced?" I asked. That had been the big fight the night before; Mom had tried to intervene but she'd given up. We'd gone with Jason into the living room to watch TV while Sharon and Dad went at it in the kitchen. Sharon had finally gone to her room, slamming the door. Then Mom had gone to her. And then to Dad.

"Of course he should," she said, slightly amused. "I'm sure he will. I know she just wants to do it because Beth Fineman did—your father *does* have a point about that. But it shouldn't be such a big deal."

If Beth jumps off a cliff, Dad had asked Sharon, would she? Sharon had said that was ridiculous.

"You shouldn't have to be in the middle of it," I told Mom.

Sharon's point, during dinner, had been that if she had to have braces, why *shouldn't* she be able to pierce her ears? It was hypocritical! I was pretty sure both Mom and I agreed with her on this. But, Mom said, she wasn't so sure about the trip to

Rocky Point. Sharon thought Dad didn't want her to go because Horowitz might be there.

"It's not because of Horowitz. Or Beth. That's not why," Mom said. "He's very worried there could be drugs there."

She doesn't know I've smoked pot, I thought, feeling bad I wasn't able to tell her. Under the right circumstances drugs could be OK. Pot didn't have to lead to heroin.

We walked through the luggage section. Suitcases the color of palm-tree husks. And travel posters. Hawaii. London. Mexico. Where would we go this summer? I love San Diego, I thought, but maybe we could try somewhere new. Mom and I often discussed different trips we might take. Although she didn't think Jason was old enough, she wanted to go to Europe someday. Dad had taken her on their honeymoon; they'd revisited some of the places Nanna had taken Dad when they'd gone before the war. In Toulouse, they'd met a man Nanna knew, a refugee from Spain who'd lived for a year in a cave. "I couldn't imagine living for a year in a cave," Mom had said. She got claustrophobic; when we went to Carlsbad Caverns she'd had to stay in the gift shop. Mom once told Sharon about a nightmare she'd had about being in a cellar during a storm. Dad said things that happened in your childhood could affect your whole life. He'd learned this from the analyst he'd gone to, years ago, in New York. What things from *my* childhood would affect *my* whole life? Maybe, because I'm already seeing a therapist, it won't work that way with me.

We walked through Sweaters, then Swimwear: rose, white, and peacock blue. "I'm feeling guilty," Mom said. I wasn't always sure where the things she said came from; maybe she'd had more thoughts about Sharon and Rocky Point. "We've *got* to get around to having Judy Weinberg over. We keep putting it off. It must be hard for her, living by herself." I nodded, and looked at the smooth, oddly smiling mannequins. I wanted to touch one—I liked the *idea* of wanting to touch one. They had *energy*. Castaneda said the world was filled with fibers. You couldn't see them. Until you learned to *see*.

Mrs. Takos, the saleswoman in the boys' department, greeted us enthusiastically. I'm on a mission, I thought: bell-bottoms. I wasn't completely sure what they were, although I'd heard them mentioned at school and on TV. I'd looked at the way kids' jeans approached the grass.

We were here for the new dress slacks Mom said I needed. Mom said my clothes looked worn. That this was disrespectful. To whom, I wondered, if you don't believe in God? And if you do, God doesn't care. Monks wear rags.

"Why does it *matter* what I wear to synagogue?" I'd tried to protest.

"We're not going to discuss this anymore," Mom had said. "We've been over it umpteen times."

Beneath the surface, I thought, she knows I'm right, but she's not going to admit it. *The Tao of heaven does not strive, and yet it overcomes.*

While Mrs. Takos found my size, I found the bell-bottoms. I told Mom I'd like to try on a pair; she seemed surprised and pleased. Mrs. Takos told us they were very popular, but I knew her opinion didn't matter and I wished she weren't there.

I went through the louvered saloon doors into the dressing room. In the three-way mirror I receded to infinity and worried whether I could be seen, in my underwear, through the slats. I slipped on the slacks and stepped gingerly outside. Mrs. Takos asked how they fit. "Fine," I said. I didn't know what fitting meant, exactly.

"Quite spiffy," Mom said, sounding somehow a little sad. "Do you like them?"

"They're fine," I repeated indifferently.

"He says they're fine," she said to Mrs. Takos humorously.

Clothes aren't important, I thought, annoyed, and then remembered I was a Taoist. I went back in, put on the bell-bottoms, and walked out.

"Very fashionable!" Mrs. Takos pronounced. "All the girls will be impressed."

Mom smiled knowingly. I went into the dressing room and put my corduroys back on.

The sidewalk leading from Norwich's had green and white sections. When I was little, I had been careful to walk only on the green ones or the white ones. I'd heard the rhyme at school about stepping on a crack.

Overcast outside. Gray sky, gray parking lot.

"I love days like this," Mom said. I agreed.

"It would be nice to live somewhere with seasons," she continued as we got in the car. Mom had gotten used to Phoenix, but I knew it had been hard when we'd first moved here; she'd been lonely. The neighbors made no effort; they didn't even have a Welcome Wagon. It wasn't like Omaha, Wisconsin, or New York. At the first dinner party they'd gone to, everyone had drunk a toast: Eleanor Roosevelt had died. Mom turned the ignition, and I turned on the radio: "Fire and Rain."

"I've heard this song before," Mom said. She liked it. I told her the story behind it—about the girl James Taylor loved who killed herself in the mental hospital. I explained that the Flying Machine was the band James Taylor and the dead girl had been in. "That must have been awful," she said. We both loved sad songs; I was glad she liked this one.

A few drops fell on the windshield.

Oh, I've seen fire and I've seen rain

I'd recently read in *Newsweek* that soft rock was coming back. I was glad. I thought about the different kinds of beauty: the classical and soft and then the harder, rougher kind. It was cloudy but the sky was luminous. Boys on bikes pumped past us while we waited for the light.

We drove down a palm tree–lined street. Mom asked what I thought would happen when the council voted on the Gunderson Ranch.

"I don't know," I said, wondering if I should try to bring up Nanna. I don't *need* to be comforted, I don't *have* to talk about her death right this minute, but I don't want to let the opportunity pass, I thought. This moment of being alone together—but I don't want to overdo it. I shouldn't bring it up unless I'm sad right *now*. It would be a waste. I don't want to exhaust Mom; she's been so patient. She probably knows I'm thinking about this. It's so hard to time things.

"I am worried how your father and sister's arguing is affecting you and Jason. It *does* have an impact on all of us."

I nodded.

"I think," Mom said, "it's sometimes hard in our family because we all *are* so close. It's special. I don't think many families are like that. It's a wonderful thing. But it can also make it hard."

"I know."

"I know," she continued, "I worry about things too much. I tell myself not to, but I still do."

I worry that you worry too much, I thought.

"I suppose my problem is I want to fix everything. And I can't. I guess I just want things to be perfect. And I'm not sure what's so wrong with that."

The window reflected her white sunglasses. What was wrong with wanting things to be perfect? Sometimes things felt perfect. I looked at the birds sitting on the phone wires. The sky was lush. I tried to picture Mom in Omaha, riding her bike to her piano lessons. Past the elm trees, the Methodist Hospital. Jason was born at Sacred Heart in west Phoenix; she'd been able to look out her window at a date grove across the street. The nurses were better there, Mom said, than at Good Sam, where I'd been born.

Jason had been such a peaceful baby, Mom said. "You were too," she'd add, reassuringly. "Sharon, on the other hand . . . *You* loved to watch the cars go by. I'd put the playpen in the front yard by the acacia, you were so happy."

That, I thought, was who I really was. Beneath the loneliness and all the other junk. Stories from before memory have more truth than the stuff I can recollect, even my very important distant memories.

The cacti looked like Gumby. I thought about the generation gap, wondering what advice to give Mom about Sharon. Parents and teenagers clashed; everyone knew this. Weird to know it was inevitable. You knew the things you did hardly mattered, but you thought and acted as if each dispute *did*—whether Sharon went to Rocky Point, whether I had to have deSoto. I don't like to think about time; I don't think Mom does either; we both think about it more than other people, I thought. I'm wasting what's left of my childhood. Failing to appreciate the time I have with Mom, this perfect time, because I worry about unimportant things.

Passing Invergordon, we spotted an open-house sign.

"Want to?" Mom asked.

"Sure," I replied. We pulled into the driveway. Mom didn't recognize the Realtor's name. When Mrs. Sklar or another friend had the listing, we didn't have to pretend we were looking seriously.

Dark cloud-waves rolled over west Phoenix as we walked toward the house, and I thought about the poems I was writing for her, about letting her see them. I was scared to, but I would. In them, I wanted to express the things I hadn't been able to say in our discussions: when two people loved each other, the feelings between them should *always* be intense. If they became normal they might soon not be feelings. "I love you more than the whole world," Mom and I used to say. If you stop saying something, it will gradually stop being true, I thought, kicking a pebble down the cement walkway in the light, wondering if she knew what I was thinking. *Love cannot become routine.* The cacti came from another planet; bits of quartz shone, in the wispy acacia shadows, like broken glass. And there was broken glass.

We entered the house, crossing the cement floors, following the Realtor. Mom looked at the unfinished countertop. Once, I remembered, I had pledged to myself that when I grew up I would live down the street from her. We couldn't marry, but I could do that. One afternoon I was trying to reach a game on the top shelf of a closet; she'd gotten it down and hugged me, and, thinking of how much she loved me, I had told myself, "I will never leave her." *I wish your soul could fathom mine.* That we could know each other's feelings, always, intensely, completely, forever. No one had an explanation for why this couldn't be.

Could the kitchen be redone? Mom asked. We weren't going to spend more than a few minutes—we wouldn't want to waste too much of anyone's time. The Realtor asked a few polite questions; Mom answered vaguely. It was fun to pretend we were buying a house. I tried to imagine the family that would really live there.

At home that evening I heard Dad in the living room turning the stereo on. Mom was out at a Jewish Family and Children's Services meeting. I felt bad he was in the living room alone.

"Hello Mark," Dad said warmly, as I put my homework on the coffee table. "I *was* wondering where everyone had gone."

"I guess they're in their rooms."

"Your sister's probably on the phone, he confided. "Yapping with that Beth. Or maybe some boy."

Sharon, I knew, never got calls from boys. "Probably Beth," I replied.

"You know," he said (as if at last given the chance to defend himself) "I'm not always sure your sister realizes I'm *teasing* her about how much time those two spend together. I may have problems with her parents. But I don't have anything against Beth."

I nodded. *An awkward silence.* But maybe it didn't have to be. Maybe it wasn't *really* awkward. Maybe if I felt it differently it would be OK.

"I do think it would be healthier for Sharon to have a *wider range* of friends," he continued. "She's got so many activities. She's like your mother in that way. She tends to overdo it. But I worry Sharon doesn't always focus. That's why I encouraged her to go back to the marine biology course. Not that I care whether she becomes a scientist. But I think it's important for her to stay with something. I want to give some guidance," he continued. "That's a father's role."

Just leave her alone.

"It's not always easy," he continued, more intimately. "Sometimes I won't know what I've said to set her off. She can be moody; she probably got that from your mother, too. I suppose that's the way women are. *We'll* probably never understand."

I wondered if I could leave the room. After a few minutes he tried again.

"So what are you working on?"

"A report for Mrs. Binder. On black holes."

"What have you learned so far?"

"Well," I said slowly, "some scientists think if you enter a black hole you go into another time dimension. Others think you just get crushed."

"Where do you weigh in?"

"Probably on the time-travel side."

"I would have guessed that," he commented, returning to his papers. I tried to think of something to say.

"But I wouldn't want to be the one who went in and found out."

He laughed, looking up. "How are you liking that class this year?"

"It's OK."

"Science was never my favorite subject either," he commented. "I remember when I flunked chemistry. Boy, was Posha mad. But then I was never as good a student as you."

"When did you flunk chemistry?" I asked curiously, trying to sound curious.

"In high school. I was spending all my time on girls and baseball."

I nodded, nervous.

"I did prefer astronomy to chemistry," he continued.

I'm more interested in astrology, I remarked in my mind, not sure I wanted to say this out loud. But I *am* interested in the science aspect of stars. Black holes are old stars, dying stars; windows to infinity. Astronomy and astrology can both be true. You can see the world in different ways.

"I'm interested in astrology, too," I ventured, sending my thought into space.

"You're not serious, are you?" he replied, seeming to know he needed to be careful with his sarcasm.

"I am," I said, humorously, careful too.

"Every time I read that column in the *Observer* it looks to me like they're just telling people what they want to hear."

"That one in the paper isn't good," I confided. "The Chinese one's better."

This sounded, I thought, a little weird. But it isn't weird. It just sounds weird *here*.

"I see," he said. We were both silent. Through the window, above the trees, the full moon. If Mom were here we would have been watching TV.

"That music is so beautiful," I said.

"I'm glad you like it, Mark. Beethoven's always been my favorite."

"I don't see how anyone couldn't be moved by that," I said.

We were silent but the silence was better.

———

The next day I got a letter from Posha. He commented on my poems and told me the trees on the farm were now all bare; there had been a slight dusting of snow. He didn't suppose we'd had any. He wondered what I thought would happen with the Gunderson Ranch. Sharon, he said, had written that she wasn't optimistic.

In my last letter I had mentioned that I was reading Castaneda. He had read Castaneda's first book, *The Teachings of Don Juan*. "I found it mildly interesting as an example of primitive animism," he wrote. "If one is looking for wisdom, I don't see that one needs to go further than the faith of your own people." I was disappointed; Posha had read the wrong book; *The Teachings of Don Juan* was really just conventional anthropology. It didn't contain the mysteries revealed in *A Separate Reality*.

The back gate opened. "Hey boy," Mr. deSoto shouted. "How ya doin', Sparky?" He was so dumb. He didn't even know Sparky was a girl. I put the letter down and went outside, where Jason was already waiting. Jump rope. Then push-ups.

"Five more, come on. Stomach in, chest out." The cement hurt my palms.

———

"All right," Ratter said to Douggy, "you got him?" Ratter grabbed my arms and Douggy held my feet. I struggled like a fish on a dock as they dragged me down the corridor.

"This is it, faggot," Ratter announced. I looked up at his gleaming tooth, his zits. We headed toward the bathroom. I kicked Douggy, who let go for a second.

"You fuck," Ratter said angrily, not to me but to Douggy.

Tightening his grip on my wrists, he said, more softly, to me, "Thought you were gonna get away? Guess again."

Douggy picked up my feet again, for a while, then dropped them, letting Ratter drag me. I struggled but couldn't get free. They're going to stick my head in the toilet. My nightmare is happening. In the distance kids played four square. Fuzzy Wuzzy was a bear, I said to myself; Fuzzy Wuzzy didn't care. Fuzzy was aware. . . . Hoffman appeared in the corridor, wearing his POW bracelet and his puka shells. His face expressed nothing. He watched, his thumbs in his belt.

I gave up struggling and decided to grin, as if this were a game I wanted to be part of.

"You fat fuckhead," Ratter said to Douggy, who had again dropped my feet and was now just watching, too. "Say your prayers," Ratter said to me. We reached the bathroom door.

Kids gathered in the corridor; Baltz came out of the bathroom. I smiled at him. He wore a white T-shirt; his legs were smooth and tan. Behind him, the stink of pee and cigarettes; the smell that's the awful truth about boys, I thought, which everyone pretends not to know. The girls' room's not like this.

"What are you losers doing?" Baltz asked. I wished he hadn't included me with the losers.

"We're not doing anything," Ratter said, brushing back his stringy hair.

"Ratter, you are the *biggest* loser," Baltz said. "You just have to beat up on the one person who is weaker than you."

Feeling half-protected, half-humiliated, I looked at Baltz: so calm, so blond, so OK-cool.

"We're just messin' around," Ratter said, his defiance subdued. "I wasn't gonna *do* anything."

Maybe, I thought, that was true; maybe he wasn't.

"Hello Mrs. Heller," Baltz said, as she came around the corner.

"What's the commotion?"

"Just doing homework, Mrs. H.," Baltz answered, smiling.

"Boys," Mrs. Heller said, returning the smile.

———

When I saw Anna later that afternoon she asked if something was wrong. But I didn't want to talk about it. I knew that the night before she'd had an aura reading at the Aquarius House. I wanted to know what she'd found out. She saw Christ and learned he was "just a man." The aura reader had gotten such strong energy from her that he decided to do something he didn't usually do on the first session: he put her under very deep hypnosis. Then an amazing thing happened. An ancient woman spoke through her. The hypnotist had never seen anything like it.

"Wow," I remarked. "Christ *and* an ancient woman."

"I know," she said. "I'm still recovering."

———

Outside of home room, I dropped my notebook on the grass. Schaeffer, in his Kawasaki T-shirt, picked up a manila folder that had fallen from it and read aloud:

> *My love is like a mountain trail*
> *I am comfortable in the warm valley*
> *with you. But on the barren peak*
> *without you*
> *cold winds may freeze my soul.*

5

ROBERT MARSHALL

"What is this?" he asked, brushing back his hair.

I thought quickly. I couldn't let him find out they were my love poems for my mother. "A special assignment for Mrs. Voigt. We're studying the general history of romantic poetry."

He seemed, for some reason, to accept this. I was afraid he would throw the poems back on the grass but he handed them to me. I wished he knew I was going to the Grateful Dead.

Later, during lunch, I read Lao-tzu.

> *The weak can overcome the strong;*
> *The supple can overcome the stiff.*
> *Under heaven everyone knows this*
> *Yet no one puts it into practice.*

I looked up and saw Martha Wallace sitting by herself, with her flute and raisin bran, at the edge of the ochre field. Martha had been at Loloma nearly as long as I; she had no friends. She had pale skin, thick glasses, unwashed hair. She'd always been called the Walrus.

When I was little I'd played troll dolls and patty-cake in the sandbox with Bonnie Wilson, I'd skipped rope with Kathy Sykes, and played jacks with Heather Morel, until one day, under the cottonwood tree, Heather asked, "Why aren't you playing soccer with the boys?" I'd never asked to play with her again. But even when the girls had let me play with them, I'd never tried to be friends with Martha. *The weak can overcome the strong.* Poor Martha, I thought; her suffering was worse than mine. I got up and walked toward her, trying to figure out what I would say.

Above, light hit a plane; a star in the day-sky—for a second.

131

"I want you to know I think you're brave," I ventured, haltingly, realizing this sounded weird.

She didn't say anything. Then, not looking up, she mumbled, "I'm not brave." She ate some raisin bran.

I started to walk away. In the distance, Ratter.

———

Sharon got into the car next to me. "I'm not sure about going to see *Christmas* lights," she announced, trying to sound both humorous and critical. "But since *everybody* wants to . . ."

"Are all those snobby people going to be at the Bufords' again this year?" Mom asked Dad as she got into the front seat, not seeming to hear Sharon.

"Same old crowd, I'm afraid," Dad replied.

Each year the Bufords had a big Christmas party. Mom never wanted to go. "All those Mercedes," she said, shaking her head. "I never feel glamorous enough."

"Pumpkin," Dad said, pulling out of the driveway. "I don't think there's anyone more glamorous."

"Pumpkin?" said Jason. "I thought she was sweet pea."

"Both," said Dad.

The world in the front seat was its own world. We came to the Cartwrights. A sled and reindeer on their roof.

"What do you give it?" Dad asked.

"I'd say a B," said Sharon.

"B minus," Mom commented.

We drove to the Johnsons. A manger in their front yard. Angels in the palm trees.

"So their average is an A minus," I said, after everyone had voted.

"Good," Dad said, "I'm glad you're keeping score. But wait'll you see this one." He turned onto East Paisano. At the end of a cul-de-sac, an entire North Pole village. The elves moved around on a track.

"Now you *might* say it's a waste of energy," Dad said. "But this person's a real artist."

The lights were beautiful.

"I think it's tasteless," Sharon said darkly.

"I think it's amazing," I countered.

Jason and Sharon wanted to get back but Dad and I wanted to go see more.

———

Several days later, at breakfast, Dad told me I couldn't go to the Grateful Dead. Mom was worried there might be drugs. But, I thought, that's the whole point! You don't understand you are ruining my life. I played with the grapefruit spoon.

———

A few days later, in the *Journal-Observer,* Jack McCarthy came out against saving the Gunderson Ranch. "Although the motives of the opponents may be noble," he wrote, "they stand in the way of economic progress." Mom was upset; Dad, too. "He should have *at least* had the decency to call me beforehand. That's the end of that friendship."

You always think you should get your way, I thought, angry about the Grateful Dead. If you want to have friends, you have to compromise, I told him, sarcastically, in my mind.

But I, too, felt bad that the Gunderson Ranch might soon

be destroyed. At the council meeting, the week before Christmas, the developers were ahead, five to four—Dad said because of McCarthy. But then, in a surprise, the mayor changed his vote; everyone applauded and slapped Dad on the back. The land would be saved.

The next weekend Mom suggested we celebrate by going on a picnic. "We've been so busy saving nature," she said, "we ought to try enjoying it." I sat next to Jason in the backseat. Even though it wasn't hot, and Mom thought we should open the windows, Dad had the air-conditioning on. I was tired of talking about the Gunderson Ranch. I thought about the Grateful Dead, wondering if I should yield and let my anger go—or express it. I had discussed this with Dr. Kurtz, omitting the part about doing acid. He'd said I shouldn't think in terms of what I *should* do. But this didn't make sense! At each moment you decided whether to hold on to anger or let it go. You had a choice—free will. And since you had a choice, you had to consider what the best thing to do was, how you were going to *be*.

The Superstition Mountains on the horizon, gray-purple figures. A motorcycle cut in front us.

"Jerk," my father said, honking. We got the finger, but I was the only one who saw. The Harley disappeared, heading north. We passed some saguaros decorated as the three wise men. *We three men of orient are, come to smoke a rubber cigar.*

"I still can't believe what Jack McCarthy did," Mom commented. How much do I love her at *this* moment, I wondered, looking at her. If you love someone, you love them *all* the time. If love starts to fade it might keep fading. Into the distance.

"Let this be a lesson," Dad said, to all of us. "Don't count chickens before they hatch."

"Why did the chicken cross the road?" Jason asked.

"Why?" Mom responded helpfully.

"So he could get run over."

"That is so old," I said, trying to be a member of the family.

"Not to mention morbid," Dad commented, as if Jason had crossed his path. He wants to keep talking about his victory, I thought.

"You can't always count on people," Dad said dramatically. "That's the way it is. The important thing to me is to be able to look in the mirror and know I've done the best I could. I want to try to make the world a *little* bit better place. In the long run the important thing is that I make the effort. Then, if I've improved the world *slightly,* someday I'll be able to look back on my life and think it was worthwhile."

"Camelot," Sharon half-sang, "in Camelot . . ."

"Honey," Mom said to Dad, "she's just teasing. Don't get that hang-dog look."

"I don't *have* a hang-dog look," he replied. "I was trying to make a point."

"We like King Arthur," Sharon said, changing her tone. She feels guilty for having made fun of him, I thought. She's been caught.

Mom and Dad continued to discuss the city council. They talked about the McGrath and Greene Christmas party, and the party at the Bufords'; Dad wondered if there would be any other Jews. They talked about the problems with the irrigation: the Smiths were getting too much, we weren't getting enough. All the yards in the neighborhood were green except ours.

I wish Mom didn't care about the lawn.

The talking never stops, I thought, but at the same time— nothing to say. Then when it *is* silent I'm afraid the silence will go on forever. We'll just sit together until the end of time without speaking. But when we do speak, it doesn't help. We're only talking to cover the silence.

"I wonder what good old Jack is going to have to say for himself at the Charros," Dad commented.

Emptiness always waits for us, I thought, like the desert. A citrus stand, a gun shop, an old man selling giant stuffed animals. Different kinds of beauty. Nanna wouldn't have considered this beautiful, but it is. She thought Phoenix was plastic. Plastic can be beautiful. Would she have come to understand?

Does anyone else feel this *energy*? How can they keep talking when *this* moves past? It's so immense, should silence everything, presence of God and we keep talking. But maybe they're as bored as I by the conversation, but know enough to keep up appearances. Maybe there's an unspoken conspiracy to pretend there's something to talk about when there isn't. Maybe that's what you're supposed to do. A part of being human I'm not good at.

We pulled into Pinnacle Peak's gravel parking lot. The desert was in bloom. The mountain was a carpet of grays and light pinks and dark green saguaros and their bright orange flowers. Stepping out of the car into the warm winter air, I heard the cactus wrens. I looked at the families getting out of the cars around us. Hiking, picnicking, doing activities, physical stuff— that's *natural* to them, I thought. How certain they seem to be about how to *be*. Not us. Some high school kids pulled up in a jeep. They weren't from my school. The girls wore halter tops. The boys' shirts were off; their chests were strong and brown.

Mom stretched in her shorts in the parking lot light. We started up toward the rocky peak. Sharon took the canteen, I carried the sandwich bag. Tuna fish, peanut butter and jelly, apple slices. Mom asked Sharon, "So is there anything new on the ZPG front?"

Sharon and Beth Fineman had begun going to meetings of the youth chapter of Zero Population Growth. She and Beth had come up with an idea: they would organize a youth march to raise money to fight overpopulation.

"It's really difficult to get anyone to do anything right now," Sharon said, sounding adult.

"It's always hard over the holidays," Mom sympathized.

"Some kids from Central High are interested, too," Sharon continued eagerly. "There's this *really cool* teacher who came to the meeting."

"The Christmas season is definitely getting out of hand," Dad said. "You should have seen the line at the bank. And they keep playing those damn jingles. I'm going to write to the branch manager. He ought to be aware they do have some Jewish customers who *might* not appreciate "Away in the Manger.""

"You do that, honey," Mom said with some affection.

He just *totally* changed the topic, I thought. He wants to bring it back to *him*. Could Mom not have noticed?

So many currents in the air. Invisible fibers. *Lines of power, lines of the world.*

"It's awful," said Sharon. "If they would just play some Jewish songs . . ."

She didn't seem to mind Dad's interruption. But she should! Maybe there weren't any currents in the air.

Jason hummed "Rudolph the Red-Nosed Reindeer." After a while we heard some trail bikes. "They ought to ban those damn things," Dad said. "People don't know how to appreciate peace and quiet anymore."

The trail was crowded; a warm, cloudless day, the first all week. "When we moved to Phoenix," Dad said, his hand momentarily on my shoulder, "we would come out here and it was really going out in the desert." The trail turned and we caught a glimpse of a pile of trash behind some Joshua trees on the other side of the parking lot. Sparkling like treasure.

"Unbelievable," my father said, shaking his head. We continued on. "People don't understand what can happen when there's too much growth."

"Maybe they're *beginning* to understand," Mom said.

"Maybe they just don't care," my sister said, picking up a crushed soda can from the trail.

Digging with my teeth into the back of my mouth, I scratched my throat.

"Will you stop making that disgusting sound?" asked Sharon.

"What sound?"

"We heard it," said Jason.

We climbed. Thistles and burrs stuck to my corduroys. I crushed some ocotillo leaves in my hand.

"It's so beautiful," my father said.

"I just think it's so beautiful," my mother said.

I couldn't say it. The words seemed so inadequate, so postcardlike. Was it wrong of my parents to speak this way? What *should* they say?, I asked myself.

We reached the last plateau before the summit, an expanse of muscular rock. Dad pointed down toward a housing development on the horizon.

"Isn't that terrible?" he commented.

"It's awful," Sharon agreed.

"Yeah," Jason said.

"They are really ruining the desert," Mom added.

But it didn't seem terrible to me; it all glimmered, the trash on the edge of the cliff, the power lines, the saguaros, the distant houses, the billboards, and the pale, glinting rocks; it is all, I thought, a surging river—of light.

—

A few weeks after New Year's, Mrs. Weinberg came for dinner. Dad blessed us, and read the prayer Mom liked so much: "A woman of valor, who can find?" Mom lit the candles; I felt the old warm glow. She'd made her famous *boeuf* carbonnade. My parents and Mrs. Weinberg talked about the old days in New York. We discussed Nixon and Beth Shalom and Watergate; Habakkuk had gone down to the water gate. Sparky barked at a car or at the moon.

III
TALES OF POWER II

I spaded Sparky's crusty manure into the wheelbarrow. Jason pointed to some dark piles by the white fence. A Sunday afternoon. Why was manure a boy's job? I had argued about this but it hadn't done any good.

Mom opened the backdoor. "Why don't you boys come in? We're ready for the family conference."

I wished she wouldn't say *the boys*. "The boys did this," she'd say, and I'd wince; the words stung. *Boys:* a chalk mark across the family, assigning me to Dad and Jason, keeping me from her and Sharon. We worked in the backyard; they did laundry.

I had asked, "Can't you say 'Mark and Jason,' like you say 'Jason and Sharon?' Why do you have to say *the boys?*" But she didn't understand. Mom didn't see anything wrong with *boys*.

I tried imagining how boys looked to her. She remembered the boys from her neighborhood in Omaha. Maybe they had been different from Schaeffer, Ratter, and Douggy. Or maybe she just pretended they were.

Sparky licked my leg. I petted her. Mom doesn't understand that when Jason, Dad, and I are together, talking becomes impossible. Or if she does she thinks it's OK; everyone does. If my mother or Sharon or Nanna were there, it was easier. No one understands this. Or admits it.

Yin overcomes yang.

The lawn was growing dark. Jason and I put the spades back on the dusty shelf in the storage shed next to Dad's tennis rackets and his college fencing foils. We went into the guest bathroom; we washed our hands, drying them on the monogrammed towels.

"Your mother and I have been discussing vacation plans. We've been thinking it might be fun for everyone to try something different this year. When I was a boy, I used to go to Camp Evergreen each summer. And boy did I look forward to it! All year I couldn't wait."

Dad's voice seemed like a car with darkened windows: I couldn't see into it.

"We thought it would be too bad if we deprived you of that opportunity. So we've gotten some information . . . you're going to be pretty excited by this."

I sank deeply into my chair. He pulled some brochures out of a manila folder and laid them on the polished wood coffee-table next to *Commentary* and *Ramparts*.

Jason picked up the pamphlet for Evergreen. He looked at it seriously and handed it to me. I examined the brochure. Tiny boys climbed a tiny mountain. They played softball; they went down a river in a canoe. I had never been away from home, except when I stayed with my grandparents. And the one time I'd tried to sleep at John Friedman's. Camp would be an endless school day; no Anna, no Mom. Douggy, Ratter, worse! There wouldn't be anywhere to hide.

"What do you think?" Dad asked, puffing his pipe.

"I think it's a good idea for you two to take a break," Sharon said.

"I'm not really sure," I said pensively, not wanting to sound upset. I knew I'd been difficult lately. "I don't know if I'll really feel *deprived* . . ."

"Sounds good," Jason said.

"Mark," Dad said, "we'll talk some more. You probably don't have too many friends who've gone to camp. But it's something most boys enjoy."

I lay in bed. I knew Mom would come to me; she'd seen I was unhappy. After Nanna had died, my mother had come to my room every night to give me an extra hug, to talk to me, to hold me while I cried. My father sometimes came, too. On some nights, when I was especially sad, I'd get up, a few minutes after she had left, and walk down the hall to their room. I was reluctant to do this too often; I didn't want to be asking for too much. But sometimes I *had* to. I would knock on their door and ask for one more hug. When my mother reluctantly withdrew her arms I felt something rip; I knew she did, too. She would hug me once again, briefly, and I felt sure we knew everything there was to know about each other, every-thing that mattered. When the second, shorter hug ended, I was comforted, a little, by the knowledge that we would hug again the next night, and every night after that, until a night, deep and dark and blue, that I did not yet need to imagine.

After several months, I began to do this less often. And then, after more time passed, my mother stopped coming to my room. We would sometimes still talk about Nanna's death, on walks, in the car on the way to Dr. Kurtz, and when we got to eat lunch alone.

I knew tonight she would come to my room.

"You didn't seem too happy."

I shook my head. "Is this *definitely* happening?"

"I was right," she said, "you're not happy." Then, carefully, "I don't think anything's *decided*."

I sniffled. Perhaps in the morning I'd discover the family conference hadn't occurred. When I was very young, I remembered, as I tried to fall asleep, I'd sometimes wondered whether everything was just a dream someone on Jupiter was having.

———

At school the next day I couldn't think of anything but camp.

———

Lilly went round in her wheel. If I'm away from Mom, who will comfort me? Why does this have to happen *now,* when my life is finally starting to get better? If she understands I know I won't have to go.

My father's footsteps in the hall, turning out all the lights— Lyndon Johnson, Dad said, had done this in the White House. I cried quietly, hoping my mother would again come. If I was too loud, Mom would know I *wanted* her to come; I wanted her to come *without* that; it was best to be hugged when you didn't have to ask. If Dad heard me crying he wouldn't like it. The house grew quiet. Was it possible she didn't know how unhappy I was?

I wanted to make time go back, to turn the clock backward, the way Mom did when she set the timer for a roast. Perhaps I could go knock on the master bedroom's door. But that would upset her; it would be childish. Why shouldn't I be childish? I thought. My mother, in her nightgown, behind the double doors. Maybe, I thought, she hadn't come to me because of Dad. The different kinds of love—you were supposed to go from one stage to another.

The air conditioning went on; the moon shone through the shutters. A symbol of the female, the yin, Anna had said. I switched on the bedside light, sipped my water, and picked up the *Tao Te Ching*. It had beautiful sumi paintings: caves, men wandering, cherry trees in bloom. To be a sumi painter one had to be completely centered.

"Be really whole," I read, *"and all things will come to you."*

———

At dinner the next evening Dad said Camp Evergreen had been the high point of his boyhood; he'd canoed Lake Champlain. "I'd think you would enjoy that, Mark," he said, earnestly, "since you like nature."

The next night my mother came to me. "Tell me what you're worried about."

I wanted to share my *real* feelings with her. I'll be away from you, I thought. "I'm just so scared." Jason, I knew, could hear us through the wall.

"Why, Mark?"

I'll be so lonely, I thought. I'll be with boys, all day, all night. I'm *barely* surviving now. I'll make her unhappy if I tell her these things. But I can't make it through a whole summer.

"I won't have anyone to talk to."

"But people like you, Mark," she responded. "You're wonderful. You're so special."

Does she really believe people think that?

"Your father thinks it would be good for you."

Of course. He doesn't understand. You *know* that. You're pretending.

"Maybe you need to tell him how you're feeling."

"I'll try," I said, angry at her in spite of myself. I wiped a few tears from my eyes.

"Mark," my mother murmured, "you know we love you."

"I know." The room was dark, her nightgown blue; she smelled of her shower. I lay my head next to her breast and heard her heartbeat. "I love you too," I whispered.

She brushed my hair and looked at the ceiling. "Maybe this *isn't* such a good idea," she murmured to herself.

My hopes rose like the moon beyond the shutters.

"It's important to have a positive attitude," Dad said at breakfast, in his annoyed voice. "If you *expect* the negative, you'll get the negative." I looked at my toast. "Mark," Dad said, "you can stop playing Hamlet." I stared more deeply into the toast. "And can you look at me when I speak to you?"

"Alas, poor Yorick," said Sharon, wearing her Mexican poncho, "pass the sugar."

———

I hate him, I thought, as I rode my bike to school. I've tried so hard to make things OK with him! Boys all day. Why do people think this is OK?

———

146

Anna and I sat on the grass. "You look blue," she said. She listened while I began to tell her about camp. But I soon felt uncomfortable and changed the topic.

"Did I tell you I got the new Castaneda book?"

"*Journey to Ixtlan?*" she asked.

I nodded.

"Have you started it?"

"A little," I answered. "I sort of want to save it."

She smiled. We both knew how powerful *A Separate Reality* had been.

I showed Anna "Cloud Mountain"; we went over it line by line. When we were done she told me about a Swiss artist who had discovered that if you looked at the sky intently you would see it was red, not blue. Later, during soccer, I squinted and, after a while, began to see the red dots.

The ball went past me.

That night my father came into my room.

"I want to talk about what you're so afraid of," he said, concerned. "I'm sorry I was short with you at breakfast. I'm just worried about your mother. She was pretty distressed after she talked to you. She thought it might help if *we* talked about what's worrying you." His voice was conciliatory. "We do need to come to *some* decision about this *fairly* soon," he added.

Maybe, I thought, I can persuade him.

"Sometimes it helps to get things off your chest," he continued. We sat on my bed, beneath my James Taylor poster. He put his arm around my shoulder.

"I guess . . . I'm afraid . . . it's going to be really bad," I said, knowing I needed to be more specific.

"Why?" he asked. "It could be different than you expect."

"I'm afraid I won't have any friends," I said, hesitantly.

"You shouldn't sell yourself short," he countered. "You're a great guy."

"It's not that," I tried again. "I just know it isn't going to be any different than school." To make my case I needed to say how terrible school was, but then Dad would say I was exaggerating.

"I think you've made *a lot* of progress. You've become a lot more self-confident lately. You're friends with John Friedman. Sometimes you discount yourself."

Don't talk about my confidence, I thought, holding my bear. He continued.

"You're probably tired of hearing this, but you know I was hesitant about camp myself. It's natural to fear new things. But it turned out to be one of the best experiences of my life. When Posha and Nanna came to get me I didn't want to leave."

James Taylor watched sadly from above; next to him, the Banana Splits poster I didn't yet feel ready to take down. One banana, two bananas, three bananas, four. The room was semilit. I tried to continue in my "reasonable" voice.

"I guess I'm afraid there won't be anyone for me to talk to," I said, knowing this wasn't what I most urgently needed to say.

"You don't *know* that," he said, impatiently. "You shouldn't *always* assume the worst."

Why don't you believe me? "I don't know it, but I've got a lot of good reason."

"Sometimes you've got to give people a chance."

"I *do* give people a chance."

"I know you do," he said, encouragingly, sarcastically, nervously. "We're just asking you to give something *new* a chance. We'll talk about it some more, all right?"

Perhaps he thought: *He won't ever listen to me. If he would, then I could help him. That's all I want. But he likes being miserable.*

Deep, dark shadows in the room. He got up, uncomfortably, to leave. I haven't, I thought, argued well. *Wise men do not . . .*

"Good night, Mark."

"Good night, Dad," I sniffled.

"Shall I hit this?"

I nodded. He turned off the light. His white shirt, in the darkness, a sail on the nighttime sea.

"Dad," I murmured, gathering my courage, "you know, I want us to be close." A softer murmur: "I want us to love each other."

Whispering of waves at night at sea; great storms at sea; I cannot see his face. "Mark," he says, "that's what I want, too."

I want him to say this in a way that's different than the way he says it. I want him to say it so it sounds like he means it. Maybe he does, he'd say he did; I couldn't prove there was anything wrong with the way he'd said it. I sensed he too, had something he *had* to say. Something he'd been holding in.

"You know," he added, "if you can, try not to upset your mother too much, OK?"

He stood in the dark waiting for my response. I buried my face in the pillow. Why can't you say something that makes us close? Why does it have to end *this* way? Why do you accuse me of hurting Mom? It's not MY fault! It's YOURS!

I was silent.

"Good night, Mark," he said, "sleep well," he added, after a moment. "You know we love you." He closed the door.

Tasting the pillowcase, I watched the clock hands turn. I'm awful, I thought.

———

I found Anna sitting with Mr. Lewis at one of the stone tables outside the cafeteria, discussing the latest faculty meeting. It hadn't gone too badly, they agreed. Mrs. Heller was easing up; she wanted everyone on her side when she went to the trustees with her plan to build an aquacenter.

"Now what does that represent?" Mr. Lewis asked, pointing to the symbol of the Tao drawn in magic marker on Anna's rice paper notebook.

"The feminine and masculine principles," she said brightly. "They correspond to the moon and sun."

My talk with Dad didn't seem important now; it had evaporated in the daylight—water on sunlit cement. Still, I wanted to talk about camp. I had thought that morning, riding my sparkly, purple-seated bike to school, that Anna could help. Now I didn't think this anymore, but I *remembered* thinking it. I held on to the thought-shadow.

I knew she was talking about the yin and yang. I felt pleased that I knew this and Mr. Lewis didn't. Did he know, I wondered, the contents of her notebook? Her book of dreams. She was seeing a Jungian therapist she had met in Hawaii; he wasn't charging her. The therapist, Don, was helping her understand her dreams in light of the Jungian archetypes. She was teaching him about Hopi mythology.

"You see, for instance, the owl," Anna said to Mr. Lewis, leafing through the pages. I was never sure how much of herself she revealed to other teachers. "Now I didn't know that this meant Athena. *You* probably knew that," she said, smiling, indicating me.

Mr. Lewis looked interested.

"Of course it would be different for you," she said. I wasn't sure if I was included in this. "For the male there are different archetypes."

Why? I want to have the same archetypes as my mother, as Anna. The feminine is more powerful. I don't want to be a boy—or be with boys.

The grass the color of shredded wheat. Birdsong mixed with light—woven together in the world like the thoughts and feelings in my mind. The clouds, Goony Golf–shaped. Past the chain-link fence one of the senior's cars, parked in the empty lot in the shade of the manzanita.

Mr. Lewis said good-bye and I sat alone with Anna. I handed her a folder of poems; I hadn't wanted to bring it out while he was there. She had suggested I let her submit them to the state poetry contest. I wasn't sure this was a good idea. *Accept being unimportant.*

"Oh good," she said. "I know what these are."

"I've got the feeling I'm probably going to have to go to camp," I said.

Anna nodded.

I wanted to be open with her, to share my feelings. But I couldn't talk about my problems with my parents; she was beyond that sort of thing.

"You know, this may turn out to be a learning experience, something you grow from."

I smiled slightly and picked at a splinter on the table next to some dried birdshit. I wondered if there was any chance Anna would ask me to spend the summer with her.

She continued thoughtfully. "Dante had to go down into the inferno before he could go to heaven. First he had to descend."

I looked up at the clouds.

"Oh, shit," she said. Time for her fifth-graders. "Sometimes," Anna said, as we got up, "there's a kind of death that precedes rebirth."

The oleander's ruby flowers—lipstick kisses left on dark green leaves. I thought about Anna's advice. "A learning experience": something my father might have said, but different coming from her. It seemed wrong that words meant different things from different people. Dad, I reassured myself, didn't talk about death and rebirth. "Are we going to have the *Amethyst* meeting Sunday?"

"I think we'll have to wait till next weekend," Anna said, her white dress rippling in the breeze. Mockingbirds watched us from the red-tiled administration building. "You were looking forward to that, weren't you?" she asked sympathetically. I didn't want her to be able to see into me like that.

———

That night I tried again to explain to my mother why I was afraid of camp, and why I hadn't been able to explain this to Dad, and why Dad hadn't been able to reassure me that camp would be OK, and why I felt he wasn't listening. I tried to explain this without upsetting her. "I don't know what to do," she said. "He's so convinced it would be good for you."

The next morning, after I'd parked my bike, walking past the parking lot's army of yellow-orange buses, I thought of all the things I hadn't said to my mother. I'd said them but hadn't said them *right*. Because I hadn't been sure what I wanted. I'd wanted to try to get out of camp *and* to get her to comfort me. They weren't the same. I have to balance carefully, I thought. I don't like being tactical with Mom. I want everything between us to be real.

Suddenly I knew exactly what the words should have been. They came to me: light from behind a cloud. I'm never able, I thought, to think of the right thing to say at the right time.

Why does it always come later? Now I knew what to say and I was *also* able to have the feelings that went with the words. I could remember the words and use them later, but by then the feeling could be gone and it would all be worthless. You're only really communicating, I thought, if you say something while the feelings are still there.

I walked, trying to hold on to the words for the feelings, and the feelings.

———

During lunch, under arrest by the pink-faced Sheriff, Douggy Dale.

"You're resisting."

My spiral notebook lay next to us on the ground. I tried to move from under his fat leg.

"Listen," Douggy counseled, "If you don't cooperate, you go downtown." He smelled of sweat and fart.

I could see, past his arm, the cafeteria, distant and hazy. The Bermuda grass' antennae gestured in the wind.

"I don't want to take you downtown." Downtown: an ant pile on the nearby berm.

"Bumpa dum, bumpa dum de dum," Douggy sort of sang.

"I want a lawyer," I said.

"I'm your lawyer," he replied. "I carry a badge." He was in his own TV show.

"Douggy, this is stupid."

"See who's stupid," he responded angrily, twisting my arm. "You're resisting arrest," he declared.

Stupid to tell him he was stupid. *Don't enter into conflict with their ideal image of themselves.*

A fly buzzed near Douggy's shoulder. I tried moving a little, but he tightened his grip. It didn't bother me as much that I couldn't move as that I couldn't do anything with the words or where they were going.

"Stop resisting."

"I am *not* resisting."

The fly buzzed near my face.

Why was it so hard to get through to him? My head, where my thoughts were, was only a few feet from his, where his were—I thought. Somewhere in the distance, school. Somewhere Martha ate lunch. Boys played four square.

Dad says to have a positive attitude. A total contradiction to say you should have a positive attitude and say you should be truthful at the same time! Mom won't be able to persuade Dad to take me to the Vineyard. My childhood can't last forever, but why does it have to end *now*? Nothing has changed except that time has passed. Time: invisible, unreal. I can't stay with Posha; he has to go to his wilderness conference at Moosewood Lake.

Douggy twisted my wrist.

"Confess now or you go downtown."

When nothing is done, nothing is left undone. I lay still, perfectly. Sharon would have urged me to resist like the Warsaw Jews.

I wondered, lying there, what show now played in Douggy's head. *Dragnet? Hawaii Five-O?* My technique was working; Douggy was getting bored. I knew soon he'd switch the channel back to *Gilligan's Island,* and I would go along with him when he called me "little buddy, little pal."

———

I sat in my parents' bedroom. "Mark," Dad said, "we're sorry you're not so enthusiastic about camp, but we've had to go ahead and make plans. We sent in a deposit to Evergreen. Now I'm sure you're tired of advice," he continued awkwardly, "but if I can give you *some,* you might remember, all you have to fear is fear itself."

———

Dear Diary:

I have never kept a diary before but at this point I have to let somebody know how I feel and so since nobody cares I will tell you. They lie!!!! They say they want to hear what I have to say but they don't. They said they wanted to discuss it with me but all along they were just PRETENDING! I can't believe it, I can't believe it.

I felt a little better once I'd written this. I lay in bed, remembering the poem Nicola had read once at Anna's: "Do not go gentle into that good night." I will not, I told myself, go gently. I cried. Far off, my father showered.

I heard their door open and then my mother's footsteps. Then she sat on the bed in the dark, holding me. I cried and gasped for breath, wanting to do as much crying as I could while she was there.

"I hate to see you feeling this way," she said. "I didn't know it would be like this."

I'm awful. I'm selfish. She can feel, I thought, what I feel I'm doing to her. It's as if we're committing a crime. Trespassing, together, somewhere in the dark.

My crying merged with the house's background noises, the climate control, the refrigerator's hum. Sometimes I tried to conceal it, or to make it seem as if I were. Crying is an art, I told myself, like everything else. I do it exceptionally well. I knew most boys couldn't cry at all; Dad hadn't when Nanna died; I was better at it than him. Sharon, Mom, and Dr. Kurtz had all said it was good that I could cry—I knew Dad knew they thought this.

I have as many ways to cry, I thought, as the Eskimos have words for snow. I read Lao-tzu and began a poem called "Butterfly Wait."

A week passed. I will try, I thought, to keep my misery to myself. At least *most* of it.

At dinner one night, Dad asked how my day had been.

"OK."

"Just OK?"

"Yeah."

"Why just OK?"

"OK's OK, isn't it?"

"You *could* make a little effort."

But saying it's OK was already not true! I don't know what you want from me. I'm not going to look at you. I looked at the toaster, out the window, at the floor. I DARE you to notice I'm not looking at you.

Dad seemed exhausted. The conversation went on. The floor, the toaster, the window—my loud silence. Sometimes Dad's eyes would almost meet mine but I'd quickly turn away; we fenced in the air.

"Mark," Dad said, "I've about had enough."

"Enough of what?"

"You know perfectly well."

"I wasn't doing anything." And even if I were, I told myself, it was hidden. So you have NO GROUNDS to accuse me.

"Well," Dad said, "you can darn well go not do anything in your room until you choose to have a more positive attitude. When you decide you want to be part of the family then you can return."

"Nat," Mom said.

"I'm sorry, but he's making life miserable for everyone," Dad said. "He can come back when he's ready to show a little respect." Jason and Sharon looked down.

I raged down the hall. The way everyone's feeling is *your* fault! You're punishing me for being quiet—I'll be quiet now; no one can hear me in my room. I hit the beanbag chair, loudly enough that they might or might not hear. Behind my stained-glass Snoopy, which Mom and Dad had bought for me in Vail, which hung in my window, the sky was as black and smooth and silent as the center of a record album. My science and social studies books lay on my desk next to the old wine bottles I'd collected. I thought they were beautiful: the way they caught the light, the words on the bottles—*Côtes du Rhône*. Why should I have a better attitude, I argued silently, when you send me to my room? All I did was not look at you. But that's dishonest; not looking is something. I want things to be the way they once were. I want to sit at the table, discussing issues. But if I go back it won't be like that.

I could hear sounds from the kitchen; plates, voices. I'm not there, I thought, but I am: it's all about me. I picked up *Ladies of the Canyon*, the only album that would work now, wondering if they could hear. Joni sang about Morgantown, how beautiful the morning was. I pictured and tried to feel it: the milk trucks and the merchants. I listened to "The Conversation."

> *She speaks in sorry sentences*
> *Miraculous repentances*
> *I don't believe her*

Tomorrow he will come to me
And speak his sorrow endlessly and ask me why
Why can't I leave her?

The boy wanted to live with Joni but his mother wouldn't let him. Lyrics could have different meanings, I thought. When she said her old man had been hit by a taxi, she might mean her father *or* her boyfriend. It could be either one.

We are stardust, she sang. It's true, I thought. We *do* have to get back to the garden. I'd tried to make them unhappy just so I could have my way.

The next day I told Dad I was sorry.

"I accept your apology, Mark."

But the next night he asked why I was looking like such a martyr.

"Because you're being such a fascist."

I was sent to my room

"Your father's very upset," Mom said.

"I know."

"Could you make a little more effort to get along with him? If you could *try* to see it from his point of view . . ."

"But he . . ."

"I know, he needs to, too. But he's been under a lot of pressure," she said vaguely and sadly.

I'm the one under pressure, I thought. I'm the one who's going to be *crushed*.

"I realize he's stubborn," she continued. "But beneath that he's very worried about your relationship."

Is that what you think or he thinks?

"Things *were* really improving between the two of you," she said, unhappily.

"I'll try," I said, meaning it.

"I want to be your friend," he would say. "You know you've really caused your mother a lot of suffering. I realize I'm not perfect," he'd continue. "I make mistakes. Everyone does. Your old man's human. But you know . . . I wish you'd realize, I am *trying*. Sometimes I get pretty mad at myself for some of the mistakes I *have* made. Some have sure been doozies. But one thing I've learned—and maybe you have to, too—is you can't always have everything your way."

Sometimes it seemed we were making progress. But then one of us would say something and we'd be back where we'd started. You still haven't even said that I'm definitely going to camp, I thought. If you'd only be honest it wouldn't be so bad! (But I knew this wasn't true.)

We all agreed *someone* was at fault; but who? Mom looked more exhausted every day. "I think the three of us need to talk together," she said. "Shuttle diplomacy is *obviously* not working." We began to meet regularly in their room, in the evening, for talks. A new, furious intimacy was developing between us, something Sharon and Jason weren't allowed to be part of.

I sat in an upright semifetal position on the edge of their bed.

"Tell us what you're afraid of," Mom said patiently. She leaned forward on the divan, a few feet from me. On the table next to her, a paperback, a jar of Pond's Cream.

"I'm not going to have friends."

"You don't *know* that," Dad intoned.

Those who know do not talk. Those who talk do not know.

"No, I don't *know* it," I replied.

"You've got to stop discounting yourself, Mark," Dad said, tolerantly. "You know there might be boys like John at camp."

"Even if there are I still won't have anyone to *talk* to."

"What do you *mean?*" Dad asked, frustrated, looking out the window.

He *must* know what I mean, I thought. I need what I've needed so much since Nanna died; what I've always needed. Someone to have "talks" with. If he doesn't understand what that means I don't know how to explain it. He stood in profile in front of the window. He's *her* son, I thought. I should be over her death. Mom and Dad have been so patient. Saying what you mean is an immense task—you're honest and then no one understands.

"I mean there won't be anyone on my level." I knew this was a mistake.

"People might *well* be on your level if you'd allow them to be," Dad said. "I don't mean this critically, but you don't always give people a chance."

"I give them a chance a *lot*."

"Well, with that attitude . . ."

"Honey."

"It's not *my attitude* that's a problem," I said hysterically. The talks I'd so wanted, I thought, have turned into such *nightmares.*

"I'm just trying to give you a constructive suggestion," Dad said, wounded.

"You're telling me . . . what attitude . . . I'm supposed to have. I don't have a *choice* about going. But I don't see why I have to act *happy*."

"We're not asking you to 'act happy,'" Dad responded, sarcastically.

Why do you always say "we"? You're the one asking, not her.

"Yes, you *are* asking me to act happy," I said. You always have to choose which point to make, I thought. Then the other point is lost forever. I don't know how anyone can ever talk to anyone.

"We're asking you to think a *little* about other people's happiness, not just your own," Dad said, pacing in front of his dresser. "You know Mark, no man is an island."

"I am not saying," I almost shouted, "that I'm an *island*." I want to be able to love you again but I don't know how—you keep pushing me. Maybe I *am* an island. I know what's coming, I thought, readying myself. He's going to say I'm spoiled. He's going to tell me I ought to appreciate how hard he works; he's going to list all the things Mom does for me. Maybe he's right. Maybe I *am* spoiled. But he is, too. I looked at my mother. Now, I thought, she feels sorrier for me than for him; but that could change. I can't attack Dad *too* much.

"Mark," my mother said, coming over to me on the bed, "we *do* want to know how you feel."

We'd had so many talks in this room. We'd planned, we'd reminisced. On her birthday, we'd served Mom breakfast in bed. We'd talked about Kurtz and deSoto and, after Nanna's death, Dad and I had talked, sometimes, in here—but it hadn't ever been like this. We'd known communication wasn't easy. But we hadn't known how fascinatingly awful and difficult it really was, the chasms, the twisted knottiness—we were showing each other this.

In the living room Sharon listened to Neil Diamond. Jason closed a door somewhere.

The conversation always moves too quickly for us to control it, I thought. We're on a wildly rushing river, but we keep talking, as if the words we choose make any difference.

Beyond the bedroom, the olive trees, the citrus groves. Beyond them, the desert. The silent darkness. Inside, Mom and Dad and me, the bed, the divan, the black-and-white TV, and Mom and Dad's ideas about a happy family, and my desire for love to be perfect, and Mom's for the same thing. And our slight hope that we can end the conversation with a truce. Use words carefully. . . .

"What I feel," I said, half-calmly, technically, "is it's too risky."

"That's being a *little overly dramatic*, don't you think?" my father said.

Why hadn't he been able to resist? I've been hearing that my whole life! Now the conversation can't end with an OK feeling.

"You don't understand!" I shouted, my voice breaking. I put my head in my hands to show I was about to cry. Sharon, in the living room, put on The Moody Blues.

"I'm sorry, but I've had enough," Dad responded. "Maybe *you two* should talk for a while. *I'm* obviously not doing any good." (His tone meant, "*I'm a monster, but I'm a martyr, too.*") He left the bedroom. Now Mom's going to think I've *made* him leave. He'll *make* Mom think that! He went into the study and started typing, loudly, dramatically. Mom held me.

"I'm sorry," I said.

"It's not your fault," she replied. "It just got a little out of hand." We sat together on the edge of the bed. I looked at the dresser, the family photos, Mom's emery board, her glass of water. Mine was a lost cause, but we believed in lost causes. McGovern, the Rosenbergs. Just because you lost didn't mean you weren't right.

Mom sighed. Even if a miracle occurred, I'd caused so much trouble they wouldn't want to go on a vacation with me. Even if, somehow, I could still change their minds, I couldn't win—I wouldn't have Mom's sympathy. Better to be the one who's hurt.

Outside, some oranges fell on the lawn. Palm fronds blew in the wind on Via Mariposa. Inside, Dad typed, and my brother, who had never complained about camp, shut the door to his room. Had I made Dad feel the way he felt? Had he made me feel the way I did? Had I made Mom . . . Where did the feelings start and end? Whose fault did Mom think it was? Sharon turned the stereo off.

"You know how much he loves you," Mom said.

———

"Your feelings are your feelings. Theirs are theirs. You're separate people."

Ha-ha, I thought.

"What I don't get about your family," Dr. Kurtz continued slowly, "is the way you all seem to think you have to make each other agree with you. It's curious. You don't seem to accept that people are individuals and can see things differently."

Don't talk about my family like that, I thought.

———

The next day Dad suggested one way for me to have someone to talk to would be to call Dr. Kurtz from camp. A few days later he sent in the rest of the money to Evergreen.

We continued to have "talks," mostly about who'd been unfair in the last talk. Each morning the argument still hovered in the air, a kind of moisture we knew could, by day's end, condense into a storm. The feelings of having been wronged, of maybe having said something wrong and needing to make up for it or justify it, of not having said something in the right way—all still there in the morning. And also the feeling that all this wasn't normal, that we ought to be able to fix it.

On many nights we argued intensely, but sometimes we didn't. One day, while we watched TV, Jason told me softly that he didn't want to go to camp either, but he thought there was nothing he could do.

Sometimes I felt things weren't so bad. My fading anger disappointed me: perhaps it meant I'd been wrong to be angry. Everyone said you should get in touch with what you *really* felt, but I could make myself feel different things. And I didn't know how I was supposed to know how the I who decided how to feel felt. Sometimes, watching the light moving slowly across the brick walls in my room, I would think about the Rosenbergs. How brave Julius and Ethel had been! I would try to be more like them. But, since Mom and Dad are getting their way, I thought, I have a right, at *least*, to be comforted. Then I can store up love; when summer comes it will protect me.

———

Dad came into my room and sat on the edge of the bed. I knew it wouldn't accomplish anything. I listened while he told me, once again, about Marcus Grosfeld, my great-uncle. He'd explored the woods. A great man; he'd given Dad piggyback rides.

He got up from the bed and walked slowly to the door. "Sleep well, Mark." His voice seemed sad.

Like a wave in the dark at Mission Beach, my thoughts swelled: He loves me and I *never* give him a chance. He'd stood up to the coach who'd called when I'd ditched PE. "Grosfeld's been skipping," the coach had said. "My son's name is Mark," Dad had answered. "Call me back when you get *that* right." He'd picked me up in the middle of the night from John Friedman's when I couldn't sleep. I'd been afraid to call but had finally decided I *had* to; I'd found the phone next to the aquarium in the Friedman's living room. When he came he wasn't mad; he'd comforted me. "It can be hard to sleep in strange places," he'd said, driving home in the car. I lifted my face from the pillow. He'd put his arm around my shoulders while we watched the returns the night McGovern lost. One time he'd taken me down to KPAK when he was interviewed; I got to sit behind the microphone. We'd had lunch at the McGrath and Greene cafeteria in the Coronado Building and he'd introduced me to everyone— the lawyers, the secretaries. He'd held me, when I was little and sick, while I vomited all night in the bathroom.

And, when I was little, he would come and sing to me. Kneeling by my bed, in his forest voice:

A capital ship on an ocean trip
Was the walloping window blinds

One night he'd stopped coming. The next day, in the car, I asked why, and he told me I was growing up. I was angry. He didn't love me the same way anymore. I knew this was what it meant, even though he wouldn't admit it. "I still love you, Mark," he said, troubled. If he still loved me, why couldn't he still come? It made no sense. His only reason: that I'd grown. But my body wasn't me.

If only I could make things be the way they'd once been, long ago. If only I could talk to him; if he wouldn't always try to change me. If only Mom understood . . .

If only I didn't have to go to camp.

If only I could stop feeling sorry for myself.

I turned on the bedside light and read the poem I'd been working on before he came in.

> *Above the clearing mist*
> *I see the mountain*
> *but not the path*
> *or maybe*
> *it is a path I do not want to see.*

———

I couldn't put it off any longer; I lay on my bed, reading *Journey to Ixtlan*. Outside, Sparky yelped at birds.

"One needs the mood of a warrior for every single act," he said. "There is no power in a life that lacks this mood. Look at yourself. You whine and complain and feel that everyone is making you dance to their tune. What an ugly feeling that must be! A warrior is not a leaf at the mercy of the wind. . . ."

I liked his stance although I thought it was unrealistic. It seemed too simplistic for the complex world in which I lived.

———

Watergate helped. It became harder to be angry; the Senate hearings were about to start. Thinking of Nixon's downfall, in the kitchen, in the yard, on the soccer field, brought the same feeling as an optimistic song: *"Even though we ain't got money, I'm so in love with you, honey."* If Nixon could be impeached, anything was possible! The world would be different when he was gone.

But, I remembered, Lao-tzu didn't care who the emperor was.

Anna mentioned Watergate once; she had a vague idea what was going on. Except for John Friedman, no one else discussed it at school. And he didn't discuss it much. No one cared about Watergate the way my family did.

———

"To be inaccessible means that you touch the world around you sparingly. You don't eat five quail; you eat one. . . . You don't use and squeeze people until they have shriveled to nothing, especially the people you love."

"I have never used anyone," I said sincerely.

But don Juan maintained that I had. . . .

"To be unavailable means that you deliberately avoid exhausting yourself and others," he continued. "It means that you are not hungry and desperate, like the poor bastard that feels he will never eat again and devours all five quail!"

———

Time for science. I walked through the warm dusty air, smelling the mown grass. Above the school a few clouds; to the west, empty sky, and then, on the horizon, lots of little stuff: electrical towers, phone poles, offices, palm trees—glinting ship masts in the sun. There are so many books I want to read. Next: Thomas Merton's *Zen and the Birds of Appetite.*

Loloma was quiet. The cactus flowers along the walkway bloomed a cartoon orange. Earlier, Anna and I had talked about the importance of not intellectualizing too much—although Anna had said she admired intellectuals. After one of the faculty meetings, Karl had given her a sign that read: *Non illegitimati carborundum.* She'd translated it for me: don't let the bastards get you down. And she'd told me about her latest dream: a key in a river, a garage burning down.

Hoffman and Tom McKnight came along the walkway in the other direction. McKnight wore a cross; he belonged to Young Life. Weird that he's friends with Hoffman, but I never know how this stuff works. Hoffman, who was short and muscular, played the drums in band. Wearing his STP T-shirt and his puka shells, he chanted to McKnight:

"Does your dick hang low?
Can you tie it in a bow?"

———

Sirica said Dean could have immunity. Magruder, too. A lot of people were upset because the soap operas were going to be preempted by the hearings. One day, at Sharon's suggestion, I looked at the ads for camps in the back of *The New York Times*. I found a camp that, along with canoeing and horseback, had an art barn. In Connecticut, not far from Posha's farm.

I revised "Butterfly Wait," making it less angry. It worked better that way. Occasionally I still used rhymes, but I wanted to give them up. There were other ways to structure poems— intuitive, hard to name.

———

Old friends, Paul Simon sang, *sat on their park bench like book-ends.* The song went through my head while I waited for Mom to pick me up to go to Dr. Kurtz. Time went by quickly, I thought. Then you were lonely and old.

Hoffman and Schaeffer walked past. Schaeffer wore sunglasses, Hoffman no expression. "Ooh," he said sarcastically, "bell-bottoms." They sat down at the far end of the concrete ledge. Carlos, the custodian, was mowing the grass; a dust devil blew past the parking lot.

"We were doin' muscle competitions in the mirror," said Hoffman. He still hates me because of the snake business, I thought.

"No shit," said Schaeffer.

Hoffman spit in the dirt. There was stuff I couldn't hear; Hoffman looked in my direction, his white teeth gleaming, his thumbs in his belt. They laughed.

"Jeremiah was a bullfrog," Schaeffer sang. Boys sometimes started singing just because they wanted to.

The lawn mower came closer.

"Got detention Saturday." Schaeffer had been caught with Baltz, smoking in the wash.

"Couldn't unhook her bra."

"Gonna go tubin' down the Salt?"

The car door was almost too hot to touch; I got in quickly. Hoffman and Schaeffer turned into little boys, then disappeared. Mom and I turned onto Fortieth Street and passed a jacaranda tree in bloom.

"I think those are my favorite desert trees," Mom remarked.

"Me, too," I said. "And I like their name."

"I wonder if we could plant one?" Mom mused.

"It would look nice."

Mom said she would talk with the gardeners. She asked how my day had been. I told her we'd had a substitute for science.

"How was she?"

"Not too good."

"That's too bad," she said, with feeling, as if it mattered. She knows that I'm leaving everything out. Why can't I be truthful and tell her what happened? We passed a Jack in the Box. Dark shadows, oleanders, cars, clouds. I want to say things the same way to different people, to Anna, Mom, Dr. Kurtz, but I can't; I'm not really whole. God is one alone, I thought, looking out the windshield at the palo verdes. And ever more shall be so. Immenseness. The office interrupted sky.

What would it be like if I really told her what had happened? Martha Wallace had gotten a better grade than me in history. Mr. Lewis had pointed out that my report on the Middle East was prejudiced against the Arabs; I'd overused the word *dirt*. I wasn't going to the dance that night that everyone, even the teachers, had talked about all day. A new kid had shown up. He rode horses and came from New Jersey. I wasn't sure whether he was going to be popular. McKnight had tried to explain to me that he was a Christian, not a Protestant or a Catholic. "You have to be one or the other," I'd said. He'd shaken his head, exasperated. I'd let the other team get a goal during PE. I'd had an idea for "Butterfly Wait," but I'd forgotten it. I kept trying to remember it, to pull it back out of the air. Baltz had said the Nazis were efficient. Douggy had called me Gilligan.

I don't know where I would begin; Mom understands, I thought, my reluctance. She's supposed to respect my boundaries. I can't say, "I felt really lonely." I can't tell her that during soccer Schaeffer yelled "Yougoddamfuckinspazz" when I let the ball go by, distracted by my thoughts. And later when Hoffman came charging down the field I was afraid to get in his way; I let him go by; I knew he would kick me in the shins. I'm such a weakling. I'm so afraid. But why should anyone kick anyone in the shins?

The reason I don't like to play with boys, I told myself, is because I don't like to get hurt. Everyone acts like this is illogical but I don't see why. No one tells the truth about sports. Boys like to play them *because* they like to hurt—they *enjoy* kicking you in the shins. I don't want to hurt anyone. Or maybe I just don't want to *get* hurt. I'm probably a pacifist for selfish reasons.

La Fonda Chevrolet. I can't, I thought, tell Mom about school. It's all too humiliating. She'll want to fix it, although there's nothing she can do, and then I'll feel it's my fault there's nothing she can do. Still, I want to be able to share it with her; I want her to be able to *guess* it.

We drove through a light. We stopped at a light. I thought about "Butterfly Wait."

The receptionist smiled; bravery's a state of *being*, I thought. *There is no power in a life that lacks this mood.* But how do you change your *being*?

"Mark?" Dr. Kurtz called. I headed down the hall.

"How are things at home?"

"Better," I told him, "but still pretty tense." We sat in silence. I know he wants me to go on and say more about that, I thought, although he would *say* that it's OK for me to talk about whatever I want and maybe I'm just imagining that these are the things he thinks are important. I gathered my courage and explained my idea: fear was something outside of you—a force. You didn't need to fear *people,* you needed to fear *fear;* you had to keep it from entering you. Castaneda and FDR, I thought, both made the same point. Dr. Kurtz nodded, looking bored. Or maybe, I thought, I just imagined he looked bored. Perhaps I hadn't been clear.

Dr. Kurtz talked about the different rates at which boys developed; I was advanced in some ways, not others.

"What do you mean?"

"You're advanced for your age *intellectually.*"

I crossed my skinny legs.

"But socially," he continued, "it's a different story."

172

I *am* making some advances! I began, wearily, to try to explain, once again, about the *Amethyst,* how Anna and Richard really *were* my peers. He thinks, I thought, I'm being conceited.

"Do you know what I think, Mark?" he asked, looking at me intently.

"What?"

"I think one of the reasons you're interested in the arts is to compensate for not being good at other things. Probably," he continued, smiling, "it's because you haven't broken the umbilical cord." He put out his Marlboro. "Are you mad at me for saying that?" he asked. "You can go ahead and express your anger. It's all right. This is a safe place."

"Your father made some calls about the camp you found," Mom said on the way home. "He talked to the owners; he seemed pleased. And, since Jason will still be going, Evergreen agreed to a full refund. I know he was worried about that."

I nodded. I'd still have to go to camp, but it wouldn't be *quite* as awful. "Things seem better between you two," she continued wishfully. They are, I thought, feeling cornered, but our problems aren't *solved.* She wants to know how I really feel; I want to tell her. But that's dangerous. Things *are* better with Dad, but I can't *just* say that. I don't want to lie. But I want to say what she wants to hear. She knows I want to tell her what she wants—and the truth. She is aware I'm aware that she's aware of this.

Why are things so *endless*?

Olive trees lined the road, their dark fruit scattered on the gravel. I was surprised she'd brought up the topic, but how else than by *talking* can we make things go back to the way they used to be? We passed some Spanish-style houses. The yards were empty; everyone was somewhere else. If I say what I really feel about Dad, she'll try to change it. We can't talk to each other the way we used to.

I knew we missed each other even when we were together. We missed the way things had once been between us. And we knew in the future we would miss each other more; we could already feel it. The different kinds of missing came and went; they were beautiful; they were in the air in the car.

I stuck my fingers out the window and felt the Phoenix wind. If only I tried harder.

Mom had told me, often, about the friends she'd had growing up. She and Evelyn would eat onion sandwiches after school. She'd told me how they'd dare each other: who could eat the hottest foods? They went to movies at the Orpheum. There were dances with soldiers; they did the Lambeth Walk.

There were animals, she'd told me, at Grandpa Vogel's store. He let her keep her turtle there. She read in the corner beneath the plumbing supplies. Grandma Vogel didn't go out much. Her brother and her husband didn't always get along. She listened to the symphony on the radio. Mom and Evelyn sat on the porch, listening to Sinatra. In Omaha, during the war.

At the corner of Osborne, another jacaranda. Trees and houses: a blur of greens, pinks, shadows. The trunks of the citrus trees, painted white to reflect the sun. In a driveway a boy popped a wheelie.

"We lived in the house with the jacaranda tree," Mom said. "That could be the first line of a story."

———

I heard Connie vacuuming in the hall. I returned to my book about Zen and the direct method. The masters hit their students—to awaken them. You had to act without hesitation. My poems have too much ego in them, too much *I*. In two months I will go to camp and die. . . . Have the mood of a warrior; control your mind. I shouldn't worry about what Dr. Kurtz says about just being myself, since there is no self. How does this no-self feel about Dr. Kurtz? If I were acting out of ordinary-mindedness, would I allow myself to be angry with him—or be indifferent?

My clothes lay around me on the floor. I thought about Baltz's comments about the Nazis. *Unbelievable.* So frustrating to be right when no one knows you are. If the Nazis were so efficient, how come they lost? If they hadn't: no more Jews or Buddhists then.

Sharon was now reading *Mila 18*, the story of the Warsaw Jews. Brigadier Funk went to see the Jews being gassed; he didn't feel a thing. To teach the German boys to be SS officers, he gave each one a puppy. At the end of their training, they were ordered to strangle the dog they'd raised. *"Jawohl, Herr Kommandant!"* And then the dogs were dead. I shivered, trying to imagine what it was like to be Herr Funk.

Maybe I should write to Posha about ordinary-mindedness. Dad said we might stop off to see him at the end of the summer. Posha and I would take long walks and discuss my ideas about Zen.

While setting the table, Jason and I decided to do the Viva test. The two paper towels absorbed at exactly the same rate. On the kitchen TV, Nixon said Dean didn't have to testify: executive privilege.

At dinner, Dad told Sharon she needed to enunciate.

"I don't need to enunciate," she said. "You need to listen."

"I *am* listening," Dad said. "You know, sometimes your father *can* be right."

There was a dance that night at school.

———

Along the canal I rode my bike in the heat, beneath billboards. I make things so unnecessarily difficult, I thought. Zen teaches that to not understand *is* to understand. *The Tao that can be named is not the eternal Tao.* The I that can be named is not the eternal I. The Mark that can be named . . .

I stopped and put the kickstand down and looked into the brown water. The problem is in the naming—naming me, as an *I,* a thing, not a process.

I saw Ratter on the other side of the canal and put the kickstand up.

———

We had a party for my twelfth birthday. Mom and Dad gave me the game Masterpiece, a Strathmore sketchpad, and the poems of Robert Browning. Sharon gave me the new Cat Stevens album plus a candle she'd made in her crafts class at Pueblo. Jason made a large card out of orange and purple construction paper and played "Happy Birthday" on the harmonica. We joked about the ugly shirt my aunt had sent.

"I bequeath it to you," I said, handing it to Jason.

"I bequeath it back," he said, making a face.

"Happy birthday to you," they sang. "happy birthday to you."

"You look like a monkey," added Sharon.

"And you *act* like one too," Jason finished. Sharon reached over and tickled me. I tickled back, and then she grabbed and tickled more. We were soon gasping on the floor. The way it used to be, I thought, looking up dizzily at the ceiling.

For dinner Mom made the special vegetable goulash she'd invented just for me.

After everyone had gone to bed I listened to my new record on the stereo in the living room. With the volume down low, I read the liner notes for "Catch Bull at Four," which explained the mysterious title: the fourth step toward Zen enlightenment.

—

The poem Anna had submitted for me won second place in the state contest. Dad drove me down to the Capitol, where the prize was given. We parked in the visitors' lot and walked past Alger "Save the Babies" Johnson, the protester who spent each day walking in front of the governor's office wearing a sandwich board covered with fetus photographs. Dad waved at him; they'd met when Dad had appeared in front of the legislature. Johnson waved back. "I don't know why he wastes his time down here," Dad commented. "These people are all *already* pro-life."

We crossed the plaza. I looked around for Anna.

"What happened to Mrs. Voigt?" Dad asked.

The superintendent of education came up to us. He greeted Dad, I shook his hand, and we entered the hearing room where Dad had often testified and the ceremony was to be held. I wondered, nervously, where Anna was.

Dad and the superintendent talked about Congressman Scanlon's speeding ticket; it had been on the news. "Probably drunk," Dad said, in his regular-guy voice, "and they covered it up. Paid 'em off."

"Wouldn't surprise me," said the superintendent, looking at me. "So your boy's a poet?" he asked.

He thinks I'm weird.

"And a very talented one," Dad answered, his hand on my shoulder, unembarrassed. Doesn't Dad know what he's thinking? I thought.

"Well, I better get this show on the road," the superintendent replied.

At last Anna rushed in. There had been a problem with the truck. We sat down. The room was filled with girls. The ceremony was brief; a girl from Tucson won first place for "Snow." Dad smiled proudly when I was handed my certificate.

When it was over we walked through the sunlight to the parking lot. Dad and Anna talked; I had brought them together but couldn't think of anything to say. I put on a bashful smile as Anna told Dad what a pleasure it was to have me as a student. We walked under a row of tall palm trees. Dad, I told myself, is being *gallant;* he told Anna teachers weren't appreciated by society.

"You are so right," Anna said. Dad pointed out the secretary of state's office and the Department of Motor Vehicles. I knew about Anna's tickets. Dad told about testifying before the legislature. Anna laughed at the Eastern Gadfly story. Dad recounted the time he'd been called an egghead, and how he'd responded, "better an egghead than a pinhead, sir," and Anna laughed at that too. I felt reluctantly proud of him. "Hopefully we'll get rid of some of these jerks next time," Dad commented. Anna agreed. I knew she wasn't registered to vote.

On the way home Dad said he liked Anna. "She must be quite a good teacher."

"Yes," I agreed.

"What do you think it is she does that makes her a good teacher?"

Why do you say things so heavily?

"What," he continued, "is the *main quality*?"

Maintain ordinary-mindedness, I thought. Words, says D. T. Suzuki, have no direct connection with life. We passed the Taco Bell.

"She's spontaneous," I said.

"I could certainly see that."

Did he mean she'd been late?

"A lot of teachers are too rigid," Dad continued. "Your grandfather was always hiring tutors for me. I remember one of them, the German tutor. Herr Fink. Boy, was he ever rigid." I don't want to hear your stories, I thought, and then remembered what don Juan had said to Carlos: *assume responsibility for your feelings*. We drove past the Aquarius House, where Anna had been hypnotized. A man with a long, blond ponytail stood in the front yard; he looked like Jesus; I wondered if he knew Anna.

"I sense," Dad continued, "you've more or less come to terms with camp? Or at least you've *begun* to," he added, sensing resistance.

"I guess."

The next day Anna told me how much she'd liked meeting my father. He knew so much. She'd been afraid he would think she was politically ignorant.

—

One afternoon the Nachmanns came over. Dad told them, proudly, about the prize I'd won. Later, when they'd left, he asked if he could see more of my poems. "I'm beginning," he said, "to think you're pretty darn talented."

I didn't want to show them to him, but I knew it would be hostile not to. I made a careful selection, leaving out "Crushing the Idols" and "Butterfly Wait."

———

"Your father knows everything about you," he said. "So he has you all figured out. . . . There is no power on earth that can make him change his mind about you."

Don Juan said that everybody that knew me had an idea about me, and that I kept feeding that idea with everything I did. "Don't you see?" he asked dramatically. "You must renew your personal history by telling your parents, your relatives, and your friends everything you do. On the other hand, if you have no personal history . . . nobody is angry or disillusioned with your acts. And above all no one pins you down with their thoughts."

McCord said Mitchell had known.

———

Dad and Sharon kept arguing—she was still mad about Rocky Point. It had, she'd heard, been amazing. Horowitz had only been there *one* day. Dad, she said, was a hypocrite; if she'd been a boy he would have let her go. "He's always *carping* at me," she complained wearily. When she went somewhere with Beth, he'd stay up until she got home, then give her the third degree. I knew she and Beth weren't secretly meeting boys, as Dad suspected. He hadn't allowed her to get her ears pierced. And he *always* asked about marine biology—it had been *years* since she'd even been interested in that. She was looking forward to Habonim, the Zionist socialist camp in the Berkshires. She'd persuaded Beth to join her. But she was sympathetic when I talked about not wanting to go.

One night we sat in the kitchen, eating oatmeal cookies, she in her nightgown, I in my pajamas. We're Bolsheviks, I thought, plotting against the czar. Or I'm Prince Alexei and she's Anastasia.

"You know," she said carefully, "I realize Mom and Dad *do* need some time off from us. It's probably important for their marriage." I wondered what she meant. "But the way they've dealt with you," she continued "has been *so* fucked."

I nodded. Outside, except for the pool lights, it was as warm and dark as Sharon's eyes.

"I've had a lot of realizations during the past few years," she confided. "Mom and Dad *pretend* to be reasonable, but then you find out they're not. It's something *I* had to go through," she continued. "Now *you're* having to. I guess eventually Jason will."

"I'm glad you went first," I said, trying to sound appreciative.

"Dad didn't used to be so uptight," she said wistfully. "Maybe it's a midlife thing. I shouldn't try to psychoanalyze. You remember how it used to be, don't you?"

I nodded. Something had changed. But what? So hard to say—and so I wasn't sure it had. But it must have; Sharon felt it too. César Chavez and the Temple Micah days. The time Dad led the creative Seder; standing in front of a fire on Squaw Peak, he'd told the story of Pharaoh. I remembered this, and the mesquite smell, and the candlelight march a few months later at the university—the nun who sang, the olive trees, the photograph of Jason holding a peace sign in the paper the next day. The songs we sang in the car: "Blowing in the Wind," "Joe Hill." On our way to San Diego.

"Yeah."

"I'll tell you what I've learned," she said, seriously. "I always had this 'Daddy' image. Then I realized it wasn't real."

I nodded.

"Or it's part real. In time you accept that. I don't think you're at that stage yet. I'm not always at the acceptance stage myself."

You go through different stages every day, I thought. But I wasn't going to point this out. I liked the way that our feelings, for the moment, fit together. "It's weird," I said, between cookie bites, "there's the way everyone thinks he is, in public, and . . ."

We heard some footsteps in the hall and looked at each other. We were quiet. Then Sharon continued, in an empathetic whisper, "I know."

"I guess I'm sort of getting to the acceptance stage," I said, wanting to go along with her theory.

"I don't know about *that*," she replied. I decided to overlook her sarcasm. You become close to people, I thought, by talking about your problems with someone else. Then you become close to another person by talking about the problems you have with *that* person.

"I've got to stop eating these," Sharon said. "You finish them. *You* need the weight."

I took the cookies.

"That stuff with deSoto is real bull," she added, intensely.

I love you, I thought, and thought of the games we'd played in the garage, years ago: she would be Ophelia. I'd be Hamlet. *"Rosemary, that's for remembrance,"* she'd say, holding the weeds she'd picked in the backyard as she fainted on the cement. Or Juliet and Romeo. I'd wear a tasseled green felt cap and hide behind the Plymouth while Sharon stood on the dusty cabinet, calling: *"Romeo, Romeo! Wherefore art thou Romeo?"*

"I'm here," I would say.

"I want to give you some advice," she continued, leaning across the blue kitchen table. "About camp. You can take it or leave it."

"All right."

"Don't cross the river if you can't swim the tide
Don't try denyin' living on the other side
All your life"

She was quoting the band America, which she and Beth loved. The fluorescent light haloed her dark frizzy hair; I ate the last cookie. I didn't understand America. "Don't cross the river"— what river?

"I'm gonna turn in," she said. I felt a little disappointed. I wanted to keep sharing.

"I'm going to stay up a little."

She headed down the hall. I wondered what she hadn't shared, and stared out the window into the darkness. Occasionally one of the thin, white hoses broke the surface of the pool and then quickly disappeared. Above the Phoenix Mountains, the sky was filled with stars. The distances between the stars, which appeared to be only inches, were vast. Lifetimes to travel between them—you'd die. Only the descendants of the original travelers would make it, and they wouldn't remember the planet they'd come from. It took years for the light from these stars to reach us. By the time it did the stars might be gone.

A thought occurred to me; before I forgot it, I needed to

write it down. On the refrigerator an oversized magnet read, "War is not healthy for children and other living things." I took down the shopping list and wrote, "oatmeal cookies." I put it back and went to bed.

———

The next afternoon I was widening the ditch around our lemon tree. Dad thought it wasn't getting enough irrigation.

"Mark, if I can give you a suggestion, it would be a lot easier on your back if you held the shovel like *this*."

I'm not that weak, I thought. I know how to *shovel*.

"OK."

"You don't need to get defensive," Dad replied. "I'm just trying to help."

———

In the car to Anna's, while Richard and Ian laughed in the front seat, I tried the Alice B. Toklas brownie Richard had handed to me. Pretty dry, I thought, as a chunk crumbled off and fell between the car seats. Would it seem stupid to try to dig it out? Or would Ian be mad if he found it later? He didn't like to waste pot. Ian had borrowed the cookbook from Nicola; I wondered if Alice Toklas's other recipes tasted better. I was eager to get to Anna's; we were going to look at some of the submissions to the *Amethyst*.

Nicola wasn't able to make it; she'd gotten sick the night before. Drew was already there when we arrived but it turned out he could only stay briefly. Before he left, Anna persuaded him to read his poem, "The Last Song of Lady Day."

It was quiet when he was done, except for the sound of Anna's dad in the driveway, working on the truck. Then Anna told Drew it was really great. Richard agreed. I sipped my tea and nodded, wondering whether I would ever be able to write anything so moving.

"I hate to read and run," Drew said, getting up. He stood in his black turtleneck (which he wore sometimes even when it was warm) in Anna's doorway. "Next time you'll all have to come up to my house." Drew lived with his mother in a tall, pink apartment building on Central Avenue. "I'll play some Billie Holiday records for you." I looked over at Richard. I knew what he thought about Drew's music.

Anna got up and gave him a hug. Leslie smiled and nodded. Richard gave an impassive wave. Ian didn't wave at all and the screen door shut and Drew's thin, lanky figure headed past the oleanders toward the Porsche his mother had given him.

Ian rolled his eyes. Because Anna's here, I thought, he's not going to show how much he dislikes Drew. "God, I'm glad *that's* over with," Richard said.

"Now, boys," Anna cautioned, humorously.

"I know," Richard said, "it's just after a while he gets on my nerves . . . those mannerisms . . . I guess he can't help himself." He shook his head and poured some wine. "I'm trying," he continued, grinning, "but sometimes he is *too* much."

I knew they thought Drew, like Mr. Nillson, was too eastern—but in a different way. Mr. Nillson was too wordy; Drew wrote about dead singers. I sipped some wine and gazed into the fire. I hoped Anna wouldn't say anything about meeting my father. We sat next to each other on the floor; Ian and Leslie were on the couch. Sometimes Anna's wide, silver bracelet glinted with the light from the fire her dad had made. Richard sat on Anna's other side, in his striped pants, smiling, backlit. I thought of how he looked when he'd sung, several years before, in the auditorium: the fat boy with a flower in his hair.

Ian could be so mean to Drew. Just what was wrong with him? Anna had said once that Richard and Ian were threatened by Drew. Maybe, I thought, it's the way he smiles. Richard smiles a lot too, but Drew's smile is just somehow wrong. Maybe it's because he talks about Hollywood. Anna had also explained that Ian "acted out" because his mother was crazy. This sounded different from when my parents said Mrs. Goldman was crazy. It was too bad Ian had a crazy Mom, but also somehow interesting. I hoped Anna would like "Butterfly Wait." I'd changed it at the last minute, taking out a lot of words.

There were some animal skulls and feathers on Anna's bookshelf, next to the New Directions paperbacks, above the TV. On her table, a vase with dried flowers; a small, fuzzy cactus on the window ledge. *Our house is a very, very, very fine house.* I wondered what it would be like to spend the summer with Anna. If it really happened I'd be afraid. I wouldn't know what to say to her in the morning when we woke up. I tried to picture breakfast at Anna's house. She'd find out what I was really like.

The light wandered across the floor. Anna began to read a poem about a mountain, the light on the mountain, and the mother goddess. It had grown out of an image in her dream book. She didn't know where the dreams were leading. Darker images were beginning to emerge. "It isn't all sunlight any-more," Anna had said, laughing.

There were different sorts of visions. Leslie's were like don

Juan's and William Blake's. When Castaneda started out he had to take peyote to have one. Later, when he became more advanced, he didn't need drugs. Then there was Zen enlightenment: satori. You studied a koan or got hit on the head. Or you could empty your mind and just let the self disappear. I'm being too analytical, I thought. Not experiencing the moment directly. I have to let the thoughts float off. *A ripple in still water. Catch bull at four.* I looked at Anna's sumi paintings hanging in wooden frames on the white walls next to a photograph of her and Karl in Colorado and one of Abbott, Anna's friend from the Hopi mesa, standing by a cliff. Abbott had taken her to the snake dance—a rare privilege; she was considered one of them.

Basho rubbed against my leg and purred. The final light of the day came through the window; the dust motes swam in the air, their shadows following on the floor.

Richard read "Fences." It was about his girlfriend Lisa moving to Los Angeles; the separation had been hard, but had led to a lot of poetry.

"It's more show, less tell," Ian said supportively. Richard didn't always use enough concrete imagery. Ian read a psychedelic poem about John Lennon meeting a dog. I kept thinking about Drew's poem. I'd been moved by it but also surprised. It wasn't like him to write about an archetype like Lady Day. Drew was changing. Maybe I should write a poem called "Lady Night." But, I thought, that would be derivative.

Anna got up. "All this tea," she said, stretching. "Don't read *anything* until I'm back." I got up, too. We'd been sitting a long time; I thought we were taking a break. I wasn't comfortable being in the room without Anna. Ian said, "What, are you going to follow her in there?"

I wasn't sure whether I should sit down or remain standing in order to disprove him.

Anna returned and Leslie read her poem. I tried to pay attention but couldn't get Ian's comment out of my head. No one else is thinking about it, I told myself.

They stare at us with buffalo eyes, which are
electric, which, burning, singe the sky

Leslie had actually done peyote. She read on but I couldn't focus. Leslie's poems were long and strange. Plus they went too fast; after a while I just saw her mouth moving. I tried to let Ian's comment drift out the window. The others listened attentively.

I looked past Leslie into the flickering orange. All this word-stuff, rushing through my head, blocking the world; can anyone else tell? I'm falling through space, trying to grasp hold of something; sometimes I *almost* can. Richard and Anna think I'm like them; they don't *know*. I want to be in the moment; I want to be pure, I don't want to think about what Ian thinks, I don't want to think about camp. Basho isn't comfortable with me; she moves away. Will Anna notice? Control yourself, your mind; remember the light on the aspen trees; be calm. *Don't* try to control yourself; let go, breathe. Remember: ordinary-mindedness. Not-self. Slow the words down, slow them down. Look at the raku pots on the wooden table, the stones on the windowsill, the darkness beyond. Return to the world. The world, made of things. Candles and bleached skulls; steamy, warm tea. The silverfish, crawling on the floor. Richard says they're ancient.

"Mark," Anna said, turning to me after Leslie finished, "do you have anything for us?" I pulled a crumpled piece of paper from my back pocket. The room had grown dark and full of power. I read "Butterfly Wait." It was quiet when I finished, except for the sounds of Anna's Dad, working on the truck, and the crackling fire.

"Genius," Anna said, breaking the silence, lightly slapping her thigh.

"Where does that *come* from?" Richard asked. It was, for a moment, as if I were on a Himalayan peak, in the thin, bracing, strong, and dangerous air. Putting on a bashful expression, I squirmed a little and petted Basho. Ian was silent; I wondered what he thought.

———

I'm still going to camp, I thought, leaving the cafeteria. I crossed the grass and then sat down at the edge of the upper field. Spring. I looked at the goalposts and the desert, pale green and brown and gray. The roofs of the houses lining the field quivered in the light, indistinguishable as souls. Birdsong and boys' shouts; in the distance, soccer. Beautiful. I shivered. Beauty is easy, I thought. It's been there all along.

I rode my bike along the canal past fenced backyards. Barbecues, pool slides, half-dead lawns. I thought about camp without feeling anything but the air against my face. I was almost in the moment. The sun went behind a cloud. Unhappiness was like that; it could disappear. I passed in back of Safeway. Other bikes had left tracks in the dirt. It was very warm. I rode past a small puddle; suddenly, I didn't feel OK. I didn't know why. I didn't know why, often, my mood changed abruptly for no reason—or for many reasons. Maybe the angle at which the light met the brown water, and the feel of the slight breeze, and the faint eucalyptus smell had somehow come together to make me unhappy. Perhaps the tiny pool reminded me of something, another brown puddle, on Nanna's farm, at the edge of her garden, near the trellised grape arbor, where Sharon said she wanted to get married. But maybe it hadn't been this; thoughts and impressions moved more quickly than a bike wheel's spokes, although at the center of the turning, a still point—if I could ever find it.

I turned my bike off the embankment onto the asphalt. Death and rebirth. A waste to spend your life being unhappy. A flock of crows burst from behind an olive tree, as if a traffic light only they could see had changed.

———

Dear Mark:

"Butterfly Wait" is quite good. I'm glad you are experimenting with free verse. However, I do feel it needs further revision. It is important to remember that one is writing in order to communicate, and you can, at times, be quite obscure. The point is, you are on your way, but I don't think you are there yet. I look forward to discussing your ideas about Eastern religions. All religions have something to teach, and they all have a great deal in common.

Much love,
Posha

What are important, I thought, are the differences.

———

DeSoto came; we tossed the ball back and forth in the heat. Jason moved gracefully sometimes, and sometimes awkwardly. Mostly I missed. "Your Dad's a good guy," deSoto said. "Done a lot for me. A lot for this town. You must be mighty proud."

I picked the ball up from the grass, wondering what he really thought of Dad. Maybe he *did* respect him. But he probably thought it was pathetic that Dad had to hire him.

"Yeah," I said.

Sit-ups on the dry grass. A cramp in my side; I slowed down; deSoto told me to keep going. Along with the pain in my stomach, another feeling—I couldn't say where. It was wrapped like a lizard on a branch around the pain in my side, in my head, in my throat, in the hot air and the yard-light, in the present light, or in the past, in memory: my body's, my mind's.

The past, wherever that was . . .

"One more," deSoto said.

"Just one more," Dad had said, standing, a few years ago, where deSoto stood now. "Attaboy," he'd say, "give it to me again. Attaboy, attaboy; keep your eye on the ball. Just keep your eye on the ball." Again and again; it wouldn't matter whether I caught the ball or not, he'd just repeat it. But the more he persisted the worse it got. Bend your knees, he'd say, even though they were bent. I don't know who he is, I'd think. He's someone different now. Not the Dad who reads about King Arthur. Not the Dad who comes at night to sing. And I don't know who he thinks I am, standing here beneath the grapefruit trees.

His voice, relentless, automatic, sad-blind, corners me in the sunlight: keep your eye on the ball. Please stop, I think. This isn't *necessary.* I know he thinks he *has* to be this way. "Eye on the ball, eye on the ball." I know he won't admit, or doesn't know, he's being any way at all. I *am* keeping my eye on the ball, I think. I'm not throwing *underhand.* Doesn't matter. He still says: "Don't throw underhand. Don't throw like a girl. Bend your knees." Everything about the way I am in space is wrong. We take a break, sit down. He asks if I ever get in fights at school. I don't answer. "If you're in a fight, don't just swing your arms wildly." He makes me show him how I would swing my arms. On the patio trying not to swing wildly. "Hit straight ahead." Please let this moment stop. "Show me your muscle," he says. I show him the muscle I don't have. We go back on the grass again.

"That's enough, guys," deSoto said. Jason collapsed on the grass, looked at me, and shook his head.

That evening Jason and I talked to Mom about deSoto. "It's really hot," Jason told her.

"We could get heat stroke," I said.

"Then we could die," Jason added.

"You're right," Mom said. "It is too hot. I'll talk to your father."

———

"I was really quite impressed," Dad said, as he gave me back the folder with my poems. "I hope you'll show me if you write some new ones."

———

I walked with my tray through the cafeteria, wondering if

"Crushing the Idols" had too many symbols. Maybe I can find a way to *balance* symbols and images, I thought, taking some Jell-O and steadying my tray. All the stanzas in "Crushing the Idols" had five lines. I was beginning to like five. A change: I'd always thought four was the best number. I'd been in favor of even numbers before. They felt rounder, more like women.

The cafeteria doors opened; some kids and light came in. The noise in the room, a low roar. I stood still, uncertain where to sit. I thought of the discussions I would have with Posha at the farm on the way home from camp. The light at the end of the tunnel, the green, leafy tunnel.

Hoffman and McKnight were sitting by themselves. Hoffman wore his puka shells, McKnight his cross. McKnight was sometimes pretty friendly to me. He'd told me on the field trip to *Peter and the Wolf* that I was going to hell because I wasn't saved. But he'd said it in a nice way.

"Mind if I sit here?" I asked.

"I'm sorry," Hoffman said, without expression, "but this seat is *saved*."

I thought for a moment McKnight was going to say something but he didn't. "That's OK," I said. I felt nothing for a second; it was like stubbing your toe and then waiting for the pain wave. With emotions, you never knew when it would hit. It could be days later, or weeks, or months. Feelings never went away, not really. I took my tray outside.

Sometimes not being wanted was a dull thud. Sometimes it felt like falling on the sidewalk, skinning your knees. I knelt on the grass in the hot sun. I shouldn't have asked them. Dr. Kurtz had told me I shouldn't think in terms of *should*. Nothing he said made sense.

———

Later, during PE, my sneaker stopped the ball. I didn't know what was happening. I kicked it and it went and it went, farther than I had ever kicked it. I was amazed.

"All right, Grosfeld!" Baltz shouted, slapping me on the back. People talked about my kick the rest of the afternoon. *Gone are the dark clouds that had me down,* I told myself, taking my books from my locker at the end of the day.

———

I sat in my beanbag chair and wrote. The room was shadowy. Outside, mockingbirds and voices and pool splashes.

Dad stood in my door in his trunks.

"Mark, do you want to come swim?"

Sharon and Jason shouting from the pool.

"Maybe I'll come out in a *little* while," I said, trying to sound friendly. First I needed to find an image of spring that wasn't clichéd.

"What's wrong?" he asked.

"Oh, nothing."

"Well you sure look as if something's wrong," he said, sounding concerned. He stood looking at me, waiting.

He's trying to draw me out. It's a trick. Or maybe not. Maybe now he does really want to know. But I wasn't even *in* a bad mood when he came in. I was just into the poem.

"Mark, what's going on?"

He wants to come in, I thought, into *me;* he wants to come in and fix me. He wants us to be *close.* I can't let him in—I'd like to get inside him too. I'd like to change him too. I looked down at the floor.

"A lot," I answered theatrically.

He exhaled heavily and turned to leave. He stopped.

"You know," he said, with half-dramatic frustration, "I've about had enough of this. You need to stop brooding and start enjoying life. You're not *so* different from other people."

"I didn't say I was."

"Well you certainly *act* like you are. You're ruining things for everyone. We've been very patient. But from now on I'm going to start enjoying myself."

I've been trying so hard and he hasn't even noticed! I just made *one* negative comment. You've been angry all along, I thought. Holding this in as if you hadn't won. But you have! You just want to win *totally!* The last three weeks I've been trying to be reasonable—what a fucking waste.

"No one's stopping you," I muttered bitterly, eye-level with his hairy knees.

"Frankly, *you* have been. You should consider what it would be like if everyone acted like you."

Or if everyone acted like *you.*

"And what it would be like if your mother and I acted like other parents. We've really gone out of our way for you. You're getting your way about deSoto. You're getting your way about where you go to camp. We're arranging for you to call Dr. Kurtz. You're getting your way on an awful lot of things."

"I'M NOT GETTING MY WAY ON ANYTHING!"

His eyes seemed weary and sad.

"Mark, it's about time you shape up and stop feeling *quite* so sorry for yourself."

"Can't I just feel the way I *feel?* Can't I at least have *THAT?*"

"Your problems are really not that great," he said angrily. "Stop using them as a crutch."

"I'm not using them as a crutch," I said, and then added, more quietly, "it's just sometimes I want to be comforted."

"We've tried to comfort you," he said, distressed, "but I don't know what the hell you want. I think you want us to baby you."

"What's wrong with that? Why can't I be babied?" I whimpered.

"You're not a baby. You're a boy." He stalked out. I sank into the beanbag chair.

I lay on my bed, holding my bear. I hate who I've become. I wish I could be a good person.

That night in the kitchen I said to Sharon, "I can't stand it anymore."

"You know," she replied wearily, "sometimes you really blow things out of proportion. I'm not saying you're wrong. I'm just saying there *are* other people in this house, and you should consider they might have problems, too. You know, you're not the only person in the world."

I poured a glass of milk and went to my room. No one wants me to be honest! I *know* there are other people in the house. Now even Sharon's abandoned me. How can people be so heartless? Especially people, like *Ophelia*, who care about strangers. Who care about evil and social injustice. But maybe I've brought it on myself. I *do* act like I'm different from other people. I *do* only think about myself. I've dragged this all out endlessly, pulling everyone into this stupid hell. *Hello, my name is Harry Cemetery.* I pointed a finger-gun at my head. The lights in the pebbly ceiling looked down like half-closed eyes on the dark room, on the poems and *Mad* magazines on the floor.

Comfort me, God.

Some moments passed. I undressed and took a bath. In the warm water, I remembered how Mom had, years before, bathed Jason and me together. We'd played with a plastic boat, splashing water on the tiles. Under the water, I couldn't tell whose legs were whose. You can't tell people apart, I thought. We're in each other. Jason, Sharon, Mom, Dad, and me. Dad is in me; Sharon is in me; I'm in Dad; Dad's in Mom. No boundaries. It's awful, really, sometimes.

I ran the towel up and down my skinny legs, drying myself off. The water moved in slow, then rapid circles, and then was sucked down the drain. I went to bed and closed my eyes.

I thought of getting up to look at Nanna's letters. I could read them—or the lines in her poems I thought were about me. I wanted to, but wasn't sure I should; don Juan had warned Carlos against indulgence. There is, I thought, a grief beneath my grief for Nanna, something vaster, more shapeless, always there. Perhaps my sadness over her is just the door to this grief. I began to get up to look at her letters but then lay back down.

Who am I when my eyes are closed? I'm voices: this thought drifted among the voices. I thought about getting up to write it down but then thought it wasn't worth it. Or there was that thought, drifting in the watery dark.

The voices were mine and weren't; I couldn't separate mine from the others; my parents', my grandfather's, Baltz's, Anna's. They aren't *caused* by my brain, I thought: you can't get from matter to voices; thoughts, feelings, souls, everything that matters doesn't come from matter. A Separate Reality. How the soul can live on, how the soul *must* live on. Ocean of souls. She is in me; I keep her alive.

I took a sip of water from the plastic cup with the faded

green cactus. Feelings—the most important things, the *real* things—can't be named. Poetry tries but is never completely successful. It can only point. Nanna knew this. A task, entrusted to me; I listened for her voice but couldn't quite hear it.

I began to float above the houses. I rose slowly over the citrus groves. I had always known how to do this. It was simple to fly; you did it with your breath. Down I looked at the TV antennae, at Squaw Peak, at the palm trees. There was the canal, the school. I tried to come down but couldn't. This feeling—familiar too. I kept rising. I would never come down.

———

I told Anna about the flying dream, how familiar it had felt. Smiling, she shook her head. "Wow," she said, quietly, and then added, lightly, "You're going to fly right out of here some day."

She told me she'd finalized her summer plans. She was going to the Milarepa Academy in Colorado Springs, to the Neal Cassady Institute for Dharmic Verse. It would be a chance to do the two things she'd always liked most: meditate and write.

———

"Mark, I'm sorry about the other day," Dad said. "I've been under a lot of pressure. You know I've been trying to communicate with you. I don't feel I always know how. But I *am* trying. The best I can."

I didn't know what to say. "That's OK," I replied, almost wishing he hadn't said this. I returned to my book.

The weeks passed. Sometimes Mom and Dad and I still "talked." Sometimes I talked with Sharon. Jason spent a lot of time in his room.

———

Now we are concerned with losing self-importance. As long as you feel that you are the most important thing in the world you cannot really appreciate the world around you. . . . All you see is yourself apart from everything else.

———

I sat reading in a green lawn chair on a Saturday afternoon; Dad talked to Mrs. Sklar. Mom, in her white-rimmed sunglasses, watered the African violets.

"We are *so* proud of you," Mrs. Sklar said. "You're really the one who saved the Gunderson Ranch. I don't think I could have stood it if they'd ruined that beautiful land. I was out on Pima last weekend. That new development, those bulldozers—it's terrible."

"They never learn," Dad said.

I felt disgusted. I wasn't sure by what—it kept shifting. Somewhere in the shadow of the disgust, I remembered Mrs. Gunderson. She'd gone to the moratorium march at the university. Dad had knelt by her wheelchair and held her hand. It had been hard to see her face in the darkness. What a beautiful night it had been. A nun sang. We'd walked slowly across the campus, holding candles, beneath the grapefruit trees.

"People don't think about the planet," Dad said.

Mrs. Sklar agreed. "But your family certainly does." She'd heard, from Mrs. Levinson, about Posha's op-ed piece.

I shifted in the chair, moving *very slightly* one way and then *very slightly* the other; I couldn't quite seem to get my position right. Sparky licked my hand; her tongue felt rough and good. I could get up, I thought, and walk through the gate, down the driveway. I could turn onto Via Paisano, walk past the lawns and the citrus trees, toward Rancho del Sud. I would reach the Chevron station. Then I could keep walking along the canal past the Biltmore. I could turn north and head toward the desert. Eventually I'd have to turn around.

"I just have to say again: you were so great at that council meeting," Mrs. Sklar said.

I was embarrassed for her; I guessed Dad was, too. Mom moved on to the zinnias, beads of sweat on her shoulders.

I returned to Lao-tzu.

A truly good man is not aware of his goodness,
And is therefore good
A foolish man tries to be good,
And is therefore not good.

There were shadows in the hedges. The patio, I thought, is *vibrant*. Who am I to judge them for *being aware of their goodness*?

I looked at the shadows. Inky holes; they seem to move. Or is it something in me? Imperceptibly, the sun crossed the sky. Nothing around me moved. Everything moved. The patio's white concrete shimmered: waves of energy; edges, lines, textures. What's beneath the whiteness? The palm fronds beyond the house fluttered, agitated. A plane passed in the distance.

Beasts in the hedges. Currents passed through the palm

fronds, down the gravel driveway, to the trash cans, toward the sky. Who am I to judge my family? Who am I?

Living, I thought, would be easy if you believed in the illusion of self. Water pulsed through the snake-hose from the house, across the yard, to the pool. I sat in the lawn chair, trying to be calm; no one could see this. Eyes closed, I saw the sun-lines in the midday semidarkness.

Gnomes, beasts, buffalo.

Were other people like me?

I opened my eyes.

"You're absolutely right," Dad said, his voice resonant in the dry air. "It's the newspaper's fault. The *Observer* is too damn powerful."

IV
JOURNEY TO IXTLAN

1

Anna wrote to me at camp. Her letters were filled with images. The Nevada desert, the drunken woman next to her on the Greyhound bus, the cowboy she'd met in Reno. Her letters weren't like my family's. They were show, not tell.

> *At the rest stop, out of Vegas two hours,*
> *a woman screams at a lizard as she steps off the bus.*
> *Johnny Cash on the jukebox in the Hub Cafe.*
> *My drunken friend from the bus bemoans lost man.*
> *Dust on everything.*
> *More ideas for the Goddess poems!*
> *Write to me at the ϓ in San Francisco.*
> *Want to hear about you.*

I didn't know how to reply. I was used to writing a certain sort of letter, the kind I would send to Posha, which always began, "How are you? I am fine," or sometimes, for variety, "I am very well." I would then go on to list my recent activities, commenting on the issues of the day that I'd been asked about, concluding with hopeful sentiments about upcoming events. Anna wouldn't want that. I needed a letter with images like the one about the bus.

After flying east and driving us to our camps, my parents spent a weekend in New York and then flew back to Phoenix. Two weeks later they flew to Boston and drove to the Vineyard. On a postcard of a lighthouse, Mom described the inn they had stayed at their first night, where they'd met a woman who'd known Eleanor Roosevelt and had met Posha. Dad wrote about the beaches, the weather, and whether Nixon would be impeached. He had enjoyed meeting Mr. Nadler, the camp's director. "I hope your summer is not turning out to be *as* awful an experience as you thought," he added. I tried to be stoic in my response. No point in arguing anymore. Still, I didn't want them to think I was having a good time.

I complained about the food and the absence of TV. I wrote, "I am REALLY frustrated I am not getting to see any of Watergate." I was, a little. On one of the first nights I imagined (as if within a crystal ball) the meetings that had so often taken place in our living room—my father, in front of the fireplace, in his white shirt and tie, discussing the Gunderson Ranch, the farmworkers, Temple Micah, and Beth Shalom. Lying on my cot, in the darkness, I contemplated this crystal ball with longing. It gleamed, like my father's face in the imagined fireplace light.

I only thought of this one night.

There were twelve boys in my cabin. One said he was part Cherokee. He had dark eyes and wore a headband. I often glanced at him. One was from New York; he lived near Posha.

One had the face of an angel. He was from New Jersey and slept in the cot next to mine. I was the youngest. The cabin was a few yards from a lake, in which we swam, in which some boys fished.

It was a hot summer and the lake was unusually low. People talked about that. At the campfire a counselor did an Indian prayer for rain. I told people I didn't think it was hot—I was from Arizona.

I tried to befriend Ira, the boy from New York. He wanted to be called Houdino, after the escape artist he admired. Ira's mother had had rubella and he was missing several fingers. He said when he grew up he was going to be a counterfeiter. He had books at home on how to do it. He hadn't brought them with him; he was afraid they might be stolen. If counterfeiting didn't work he was going to design stamps. He got short-sheeted. He was called Houdino—with derision. I felt sorry for him, but after the first week I realized we didn't have much in common. Ira was, as Anna would have said, very left-brain. He didn't listen when I tried to discuss spirituality. I wouldn't become too friendly with him. I would be a little friendly, but not too.

My mother had sewn my name into my undershirts. She had written it with a felt-tip pen on the inside cover of the books I'd brought with me. These included *The Teachings of Chuang-tzu*, *Journey to Ixtlan*, and *The Catcher in the Rye*. I'd brought *The Catcher in the Rye* because I was afraid the other books might look too weird. I tried to read it on the plane but kept wondering what Holden Caulfield would have thought of me.

I wasn't sure how I would explain *Zen and the Birds of Appetite* if someone asked about it. I kept it under my cot. I kept *Journey to Ixtlan* on the ledge above my pillow. I was comforted each time I opened it and saw my name in my mother's writing. Kevin, a counselor from another cabin, saw me reading this and called me the resident intellectual. He reminded me of Richard; they both had beards and dirt-brown hair. Kevin sort of liked me but said I was strange. He went to Amherst and was reading *A Portrait of the Artist as a Young Man;* he talked with John, our counselor, about which girls they'd like to fuck. It was rumored John had done "it" in our cabin the previous summer, while the boys, supposedly asleep, were listening.

The boy with the headband had a tape player and two tapes: Elton John and Neil Young. *See the lonely boy, out on the weekend.* I would picture the lonely boy, in blue jeans, with his pickup, and feel somehow stirred, as the wind stirred the pine trees and the late afternoon light drifted into the cabin where I lay on my cot, reading or not reading. *She got pictures on the wall, they make me look up.* What were the pictures? John, the counselor, had a Jethro Tull tape; he talked about music with the boy with the headband, and I knew that sometimes they smoked Thai stick in the woods behind the cabin with Kevin and some of the other boys. I didn't like being excluded; I wished they didn't assume I didn't smoke. But I didn't really want to get high with them. It wouldn't be like the *Amethyst.*

I tried to think how to describe camp to Anna. But when I sat down to write on the steps of Cabin Seven, I never felt centered enough. I watched the squirrels dart past on the grass. I rolled pine needles along the wooden slats. I wanted to just be there in the moment, but other moments kept rushing in. I was missing the immediate Now. I thought of all the people Anna was meeting at Milarepa. When she got to San Francisco, she would get together with Duncan; perhaps someday she would introduce me to him. Clouds passed. I didn't like the sound of the letters I began. They weren't like Anna's; they didn't have the right tone. Maybe she wouldn't care about this as much as I feared.

The sun was setting. The lake, I thought, was a flickering jewel. Was this image too forced to put in a letter to Anna? I heard the shouts from the water. I looked at the trees' reflection in the orange water, which merged with the real trees: an inkblot on a folded piece of paper.

———

Posha wrote to me on his law firm's stationery.

It was great to hear from you. I'm looking forward to seeing you in a few weeks. And I was quite interested to hear some of your thoughts about camp. You sound quite resigned. "This too shall pass," you write. It is certainly natural, Mark, to experience some anxiety when encountering a new social group. But it is important to remember that Man is a social animal; learning to overcome these anxieties is part of the maturing process. I also wanted to thank you for sending me the Amethyst. *It is most impressive! And, of course, your poems are quite good. However, I do wonder why you insist on referring to yourself as "i"? Why not "I"?*

Outside the cabin someone was hammering and a tape played "Rocket Man." Turning over on the cot, I finished the letter. Posha corrected my spelling errors. "It sounds like you are reading some very interesting books. I look forward to discussing them." In closing, he reminded me of Cicero's advice about a sound mind in a sound body.

I argued in my head with him about the importance of the body. Wasn't it just a part of the illusory world? Didn't it exist, in a sense, in the mind? I knew that if someone were to listen very patiently I could prove this. I wrote a carefully worded response about "i," saying I did not want to give too much importance to the self.

The hammering stopped. Man didn't have to be a social animal, I thought; there were other ways to look at it. I had to fill up the page. I told Posha I was glad we had finally gotten some rain. Had they gotten rain? Everyone thinks it's hot here but they're not from Arizona! I told him how sorry I was to be missing Watergate.

———

Although at home I always sat when I went to the bathroom, at camp I knew I had to stand to pee. "You're the only person I've ever known who shits and pisses separately," John, our curly-haired counselor told me, quite amused. Anna sent me a letter describing her arrival in San Francisco and the graffiti on the walls at the YWCA. She enclosed a sheet of white bond paper with advice she had typed from the *Tao Te Ching*. A passage I knew well:

> *Yield and overcome*
> *Bend and be straight.*

———

It was two weeks until I heard *fag*.

"How ya doin', fag?" a boy demanded for no apparent reason while I sat beneath a tree during free time, writing to my parents. I did not respond. He didn't say it again. Odd how this word had followed me, all the way across the continent, the way the moon had trailed us past the airplane's silver wing.

I sat on a hill, in a tree's shade, next to some white flowers. They bloomed without being aware of their blooming. Why couldn't I be like that? Their petals and the grass were slightly damp. I didn't know what kind of flowers they were. In a month I'd be at the farm with Posha. We'd take long walks, discuss ideas. I'd explain Zen and Thomas Merton. And ask questions. Who were your greatest influences? I know mine, I thought: Nanna and Anna. Sometimes, on our walks, he would ask me who my favorite presidents were or quiz me about plant names. I sat near some skunk cabbage, in the bright sun; I guess I don't think names are *important*, I said to myself, imagining our conversation. Skunk cabbage. That isn't what it *is*, that's what it's *called*. A writer at ASU had told Anna it would be good for her to include more plant names in her poems. He'd told her to buy a field guide. Anna thought he was wrong; I agreed with her. Still, I thought, the names *are* sort of beautiful. Skunk cabbage. *I stuck my head in a little skunk's hole. And the little skunk said, "Well, bless my soul."*

A breeze came out of nowhere—a Christian argument for God. You could see God's effect: leaves blowing. But you couldn't see the wind or God. It wasn't the *best* argument. The blades of grass on the hill in the wind crossed each other, sometimes, like fingers, caressing the air. Sometimes they gestured wildly.

———

Everyone was excited about the upcoming canoe trip. But I was afraid to go. I had never canoed. I didn't want to think about whether or not I should go. But during the days before the trip, I could hardly think of anything else. Why couldn't I control my thoughts? I would decide I should go. I *should* go because I was afraid of going. But I ought to do what I wanted. I should listen to myself and follow my instinct. My instinct was to *not* go. But wasn't that *fear*? How could I grow without conquering *fear*? I knew this decision wasn't that important. But the universe was watching me. I signed up for the trip. I began to imagine what the day would be like: the discomfort of crouching in the canoe, the humiliation of mishandling the paddle, the sunlight, the shouting. I ought to have the inner power and sense of detachment to cope with these possibilities. But why should I have to prove this? After all, not everyone was going. On the morning of the trip I told John I wasn't feeling well. He shrugged his shoulders, indifferent. After everyone had left, with the camp nearly abandoned, I felt glad I hadn't gone. I stayed in the cabin and read. In the afternoon I began to feel melancholy. I should have gone. I went down to the meadow and did some drawings of the dandelions and the Queen Anne's lace. I walked around the lake. It was, I thought, a mirror of the bright blue sky. I wanted my mind to be like that: empty, like a mirror. I sat down on the little dock and wrote to Anna about the lake. Then I wrote to Jason at Evergreen and Sharon at Habonim.

I got up and began to walk, using a stick as a cane as if I were Posha. Could you send thoughts to people through space? How far away Loloma seemed. Next year, I wouldn't be in Anna's class, but we could still talk between classes and after school. I headed back to the cabin.

The next day everyone talked about the canoe trip. I repeated my excuse about having been sick. I had let myself be governed by my fears. Maybe it *was* my fault I didn't have friends. After all, I would have survived.

The canoe trip was on a Sunday. I had to wait until Wednesday to discuss it with Dr. Kurtz (once a week I called him from the privacy of the director's office). I spoke into the black telephone, underneath a pair of antlers and a wall with framed certificates testifying to the camp's excellence. Dr. Kurtz and I talked about fear. He said I should give myself credit for having gone so far as to sign up. Sometimes the glass was half full, not half empty. I should look ahead, not behind. I should change what I could change and accept what I could not: a wise man had said this. Hanging up the phone and leaving Mr. Nadler's office, I felt frustrated; I thought of the things I hadn't said. They seemed to multiply more quickly than I could ever express them. Even if I remembered the thoughts next week, by then everything would have changed. I walked through the Nadler's living room. Mrs. Nadler gave me some of the cookies she'd just baked. Outside, Mr. Nadler was standing with a hose in front of the geraniums. He waved. It would be seven days until I talked with Dr. Kurtz again. If I *really* needed to I could arrange to call him sooner. I knew I wouldn't.

———

I stood on top of a small hill looking out at the rolling country, at the power lines, and the Housatonic. It led, eventually, to my grandparents' farm, where I would be in a month.

I have mixed feelings, I thought, about the East. It's easier to appreciate beauty here: it's all around. The dense green trees, the grass, the lake, the flowers. Buttercups and gold-enrod. But in a way it's too easy. I don't know, I thought, if I could live in the East. I'd always be overwhelmed! Wisdom's in barrenness. Maybe, because beauty is so available, it doesn't affect people here the way it affects me. Perhaps it does, but then it's odd everything doesn't stop from the beauty. Maybe you get used to it; I don't want this to happen to me. It's better to be from the West, where you have to *look*, make do with less. Where you learn to make something out of nothing.

Sometimes, even when surrounded by dense green trees, ferns, and soft, flower-laced meadows, I couldn't feel their beauty. This was, I knew, because I wanted the feeling too much. Thomas Merton said the self stood in the way: beauty, like grace, was all around. Merton had been a poet and a Trappist monk who studied Eastern thought. He'd written about Zen and the problem of the ego. Zen had practical methods, like the koan, for getting rid of it. The self was brought to a sudden crisis and then you experienced the world directly. Satori. You learned to *see*.

A dragonfly hovered near me; I walked away from it. The mountains were soft and blue in the distance. My parents would be coming in a week and a half for visiting day. They would drive all the way from the Vineyard to see me. I wondered how many of my true feelings I would share. Should I try to be happy for them?

Some stray clouds felt their way across the sky. I remembered the famous story of Huineng, which Merton's friend Suzuki told. Before Huineng, it was believed that the mind was a mirror; through meditation, you could get rid of the dust on the mirror. The dragonfly followed me. Huineng wasn't even a monk, just a rice pounder at the monastery. One day there was a contest to select the fifth patriarch's successor. The leading contestant, Shen-hsiu, wrote a verse for the contest:

> *This body is the Bodhi-tree,*
> *The soul is like a mirror bright;*
> *Take heed to keep it always clean,*
> *And let not dust collect on it.*

Everyone thought Shen-hsiu had it won. But then, in the middle of the night, Huineng wrote his own stanza alongside Shen-hsiu's:

> *The Bodhi is not like the tree,*
> *The mirror bright is nowhere shining;*
> *As there is nothing from the first,*
> *Where can the dust collect?*

Nobody could believe it had been written by the rice pounder. He became the next patriarch.

I wasn't sure exactly what was meant by "the Bodhi." I picked some flowers and walked down the hill through the tall, yellow-green grass.

The master was asked, "What is the meaning of the first patriarch's visit to China?"

"The cypress tree in the front courtyard," came his reply.

In other words, just things. The coming year would be a good one. The next *Amethyst* would be better than the last; we'd all grown as poets. I'd come, I thought, through the darkness. In eighth grade, my real journey would begin. I could not know where it would take me. There was so much beauty. Leaves and flowers and light and clouds and grass. As if I were Moses, I looked down at the camp, as if it were the coming year at school, the Promised Land. Light voyaged through the clouds; I saw some boys playing tetherball; a feeling of peace passed through me. I dropped my bouquet in the tall grass and headed down.

Back in the cabin, I opened my mail. Jason wrote: "I am having a good time. I've climbed a lot of mountains. It's really beautiful. I hope you are having a pretty good 'camping experience' too."
There was also a letter from Sharon from Habonim.

I've met a lot of wonderful people here. I'm getting some new perspectives on life—I think! I'll be really sad to leave. But at the same time I can't wait to get to the farm. I'm really looking forward to having a chance to talk to Posha. Now I hope you won't be mad, Mark, if I give you some advice. When we head home, don't reproach Mom and Dad about the summer. They may not be perfect, but you know what? No one is. I keep learning that life can be pretty complicated. They're having to learn how to be parents just as much as we're learning stuff. So don't make them suffer. You can be honest without going overboard and blowing everything incredibly out of proportion. I'm sorry if this sounds like a lecture to you. I want to be your friend.

Then she told me about the Shalom Aleichem play she'd been in.
Maybe she was right. I had caused suffering. But how did you know the right proportion? Maybe going overboard is just being honest.

———

I slept with my arms beneath my blanket. The angel face in the next cot asked, "What are you doing, jerking off?" Then I slept with my arms on top of the blankets. I wasn't sure if this was what I *should* do. Did it mean I was admitting he'd been right? And I also thought that possibly I was *supposed* to be jerking off. I wasn't sure how his question had been meant. He had told me, on one of the first nights, about his girlfriend's tits, how she let him suck them, and he asked what base I'd gotten to. After a few days he'd begun to ignore me.

Sometimes at night, after the campfire, before lights-out, I would walk down the steep trail that led from behind the dining hall past the cabins toward the lake. Tree roots, like strong boys' limbs, crossed the path. I tried not to trip. I thought about Castaneda. Like him, I was gathering power. I walked carefully past boulders and ferns that merged in the darkness, which itself seemed to merge with the silence. The path was damp. I felt at moments that the night was about to tell me something, but I knew that the darkness was all that was going to be revealed, and that I had to accept the simplicity of this. I remembered what Anna had told me about Dante: one had to descend before coming up. This experience, this steep downhill walk, had meaning. The trail was a metaphor. Conquering fear? Perhaps, I thought, I shouldn't think of it as a metaphor. I should experience it directly. Remembering don Juan, I thought, *This is a place of power.* The trees were like tall old bearded men, watching. Something fluttered in the darkness. I stopped and felt a stone's coolness. I decided to allow myself the indulgence of my thoughts. Branches, like boys' arms, were in my way, but I slipped past them. Spruce needles brushed my face. The path was slippery. I could make out the velvet sky through the dense interlacing of the trees.

I came to the end of the trail. It opened onto the meadow. The ground squished beneath my Keds. The lake was a dark eye, the only seeing thing on the face of the earth.

I returned reluctantly to the cabin. Entering, I was signaled to be quiet. The boy with the headband perched on one of the rafters, his belt unfastened. There was suppressed laughter when the cabin's screen door opened and Houdino walked in. He seemed momentarily perplexed by the silence, and then by the piss that came streaming down on him.

In the morning the sun, filtering through the pine trees, made patterns of shadow and light on the dirt outside the director's office. We waited for the mail. I looked at the T-shirted breasts of the girl next to me. I thought this was something I was supposed to do. The boys in my cabin always talked about her breasts. The light played on them as if they were gentle hills. "What are *you* looking at?" she asked, not gently. I wanted to disappear; I didn't know what to do with my hands, my eyes, my thoughts. I felt perverted and I stood still.

———

My parents arrived for visiting day. They stayed at a motel near the Housatonic. We ate lunch in the coffee shop. In the evening I would have to return to my cabin. I didn't want to think about the way these short hours were passing as I sat across from my mother in the coffee shop. It felt wrong that we should be talking about what to order when there was such a short time. I did not wish to think about this but I couldn't help it. I wanted to appreciate the time, to not be so aware of its passing. A fly hovered near the milk container. I looked at my mother and I knew she felt the way I did. I couldn't prove it; I knew it. We would both cry when they had to leave.

Outside the large glass window, the river I had not canoed rushed by, dazzling in the light. Dad asked if Mr. Nadler was a good camp director. I talked with him about Watergate. He asked if I'd made friends and if I'd heard from Mrs. Voigt.

Mom said she wanted to collect some pinecones and take them back home. I sipped my iced tea. Back in the hotel room she was able to fix the zipper on my windbreaker, which had been stuck for weeks.

When their rented Ford disappeared down the dirt road, leaving me back at camp, I felt sadness rising up in me. But it soon began to recede. In a way I regretted this, but I realized camp was more than half over. I had passed "the hump."

One night at campfire a girl sang "Daniel," Elton John's song about his brother, who had flown in the night to Spain. Her voice drifted off into the darkness, toward the mountains. I'd always loved this song. What were Daniel's scars and why had they not healed? I'd long felt I was on the verge of discovering a clue hidden somewhere in the song.

The girl who sang had seemed no different from any of us. But now she voiced a hopeful sadness, which I sensed we all shared but which was normally hidden. I looked toward the distant lights of the Piggly Wiggly. I knew this feeling we had would vanish in the next day's light. Why were things like this? Why tomorrow would it all be gone?

The next few weeks passed quickly, which was weird: I'd spent so much time thinking about camp and now it was almost done. A girl from Michigan befriended me. She had a friend who had a cousin who'd gone to Loloma. I wasn't really sure why she liked me; it seemed arbitrary. *Learn to be there among them*. She said that God was the ground of all being. She wore a necklace with a fish and thought I was "interesting." Kevin, the counselor, said she had a crush on me, but I couldn't tell if he was joking.

There were still many days when I didn't feel centered. I knew that the fields were beautiful and that I thought too much. In the distance the mountains were always a pale blue-green. And then there were mountains beyond the mountains. Sometimes I regretted that I wasn't more homesick, that I had become used to camp, that it wasn't as terrible as I had anticipated. I wondered if I felt things deeply enough.

Ira didn't stay the whole seven weeks. I'd wondered, after he left with his mother on visiting day, whether I would see him again in the future. I often thought about what it would be like when I met people in the future. The possibility surrounded each encounter like the haze on the meadow at dawn. How would these meetings unfold? Would the people who had teased me apologize? Would I apologize to Ira? I *should* have been kinder to him. Even if I didn't like him, I should have tried to be his friend. I wondered if I had bad karma because of this. I tried to anticipate what it would be like when I saw Ira, and the others, on the streets of the future. I rehearsed over and over: *"Didn't you go to camp . . . ?"*

I had adapted. I was learning to just be there among them. Walking through the tall grass, I thought that, in a way, I'd been wrong about what camp would be like. I did not want to admit it. This was because of my ego. I tried to let it go. Past the trees, toward the sky. Thistles stuck to my socks and legs. *Yield and overcome.*

2

I woke in the room with the dark wood walls that had been my father's once. Above my head, a drawing of Roosevelt. On the bedside table, next to a glass of water, the notebook with my poems.

I heard Jason, Sharon, and Posha downstairs. Doors opened, silver clanged. How lovely, I thought, to wake knowing my family was there in the house. Light came through the lace curtains. I went to the window, sat on the daybed, and looked out past the pear tree's wet leaves: rain the night before. The barn was glazed deep red; there were puddles in the road. I felt sluggish; I had to go downstairs but didn't feel quite ready. I lingered for a moment, looking out at the trees and the hills.

Everyone was seated at the table. "Look who's joined us," said Posha.

"Hello, bro," said Jason. Pearl, the cook, brought the oatmeal in, and I spooned brown sugar on it. A fly buzzed outside the window in the garden. My father looked through the paper.

The day before, Mom and Dad had picked me up at camp. Driving down, they were cautious; they didn't ask too many questions. When we got out in front of the old stone house, Mom gave me a long hug. She knew how I felt about being at the farm.

Posha had come out the screen door; he'd stood there waving, wearing a light-brown windbreaker. I carried my suitcase up the sloping lawn past the old, rusted pump. "Can I help you with that?" Posha called.

"No, that's OK." How beautiful it is, I thought. I can feel her in the air.

I put my suitcase in the front hall and walked around the house, assuring myself I was really there. I went out the back-door, into the garden; I walked to the grape arbor and looked at the hill I'd rolled down when I was little. Yes, I was there.

I looked at Dad, reading the paper; I knew he wanted to make up for the past.

Sharon was right. Even though Mom and Dad had been wrong about camp, I had blown it out of proportion. I shouldn't expect things to be perfect. I'd grown over the summer. I'd made a resolution in the car: from now on, what they do and say won't matter to me so much. A new morning.

"So, has everyone figured out their plans for the day?" Posha asked.

"Sharon and I were thinking of going into town," Mom answered brightly. "Mark, want to come?"

"I'm not sure."

"Give the boy a chance to wake up," Dad said.

"I want to look for that old Parcheesi set," said Jason.

"It's in the attic," Posha replied.

"We better get into town soon," Mom said. "I need to go to the market. Pearl gave me her list. The bakery had some nice pies. And I noticed a new antique store on Ridge Street; Sharon and I were going to go inspect. Jason, have you changed your mind? Do you want to come with us? Mark?"

"Now, everyone can't go," Posha said. "I'll need one of you boys to help in the barn. We might need to replace some planks, and I want to bring some wood in from the shed."

"I'll be glad to help, Pop," Dad said.

"I'll need a young person, too," Posha replied impatiently.

"Mark?" Mom asked.

It would be lovely to walk through Walton's tree-lined streets with Mom and Sharon. Lovely to go to Newton's market; Mr. Newton had been a friend of Nanna's and he sold many specialty foods you couldn't get in Phoenix. The ice cream shop next door carried experimental flavors, like banana-guava.

"It's a Saturday," Posha said. "The traffic is going to be horrendous. It's turning into a tourist town."

"That's so awful," Sharon said. "I wish Walton wouldn't change at all, ever."

If I went with Mom and Sharon, I could go to the bookstore while they stopped at the antique shop. But Dad and Jason might come, too—maybe I should stay and be alone with Posha. We could go on a walk. If I waited until the afternoon, everyone would go on a walk together, and there would be no chance to talk with him. But if Jason or Dad stayed behind I wouldn't be alone with Posha. Maybe it would be safer to go into town. If everyone went to town, Posha would be angry because no one was helping in the barn.

Boots came in from the kitchen; Sharon petted her. I looked out the window at the garden; cloudy again. I didn't want to speak until I knew who was going into town. But I didn't want them to know I was waiting for them to decide—they knew anyway. The light came in through the lace curtains; the dark wood table gleamed. I stirred the brown sugar and cream in the oatmeal in the dark brown bowl.

Jason ate Cheerios and looked at the comics. If Dad stayed to help and the rest of us went he'd be hurt. I knew Mom didn't want this; I didn't want her to think I didn't want to be with Dad. It isn't that I don't want to be with him, I told myself. From now on, I'm going to be a loving person. But things won't be the same if he's with us.

Everyone, except Posha, I thought, understands what's happening. We're *always* choosing and pretending not to.

"Interesting piece on Howard Baker, if anyone wants to take a look," Dad remarked.

"I do," I replied, as if being interested in an article made up for not wanting to be with him.

"We went to Howard Johnson's one night at camp," Jason said.

"I hate that place," said Sharon.

"I love it," said Jason.

"Baker's quite an interesting figure," Dad continued. "Rather a *courageous* figure. He could . . ."

"He knows which way the wind is blowing," Posha said, gruffly. "I wouldn't make him out to be *courageous*."

"I'd like to see it," I repeated softly. Dad handed me the front page and buried his head in the financial section.

"Jason," Posha said, "when you're up in the attic looking for that Parcheesi set, see if there's another catcher's mitt. We'll need it for the game."

Damn, damn. Uncle Harold, Aunt Beth, and my cousins, Tom, George, and Matt, were coming down from Boston in a few days. We would have the annual baseball game. I wished they weren't coming, although Mom and Sharon seemed happy that they were.

Dad had said the house would be too full. I agreed with him; Jason, Sharon, and I would have to share a room.

"So who wants to go into town?" Mom asked.

"I've never seen such a bunch of indecisive people," Posha said. An insect buzzed noisily outside the window, around the delphinium. "The day's going to be gone," he warned, humorously, gruffly.

Why I wondered, are we such do-nothings? Limp, paralyzed, we sit; we can't move. Posha must be disappointed in us. He's always up before eight.

"I'll go with you," Jason said.

Now if I go, Posha will be angry because neither Jason nor I will be staying to help in the barn. He'll think we're lazy. It's worth spending *some* time in the barn with Dad and Posha if, later, Posha and I can take a walk alone. Then Dad won't think I'm avoiding him. Plus I don't want to go to the antique shop.

"I'll stay," I said. Another terrible decision, I thought.

The air washed my face; we crossed the damp grass. "Pop," Dad said, trying, it seemed, to be casually self-assured, "I'd like to talk to you later on a little more about the trusts."

"All right," Posha replied impatiently, coughing phlegm. "You should have been here in the spring," he told us. "The lilacs were amazing."

Dad seemed annoyed, but held it in. We walked silently past the garden.

It was dark and damp in the barn. "I don't think these planks are so bad," Dad said. His voice, with Posha, seemed less like Posha's than usual.

"Someone could get injured," Posha replied.

I held a flashlight. The straw crackled; shafts of light, sneaking into the barn, lined Posha's and Dad's plaid shirts. When I was little a bee had stung me here, but I hadn't cried; Nanna had said I was brave.

Back in the house, the phone rang. Jack Buford, from Valley Tech. Dad picked it up on the hallway phone, next to the coatrack. He wrote on a yellow pad.

"Even when we're on vacation, he's never away from work," Mom had said. "I wish he would let someone else handle some of it."

"Up for a walk, son?" Posha asked. We went out the front door, through the shadow of the old oak, to the gate in the fence, next to which, in the sunlight, a patch of daylilies bloomed. "Better go up the hill," Posha said, gruffly, warmly. "I suspect it's too wet down in the valley."

"I think so," I said.

"Maybe tomorrow we'll try the valley," Posha continued, "if it doesn't rain again." We went past the vegetable garden and turned by the barn. Cornflowers by the side of the road, puddles in the middle. A light and then cloudy, warm and then cool, summer day. "It's awfully good to see you, Mark," Posha said, his hand clasping my shoulder. "I've the feeling you've grown a lot this year."

"Oh, I guess," I said, a little teasingly.

"I do hope you'll show me some of the writing you did at camp."

"I haven't really *finished* anything yet."

I asked about the conference at Moosewood Lake; it had gone well, he said. He'd send me a copy of the paper he'd given. He asked if I was looking forward to seeing my cousins. I said I was. We turned in the direction of the cornfield, and with each step on the spongy grass, I tried to think of a way to bring up the subjects I wanted so to discuss. Zen, the empty mirror, Nanna. They moved through my mind like the restless butterflies hovering above the meadow in the breeze, enormous to them.

"I'd be awfully interested to see those poems when they're finished. I'm sure you made good use of the experience—which

I gather wasn't as bad as you feared?" His voice stepped carefully, as if the topic were a field perhaps too soaked to enter.

I looked toward the meadow, filled with Queen Anne's lace moving slightly in the wind. There, in the mowed corner, if it didn't rain: the baseball game. "In some ways it was bad, in some ways it was OK."

Posha made a noise; in a book, I told myself, that would be "harrumph." We turned onto the tree-lined path that led up the small hill to the cornfield. The ground was drier here. Green light above, shadows and red dirt and tractor tracks below. Light blue ahead, and the sound of hammering and men's voices coming from behind the row of trees that marked the edge of Posha's land. They were building houses on the old Brown farm.

"We tried to stop that," Posha said, pointing with his cane, "but the town granted the variance." Old Mr. Brown had sold to the developers; soon after, he'd died. The sound of the hammers mixed with the birdsong and the leaves rustling in the wind, shaking droplets on our heads.

"Your grandmother wouldn't have liked to see that," he said. "She loved this place so much. Quite a lady, your grandmother."

Yes, I know, I thought.

"Sometimes," he continued, "I'll think of something I want to say to her. She'll think that's great, I'll think, and then I'll realize I can't tell her."

"Yes," I said, "I know." That's it exactly, that feeling. I loved Posha. We came to the end of the tree-covered path. The cornstalks towered above us.

"We'll have to head back soon," Posha said, looking at his watch. "But what do you say we go a little farther—up to where you see the river?"

"OK."

"So do you think you'll keep up with any of the boys you met at camp?" Posha asked.

I tensed. I brushed my hand against a tree's bark. "Maybe there's one," I lied, imagining writing a letter to Houdino. We would have to go back to the house soon. I knew I had to change the topic.

"You know, I wanted to talk to you about some of the ideas about Eastern religions I wrote to you about in my letters," I said daringly, hoping he would not criticize me, as he sometimes did, for *"you know."*

"Yes, I wanted to hear about them," he said seriously.

"I think they have a lot of interesting ideas. They have a lot to say about what the self is."

I was saying it wrong—because I was afraid to say what I meant. I tried again. "I mean, about the illusion of self."

"I'm not really sure what that means, Mark. What illusion?"

"There's this image of the self being like a mirror," I began, and then hesitated. Everything I'm saying is completely wrong, I thought desperately. I'm blowing the opportunity. I don't even believe the self is a mirror. But I have to explain that concept first.

We came to the field's upper corner. Through an opening in the trees we could see the Housatonic. Here, Nanna had had the inspiration for the "Housatonic Elegies." We stopped and looked beyond the silos and the willow trees at the tiny, winding river.

"I know there are very high forms of Hindu spiritualism," Posha said. "The Gita, for instance. But there are also the most revolting forms of superstition. I suppose that's true in the West, too. But I don't know, as I've said, what you can find in the Eastern faiths that can't be found in the religion of your own people."

"I'm more interested, I guess, in Buddhism," I said, nervously, quietly.

"I think we better be heading back. They'll have returned from town by now. Pearl will want to get lunch on. I hope we'll have an opportunity to talk about this more later."

We walked back down the hill, down the tree-covered path, past the storage shed. I quietly tried to figure out what to say next. Posha wasn't Nanna; I shouldn't expect him to be. After a while Posha broke the silence. He was bringing a lawsuit to stop the SST. He'd given a paper about it at Moosewood Lake; no one yet knew the consequences of the supersonic plane; there hadn't been enough studies. I tried to remember all the things we hadn't gotten to discuss: Huineng and the mirror and the concept of no-mind; I wanted to be sure, the next time we talked, to have the right words ready. I also wanted to pay attention to what he was saying about the SST; that, too, was important. What happened, I wondered, to my ideas about Zen when they weren't in my mind? Since there was consciousness only, if they weren't in my mind, did they exist?

"Could it affect the ozone, for instance?" Posha remarked.

"Who needs to get anywhere so fast anyway?" I asked, thinking perhaps this might lead back to the topics I *really* wanted to discuss—but it didn't. I murmured to myself, not quite audibly, "the metaphor of the mirror being consciousness is still a form of the illusion of self." I repeated my ideas to myself, silently; I would remember them when we had another opportunity to talk.

The opportunity, for some reason, didn't come. The next

two days went quickly. I didn't have many chances to be alone with Posha, and when I did, I let them slip away. Then the cousins from Boston arrived. On the same day a professor from the University of Connecticut came up. Mom said she was glad Posha had a lot of visitors. He was lonely; he missed Nanna so much.

The professor was writing a book about the Brain Trust. Mom brought iced tea out to the garden, where Posha and the professor sat at the glass table. Posha smoked his pipe. The cousins and Sharon and Jason and I sat on the garden's brick border, in front of the phlox and the nasturtiums. I kept looking at the flowers, trying to remember their names. Mom and Aunt Beth pulled their chairs up to the table. Posha talked about the London conference; the professor and Mom asked questions. The cousins got bored and went somewhere, but Sharon and Jason and I stayed and listened. I couldn't imagine just getting up like that—we might appear uninterested. But no one seemed bothered when my cousins did.

There was hardly a chance to be alone with anyone. I wasn't comfortable around the cousins, who seemed so sure of themselves. They talked about sailing and bands I hadn't heard of. They helped Dad and me and Posha in the barn. We went on long walks, Posha leading the ten of us down through the valley where the skunk cabbage grew. The cousins discussed ecology with him.

Tom, the oldest, who'd finished a year at Harvard, Posha's school, had spent two weeks in the Galapagos working on a turtle census. "So explain again," he asked Sharon, as we walked through the high grass, "why the three of you went to different camps. Seems kind of weird."

Everyone was quiet for a moment; I looked at the muddy ground. Mom said, "Well, all three of them had different interests. Sharon, for example, was interested in Zionism. . . ."

The discussions at dinner were lively. We talked about Watergate, and Posha and Sharon debated the future of the kibbutz movement. Afterward we played Parcheesi and charades in front of the fire. Mom and I were on the same team. I gave her *Planet of the Apes*. "What in the world?" Posha said as she mimed ape gestures in front of the fireplace. *"The Madwoman of Chaillot?"* guessed Uncle Harold. Then Cousin Tom got it. Jason gave Sharon *The Sound of Music*. Posha gave Dad *David Copperfield*. No one got it. "I was a policeman," he explained, later. "A 'copper.' *I* thought it was pretty good."

The cousins rose early in the morning and so we did, too. Once, after breakfast, I went on a walk down to the brook with Mom and Sharon. We went along the white fence, which leaned with the hill's curve, and passed Mrs. Bennett, watering her daisies. She waved at us. Mrs. Bennett was nice, Mom said. She'd never gotten along with surly old Mr. Brown. "Who would ever believe Posha had a neighbor named Farmer Brown?" Sharon remarked, kicking a pebble down the dirt road.

"I know," Mom said. "You wouldn't believe it if it were in a book."

"You could write a mystery," Sharon said. "The murder of Farmer Brown. And Mrs. Bennett did it. Who would ever suspect?"

"Sick," I said, happy. This is a good walk, I thought, as we continued down the hill. Sharon picked some cornflowers even though Posha had said we shouldn't. Posha, she remarked, was loosening up. Jason and I no longer had to wear jackets at dinner. He was mellower, Mom agreed, since Nanna died. He no longer got so angry with people if they made mistakes or overslept. We discussed what it felt like to be at the farm. I tried to recapture the feeling I'd had a year before, the first time I'd been back since Nanna's death, when I'd taken this walk, the way I'd remembered her then on this fern-lined road. She was in the air now, I thought, and then she wasn't, and then she was. The field was full of Queen Anne's lace. I shouldn't try to remember, I thought. Let it happen. Let go. I loved Mom and Sharon.

We came to the little bridge. The brook rushed under it. "This place is so beautiful," Sharon said.

I looked at the willow tree and did not feel Nanna's presence. What, I wondered, if someone no longer lives on through you? My task, to keep her alive. I looked again at the willow and kicked a pebble in the brook.

Later that day Sharon took a long walk with Tom. When she came back, Jason and I, who were playing Parcheesi on the porch, teased her. "You've got a crush on him," I said.

"Bug off," she replied.

I hoped it would rain the next day so the ballgame would be canceled, but it didn't. Dad made a run, Jason got to third, and Posha and I both made it to first. Mom decided to just watch. Sharon played on the cousins' team, which easily won.

At least I hadn't struck out. Afterward, I went up to the bedroom. I was going to read Thomas Merton, but instead I looked at the pear tree in the window and let myself feel sad.

That night, before bed, I walked in the darkness around the old stone house. Perhaps Nanna would come to me. First I went to the grape arbor, then I stood outside the living room window. My parents were reading; my cousins and my sister played cards, arguing loudly. Uncle Harold and Aunt Beth looked through the guest book. I knew they were remarking on all the famous signatures; Sharon and I had done the same the night before. My brother sat next to Posha, answering questions. Life, inside, was going on; I didn't want to be part of it. I walked down the porch steps and went a little way down the dirt road. I looked back up the hill. The house, in the dark, was lit like a ship on the night sea, a ship of life, sailing on. I didn't want to go on it. I wanted to stay behind, in the darkness, where Nanna might still come. I walked a little farther down the road and looked at the soy fields and the woods. Maybe she would appear, a figure in white in the darkness. Maybe she would have a message. The moon rose above the distant power lines, I shivered in the cool night air; I saw some fireflies, but Nanna didn't come. I headed back to the house.

3

Time passed. Many philosophers said time was an illusion; it wasn't something you could touch. A word, a mental phenomenon—it *appeared* to pass. Still, I was, in some ways, excited by the beginning of another year at Loloma. Eighth grade. The familiar feeling of newness, but a different newness— more complex.

In science, we had a new skeleton. The old one had fallen apart. With the help of Schaeffer's dad, Mrs. Binder had gotten it replaced.

"I want you all to meet Bones the Second," she cheerfully told us.

"You could have saved some money," Hoffman said flatly, his thumbs in his belt. "Just use Grosfeld."

"Ha-ha," I responded.

"Hoffman, you're such a moron," said Bruce Waterson, the new boy who had shown up at Loloma toward the end of spring.

"Boys," said Mrs. Binder, "let's not make a bad impression on Bones."

"I can't believe that biddy has a job," Friedman whispered, rolling his eyes. Maybe, I thought, John and I will start to be friends again.

"I know," I whispered back. "We should just dissect her."

"Hoffman is a jerk," he added. "Don't mind him."

"I don't."

When he'd first arrived at Loloma, I'd thought Bruce Waterson *could* become popular. He seemed to be, for a couple of days. He was from New Jersey and said he'd done a lot of drugs. He had dark hair and eyes and talked a lot. Probably, I thought, too much; some people said he was full of himself.

But a few of the girls seemed to like him. He rode Arabian horses; so did they. But then one day Schaeffer told everyone he'd seen Bruce in the library reading *Vogue*. Bruce denied this and called Schaeffer an asshole. Schaeffer hit him and they were both sent to Mrs. Heller.

McKnight backed Schaeffer up, saying Bruce had been wearing cologne. "I *definitely* smelled it."

"It was aftershave," Bruce insisted to Heather, one of the girls who rode. (Her family owned a horse ranch up near Payson.)

After that, she started avoiding him, although sometimes they still talked.

Bruce began to get into a lot of arguments. Then summer came. Then the first day of science. One afternoon, a few days later, I found him sitting beneath the mulberry tree outside the white stucco library.

"Mind if I sit here?"

"No." He didn't look up or seem friendly. Maybe this is a mistake, I thought, as I knelt in my corduroys on the grass.

"That science class really sucks," I tried again.

He still didn't look up.

"I don't know why they let her teach," I continued. "She's so pathetic."

He looked at me.

"She's not bad. There are people here who are fucked up. She's old," he said, sincerely, "but she's sweet. If you talk to her. People judge so superficially."

I *had* judged superficially, I thought. And I'd said something I didn't even mean just to try to make friends with someone.

"I know," I said. "She's not the worst."

I don't know, I thought, how to *be*. What I said was pathetic.

I'm trying to go along with his approach to being but I don't know what it is yet. All I know about are the horses, which I don't know anything about.

"I mean," Bruce said, "compare her with Mrs. Heller. *She* is evil. Or Mr. Lewis. Or Coach Johnson."

"Mrs. Heller is Satan," I replied. Was this too strong? How quickly moods change, I thought. Everything is maybe OK now. Hope comes so suddenly, like an angel, no one talks about the way hope comes and goes *quickly*. I don't know if it's like this for everyone.

Maybe I'm *making a friend*. Each gesture—the angle at which I sit, what I do with my head and with my eyes, what I say—and the angle at which I say things: rolling dice.

"She is!" he agreed emphatically.

Mentioning Satan had been OK.

"Mr. Lewis isn't evil in the same way," he continued. "He's a fucked-up loser—which is *different*." He thinks a lot in terms of good and evil, I thought, nodding

"Is this the only school you've gone to?" Bruce asked. He was bigger than me, not strong, not fat. His face was sort of chipmunklike.

"Unfortunately." This sounded right. How much, I wondered, do other people hear themselves talk at the same time that they're talking? The mulberry's shadow had moved a little and I repositioned myself on the grass to try to get back in it.

"It *is* unfortunate. Because you can't compare. *You* don't know how bad this place is. How stupid people are. And how superficial. I don't mean you," he said, as if I thought he'd accused me. "I think you're probably one of the *few* people who's not like that around here." He looked at me with his obsidian eyes. "It wasn't like that at my old school."

I listened, moving slowly with the shadow. He'd wanted to stay in New Jersey, but his mother had married his stepfather, given up her modeling career, and moved to Phoenix. He could have stayed, he said, and lived with his grandmother. He described her house. I thought of mentioning something about Nanna but decided to wait.

"And now," he said, "my stepfather wants to put her in a nursing home. I'd do *anything* to stop him."

"That's terrible," I offered, and felt bad again about what I'd said about Mrs. Binder.

"He made her sign these papers. I couldn't believe my mother let him. But she just sits around and thinks about herself."

I nodded, shuddering at the thought. Only the start of the year and already I am making a *friend*. And this is only the beginning. Bruce and I will do things together. I'm not sure what— maybe climb a mountain. But that's only part of what's going to happen. I will grow as a poet. I'll show my poems to Jack Osborne, the poet Anna met at Milarepa. In a few years, San Francisco. Maybe Anna and Karl will move there too. We'll all live in a house together. *Be sure to wear some flowers in your hair.*

———

The world was changing. One Saturday night, Sharon and I sat in the living room watching the news. Nixon fired Richardson; he fired Ruckelshaus. A man we hadn't heard of fired Cox. The FBI sealed the prosecutor's office.

"Do you think there's gonna be a coup?" I asked Sharon.

"I don't know," she said. "It's a real possibility."

———

Bruce and I weren't on the same team in PE, but when we had track everyone would run together. Bruce and I would run alongside each other, and when we passed the cottonwood tree we would, sometimes, cut away to the wash, where, sitting on some rocks, in the heat, we discussed everything that was wrong at Loloma. Sometimes Bruce talked about horses or Khalil Gibran. A few times I talked about *my* ideas about religion. Bruce seemed interested. But then later, sometimes, he would tease me about things I'd said. I knew he didn't mean anything by it, but after a while I decided it was probably better not to discuss my ideas—at least for the time being.

Occasionally Bruce would want to hide in the wash when I wasn't sure it was safe. Sometimes Coach Johnson caught us and we had to do push-ups.

"You two are pathetic," he'd tell us. "You're both spoiled brats."

"You're the one who's a *PE coach*," Bruce would say.

More push-ups.

———

Dr. Kurtz had asked me to bring in the drawings I'd done at camp. I doubt, I told myself, he's going to be able to interpret them; a few weeks before I'd told him a dream about wandering down a dark path in a forest. "A sexual dream," he'd said, looking knowing and triumphant. "Entering the forest—entering a woman."

The way he interprets things, I thought, sitting in his waiting room, doesn't have magic. But I shouldn't just dismiss his years of scientific training. There are different ways of seeing the world.

"Mark?"

As I told him about Bruce he half-smiled.

"What do you think there is about him that allows you to be friends?"

Why do you ask the question that way? It makes me sound weak. When I'm being strong. It makes it sound as if Bruce isn't that important. But maybe, I thought, I'm reading stuff into stuff. I wanted to hold on to my sort-of-good mood.

"I guess it's that he wants to be friends with me," I said, accommodatingly. But, I thought, that's not it. I want to be able to talk about things in my own way.

We sat in silence.

He spoke carefully, as if taking a risk.

"I don't feel you're completely here, Mark. I'm wondering why."

"What do you mean?" I asked, stalling.

"I don't feel you're connected to what you're saying." He seemed to be trying something new. "What are you thinking, Mark? What are you *really* thinking?"

About whether I'm *here*. I *was* present in the moment! Although now I feel I'm *not*. *You* made me feel not here by saying I wasn't.

The room felt without gravity: a white hole. Maybe, I thought, you're right—maybe I'm not *totally* here. But that's because I was mad about your reaction when I talked about Bruce. But maybe I just imagined that. You'll deny it if I bring it up; then we'll have to spend time talking about *that*. Why is this so complicated? Maybe *unconsciously* I was madder than I realized, even though I thought I didn't care that much. I was trying not to be angry. I don't know what I feel, or what I'm *really* thinking. I thought I felt OK when I came in. This is stupid and unnecessary. But I have to be fair—maybe we are getting to something in my subconscious. How are you supposed to know when a feeling becomes a feeling, a thought becomes a thought?

Maybe I'm just here because you want Dad's money.

"I sort of felt, I guess, that you didn't really believe me when I was talking about Bruce."

I want to go home.

"Why did you think that?"

"I don't know. It was just . . . well . . ."

This isn't like the silence of the woods, I thought. It isn't powerful. It's dead.

"Maybe we can go ahead and look at your portfolio," he suggested. Reluctant but relieved, I placed the ink drawings on the floor. A pond. A field. A fence. Some trees. He got down and looked at them. They weren't, he said, what he'd expected.

"All right," I said, wearily, eagerly, "I'll tell you what they mean."

———

"My mom's a Scorpio," Bruce said one day. "Which is why she's so self-destructive. But she and I have a close affinity. We're both water signs." Bruce, I knew, was a Cancer.

"But that's also why I have an affinity for you," he continued. "You're Aquarius. Which is air, but it's also sort of water, because you're the water carrier. Which explains why you're so good." I was glad to hear he thought I was good. I was still worried he might think I was bad, because of what I'd said about Mrs. Binder. "Aquarians are always good. And they're fair. It's both your strength and your weakness. You don't stand up to people."

I *do* stand up to people, I thought. I didn't want him to think I was *too* good.

"Where does your Mom take you shopping?" he continued, looking at me critically. "We go to the Biltmore Fashion Plaza. I'll take you there sometime."

———

I started to work on a poem I'd begun at camp. I wrote about the dark path. The boulders, the lichen, the trees. I was excited about the symbolism. But I was careful not to be too symbolic.

———

Bruce took up ceramics. Anna taught him to throw on the wheel and said he showed promise. He spent hours perfecting his glazes. I thought his bowls were beautiful. He wasn't good at cleaning up, and sometimes Anna had to chide him, "Is this how you would leave it if you were at home?" But if Bruce were at home, I knew, his maid would clean it up.

Bruce brought some albums to play while he worked on the wheel. Richard reluctantly allowed him to put on Carly Simon and David Bowie. Bruce's favorite song was "Space Oddity," which he played over and over. Major Tom, on one of his voyages, lost contact with Ground Control. He floated through the dark galaxy, unable to communicate. Like "Rocket Man," it was about being lonely in space. Richard had no opinion about David Bowie but said he hated Carly Simon: she was commercial and a bad lyricist.

"I know," I told him outside of Bruce's presence. "What the hell does she mean, *'you probably think this song is about you?'* It *is* about him. It doesn't make any sense!"

Sometimes when I was listening to a song on an album I knew well I could already hear the next song before it began to play. I had the same sense at school one day walking toward the library: I knew I would see Bruce. Then there he was, sitting under the mulberry. My intuition is becoming more powerful, I thought. It is as if I can somehow look around a corner before I come to it, seeing, just inches, into the future.

I'm someone who can survive things, I thought, walking through the warm air across the parched grass. I was pleased with this thought. Kneeling down next to Bruce, who sat semi-cross-legged writing furiously in his notebook, I remembered our conversation just a few weeks before. This memory already had a nostalgic glow. The mulberry tree was like the Bodhi tree where the Buddha attained nirvana. I knew I was sort of daydreaming, but it was pleasant to think of things around me being like things I'd read about. I crumpled a mulberry leaf in my hand.

"Mr. Lewis is a fuck," Bruce said. "He threw me out of the library. I wasn't doing anything."

"Nothing?"

"Nothing!"

"That's really shitty," I said, shaking my head. Bruce probably had been doing *something* in the library. He's always getting into quarrels—but that's because he has *feelings.*

"Guess what?" Bruce asked.

"What?" I picked a blade of grass and rolled it between my fingers.

"I'm going to learn to meditate."

I was pleased. I'd tried to explain Zen during PE. A light wind blew. Bruce squished an ant making its way across his spiral notebook's vast aqua plane. Its soul, I thought, is gone.

Bruce continued. "I saw this guy on TV. He could float across the room."

I felt disappointed. The purpose of meditation isn't to float across rooms. That's an outward manifestation. Spirituality isn't performing tricks. But Bruce has to proceed at his own pace.

"How long did he stay up?" I asked politely.

"Just a few minutes," Bruce said. "But that isn't the point."

I brightened inwardly.

"If you practice you can get what you want. If you really learn to control your mind, there's no limit. We only use a fraction of our brains. Like, if there's this horse I want to own, if I really learn to meditate, then it will come to me, instead of me having to try to get it."

"There are a lot of different ways," I said, disappointed again.

"You know what I like about you?" Bruce said. "I like that you're so individualistic. Most people here aren't individuals. You're at least yourself."

I sensed something ineffable emanating from Bruce. It didn't matter that he was materialistic, that he didn't understand meditation. Or liked Khalil Gibran. Emotion floated around him, a bluish aura, a shadow in the sunlight. Like hearing, on the radio, a new, original group.

———

Jason and I pulled weeds in the backyard. Little sticky, hairy trees. We kept digging them up but they kept coming back; full of energy. So were the dirt and grass. Everything you need, I thought, you can find in your own backyard. The way of the Tao. Posha's wrong; you don't have to travel the world. It's all right here.

I tried to think of something to say to Jason. It doesn't matter, I thought, if there are weeds or grass; weeds are more beautiful! I remembered how, when I was younger, I'd tried to prepare myself for different moral dilemmas. Anything *could* happen. The Nazis might take over. What would I do if the SS came into the backyard and put a gun to my head, making me choose between Mom and Dad? I could refuse, but then they'd kill both of them—and me, too. My parents would look at me; there'd be no way out of it: I'd have to choose Mom. Then the men in the black boots would take Dad in back of the garage. It would be terrible; I wouldn't know how to go on living with Mom afterwards; she'd be so upset by what I'd done to Dad—by how, in the last moment, I'd hurt his feelings. I might choose Dad just to make sure this didn't happen.

Mom opened the backdoor and called, "Why don't you boys come in? Your father's off the phone. We're going to have the conference."

"What do you think *this* one's about?" Jason asked.

We went into the living room. Dad asked Sharon to turn down the Weavers on the stereo. "As you know," he said, sagely, "we've been getting a lot of advice." State Senator Del-Blanco, Mr. Nachmann, and Posha, among others, were urging him, he told us, to run against Congressman Scanlon. "I know if we do this," Dad said, "it's going to have an impact on everyone. So I want all of your input."

"I'm wondering," Sharon asked, "whether you think you could win?"

"A lot of people don't like Scanlon," he responded.

I traced a pattern in the carpet.

Scanlon, Dad continued, wasn't popular with the Mormons or the real right-wingers. He came from a powerful, old Arizona family. His father, Jim Senior, owned half of Yavapai County. He'd bought the Republican primary two years ago when the Fifth District was created.

We know that, I thought.

Although Scanlon had voted, for the most part, very conservatively, some Republicans were suspicious about his personal life. There were rumors he'd shown up drunk at committee meetings. Rumors about trips to Las Vegas. And his marriage. His wife, Althea, a former Miss Arizona, was planning, people said, on leaving him. She spent most of her time at their condo on the coast.

"So you can hit him on that?" Jason asked.

"I wouldn't want to run a dirty campaign," Dad said. The rumors on their own, he thought, would weaken Scanlon. But it would be tough. Scanlon had all the money he needed. Like his old man, he could be ruthless. And of course, in Arizona, the Republicans had the advantage. No matter what happened, they nearly always won.

"I do know," Dad said, "we'll get strong support from Jane Hanson and the teachers. Which should be useful in getting out the vote. That's always one of the main problems."

Sharon looked at Mom.

"I do have some doubts," Mom said. "But I realize it's natural to have *some* doubts before a big decision."

"What do you think, Sharon?" Dad asked.

She said she'd support whatever Mom and Dad wanted to do. Jason agreed. I sat on my side on the floor. Why run for

Congress, I asked myself. It would be normal to start with city council or something. *Those who know do not talk, those who talk do not know.* But it doesn't matter to me what he does. Best to *expect* to lose; then you aren't disappointed.

I felt the sun on my face and, for a moment, a sense of Anna-ness that I wanted to hold on to.

"If we do go ahead with this," Mom said, "I'm going to have to quit the counseling."

"Do you have to?" Sharon asked.

"I don't *have* to," Mom said edgily. "But I choose to."

Sharon looked down.

"I might have to see if Connie could come in a few more hours each week," Mom added thoughtfully.

Sharon and I looked at each other.

"I bet she'd be *glad* to," said Dad.

"You look hesitant, Mark," Mom commented, sounding concerned, trying, I sensed, to shift the mood.

Outside, on Via Mariposa, a high school student revved his engine. I want the best for everyone, I thought. I want to be full of love.

"I have *some* hesitations," I said, using my reasonable-person voice, "but it's your decision."

"We want this to be a *family* decision," Dad emphasized.

———

"Soon," Mr. Lewis said, "everyone will live in a megalopolis. There will be one giant city running from Boston to Washington. Does anyone know what that city will be called?"

"He's such a retard," Bruce muttered.

I nodded and stared out the sun-streaked window.

Although the odds are against it, I thought, it's *possible* Dad could win.

"Bowash," Mr. Lewis said.

It might be good to live in Washington, I thought, looking at the gray-green acacia. Cherry blossoms, green trees, seasons: spring, winter, fall. We would live in a city; there would be more kids like me; they would write, play the piano, read Dostoyevsky. But they'd only be like me in a left-brain way. I'd become left-brained and lose everything that mattered. Better to be from the desert, the source of my power.

Bruce passed me a note. Fuckwash City. I began to doodle, on the note, a map of Fuckwash City.

Later that day I found Anna. I told her I wanted to talk in her office. She closed the door.

"There's something I need to tell you," I said.

"Yes?"

"I don't know how to tell you this."

"Why don't you just say it?" she asked, a little impatiently.

I leaned forward. "My father is running for Congress," I whispered.

Dr. Kurtz asked, that afternoon, what I thought of Dad's decision. We still hadn't talked about the stuff that had gone on in the session a few weeks before; it had been lingering—I'd thought maybe we would today. But now this, I guessed, was more important.

"I'm trying to live and let live," I said.

"But how do you feel about it?"

"Kind of mixed. I mean, you can look at it different ways. I'm sort of hesitant in some ways."

"Why?"

I just don't want all the changes, I thought. I'm entering a new world and this will get in the way. If it didn't involve me, that would be OK; if it was just Dad's thing, but it won't be, even if I try not to be a part of it I'm going to have to be; I'll have to be on TV, which will be terrible; what will Anna think; what would Allen Ginsberg do in this situation; maybe I should refuse to take part, but I can't, that would be egotistical, there would be conflict with Mom and Dad, and so even if they *say* I don't have to take part I really will, I'll have to wear a coat and tie, everyone at school will see me and think I'm an *idiot*.

Maybe I am strong enough now not to care.

I pictured myself being interviewed in a coat and tie. I would look intelligent, say intelligent things. *The young diplomat.* Dad, a star congressman, would rise quickly. He'd become a senator; soon the speculation about the White House would begin. Posha's farm: the summer White House.

Cherry blossoms. Light on the river. The sumi paintings I could do. How do you know what you *really* want, I wondered, trying to imagine Dad winning, Dad losing. Looking inside yourself, I thought, was like looking into the future. Maybe I can write a poem about this. *I look at the horizon, and try . . . to tell the mountains from the clouds.*

Was it possible, Dr. Kurtz asked, that I was anxious about having to end therapy if Dad won? That doesn't have anything to do with it, I thought. But then I wondered: maybe this fear was hidden from my consciousness.

———

"What can I do to live like a warrior?" I asked.

"You have no more time for retreats or regrets . . . work for patience and will . . . ."

"How does a warrior work for them?"

Don Juan thought for a long time before answering. "Will is something very special. It happens to us mysteriously. . . . Perhaps the first thing that one should do is to know that one can develop the will. A warrior knows that and proceeds to wait for it. Your mistake is not to know that you are waiting for your will."

———

Bruce saw me with Martha. "What were you doing talking to the Walrus?" he asked when I came up to him. "Goo goo g'jew."

"What do they have in the cafeteria?" I asked, trying to change the topic.

"Don't worry about *that*," he said. "Come with me."

"I haven't had lunch."

"Oh, come on. This is important." I wasn't sure I wanted to go with Bruce, but I followed him down the corridor. On the grass some fifth-grade girls skipped rope ferociously, pushing the air aside.

"So who do you think the two most disgusting people to imagine fucking would be?" Bruce asked.

I tried to think about this. Douggy and Martha. But I didn't want to be mean to Martha.

"I'll tell you who," Bruce said. "Carlos the janitor and Mrs. Heller."

I got the image in my head. Bruce began to sing.

"She's got electric boobs
They're more than Sue's
You know I read it in a magazine."

I hoped no one would hear him. We came to Mr. Lewis's empty classroom. The walls were lined with pictures of the presidents and a map of Arizona. I wondered what we were up to.

Bruce began to turn the desks over. A protractor fell on the linoleum; he picked it up, waved it around, put it down. He found a magic marker and drew fangs on Kennedy and Nixon. *"Cherokee people,"* he sang, *"Cherokee tribe."* He wrote, on the cactus-colored blackboard, "Lewis Sucks." We're being *rebels,* I thought, as I started turning over chairs. I'm Ginsberg, he's Kerouac. I'm Simon, he's Garfunkel.

—

Dan Baltz had a party. Schaeffer passed out. His dad grounded him. Schaeffer was really pissed. He was suspended from rugby and wasn't allowed to go to Cheryl McCrae's party. I thought I overheard Baltz talking to Cheryl about getting some acid for the party, but I wasn't sure. Bruce asked Cheryl if she was going to invite him. She laughed.

Mr. Lewis didn't know who'd vandalized his room. Bruce and Ratter were both called in but neither would confess and Mr. Lewis didn't do anything. Sometimes I felt weird when I talked to him. After a while everyone seemed to forget about it.

One afternoon, walking to class with Bruce, I saw something gleaming in the grass. I leaned over and picked it up. A peso.

"That's weird," Bruce said. "How'd that get there?"

"I don't know," I said, putting it in my pocket.

Light everywhere. Bruce returned to the topic I'd briefly interrupted: his old school, how he'd done coke. Perhaps finding the coin was an omen, a good one, the kind Castaneda sometimes had. Maybe Bruce was my *ally*. I thought about telling him my father's plans, but I didn't want the whole school to know. It was going to be embarrassing, but it wasn't something, like seeing a psychiatrist, that I could keep secret. I could tell him—or wait to tell. Someday, years in the future, when an article was written about me in *The New York Times Magazine*, the writer might mention that, in eighth grade, I had met Bruce Waterson. I imagined a small picture of Bruce. Maybe they would find and interview him, along with others who had known me during my Loloma period. Perhaps I would remember to tell the writer about the coin.

By the water fountain, a boy held a girl. "Please help me," she pretend-screamed, giggling. Bruce told me about the dangers of water fluoridation, which his stepfather had explained to him. I'm tolerant, I thought.

"He's such a son of a bitch," Bruce said.

"Yeah," I replied, thinking about the water fluoridation, feeling a little confused. Didn't Bruce *agree* with his stepfather about that?

"*You* don't know." He sounded sort of angry. "He beat me with the belt last night. Again."

I wasn't sure whether this was something he'd already told me that I'd somehow misunderstood. Maybe he'd hinted at it. How terrible of me to have missed this. I pictured his stepfather taking off his belt. His eyes were cold and his face was hard. Dark and tall, he made Bruce lean over a chair. Or maybe Bruce had to stand against a wall in their living room. What did it feel like when the belt hit? What was it like to wait for it? I wondered if he wanted me to ask him questions. He was standing right next to me but I didn't know how to find this out. The horse on his belt buckle glinted in the sun.

"That's awful," I said.

"He's an asshole. If somebody killed him, think I'd care?"

Bruce's stepfather, I thought, is cruel. Lots of boys' dads, I knew, belted them. I have nothing to complain about.

A wave of feeling toward Bruce rolled through me as we walked past the acacia. Thrilling that he'd told me this. Maybe *that's* what the peso meant. It all *felt* predestined. My mother and Anna thought I was someone who could be confided in. I'd always known it was only a matter of time before other people realized this, too.

Because Bruce has trusted me, I thought, I should trust him—but I didn't have anything dramatic to confide. Bruce has a real life, I thought; I don't. No one hits me with a belt. Too bad, I thought, ashamed of the thought. A whiff of smoke in the dry school air. A piece of broken glass in the grass. I told him about Dr. Kurtz. Except for Anna, no one else knew.

4

One night we went to dinner at the Nachmanns'. They lived on Camelback Mountain, at the end of a steep driveway off Rocking Horse Road. Through their dining-room window you could see the lights illuminating their kidney-shaped pool and the boulders.

Mr. Nachmann had agreed to be the campaign manager; Dad said he wanted someone he could trust, someone aggressive who could raise a lot of money. Mr. Nachmann had served on the Democratic National Committee and knew important people in the party. Senator DelBlanco and Mrs. Hanson would be cochairs.

Mrs. Nachmann served a salad on glass plates: lettuce, cucumber, and carrots. Mr. Nachmann told Dad about a consultant from Washington he thought Dad should hire.

"What are your campaign themes going to be?" Mrs. Nachmann asked, poised and cheery.

"I think it's important to keep to the center," Dad said, pondering the question.

"Maybe 'good government,'" Mom said, playfully and a little self-doubtingly, like a semi-confident high school girl.

"How about just 'change,'" Dad said.

"What kind of change?" Mrs. Nachmann continued.

"How about economic justice?" Sharon suggested.

"I don't think people in this district are too concerned about that," Dad said.

"Maybe they should be," Sharon replied.

Eating the last cucumber chunk on my plate, I remembered a dinner conversation from several years ago. Sharon and Dad had been debating what to do about poverty.

"Why not have lots of taxes on the rich?" I'd suggested.

Sharon had looked at me with pity.

"We *are* the rich," she'd said.

One afternoon at Safeway, I asked Mom whether we really were rich. "I've been poor and I've been rich," she'd said, sort of automatically, "and it's better to be rich." Then she added, while we picked out cereals, "I'm not sure if we're *rich.* I'd say we're more *upper middle class.* When I was growing up," she continued, somewhat to herself, "we were middle class, I guess. Or sometimes lower middle class." While I took down the Cocoa Puffs, she told me about her cousin, Aunt Sylvia's daughter, who lived in Dundee. "She would always ask: so how often do you have steak at *your* house? I couldn't stand her."

We have steak pretty often, I told myself, although I never eat it. Through the living room window the lights of the city spread out beneath us like a golden dress. The Nachmanns' friends the Porters were multimillionaires. They had a ranch and lots of cars and once a year they threw a party.

Mr. Nachmann, ignoring Sharon, told Dad he should be sure to focus on Scanlon's ethics. And local concerns. Water rights . . .

Beyond Camelback Road, the canal crossed Phoenix: a dark belt. Then the dry Salt River, and beyond it South Phoenix, where most of the Chicanos lived. It was almost another city; I'd only been there once. Years ago Dad had taken us to see, he said, how those who weren't as fortunate lived. It had been near dusk. I remembered now, looking out the window, the embarrassment I'd felt then. Chairs and chickens and trucks in the yards. The same trucks I saw parked in front of the lawns in our neighborhood when the orange pickers and the mowers came. Old cottonwood trees, tall and shady. It was quiet. It hadn't seemed that bad; it wasn't like the slums on Cronkite. Still, sometimes I wondered, years later, why everyone didn't come across the dry river and walk into the homes on the mountain and start taking stuff. Why shouldn't they? I pictured the police forming a line to stop the people coming from South Phoenix. It would be easy to get around.

They continued to talk about Dad's media strategy. What colors, I wondered, should he use? I hoped it wouldn't be something boring, like blue. Maybe purple—that would be new. Maroon—like the shadows of desert mountains. The billboards, the bumper stickers, the buttons: they should all be that color. My parents and the Nachmanns had moved on to a discussion of the temple. Mom and Dad were worried that if Beth Shalom grew too fast it would get taken over like Temple Micah.

This isn't real, I thought. It isn't about *things*. I looked at the things in the Nachmann's living room. The sofa, the lamps, the walls, the plants. Their living room resembled ours, I thought, like a cousin's face with familiar features, similar to your own, but still somehow different. Mrs. Nachmann had overcooked the chicken. Our house is better. There is just something wrong about their house.

Dad talked about how once, on their way back from a conference in Seattle, he and Rick Goldman had had to change planes in Las Vegas, where they'd been stuck for three hours with Rabbi Horowitz, who was returning from some kind of meeting in San Francisco. He'd gone on and on about gestalt. "That's when I started getting *seriously* worried about him," Dad remarked.

"That flight used to be delayed all the time," Mom said, shaking her head.

"You think that's bad," Mr. Nachmann said, "I was stuck in Denver five hours once."

"That's why I call it 'Hughes Air Worst,'" Dad said.

No one had seen Howard Hughes for years. He might not even be alive. Karl said he wasn't: he'd been murdered by the CIA. If he was alive, he was the richest man in the world, but also the loneliest. His fingernails, Bruce said, were nine inches long.

"I used to call them Trans-Dogpatch," Mr. Nachmann replied.

Dad laughed.

Their conversation moves quickly, I thought, but never goes anywhere new. All false, but how can I prove this—with which word or phrase? They all *seem* false. Every word Dad says, every word he doesn't, every breath, every movement of his hand, every word of Mr. Nachmann's, of Mom's, and of mine; falseness fills the room—an invisible gas. Maybe I'm imagining it; maybe it's in *me*.

"I was wondering," Mrs. Nachmann said, "have you heard from Estelle?"

It had been quiet for some time on the Mrs. Goldman front.

"No," Mom said. "I really do have to call her."

"You've been very patient, Jean," Mr. Nachmann commented.

"Jack treated her awfully," Mrs. Nachmann said, impatiently.

Mom nodded.

"He was *very* patient with her, Barbara," Mr. Nachmann remarked, correcting his wife. I wondered if Dad would say anything. Mom didn't like it when, on occasion, he defended Mr. Goldman.

"Until she got a little too old," Mrs. Nachmann rejoined. "You men will stand up for each other no matter what."

"We better," Dad replied, as if to lighten the conversation. "Now that you're all reading *Ms* . . ."

Mom's face seemed, perhaps, to tighten.

"It's a great magazine," Sharon said.

"They do have some very interesting articles," Mom said, her tone half light, half dark.

"Isn't that what they say about *Playboy?*" Mr. Nachmann asked.

"*Right,*" Mrs. Nachmann replied.

A few nights before I'd watched a nature documentary with Mom and Sharon. Men in trucks went up dirt roads into the African hills. The little chimps played and swung from branches; a mother nursed her young. "They're *so* cute," Sharon said, between Wheat Thins. "When the male chimp enters adolescence and reaches the size of the adult female," the narrator remarked, "we witness an extraordinary change. Before he was playful; now, almost without warning, he becomes brutal and violent. We may wish to believe civilized humans are different. Some argue violence is caused by society. But our ancestors were woodland apes."

I looked at Mom and Sharon, wondering whether they were thinking, *Mark: male chimp.* One screeching monkey slammed another to the ground. Boys will be—but I'm not. Or maybe I just don't want to admit it. I *am* angry so often. Can't fool Mother Nature. A cloud of dust rose above the jungle. "This behavior serves an evolutionary purpose. The females are attracted to the more violent apes." Maybe they think *I* should be like that.

I'm almost as big as Sharon. I know Mom has to look at me differently now—or thinks she should. I've changed, but into what? I took some Wheat Thins from the coffee table. She knows how to love a little boy, I thought. Maybe when she was a girl in Omaha, playing with dolls on the porch, or in the hardware store, beneath the wrenches and plungers, she'd dreamt of a baby boy. But could she have dreamt of me as I am *now*, as an *ad-o-lescent*? The way we've always been together has to end. We pretend there are reasons for this but they aren't *ours:* my body changing, time—what do they have to do with us?

The pool lights reflected strangely on the single lemon tree in front of the dark pink boulders in back of the house. Dad, Jason, Mr. Nachmann, and I all, I thought, have penises. Weird to know everyone in the room could be thinking about this, maybe, in some way. I drank my ice water. Giving birth must be awful—someday Sharon will have to. Once I'd thought she'd be the first person I would have sex with. It had seemed to make sense: we knew each other so well. Now I knew it didn't work that way. Someday, I thought, I'll get married. We'll live in a small house in Colorado or Massachusetts, where the leaves will change in the fall and my wife will give birth. I felt sorry for her. Bruce had said Catherine the Great used to get fucked by a horse. No one in Russia could satisfy her.

"They had an interesting article about intelligence," Mom continued, with a little defiance. "The old way of defining intelligence didn't take emotions into account."

"So you're saying women are smarter," Mr. Nachmann said.

"They just may be," Mom said. I didn't want to be outside of her alliance with Sharon, but I knew I was.

Sometimes Mom and Sharon complained about the line for the ladies room. Men had it better, they said. But if you were a girl you got a private stall. Bruce said Schaeffer and Heather were going to ball. I wondered if balling was different from screwing. It sounded *rounder*. Maybe you moved differently. Or did it with your balls.

Jacking off versus jerking off. I want privacy when I go to the bathroom. I don't like standing next to Dad or Jason. Everyone pretends being a boy is OK. They know it's disgusting.

I thought of the czarina's stables and the story Bruce had read in the *National Lampoon* about the hippies fucking, which he'd told me while we were in the wash ditching PE. I looked at Mrs. Nachmann's string of pearls. Bruce's grandmother had known Pearl Buck. Buckminster Fuller had built geodesic domes. He said they were the perfect structures. They were building them out near Bell Road in the desert north of Phoenix.

After dinner everyone moved into the living room. Mr. Nachmann and my father discussed strategy; we listened. I don't want to be interested, I thought. I'm not part of this. I looked out the window at the valley's lights, gathered my nerves, and asked if it would be OK if I took a walk. I expected opposition but there wasn't any. The discussion grew more animated as I slipped out the backdoor.

Down the Nachmann's steep driveway to their mailbox. It was good to be out of the house in the cool, dry air. I turned onto a small dirt path and thought about "The Path." There were barrel cacti, organ pipes, and prickly pears, but in the night they were just dark forms.

Yucca. Ocotillo.

What I perceive is real, I told myself. Get beyond the *names*. I wanted to get as much distance as I could between myself and the discussion in the house.

I walked along the dirt path. To the south, on the horizon, aureoles of light, white, yellow, red. There were radio towers and, in the distance, the tiny Papago Buttes. And the far-off traffic.

To the north, the mountain rose abruptly beyond the houses. Shrubs and stones. On the ridge, I saw a figure moving slowly toward the summit.

I stopped.

A dark, hunched silhouette moving along the mountain's spine. A man, in the moonlight, climbing? He stopped moving. Maybe just a rock outcropping, I thought. But then it started again. From this distance you'd barely be able to see a man. It can't be human. A giant? A sorcerer? An *ally*? It stopped moving. Or maybe it was just moving very slowly. And then it *definitely* moved.

In me, a shudder. The figure began to move backward, away from the peak. Perhaps it isn't moving at all. Maybe it *is* just a man. But no, it's much too large. It starts forward again. I know for certain it's not human.

But it could be a saguaro. I waited for something to happen. Nothing did. I continued to stand still.

I can't feel much of anything right now, I thought. School, Dad, politics, Bruce, Mom, Pearl Buck. It's probably a saguaro. But if I could *see*, it could be an *ally*. Sometimes an *ally* or a sorcerer appears as a tree or a cactus. I'm always half-believing—my family's fault. It would be different if Anna were here. Or maybe not.

The dull falseness I'd felt at dinner was still in me. I wanted to be rid of it, but it wasn't enough to leave the house. There was a faint scent of creosote in the desert air; the dullness was *in* me. I kicked a beer bottle lying along the path. Where did the path lead? Perhaps if I went far enough into the darkness, away from the houses, I would change. I would lose myself . . . but I knew I wouldn't; my self would follow me.

Prickly pear.

My real life will begin soon. There ought to be power in the darkness. I want to feel something unique; I want my feelings to be like the spotlights on the cactus outside the Nachmann's home. But they aren't.

I want to see a figure on the mountain but I don't.

I don't know where this path is going.

The clouds in the night sky were mysteriously white, white as day clouds, milk spilled on a dark cloth; many layers of clouds. Something moved through the creosote. *Jackrabbit*, I thought, was just the name we gave it; words make you feel but can also stand in the way.

The first time I'd thought I couldn't feel: the summer when we drove through the western states, the summer Nanna was sick, the summer before I met Anna. In the back of the car I'd studied the maps, fascinated by the names of the towns: Washington, Cedar City, Monticello. Walking in the morning through the parking lots outside the Best Westerns, I sensed the auras of their names. It was like the idea of reincarnation, the way you could pick up the faint presence of another existence in a person—or the name of a town.

Florence. Monticello.

We spent a week, that summer, in Vail. A mountain rose steeply behind the rented chalet. Through the kitchen window you could see nothing but its dark earth and the buzzing flies, the shimmering yellow leaves. I was excited to be in a place that was so beautiful. On the first morning, I walked up the mountain in back of the house, expecting to be filled with feelings as strong as the light on the aspens. I knew

I was in a *very beautiful place*. I waited. But I couldn't really feel anything.

This not being able to feel was a sort of feeling itself. I thought that, like a cold that causes you to miss a perfect day, it would pass. It did.

The path had led to the back of another home. Spotlights on some yuccas, another pool. Beyond the house I could see again the red and white lights of the distant traffic. A dog barked in the black yard. I turned back toward the Nachmanns'.

5

I sat in Anna's office. The sun made its way across Nicola's pillows and the Hayden's Ferry Crafts Fair poster. Karl, Anna told me, was going to Colorado for three months. He'd never been away that long. At first, she said, she had been upset. She'd called Don the therapist; she had, she said, thought of calling me. After talking to Don, she'd realized that in the long run it was good. It would strengthen their marriage. "I guess sometimes you shouldn't trust your first reaction."

"Maybe it's sort of programmed," I ventured.

"I think maybe you're right," she said, looking at me intently.

Bruce's voice in the art room. He knocked on the door. Anna smiled at me. Bruce came in, Anna asked him how he was, and the two of them started talking about his pots. Anna told him she wanted to show him how to do raku. But mostly Bruce talked. He can talk *a lot*, I thought. I was a little concerned (as I usually was when the three of us were together) whether Bruce was making a good impression. They discussed raku. Maybe, I thought, there are ways in which Anna has more in common with Bruce than with me. He's less self-conscious than I am. But I know I'm her favorite. I wished he hadn't come in; Anna and I hadn't gotten to discuss the letter she'd received from Jack Osborne.

"So Mrs. Voigt," Bruce asked, "what did you think of those people yesterday?" There had been a presentation, the day before, by the Society for Creative Anachronism. They'd given a jousting demonstration outside the cafeteria; Baltz had spent the rest of the afternoon talking about wenches.

"History wasn't really my best subject," said Anna, diplomatically.

"I think they should be put in a loony bin," Bruce said.

I agreed.

On the grass, next to Bruce and me, later that day, dead oleander flowers in the sun. Frail paper trumpets, I thought.

"Let's analyze someone," Bruce said.

"Who?"

"How about Heather? She's really a complex person."

"Yeah," I agreed. I felt doubtful but played along. "Why do you think that is?"

"On the one hand she's nice. But deep down she's also insecure. That's why she sometimes acts like a bitch. It's really because she's so competitive with Cheryl."

Did Heather have a *deep down*? Bruce sees the world differently, I thought. He thinks about horses, and Heather, and Mrs. Binder. I looked at his shadow, bluish in the grass.

"Cheryl's the one who's really the stuck-up bitch," Bruce continued. "She thinks she's so great. Just because she's got those boobs."

Why do you care so much about any of this? Heather was just a little nice to you a few times. And now you want to make a big deal out of it.

"Cheryl's probably got some weird stuff going on deep down, too," I said.

"No," he said, as if I'd said something quite dumb. "She's just a bitch. Did you see those jeans she was wearing today? She was *poured* into them."

"I know," I said, wondering what that meant.

The next day I sat again in Anna's office, on the couch with Richard and Ian. They were talking about Paula Swanson and Beth Rawley. Richard had been complaining about how hard it was that Lisa lived in Los Angeles. I was glad when Anna came through the doorway.

"Will a week from Sunday be OK for everyone for the meeting?" she asked. Richard and Ian nodded. I nodded too, casually, pretending it was of slight importance. I was frustrated we weren't having more *Amethyst* meetings.

Richard and Ian left. Anna and I were alone. I tried to guess her mood. Hoping my voice sounded sympathetic, I asked how she was doing; I couldn't *feel* the sympathy once I started to speak; it seemed to evaporate in stage fright. I wondered, while I spoke, if I was being sincere.

"How am I doing about Karl?" Anna responded.

I nodded.

"I woke up early this morning while he was asleep. I drove up to North Mountain—it was still dark. I watched the sun rise. You know what I realized? I hadn't recognized what this is for *me*. It's an opportunity to get my own work done."

I was glad Anna was thinking in terms of her work.

"It will help me learn to be *really* independent," she continued. "I think I'm independent, but maybe I'm not *so* independent as I thought." She laughed.

"It's a good thing you went up to the mountain," I said jestingly.

"When I'm sixteen," Bruce told me while we ate lunch, "my Dad's going to take me to Las Vegas. He's going to get me a prostitute. I'm going to fuck her." I tried to picture Bruce fucking a prostitute in a hotel room in Las Vegas. The woman, the slot machines, the neon signs. Hard not to think about: slot, slut. Someone, I saw, had scratched a peace sign on the picnic table. Beneath it: "footprint of a chicken." Douggy Dale munched a hamburger at the same table, although not exactly next to us.

Beyond us, Phoenix quivered. Some of the boys walking past really walked like boys: Baltz, Schaeffer, Hoffman. Others combined gestures: Matt Culligan, Tom McKnight, Billy Page. They were boyish, not boyish: awkwardly put together but still sometimes graceful. They all had different auras.

I felt uncomfortable.

Cheryl McCrae came up to us. She wore a pink sweater. "What's this," she asked, "the queer convention?"

Bruce threw a french fry at her. "What's your problem, you fat fucking slut? You fuck horses, don't you?"

I drank my milk. A BB gun went off somewhere. Bruce and Cheryl glared at each other. Douggy looked down at his hamburger.

———

I stood on the edge of the patio, holding the splintery shovel, taking a break from my chores. Warm and cloudy. Mom and Dad were talking to Mrs. Sklar; she'd "just dropped by" after her violin lesson. (She was in an amateur chamber group; Dad said they played terribly.) Sharon, in her terry-cloth shorts, lay in a patio chair reading *The Hobbit*.

Mrs. Sklar offered to be the volunteer coordinator. How, I wondered, does she see us? Everyone has a different vision of reality. They can't *all* be true. No one seems to notice that there are so many versions. They act like they live in the same world. Different people's dreams of what the world is like float separately above the world; white clouds, indifferent to one another, occasionally passing accidentally close, then floating off on their own courses. Anna's dreams, mine, Dad's, Bruce's.

Dad told Mrs. Sklar about Stan Rouse, the campaign consultant Mr. Nachmann had recommended. Dad was hiring him. Rouse had managed an upset in Colorado two years before. Colorado, where I would live when I left home. Where fish leapt in the rivers; where light fell on the aspen trees.

The sun moved behind some clouds and then emerged and then hid again. I moved in and out of feeling normal, a part of my family, a part of *things*. I clutched my shovel, listening while Dad told Mrs. Sklar Mr. Nachmann's fund-raising idea: a telethon. They might get several candidates to go in on it. The Nachmanns knew a retired movie star who lived out in Carefree. There was also a country singer he might be able to get.

"We need someone like Robert Redford," Mom said. Dad and Mrs. Sklar agreed he would be great and it might even be possible to get him. Sharon liked the idea, too. "If you can't get him," she added, "try John Denver."

"Who would you suggest, Mark?" Dad asked.

"I don't know." Alan Watts, I thought. I need to be away from them. Sharon has such bad taste; she doesn't understand the Grateful Dead. I walked around the patio's edge with the shovel, looking for Sparky's manure. Beyond the humming gray-green pool filtering machine, an area of well kept grass. I moved farther into the yard, further into my thoughts.

I'm a grayness. People don't think I think the things I think. The voice they think is mine isn't. The one I hear mumbles fragments, slips in time. A shadow voice. When I use the voice they expect, everything's lost. We don't think the same things are real. If they heard my voice, they wouldn't think it was real. They don't *want* to have to think that. I don't want them to have to think that. I don't think I'm real, either. No one would believe someone like me exists—if they heard my voice, my thoughts, whatever this stuff is.

But the mumbling *is* real. I hear it all the time.

Blahhbittyblahh. Col-o-ra-do-o, Mountain Mama, take me home, I-love-you, hate-you, God-Mom-Dad-Baltz-PE-The Universe.

A piece of Sparky's manure stuck to the shovel when I tried to shake it into the wheelbarrow; I shook it again. Dad, I thought, is bored by Mrs. Sklar. Mom gets bored easily, too. She'll say, sometimes, after a party, "those people were so dull. I thought I was going to lose my mind." She doesn't realize, I told myself impatiently: life is *like* that. Mrs. Sklar isn't so bad anyway. I don't get who Mom and Dad like versus who they don't. *I'll* sit at lunch with anyone who'll let me. Boredom doesn't bother me, maybe because, unlike Mom and Dad, I was born in the desert. The desert, I thought, teaches you to conserve experience like water: you never know when you might run out.

A chewed plastic bone lay in the weed grove; a dead bird in the pale grass. An omen? I noticed some faint lines by the fence. I looked, waiting to see if they intensified. But I knew I wanted that too much. When you looked for something you didn't find it.

Quiet. Leaves stained other leaves with shadows. I remembered how I'd worried, years ago, about what would happen if the liberals won and there were no more wars or pollution. It would be boring if the world became heaven. You had to practice being bored and learn to see things in the boredom. I headed back to the patio.

"There are these clicks on the phone," Mrs. Sklar was saying. "If they're wiretapping me then who knows what's next?"

"Sounds a *little* far-fetched," Dad said, blinking in the bright sun.

Birds as dark as Mrs. Sklar's ideas about the government circled overhead. Do I observe because I'm distant, I asked myself, or am I distant because I observe?

———

Bruce and I worked together on a project about Mars for Mrs. Binder. I did most of the work but didn't mind. I wondered why I still cared about getting good grades. I should be beyond that. One day Bruce wore a POW bracelet to school; no one made fun of him for wearing a bracelet; Hoffman had one, too. Bruce seemed to be getting along better with people. He wasn't getting in so many arguments. Anna thought that maybe the time he was spending throwing at the wheel was helping. I agreed. Sometimes he and Heather talked. Boys still avoided him. One day, on our way to the cafeteria, I told him I was a vegetarian. He told me he was thinking of becoming one.

"So are you still allowed to eat fish?" he asked.

"You can do whatever you want," I replied, slightly impatient.

"So speaking of fish, what girl in this class would you want to fuck most?"

Squint and endure.

"Oh, I don't know."

"What about Heather? Don't you want to feel her tits?"

That's like saying you don't like homework, I thought; it's that creative. And mean, too. Don't you claim you *like* Heather? So why do you talk about her this way? Ridiculous to imagine either of us doing anything with her. This conversation is so stupid.

I looked over my shoulder and saw the acacia. I wanted to turn and look again; I wanted to see it in the same specific, hazy light. But I didn't want Bruce to see me turning around. We kept walking and I forgot the urge. He walked very close. "Come on, don't you want to feel her tits?" he repeated, while we crossed the withered grass. "Big, firm titty-boobs," he continued. "Come on, Mark, don't you want to?" He leaned into me, unable to restrain himself.

"Oh, I guess Jane Patterson," I said. A somewhat plausible response, I thought; she was plain and kept to herself. But it was, I knew, a nonanswer. I wasn't playing along.

"Oh yeah," he said, a little brutally, "you probably want to fuck Martha Walrus."

"Shut up," I said, in an almost friendly voice. We kept walking.

———

Dad signed a lease for a campaign office; I was disappointed. It wasn't like the McGrath and Greene offices in the Coronado Building. It didn't have big windows or wood-paneled walls. It was next to a Laundromat, a dentist's office, and a sandwich shop.

———

I listened to the radio: *Little Willy, Willy won't go home.* You couldn't push him around. He shimmy shuffled, in his dirty jeans, through the parking lot in back of his school. He was free and wouldn't go. *Try tellin' everybody but, oh no.* Why couldn't I be like Willy? Willy was like Bruce.

——

Stringy-haired Ratter. Backlit, at the edge of the yellow field.

"Hey, Grosfeld, over here."

He hadn't picked on me in a long time. I'd thought this meant I'd outgrown this problem, that, somehow, I'd found the answer to it. I wondered if I should ignore him or if that would make things worse.

Shouts from the soccer field: "Give me an L. Give me an O. . . ."

"What the fuck is your problem?"

"I don't have a problem," I answered and kept walking. I felt *strong* for a moment, then that feeling went away and I tried to get it back. Sharp, dark grass shadows—in the grass; dust on my mouth's roof. The roofs of houses, across from the school, vibrating.

"I don't have a problem," he mimicked, disgusted. "Wait till after school."

I hate you, I thought, and headed toward the cafeteria.

After school, I rode my bike down the canal. Ratter hadn't done anything, but *fear* had followed me all afternoon. The ground was pebbly, uneven. The phone call from death row: *I'm sorry but the governor is out now.*

The sun pulsed, my heart pulsed, my head pulsed. But the eucalyptus scent was beautiful. The energy of the trees, pouring toward the sky; the canal, Anna says: my private river.

Dust and olive scent, mixed with the eucalyptus; so many scents; my mind turns more quickly than the bike's wheels.

Since camp, I'm more realistic and willing to compromise, I told myself, aware I was telling myself stuff. I'm not sure what to do about the problem of whether or *how* to believe things you say to yourself—trickery—when I talk to myself, as many interruptions as at dinner! I tried to hush a part of my mind and returned to my conversation. What will this year *mean*? Should I ask Bruce if he wants to come to an Amethyst meeting? It's sort of odd that I haven't. Maybe he's waiting. Maybe he doesn't care but still wants me to ask. But if he came he'd start talking about Khalil Gibran. Maybe I could ask him and then he'd say no. But what if he said yes? I wish this wasn't so *complicated*. Maybe Changing Times Books can carry the *Amethyst*.

Anna says sometimes you go through periods when you don't know where you're going. That's process. It usually means you're on the verge of something major but can't clearly see it—yet.

There are things in your mind but not in your consciousness. Where? Invisible. Kurtz says I'm secretly afraid of stopping therapy. But maybe I'm secretly ready for it.

Mountains in the dirt embankment; mesas, ridges: a map, a small version of the whole desert. Bits of broken glass, eucalyptus leaves, dog hair. Ratter doesn't bother me. I'm *harder*. That's what happens. Something lost and something gained. Living everyday. I've always known I would survive. When things happen, I thought, they always seem familiar.

Preja Vu.

I pedaled and searched for a memory of Nanna's farm. It wasn't easy to make the memories come alive. There was so much light around me, and in my mind, and in that light I wanted to find a *particular* light, the light on the cucumbers, on the white picket fence. If I could just remember how it felt to be there I could put it into poetry. In the moment when you found the words, you were, I thought, going outside of time. Where one wouldn't die. Where, I thought, riding through the fluttering eucalyptus shadows, *maybe* Nanna might not be dead. Such a blissful feeling, finding the right words. It made regular life worthwhile. Along the embankment, some dead birds. A pattern? I wondered. Birds equaled prophecy.

I am being followed by dead birds.

I remembered Eliot's poem: *I Tiresias, have foresuffered all.* The footnotes explained that he was the most important person in the poem, even though he was just a spectator.

I rode past Safeway. In the parking lot, some seventh-graders leaned against a truck, smoking. Maybe, I thought, once I finish "The Path," I should try writing something long, like "The Waste Land." I now know what this year will mean! I pedaled home.

———

Mrs. Hanson put together a fact sheet. It included a list of quotes from prominent people about Scanlon. "He's one of the least ethical men I've ever met," said the Mormon ex-mayor of Tempe, a Republican. Dad said it couldn't be used, not as it stood; some of the quotes implied stuff that couldn't be proven. Mrs. Hanson agreed, but she also told Dad there were rumors about Scanlon and a call girl in Las Vegas. She and Mr. Nachmann were going to look into them.

———

One morning Bruce told me his stepfather had used the belt on him again. "You're the only person at this school who is OK," he said. "Everyone else is full of shit. You're my friend to the end. Friends to the end, right?"

"Yes," I said, with feeling.

Later that afternoon, someone put a dead frog in Martha's locker. She took it in to show Mrs. Binder. "Why are you bringing me this?" she asked, upset.

I stood on the soccer field, in my blue shorts, waiting not to be chosen. My neck was tense. Death, don Juan said, was an adviser. It sat hovering above your left shoulder. Where? I turned my neck, quickly, slightly—nothing there. As if to check, I did this twice again. I felt less tense. The field glared, the tension came back; I wanted to turn again. I did, feeling stupid, hoping no one would notice these odd, jerky motions. It was almost as if my neck turned itself. Two teams formed: the shirts, the skins.

———

At last: the reading at Anna's. Drew couldn't come; he had a rehearsal for *Bye Bye Birdie*. Anna had the house to herself: Karl had left for Colorado. Anna and Nicola discussed how good it could be to be alone. Anna hadn't realized how much she had missed this. She had gotten a lot of work done; the revelations were coming quickly.

"The dams are unlocked," she laughed, and I guessed that this was an old joke between Nicola and her. Nicola put a scratchy album on Anna's record player. We listened to Dylan Thomas: *I see the boys of summer in their ruin*. Schaeffer and Ratter: they were in their ruin.

The record played on but I couldn't pay attention. My mind circled like a needle caught in an album's center, the arm unable to lift. Then the record stopped and Richard read "Wind." It derived from but was not haiku. Ian read a long work called "The Tangerine Snail." Leslie read "Distant Traveler."

He wants to be with us
Without knowing who he is
The stranger
He must protect himself
From our dark eyes.

I wondered if it was about me. Anna praised Leslie for having pared the poem down. I read "The Path." Richard and Anna thought it was great. Nicola talked about her tarot reading; it had told her a lot. Richard opened a bottle of wine, and I stared into the mysterious blue in the center of the fire.

Later that evening I could not sleep. "The Path" was about the way my self was dissolving. It was more intense than anything I'd written before. I could see where I was heading but it couldn't be put into words. I dressed, listening, trying to tell if anyone was still awake. I only heard the house's quiet sounds. I turned off the alarm system and went out through the patio door.

The lights shone on Dad's barbecue, Mom's marigolds. Past them, darkness. The shapes of the citrus and the olive trees emerged; I heard the whoosh of the pool-cleaning hoses and the ceramic wind bells' clink. Mist rose from the water into the cool March air, into the darkness.

During the day, shadows are doors of not-doing. But at night everything is a shadow.

The power of the darkness on my skin, entering me everywhere, moving through me, turning me inside out. Almost unbearable; I felt perfect, I was the darkness. No longer Mark. The spotlight of Earnhardt Chevrolet swept slowly like a sword across the sky. Leaves from the citrus trees blew onto the patio. You didn't always know when you were gaining power.

———

"So do you comment on and critique each other's work?" Mom asked. We were in the kitchen making root beer floats.

"Sort of." I knew she was curious about the reading. I wasn't sure whether I wanted to talk about it. If I did, it might lose its magic.

"I don't know," she mused. "I'm not sure how I'd feel about people critiquing *my* work."

"How is *your* writing going?" I asked. She'd recently started an article she wanted to submit to *Ms.:* "Notes of a Candidate's Wife."

"It's hard to find the time," she replied. "I guess I'll never write the great American novel."

I wasn't quite sure how seriously she meant this. I, too, wanted to write a novel. I took five mottled-green Chevron station glasses from the cabinet and placed them by the blender. If anyone were to write about our family it should be Mom. She knew everything. The light passed through the glasses, staining the counter green. "The trouble is," Mom continued, "I'll think of a first sentence. Then I don't know what to do after that."

"First sentences are important," I said.

"Maybe I could write a novel with just first sentences. A series of great first sentences. What do you think?"

On the counter across from me, a box of Lucky Charms, Dad's sunglasses, and Jason's catcher's mitt. And Sparky's leather leash. The feeling of being in a squarish space, in a white room. "But then," I said, "the second first sentence wouldn't be a first sentence."

"You're right," Mom said, playfully, seriously, moving toward the refrigerator. "So much for that great idea. I guess my real creativity comes through cooking. When I'm cooking, I think I get some of the same satisfaction a writer gets. I think it *is* an art."

I wondered if she really believed this. I thought of the way I felt when finishing a poem. In the moment of completion *you* were complete; you had an epiphany; cooking can't be like that, I thought, and then thought maybe it was.

"It probably hasn't been valued as much," she continued, "because it's what *women* do." She paused, then mused, "I guess the hard part of a novel must be coming up with a plot."

How she darted, like a hummingbird, mood to mood, thought to thought. I was still arguing in my head about cooking. But she was right: how were you supposed to come up with plots? Poems were just feelings and images; they didn't need plots. The light coming through the window, the kitchen smelling of ice cream and burnt toast: these are the things I'd want in a novel. The way the house feels on a Sunday morning. Dad's tea, the sound of Sharon drying her hair in the bathroom, the not knowing what to do with the day feeling, the feeling of being in a room with other people, the shifting fields of tension in the air. Would I be able to describe how I'm thinking about describing this moment, how I think about the things I would include if I *were* to write about it, how I think this is not a good way to think, and how I wonder if Mom knows what I'm thinking and how I think maybe she does?

Novels lie, I thought. You change things. I want my real family to live forever, not some made-up people.

"Maybe if you were with other writers you'd get ideas," Mom continued. "It must be good for you to have a group like that."

Sometimes she understands me too much. If I share Anna's world, it will dissolve in Mom's watery light. She wants to dissolve it, maybe.

"So do you think the telethon is going to happen?" I asked, immediately regretting having said this.

"Oh, who knows?" she said, dropping that topic. "Your father likes 'Here Comes the Fudge.'"

I nodded.

"How do you think Anna feels about Karl spending so much time in Colorado?" she asked, an edge to her voice.

"I don't know. I think it's how they both like it." I'd tried to explain their relationship before but it was difficult. I didn't want to tell her Anna had been upset about Karl going away. I could tell her Anna thought this would be good for her as an artist. But somehow, with my mother there, I wasn't sure I believed this anymore. I could scent her doubt in the air; she's criticizing Anna, I thought angrily, for a moment. People say you're born alone and die alone—but we *feel* we're in each other.

I didn't want Mom to think Anna was lonely.

"It must be a hard situation," she said, sympathetically.

"I don't know." I tried to scoop the ice cream but it was too hard.

"You can let that sit," she said.

I still wanted to tell her about the reading.

"I think I'd like to do something tonight," she said determinedly, turning on the blender. "Your father needs to take a break."

She's always thinking about *him*, I thought. She's always feeling sorry for someone.

"Such as?" I asked.

"Oh, I'm not sure. We could play a game. Maybe even," she added tentatively, "charades."

"Maybe we could build a fire," I suggested.

"Did Anna have a fire last night?" she asked, knowing.

6

Just as the blade of a knife cannot cut itself so we cannot experience consciousness directly as an object in front of us. Introspection can thus never hope to meet the subject face to face. The final subject is completely beyond our experience; it is not really of this world. To try to get at it would be to attempt the impossible. This is exactly what the yogicarins set themselves out to do.

I was disappointed to see Connie's dusty, blue Chevrolet in the parking lot; I wanted Mom to drive me to Dr. Kurtz. Now Connie came five days a week; Sharon had scheduled activities—youth group, volunteer work, ZPG meetings—so she'd be out of the house when Connie was there. Connie was enthusiastic about Dad's campaign; she had told Dad that she and Lloyd wanted to host a coffee and make phone calls. I sat quietly as we drove down Claremont.

"You're lucky your parents send you to such a good school," Connie remarked as we passed the Frontier Bank's glittering fountain.

"I know," I responded uncomfortably.

"I wasn't much of a student but I'm reading a lot now. I want to make up for it," Connie said, more talkative than usual. I wondered whether she knew what kind of doctor Dr. Kurtz was.

I noticed a book on her dashboard: "Christianity and Rebirth." At the Chevron station, red and blue pennants flapped in the wind.

"Do you believe in reincarnation?" I asked.

"I don't know," she said. "I want to learn about all the different paths. I was raised Baptist but I know there's a lot more out there. I want to learn about the Jewish faith, too. I asked your mother to give me some books. I don't think the Jews believe in reincarnation, do they?"

"I'm not sure."

Connie turned at the Valley Ho; birds flew toward the mountains. Light made sharp shadows in parking lots and in the distance drowned things in haze. Energy moved through me; I'm on the edge of *something*, I thought. I wanted to touch the seat belt.

I wanted to talk more but we'd already reached Dr. Kurtz's. I got out of the car and walked up the driveway, kicking the oleander flowers that lay on the dark asphalt ground.

We talked for a while about school. Then, after a moment of silence, Dr. Kurtz leaned back in his chair. "Have you begun to masturbate?" he asked, taking out a Marlboro. *Masturbate:* the word seemed hazy, technical. I hadn't had any sperm yet, so I wasn't sure, but I did touch myself, so maybe I masturbated.

"Yes."

Dr. Kurtz looked unconvinced. "Do you have fantasies?" he persisted.

I wasn't sure: when I thought of fantasies I imagined the casino lights I'd seen when we'd driven through Las Vegas. I did try to think about sex—I knew I should. Under the covers, in my room, I would touch my penis. Something was supposed to happen. It was like doing exercises. Posha had shown me a sit-up routine I sometimes tried before bed. But like Posha's method, I wasn't sure I was doing it right. What was I after? I knew how, when writing a poem, to focus on a significant memory: the smell of the freshly turned earth in my grandmother's garden, the light in the aspen trees at Vail. Once the memory came alive, once I could really feel it, then the right words would, with a little further effort, come. I sensed, lying under my soft, green blankets, that this process was the same, but in reverse. I wasn't looking for something that had disappeared, but for something that hadn't emerged. It would—I knew how to explore the darkness. At Halloween, Sharon and I would sometimes go to neighborhoods we didn't know to collect for UNICEF. I'd walked without a flashlight, at camp, in the woods behind the lake. It was good, I thought, not to know where you were. How you gained personal power.

I could hear the strange night noises of the house. The unexplained humming, the sounds of shutting doors, slippered footsteps, Lilly on her wheel. I could hear all of that, and the voices of Loloma, the laughter as Schaeffer moved his clenched hand up and down over his opposite thumb in the back of the science room.

I would touch my penis.

My knees turned the blankets into temporary hills—fluffy humps like the Papago Buttes. The future's in the valley, I would think, not *longing* to arrive, but curious. I knew I should use images to get there. The Tibetans meditated on the mandala, Christian mystics such as Meister Eckhardt used Christ suffering on the cross, and I used images from the school day. I sorted through them. Heather Morel walking through the parking lot. Cheryl McCrea in front of her locker. Dan Baltz.

There were moments when I wondered whether other kids from my class, in other rooms, in darkened houses on Ventura, on Monterosa and Montecito, were also putting together the bodies and faces of their classmates as they cut and spliced their way into the night. There were probably just a few kids used in this way, whose images floated in sleepless heads throughout the East Valley. Like powerful sorcerers, they traveled without leaving their beds. While they lay more or less still, their faces floated above the darkened citrus groves and the eucalyptus-lined canals, above the service stations and the winding asphalt streets, into our heads.

My green blankets would now and then give off static sparks. Perhaps Lilly, tiring herself as she went round and round in her wheel (which reminded me, sometimes, of the Ferris wheel at Legend City) could see these sparks. Perhaps to her they were distant fireworks, like the ones set off at the party my parents had taken me to for the opening of Big Surf, where they'd served everyone banana-and-peanut-butter sandwiches.

Sometimes I would come up with an image of Dan Baltz and Cheryl McCrae. This seemed to work better than when I just used Cheryl. Dan wearing shorts, lying on top of her in the dark on the beach at Big Surf, his butt moving up and down in rhythm with the crashing of the giant artificial wave. Her blonde hair would lie in the sand. I pictured her legs. I would try to think about Bruce with the prostitute in Las Vegas. I imagined a dark-haired woman on a hotel bed, and Bruce taking off his belt (the one with a silver horse on the buckle) and then I would picture the lights outside the hotel's window, and the large television set they'd probably have in the room, and I would remember our trip through Las Vegas two years before, and the Circus Circus Casino, and then I would try to return to the image of Cheryl and Dan or Heather and Dan at Big Surf, but then it all would start to blur.

The birds chirped in the atrium. I thought about Dr. Kurtz's question. "No," I said. "I don't think I do. I don't think I have fantasies."

—

When the session was over, I walked out through the waiting room past the sullen, older boy whose appointment always followed mine. Seeing me, he put down his *Sports Illustrated* and waited for Dr. Kurtz to summon him down the hall. I wondered what his problems were. I was certain they were worse than mine.

I left the office and walked down the driveway through the purple shadows and the waning afternoon light. A woman with a stroller stood next to me at the curb where I waited to cross Civic Center. I wondered if she knew whose office I had left. I squinted at the passing cars. My father would be late picking me up. He was meeting with Mr. Nachmann and Senator DelBlanco. I was to wait in front of the library.

Outside the library some old men sat on benches reading the *Journal-Observer*. There were a few three-speeds parked in the bike rack. One of the old men tossed a cigarette butt on the concrete and looked at me. I went inside.

The white stucco building was cavernous. I didn't come here often: we had so many books at home. Years ago John Friedman and I had checked out some joke books and once I'd come with Bruce: he'd wanted to get a copy of *The Happy Hooker*. I crossed the brown carpeting to the card catalog and found what I was looking for. Checking out the books, I avoided the eyes of the white-haired volunteer. I looked at the names on the inserted card to see whether I knew any of the people who had previously checked them out. Somehow I hoped Anna's name would be there, although it didn't make sense for her to use a library on this side of town. There were only a few names. I tried to decipher their script, wondering who they were and where they lived.

I knew they would be quite unlike me. But they were on the same path. Donald van der Heusen. M. Gablik. Who were they? Would we one day meet?

I went out the glass doors and walked past the old men on the bench. I wanted to sit in a place of power. In the distance there were some kids on bikes. I walked over to the steps that led down to a newly built lake on which there were some swans—my parents had given a donation to help buy them, and our name was on a nearby plaque. I sat on the steps. I had taken out several books, but the one I sensed was most powerful was a small, black, jacketless volume. *Buddhism: Its Essence and Development.* I had another twenty minutes to wait. I sat on the concrete steps leading down to the dark lake beyond which the traffic rushed on Civic Center. I now understand, I thought while I read, something no one else in my family knows, which will separate me from them forever: it *is* possible to escape from suffering. Nirvana *is* attainable in this life. One must, the book said, accept that there is no happiness in this shifting world. I knew at once that this was true. Something passed through me, a sense of the beginning of a momentous crossing, as I sat, closing the book, waiting for my father, watching the swans.

7

"I have something I want to talk to you about," Anna said. I waited expectantly.

"Karl asked me to send him some magazines. You know, those dirty comics. I was looking for them, and I found these letters this girl had written him."

"Who?"

"One of the life-drawing models."

"What are you going to do?" I asked.

"I don't know," she said. "I think this must mean it's over." Her face didn't show any pain. "What do you think I should do?"

I needed to say something. "I think you should wait and talk to him and see. It could be it's just a one-time thing. Maybe it'll pass." I felt like an astronaut moving, in a puffy suit, through space, without gravity, direction, or light. I hoped I'd sounded mature.

"You are so wise," she said. "I don't know how you can know so much for someone so young."

———

Bruce's efforts to be accepted (which had seemed to be succeeding for a few weeks) began to backfire more and more. He doesn't realize, I thought, that Heather will talk to him every now and then. She's not going to talk to him *every day*. He shouldn't always barge in. I'd sometimes like to be able to go to the art room and talk to Anna and Richard alone. But he's always there.

One day Bruce came up with an idea: a beauty pageant. He would be the judge.

"I don't know about that," I told him. It's weird, I thought, how people will all of a sudden just say something that makes *NO* sense.

"I didn't ask *your* opinion. You're so negative."

"You did too." I wasn't sure whether he had.

"*NO*, I did not. Stop being so critical."

"I am not . . ." I said this sadly, looking down.

"I know you're not. I was just kidding. Didn't you know?"

He hadn't been kidding about the beauty contest. He continued to talk about it. People groaned. This went on for a couple of days, until Mrs. Heller remarked, in front of a classroom of kids, that he should stop trying so hard to get attention.

In line at the cafeteria, Bruce said to one of the elderly women who served dessert, "I prefer strawberry." Everyone ridiculed this. "I *prefer* you go fuck yourself." "I *prefer* you disappear." "I *prefer* you shut up." "I *prefer* you go hang out with the other fags."

—

The four noble truths: All is suffering. Suffering is caused by desire. It is possible to escape from desire. The way to escape from desire is to follow the tenfold path.

I paused and put down the small black volume. The Taoists hadn't taught that all is suffering. Buddhism was more radical.

In Zen, enlightenment came abruptly, out of nowhere. It came through a koan. It came when you were slapped by a master. In Mahayana, it came through practice.

I wondered whether all *was* suffering. Sometimes I felt that way. But other times I didn't. Birds chirped in the citrus trees.

The Buddhists said that if you did not realize that all was suffering it was because you hadn't looked deeply enough. Were all pleasant things an illusion? I looked at the crimson clouds above the trees. I could smell the orange blossoms in the cool, dry air. Some kinds of suffering, the Buddha taught, were obvious. But others were concealed. I tried to imagine the skull beneath my skin. Shadows lengthened on the patio. Inside, Mom made dinner. Some things were pleasant but caused suffering to others. Some things were pleasant but made us anxious because we were afraid we would lose them. Other things seemed pleasant, but they did not satisfy out inmost soul.

Mom had planted a jacaranda tree; it had a few blossoms. The Buddha had started his life as a prince. The birds chirped. One day Prince Gautama saw the suffering around him; he could no longer stay sheltered in the palace. Sparky leapt at the birds and they flew away. Gautama left his kingdom and wandered for six years. One evening, underneath a tree, he found enlightenment. Jason dribbled a basketball in the driveway. Some of the birds sat on the roof, some of them in the trees. A chalky moon rose above our house.

The Buddhists believed the self was an illusion. It was because of this false belief in an *I* that we became attached to things. This was how the cycle of suffering began. If there was no *I*, who could do the desiring?

——

Bruce and I sat at the table next to the kiln. Anna and I had just praised his bowls. Heather Morel sat at the other end of the table working on a watercolor. Schaeffer had been in earlier, touching her ass, discussing rugby and the boondocker he was planning.

Bruce tried to get Heather into a conversation. He started

talking, once again, about how popular he'd been at his old school. "I used to go to *lots* of parties."

"Oh, yeah, sure," said Heather.

Bruce ignored her. "I asked my mother if I could have a party," he said. "She said it would be OK as long as nobody got any sperm on the curtains."

How would the sperm get on the curtains?

"You are such a freak," Heather declared coldly, brushing back her hair. "You are *so* totally full of it."

"I'll show you what you're full of," Bruce said, rolling out a log of clay. "This is what you're full of: Schaeffer's dick. This is how big it is when you suck on it, isn't it?" He waved the clay in the air until it plopped on the floor.

"Ohmigod," said Heather. "I have *so* had it. You are the most abnormal person. Why do you exist?"

Not long after, Bruce was sick and missed several days of school. People joked we might get lucky—he might die. I, too, was sort of glad he wasn't there.

———

From someone's radio, near the bike racks, Elton John. The boy danced with Suzy in his old blue jeans. With a hard-on? He remembered when he was young. I was supposed to be young but I was missing out on it. I walked through the hazy morning air, past the trees, gray and crocodile green.

I sat eating lunch at one of the picnic tables behind the cafeteria, alone. Usually I ate with Bruce. I would, I told myself, be more popular if it weren't for him. A fly buzzed near me. I drank my milk.

Am I existing in the right way? I wondered. I'm *always* thinking about this. I ate a soggy string bean. Fish sticks. "Fish dicks," Bruce called them. Everyone would have thought it was funny if someone else said this, but not when Bruce did. It didn't matter what you said, it mattered who said it. If you said the right thing in the right way, enough times, who you were might change. The sun attacked the stucco buildings and the white pathways and the pale grass and, at the far end of an oleander hedge, the picnic table where John Friedman sat with Schaeffer. I thought about the time when John had been my friend. We'd made jokes about Nixon, and had (along with Martha Wallace) gotten the best grades. Before Tim O'Donnell had moved to Wisconsin, we'd all gone to see *Planet of the Apes*. But then John had gone out for football. I'd felt betrayed watching John, who used to hide with me in the shadows of the bleachers, doing push-ups after school. But, I thought, our separation had been kind of inevitable. John was always "proving" God did not exist. Of course Buddhists don't really believe in God either, I told myself, but they aren't atheists. God is a Western concept. Buddhists believe in pure consciousness: the void. *Mind-only*. John thinks the world is made of atoms. But when you become enlightened, I imagined explaining, there's nothing but awareness.

Sometimes, I thought, John still *does* eat lunch with me. Just not with Bruce. I got up from the table to go join him—and Schaeffer. I hesitated, almost putting my tray down. I know I should follow my instincts. That's what everyone *says*. But what are they? I stood still, next to the picnic table, trying to *sense* them. Like looking into the glare of headlights. *We cannot experience consciousness directly as an object in front of us. The blade of a knife cannot cut itself.* The fly circled my face. I can't sit down now, I thought. The mind is like the sky, the sky is like the mind. I began to cross the grass.

Silently, I repeated Dr. Kurtz's advice: don't assume they will reject you. Walking by the oleander hedge, I thought about the different forces inside me. Which side, I wondered, would win? One day, when *The New York Times* or somebody writes about me, I thought, they'll say "fear and the equally great need to conquer fear were always at war within him."

The faint, dry, desert smell in the air: rocks, cactus, dust, sun, cottonwood. Maybe *courage* and *fear* are struggling inside me. I can feel the forces but can't see them. So I don't know what they should be called. Weird how people talk about people having *sides* to them. How do you see your sides? I remembered the four noble truths. Detachment: if you do not desire things they will come to you. I desire not to desire that they'll accept me. My left brain sets so many traps! Only the rational mind, I thought, fears contradictions. Schaeffer's trombone case sat beside him on the grass. Wearing his Kawasaki T-shirt, he drank a chocolate milk and listened while John recited "American Pie," proving he knew the whole thing. Schaeffer looked annoyed as I set my tray down.

John finished. I said, "It's supposed to be about Kennedy." Sharon had told me this. "You think you're really smart, don't you?" Schaeffer groaned, drumming his fingers on the picnic table. "Well, OK, let's see. For instance, do you know what a levee is, for instance?"

I thought I knew—where the Chevy had been. But I

wasn't *sure*. Perhaps there was a sexual meaning to levee—the word *was* similar to Levis.

"He doesn't even know what a levee is." Schaeffer's disdain was as endless and unexplained as the desert. I couldn't read Friedman's look.

"You know, for someone smart, Grosfeld, you're pretty stupid," Schaeffer continued, brushing back his Jim Morrison hair. "If you're going to be weak, don't be stupid. OK?" He said this as if he'd proven an irrefutable and important fact. He got up and John did too. They took their dark-orange trays and left.

I sat for a while. Then I, too, got up and took my tray. It had been a mistake to go over to them, a mistake to say what I'd said. How can you act on your instincts when your instincts are always changing? How can you *not* be self-conscious when everything you do is wrong? Schaeffer and John now stood with Tucker, yards away, laughing. At me, I know. What the Buddha says is true. All *is* suffering. Sometimes I'm able to trick myself into thinking this isn't so. But now reality stands revealed: *All is suffering, all is ill.*

Walking past a row of lockers, I sensed that some of their numbers were bad omens; I tried not to look at them but they sort of whispered to me.

I passed Dan Baltz, surrounded by a group of laughing kids, and thought about the conversation I'd had, so many times, with my mother. Lying on the white comforter on her bed, she would listen intently, and tell me other kids really did like me. Sometimes, she said, you didn't find this out until years later. It would seem incomprehensible to both of us that this could not be true. We would turn on *Marcus Welby, MD* and settle in next to each other; everything would be all right. The desert light now gleamed off the gray lockers. Mom, I thought, doesn't know that all is ill.

But perhaps she did.

———

I thought if I tried to spend less time with Bruce he might not notice—but he did.

"You're being *weird*, Grosfeld," he said. "What's wrong?"

"Nothing's wrong. I just want to be by myself a little."

"Come on," he said. "You've been acting really *mental*."

I'm not mental, I thought.

"Admit it, Mark."

"I don't have anything to admit." I wanted to sound lighthearted.

"Come on," he said, grasping my arm. "You're thinking about your girlfriend, aren't you? You're so in love with the Walrus. When's the wedding?"

I continued, for a few days, to try to keep some distance. I wanted to show the personal power I was developing. Then John Friedman told me he thought it was a good idea to avoid Bruce. I didn't like it when he said this. Bruce was, after all, my *true* friend.

"Bruce, I'm sorry I've been acting a little weird this week," I said, one afternoon.

"Don't worry, Mark. I'm not mad. I forgive you." He put his arm around my shoulder.

But you ought to apologize, too, I thought, for the Walrus stuff. You were acting weird, too. The next week Mrs. Binder returned to school after having been away for several weeks.

She'd had an operation on her foot. Bruce suggested we buy her a present. You have a *good heart*, I thought. I just want to be good but I'm not. We rode our bikes down to the Biltmore Plaza. Bruce picked out a piece of stained glass I thought was too expensive.

Riding back, past houses with pampas grass and log fences, Bruce talked about how terrible school was, how some people were OK, like me and Mrs. Binder. I had trouble paying attention. I wanted to be in the moment but my thoughts interfered. He rode ahead when we reached the canal. *"Gypsies, tramps, and thieves,"* he sang, his voice mixing with the sounds of traffic. I caught up with him and we turned off the embankment. A radio played in an empty car, like a voice from a tree in a fairy tale. The houses we rode by seemed normal, their normalness weird. Gray houses, white houses; small green oranges on the large, green, well-kept lawns. As we rode, he told me about Khalil Gibran. I listened patiently. I'd given up on discussing metaphysics with Bruce. He told me that even though he sometimes had problems with her, he really liked Mrs. Voigt.

"But have you ever noticed something?" he asked.

"What?"

"You know how wide her hips are? She must get fucked a lot."

Oh, fuck you, I thought. I'm not being very Buddhistic. But Bruce is attached to things and he draws me into states of attachment when I want to be indifferent. Was it true about Anna's hips? I tried to think about something else. The mailboxes shone in the sun. Pyracantha, geraniums next to a wall. The flowers in the shadows bloomed like madness in the spring. Richard had read Baudelaire; I would read him too. *Aqualung my friend*. Bruce was not my friend.

"What's a matter, Mark?"

"Nothing."

"Oh, come on, tell me what's a matter."

———

Curled comfortably on my bed I read. Alan Watts's *This Is It* had the famous essay on Beat Zen and Square Zen. There was another on LSD and satori. We believe, Watts reasoned, that man is a self-conscious, self-controlling organism. Yes. Self-conscious, for sure. . . . We believe, he says, that there's a little man inside pulling the strings. I drank my 7-Up. Who, for instance, decided to sip the uncola? But does the little man have a little man inside, pulling *his* strings? Who controls the controller? *When I can no more identify myself with that little man inside, there is nothing left to identify with—except everything!* Yes. Everything.

———

Stan Rouse, the consultant, flew in from Washington to help plan Dad's announcement. He told us about the campaign he'd run two years ago in Colorado. He'd made some half-hour commercials, something, he said, no one had ever tried. I listened hopefully as he described how the commercials had turned the race around. The Democrat had been fifteen points behind when he started. The commercials came out in October. The election ended up so close he wasn't even sure his candidate had won until the next morning.

Our district, Rouse cautioned, was more Republican than the one in Colorado. Still, technically, there were more registered

Democrats. The problem was they didn't vote—especially in South Phoenix. If something could be done about that. . . . There were rumors that Althea was going to ask for a divorce. There were rumors that she'd been threatened. If some of this came to light . . .

"But it shouldn't come from us," Dad said. "People are tired of dirt. They want someone who cares about the issues. The best way," he continued, "to bring up *his* problems is to show the contrast with *our* family."

Rouse, smiling, looked around the table at Sharon, Jason, and me. Sharon looked up at the ceiling.

"That's why I like your idea for the half-hour commercial," Dad went on. "It can include the family. People want to vote for a moderate who has substantive opinions on the issues."

People want dirt, I told myself. Still, I felt a warm glow in the room. The old, warm glow, I thought, listening to the Soleri bells, clanging in the wind. The wind that came from far away, from somewhere past Bell Road. I looked at the zinnias Mom had arranged in Aunt Sylvia's silver bowl. If all the factors come together, I thought, it could happen. We could win.

"You're absolutely right, Nat," Rouse said. He doesn't mean it, I thought, noticing how many olives Jason had taken from the salad.

Rouse looked at Sharon. She smiled at him. "Your father's told me you're the scientist of the family. He says you want to be a marine biologist."

"I don't know where he got *that* ancient news."

Rouse looked relieved when Mom brought out the duck à l'orange.

"This is the best I've ever had, Jean," Rouse exclaimed. "Delicious."

After he left, Mom told Dad she worried he was spending too much on Rouse. The commercials could end up being costly. "If I'm going to *have* a chance we're going to have to *take* chances," Dad said.

———

"Hi Connie." I stood on the steps of the living room while she vacuumed.

"Hello Mark," she said. I wanted to continue the reincarnation discussion we'd started on the way to Dr. Kurtz, but I didn't know how to bring it up, or if I should: I knew she had work to do.

"So your Dad's going to be making the big announcement," she said.

"I guess so."

Mom entered from the dining room and she and Connie began to discuss what needed to be done around the house. I went to my room. I want my new poem to be open in form. A series of fragments. In the past I've probably been too concerned about a meaning I can explain.

I lay the pieces of paper with the image fragments around me on the floor. Sitting in my beanbag chair, I thought of ways to structure the project. I could title each section after a different tarot card. The most important was the Magician. On his table sat a cup, a sword, a pentacle, and a wand. He was surrounded by white lilies and red roses. Above his head, the infinity sign. One hand pointed toward heaven; the other, earth. He brought the two forces together. In my poem *I* brought forces together. The poet, too, was a magician. Bird imagery would run throughout. There was a part about Egypt.

Different sections would describe the magician's travels. Finally, he would go *beyond* magic. I wasn't sure how. I'd have to follow my intuition.

8

"Now *who* is it you're planning to go see?" Dad asked. We were on our way to get haircuts.

"This writer," I said vaguely. "Someone Mrs. Voigt knows," I added, still reticent, but feeling I should give him more. We were going, in a few weeks, to hear Jack Osborne read at the university. Anna had called the night before to tell me. Perhaps, I thought, he might also come to an *Amethyst* meeting. One evening, at Milarepa, in the middle of a reading, he'd looked into the crowd and said, suddenly, pointing at Anna, "there's a woman here who is a see-er." They had never even met before! If I tell Dad this, it will become tarnished. I still have so far to go to reach *Unconcernedness.*

The night I met Jack Osborne could turn out to be an important night.

Anna had also had other good news. She'd talked to Karl; he'd agreed to come back to Phoenix and go with her to see Don, the therapist. Don had hypnotized her two days before and seen a white aura around her, from which he'd known everything would be OK between her and Karl.

Dad and I, in our sunglasses, faced the glare; I felt we felt like shadows in the light. His face was as smooth as a stone I might save from the beach. He seemed to be searching for something to talk about. Maybe, I thought, we could discuss media strategy.

"So are you making any new friends this year?" he asked.

Why do you have to use that false optimistic voice, I asked silently.

"Well, I think I'm making some new friends."

"Do these friends have names?"

"There's Bruce."

"Just Bruce?"

"Bruce *Waterson*," I answered, more sullenly than I'd intended.

We were buckled in. I'd given Dad old news. It was all pointless. I wasn't sure I was even going to be able to stay friends with Bruce.

"You don't have to get that tone," Dad said, after a minute.

There are some beings who, after attaining enlightenment, choose to return, to be reincarnated, in order to help others attain salvation. These are the bodhisattvas.

"What are Bruce's interests?" Dad asked, more softly, trying to make up for having gone, in tone, too far.

"He rides horses."

Dad was as unable as I to do anything with this. Neither of us wants things to go back to the way they were pre-camp. Still, if there's a problem between two people, someone has to be right, someone wrong. I can't see any way out of this. The blame goes back and forth, silently. We drove by plastic chairs on yellow lawns. We're trying, I thought, to act as if things are better than they are.

The Saguaro Cleaners, lightwashed; in front, a pink wall, a flower bed with pink snapdragons, a small puddle. I was reminded of something but wasn't sure what. Where had I had *this* feeling? Maybe at the dude ranch in Wickenburg, maybe in San Diego, maybe at Mrs. Gunderson's. I tried to remember these places exactly. Picture *just* the way the flowers lined the walkway in San Diego, and the yard with the old fruit trees, and the ziggurat steps that led down to the beach past the avocado stand; picture exactly the wall's outline, its white-ochre color, and the smell of the ocean air and the gray clouds in the morning above the sand-swept walkway. . . . I knew that once I captured the image then the feeling that was in the memory-picture, the real thing, the *essence,* would break through. Suddenly I felt I had it—it was as if I'd bitten into a fruit I'd grown with great care on a tree in my mind and was tasting its sharp juice. The taste was intensely beautiful but I knew it would only stay with me a few moments; I wanted to put it into words so it would last. If only, I thought, I weren't in the car with Dad. It took all my concentration to hold onto the feeling, and to compare it with the feeling I'd had when we'd driven past the cleaners.

"So would Bruce like to go to a Suns game?" Dad asked. I let go of the image. "Or if there's someone else you want to invite . . ."

How shadowy, how hopeless. Dad and John Friedman and I had gone, years ago, to some Suns games. Dad liked John; when he came to our house they'd talk basketball and politics. Still, I thought, Dad was reaching out. A good moment to be a bodhisattva.

"A lot of people don't get along with him," I confided. A high-wire act.

"Why is that?"

"I don't know," I said, and then wished I'd said more.

A woman rode a horse along the roadside in the shadow of billboards and palm trees. Ahead, road mirages. I touched the seat belt, feeling its texture. Then I stopped touching it, and then wanted to touch it again. I didn't, but thought about touching it. Even when I wasn't touching the seat belt, I could make myself imagine what it would be like if I were.

"Well, you can't pick friends based on what other people think: that's part of friendship. *'This above all: to thine own self be true.'* You know where that's from, don't you?"

"Hamlet," I mumbled. We passed Safeway.

What do I expect from him? It isn't his fault. He doesn't know the situation. You can't expect people to be mind readers, Dr. Kurtz had argued, although I knew there were people who were.

A shopping cart had been left in an empty, weed-filled lot next to the Dairy Queen. "Now what some people forget," Dad said, thinking out loud, "is that it's Polonius who says that. Not Hamlet, but the old fool."

Maybe, I thought, I should have attempted to explain my problems with Bruce. If Dad knew more, we could, possibly, talk about it. In the future, when I looked back, when I thought about my relationship with my father, what would I think? Weird to be thinking about how I'd think about *my relation-ship with Dad* while I was sitting next to him. Maybe I would think I hadn't stood up for myself. In his youth, they'd say, some day, Mark Grosfeld never rebelled against his father. Never became his own person. Or maybe I'd realize too late that I'd made too big a deal out of little things, that I'd made every-thing unnecessarily difficult. And there he is next to me. Is Dad too always trying to figure out what's going on between us when we're together? Odd that whenever I'm with him I'm trying to figure this out, that *this is always going on.* And my awareness of Dad's awareness that I'm trying to figure out what's going on between us—this is *also* always going on.

The awkwardness: an endless series of reflections. We passed the Bike Barn and the Xpress Lube. Dad, I thought, is a sentient and infinite being, too. *One should learn to treat all people alike and to steadily diminish one's personal preferences and antipathies.*

"Oh Lord what fools these mortals be," Dad jested, entering the parking lot. A Jaguar was trying to exit the entrance. "They couldn't have done a *worse* job designing this mall," he said. We got out in front of Thrifty's and walked past the ride-for-a-quarter carousel horse and the bubblegum machine, into the shadows of Bob's Squaw Valley Barbershop.

The Squaw Valley Mall was run-down. Dad says he keeps coming to Bob out of loyalty. "I can trust him. Like your mother with Trevor." But it's *not* like Mom with Trevor. Mom comes back from Paris Fashions full of Trevor's stories. How his son's been arrested, how his wife might need an operation.

Recently Mom had started taking Sharon. I wish I could go with *them,* I told myself. It's Mom's fault I have to be here. Dad wants to believe this is the same. Later, Mom will play along, asking how our "expedition" went. Then she'll comment on the difference: when women get their hair done, it's like a soap opera or seeing a psychologist. Although sometimes, she says, *she* feels like the psychologist, giving Trevor advice about all his problems.

"How's business?" Dad asked Bob.

"Not bad."

"Think that new McCrory's is going to bring in traffic?" Dad inquired, like a well-meaning country squire discussing the grounds with the caretaker.

Bob said it probably would. Dad asked what he thought should be done about fuel prices. Bob didn't know, but he believed the Arabs thought they could push us around because Nixon was in so much trouble. I was relieved he didn't blame the Jews.

The night before, Mom had had an idea for a brochure. We were sitting around the kitchen table while she scooped out ice cream. "One for you, one for me, one for the Museum of Natural History. How about: 'Nat Grosfeld: A Vote for Change. Seventy-four reasons in '74?'"

"That's going to be hard to come up with," Dad said.

We began to try to list them. There was everything he'd done for the environment, founding ACEL, stopping the dumping of toxins in the Colorado, the Gunderson Ranch. He'd been a Valley Man of the Year nominee. There was the work he'd done for the migrant farmers; his suit against the nursing-home owners.

Dad said he didn't want to come off too left-wing. "The first thing should be: 'He'll return honesty to Washington.'"

"Don't forget the temple presidency," Mom said.

Dad started taking notes.

"The United Jewish Appeal?" Mom asked.

"Don't want to have too much Jewish stuff," Dad replied.

"You are who you pretend to be," Sharon said.

"Sharon," Dad said, "can the condescension."

"Ooh," I said, unable to resist, "canned condescension."

"Both of you," said Mom.

"I didn't start it," Sharon said. She got up and took out a jar of butterscotch sauce.

Dad wanted the brochure to include a picture of himself in his army uniform and several pictures of the family. On the tennis court. Climbing a mountain. Then there should be a list of his other qualifications: the Charros Club, the Businessmen's Roundtable.

"He led the effort to get rid of the weeds," Jason intoned.

"Not a small accomplishment," Dad replied, sort of humorously.

"Who accomplished it?" Jason asked.

"He reinforced the berm; he organized the garage cleanup," Dad said, in a baritone, ignoring Jason's question, trying, too late, to preempt our mockery.

Sharon, Jason, and I sat still, uncertain whether to continue.

"He was a great outdoorsman," Sharon declared, meaning that he wasn't.

"Stop it now," Mom said, almost pleasantly, as if she were still going along with the none-of-this-is-too-serious idea.

"He put up with some lazy brats who didn't appreciate him." Dad tried to say this as a joke.

"Who cleaned the garage?" I asked, feeling pathetic.

"Everyone stop it *now*," Mom said angrily. We were quiet a moment. That was so dumb of me to say, I thought. I can't stand the way we're stuck with each other for one more second.

"The Boys' Club presidency," Dad remembered.

The year he was president I'd had to go. "I want you to give me reports on how it's run," he'd joke, dropping me off at the Saguaro branch each Saturday afternoon. I tried to learn to play pool. At least that was indoors. Most of the boys played basketball outside in the heat. There was a fish tank. One of the counselors got mad because I scratched the pool table; he didn't know Dad was the president. I sat in the corner. After a few weeks I stopped going.

"I don't know," Mom said. "Maybe we better just aim for forty-seven reasons."

"That will cut down on the cost," Dad said. "And save some trees."

Bob, the barber, asked Dad what he thought about *Time's* selection of Judge Sirica as man of the year.

He doesn't care about this stuff, I said to myself; he just knows it's a topic Dad will like.

Dad said he thought Sirica was a good choice. But he thought they could have included several other important Watergate figures, like Senator Ervin and Archibald Cox.

"Hmm, that's interesting," Bob said, sounding intrigued. "*Men* of the year. Now there's an idea."

Dad seemed pleased with this response. The fluorescent lights' reflection shimmered on the dingy linoleum floor. Enlightenment could be sudden: the sound of one hand clapping.

The sound of my father and Bob talking. The sound of the razor's buzz, like the hum of the crop-dusting planes that we heard when we drove past the Indian reservation, like the whirr of the helicopters that sometimes crossed the suburban sky. Dad continued to try to get Bob's opinions about the issues. Al, who cut my hair, was mostly quiet, but after a while he asked (as he always did) where I went to school. I was embarrassed: Loloma was private. Al asked me how I thought the Suns were doing and I said I thought they were doing pretty well; then he stopped talking. I drifted into the cave of my silence, surrounded by the razors' humming and the sound of the scissors cutting, and the words of the customers and the barbers. My black hair fell on the white cloth: ashes on a snowy mountain. I looked at the oil seascape on the fake wood wall. It was beautiful. I knew it wasn't really art, but then Anna often found things to praise in surprising places; she had pointed once with admiration at the cowboy mural on the First Valley Bank building. This was like that. My father, I remembered, had admired the same mural. Their views shouldn't overlap, I thought, troubled. Their *essences* are different. It was amazing, the way the light came through the waves in the painting on the wall.

"You know, Mark" Dad said, in the car on the way home, "I've been wanting to tell you: you seem to be have grown much more self-confident lately."

"Thanks." That again.

After a minute: "Are you still friends with John Friedman?" He can't ever let *anything* go, I thought, my nose against the window. I've been trying so hard to be *indifferent*.

"Yeah," I said, trying to conceal my irritation, "we're sort of friends."

"Sometimes you have to reach out to people," he instructed. "Let them know you're still interested in being friends."

I don't tell you what to do, I thought, wearily.

Phone wires rose and dipped like my father's signature. Birds marked up the sky. The largeness of the sky contains so much. You can't say enough about it, even though there's nothing to say. The expanse of space, the desert light, always there beneath events—like the whiteness of the page beneath words.

"I know," I said. "I do."

"I know you do."

You say one thing, but your voice says the opposite. You don't believe me. But maybe, I thought, he's not being sarcastic. How could you ever tell? And maybe, after all, he was right. John *had* been friendly at the beginning of the year. I could make more of an effort. *If the Buddha nature is really present in all, then all are equally near Buddhahood.*

At a nursing home, an old woman sat alone on the terrace in a chalk-green nightgown. How lonely she must be, I thought. I'll end up like her. Maybe I can use the image in my long poem.

"Sometimes a good way to be better friends with people is to do activities with them."

"I *do* activities with people," I mumbled.

"I didn't say you didn't. I'm not telling you you *have* to do anything. It's just a suggestion. You should be willing to listen to suggestions. You know sometimes things you think you aren't going to like turn out not to be so bad."

"Sometimes I'm right."

"You won't like my saying this, but you thought camp was going to be the end of the world but it wasn't, was it? You may not have *loved* it," he added, "but it wasn't *that* terrible, now was it?"

The house in San Diego. The flowers. The light on the wall. Recall it *exactly.* The feeling is in there. . . . Felicia Goldman had group sex. We pulled up to the driveway. Dad opened the mailbox and took out *Consumer Reports.* I got out of the car and walked up the unswept cement steps. Dad went to check a broken sprinkler head. I entered the quiet house and walked past the Chagall posters to my room. I lay on my bed. I thought about the Jack Osborne reading at the university, and the upcoming *Amethyst* meeting, and I leafed through my tarot book. The Empress. The Hanged Man. *Self-surrender leads to transformation,* I read, as Lilly went round in her wheel. Could you be a Buddhist and an artist? Art was egoistic, but Buddhism wanted to get rid of the ego.

Dad's ego. My ego. I stared at the light shifting on the wall.

—

The Spanish Club came back from Baja. Everyone had gotten really stoned. Tom McKnight told me it was definite I was going to hell because I wasn't saved. Baltz and Hoffman magnifried ants. When Bruce tried to get to his locker one afternoon, some kids stood in front of it and wouldn't let him through. He shoved Cheryl McCrae. Mr. Lewis came out of his room. "That is no way for a young man to behave!" he hissed at Bruce.

"But she . . ."

"You do *not* hit girls!" Mr. Lewis said, shaking his fist vaguely. "We're going to march on down to Mrs. Heller's. Now."

———

Mom asked Dad if he wanted to come with her; she needed help picking up the campaign stationery from Vista View Printers. She also wanted to get some cheese; Senator DelBlanco was bringing some important people over later that afternoon.

"I'm sorry," Dad replied. "I've got to finish this fund-raising letter."

"I'll go," I said.

Lush green yards—almost, I thought, like yards in the East. Green shrubs, bushes, and trees; green, green; and green street signs. Via Paisano; Rancho del Sud. In her white sunglasses and scarf, checking the side-view mirror, Mom looked, I thought, like a foreign movie star. She began to talk about the temple; she felt guilty we hadn't been to Beth Shalom for a while. And she was worried about Mrs. Goldman, who'd again begun to call at weird hours. Mrs. Goldman was getting counseling from

Rabbi Horowitz; Mom wasn't sure this was a great idea. The cars on our left had tiny suns in their windshields. Sun after sun after sun, coming toward us on North Jacinto. The world is filled with traveling pools of light; a golden haze. "I want to get my hair done before your father's announcement," she said. "I want to look snazzy."

We turned a corner; irrigation in the yards. I looked at Mom. Is she as normal, I wondered, as she seems? "I haven't seen that irrigation man for a while," Mom commented. "I wonder when he's going to come." An aluminum garbage can, cactus ribbed, in a white driveway in the light. Mom told me Scanlon had gotten drunk at the Phoenix Club and made jokes about the Mormons. People had overheard but, as usual, no one was willing to come forward.

We pulled up in front of Cheese 'N Things. A slight, dry breeze. The scent of dust and citrus, maybe sage, and gasoline. The Plymouth's hood reflected the clouds and us. Darkly, bluely; a pool. "There are so many rumors," Mom said.

I hope there will be poof, I thought as we went inside. We sampled the Havarti, the Gouda, and the Brie, and then agreed on cherry gourmandise. And some *lahvosh*. Afterward, before the printers, we stopped at the bookstore.

While Mom chatted with Mrs. Briscoe, I looked through the New and Selected Titles. Noticing an enormous moth floating above an umber desert, I picked up *Tales of Power*. I felt troubled, remembering the end of *Journey to Ixtlan*. Hadn't Carlos talked to the luminous coyote? Hadn't he had his vision? Don Juan always made fun of Carlos for keeping his notebook. Carlos wasn't able to experience anything directly; he always had to write about it. The only use of books should be to get beyond books. I knew my attraction to them was a weakness. It was a lot easier to read than to be in the moment. But at the end of *Journey to Ixtlan*, Carlos had *seen*. He couldn't continue writing after *that*. Maybe, I thought, I'd remembered wrong.

I brought *Tales of Power* over to the cash register. Mom was buying a Bernard Malamud and *Portrait of a Marriage*, which, according to Mrs. Sklar, had gotten a good write-up in the *Times*.

"I don't know when I'll have time to read this," she told Mrs. Briscoe. "But it's hard for me to resist."

———

Metaphors are so difficult, I thought, sitting in my room. Dark as . . . what? You have to have the feeling of *really* capturing something. Then you're getting at the essence; through this you transcend; it requires the right state of mind: openness and calm. And not thinking about "the right state of mind."

How many metaphors? How many symbols? What's the *balance*? Where do the words fall on the page? Listen for this. It didn't come today because you couldn't empty your mind. Because you were thinking about school, Bruce—all that *junk* stands in the way. Keep searching for the invisible rhythms. The spaces; the ebb and flow. Hear the whispers coming from somewhere else. Allow your mind to *be* the poem. Don't cast your shadow on yourself. Be a flower that blooms without being aware it is blooming.

Then put it down on paper—immediately!

Listen for gusts of thoughts and feelings; when there is no separation between your mind and the universe, it *is* the poem. Then it's not even *your* mind. Not really.

Sometimes there are torrents of voices and energy.

Perfect mind, perfect poem. Perfect the mind. Then you will be in another place. Outside of time.

> *Stumble through the darkness on the roots*
> *of the trees. The unseen trees.*

That's not it. Remember how it *felt* on the mountain.

> *Stumble on the roots*
> *In the darkness*
> *Of trees you never met.*

Closer. But not it. The spaces and the mind-rhythm.

> *The lights in the distance*
> *Like candles.*

No. What were the lights *like?*

> *chromosomes*
> *of light*
> *Above the path.*

That was it! I had *seen* that. The image had come to me! I hadn't forced it. "The Path," I thought excitedly, is about my spiritual journey—but also about writing the poem. If I could just work *this* idea in, too. Only connect, Anna had told me. I could use mirror imagery in "The Path" to convey the idea of the poem itself being a path. I need to connect *that* to the image of the path. In a real way. I knew I could do this if I thought hard enough—or *stopped* thinking hard enough.

I wanted a little more inspiration. I put on Cat Stevens.

Oh I'm on my way, I know I am, somewhere not so far from here

I, too, was on my way, I thought; I, too, did not know where. A traveler, like Carlos, like Cat, like Eliot, in his *really* hard *Four Quartets*.

Life is like a maze of doors and they all open from the side you're on

I looked at my desk, at my stained-glass Snoopy. I will be there soon, I thought. Somewhere not so far from here. Maybe *here* even—but the other side of here. My poetry will lead me. I'll soon go through that door.

———

"What happened with Mrs. Heller?" I asked Bruce.

"Nothing. She doesn't like Mr. Lewis. She said he was wasting her time."

I knew Bruce's mom had given money to the Loloma Aquacenter fund.

Bruce asked to look at the book I was carrying. I showed him my copy of Chuang-tzu.

"I want to read this some time," he said.

"OK," I replied, adding, a little reluctantly, "do you want to borrow it?"

"Ah so," Bruce said. He kept saying "Ah so" all afternoon and the next day.

"Cool it," I said.

"Ah so, Confucius say cool it."

"Bruce."

"Ah so, asshole, ah so. Mark, I'm kidding. You're my friend to the end, ahh-sole."

This bothered me all afternoon. "Bruce," I said the next day, "can we talk about yesterday?"

He looked at me with feeling. "What's up, Marky?"

"The stuff you said about Confucius," I said, and felt stupid.

"Mark, you take things *way* too seriously."

"Yeah," I said. "I know I do. Sometimes I just wish you'd . . . I don't know . . . sort of, like, not *push* so much."

"You are weird," he said. I looked down.

"I'm sorry," he said. "You're not weird. I mean you really are the least weird person. It's all the stuck-up people like Dan and Cheryl—they're weird."

This was, I thought, a daring thought. The world can change.

"But Mark, when I asked if I could borrow that Chinese book, you should just have *let* me borrow it. If you ever wanted to borrow *The Prophet*, I would just *give* it to you."

"But I told you you could! You can borrow it. You can have it *now*."

"I don't want to borrow it *now*," he said. "I was just making a point."

"OK," I said, thinking perhaps he did have a point. I hadn't wanted to lend it to him. He'd seen into me. I thought that maybe I should ask if I could borrow *The Prophet*—I didn't want to, but I thought he wanted me to.

"I can get some coke," Bruce said. "You should come over to my house and we'll do coke."

"OK."

———

Bruce, I thought, could sense that I was trying (as Dr. Kurtz had suggested) to have a little distance. I didn't want him to feel that. So I spent even more time than usual with him. And resented it. One day, after he'd seen me reading Castaneda, Bruce said (rather loudly, during homeroom), "You really love spics. You want to be Rabbi Spic."

"Oh, God," I said. "That's not funny."

"You mean you don't like spics?"

"I don't like the *word*."

"You can't take a joke," he replied.

I'll have, I thought, *the mood of a warrior*. When Bruce saw me avoiding him, he would treat me with haughty disdain—or torment me. "Hey Marco Polack," he would say, "what's your problem?" But then, on other days, everything seemed fine. Bruce, I thought, is able to forget the day before; I can't. Sometimes he avoided me. He began to hang out with new people. There was Debra, an older girl, who Ian said did speed. Sometimes I saw him talking with a crater-faced seventh-grade boy whose father was in prison for land fraud. Sometimes I saw him with Drew.

On one of our better days, while we sat together outside the cafeteria, Bruce told me he'd started to write poems.

"Can I see them sometime?" I asked. "When you want to."

"Yeah," he said. "Just wait till I'm done. Then I'll show you."

"If you want to. I'm sure Mrs. Voigt would be interested in seeing them."

"I don't know," he said.

———

"What am I going to do about Bruce?" I asked Anna, as we

sped down the Galvin Parkway on our way to hear Jack Osborne read at the university.

"He's really been giving you a lot of problems lately, hasn't he?"

"Yeah." I shook my head regretfully.

"He's been having a hard time," she said. "I can see it. His home life is tough. His parents aren't as supportive as yours. They're not so liberal." I wished she hadn't said this. She continued. "I don't know what to do for him. He *does* make things difficult for himself."

"I wish I knew what to do about it," I said.

"There may not be much you can do," she counseled. I wondered what you were supposed to do when there wasn't anything you could do. The road curved; Tempe's lights and blackness came in view. I wondered if I should invite Bruce to an *Amethyst* meeting. Maybe he was mad that I hadn't. He hadn't *said* so. But maybe that was what he was thinking. Would Anna want me to invite him? Was it too late for that now? The whole idea was probably stupid. I couldn't picture Bruce in Anna's living room with Richard and Ian.

"I talked to Karl last night," Anna said.

"And?"

"He's going to come down for a week. I'm a little nervous." She didn't sound nervous. "He seemed apologetic. He had some difficult things to say about me. But I think we're maturing."

We drove past the low, tangled creosote. I wondered what difficult things Karl had said to Anna. She began telling me a new dream. A key floating down a river through a grove of birch trees. A fish that spoke. Villagers who came from the hogans and gathered on the leaf-strewn banks. Then, in another dream, she'd met a rancher. He had been her guide, taking her through a gap in the mountains. She had written to Duncan; he'd written back telling her it was important—she had to go on.

"It sounds like you really do," I said, afraid my words lacked clarity. I want to speak, I thought, the way Robert Duncan would. But instead I hear Dad's echo, his voice in mine. Can Anna? She'll think the voice is dull; she'll humor it. But she's often told me how much she respects my parents.

I wonder how she really sees them.

Saguaros seemed to watch us speeding past. I saw Legend City's glimmering Ferris wheel, and the moon above the Papago Buttes and the spectral white tower of the Hayden's Ferry mill.

"I'm not going to mention this to Richard and Ian," Anna said, "But Frank Lewis told me he's bisexual. I guess I expected it. I didn't know what to say. It isn't something I've had any experience with."

"What did you say?"

"Not much. I felt he wanted me to say something."

"Maybe he shouldn't expect that from you."

We passed the rose garden in front of the Shepherd's Way Church. "Look," Anna said. On the white concrete wall, a gray cat, caught in the headlight's eyes. I am about to meet Jack Osborne, I thought. What will happen? What will I say to him? What will he say to me? Perhaps he'll pick me out of the audience, the way he'd picked Anna at Milarepa. No, of course that won't happen. He and Anna were planning to drive to the desert the next day.

Maybe when I'm older Anna and I will drive into the desert. Perhaps things with Karl won't work out. Maybe, someday, Anna will go out with me. It's possible, but I have to wait.

I studied the line of Anna's neck. Patience, Mark, I thought, looking at the olive trees against the dark sky. The yuccas on the mountain in the headlights: glinting emeralds. A *metaphor*. Why can't I see things as they *are*?

I'm so impatient.

"What is in that head of yours?" Anna asked, brushing my hair.

It was hard to follow Jack Osborne's poems. After the reading, Anna introduced us.

"Oh, I've heard about you," he said.

"And I've heard about you," I said. The right thing to say? He seemed, I thought, about to say something more, but the head of the English department came up and began to talk to him. There were a lot of people I didn't know who knew Anna; she spoke to them, and I wondered at the way she (like don Juan) could move so easily from world to world.

———

"You're not seriously going to wear that tie?" Mom asked as we were about to get in the car to go to Frontier City. She made Dad change it; he was afraid he'd be late for his own announcement, but we got there early. Senator DelBlanco introduced him. My allergies were bad; I tried not to sneeze while Dad spoke. Reverend Stephens was in the audience with some people from the UFW. Phil McGrath came, along with most of the ACEL board. We wore cowboy hats and were the second item on the news. A few days later KPAK ran a story about Congressman Scanlon's Phoenix Club remarks. He called the KPAK reporter a liar.

———

One day John Friedman sat with me at lunch. "I know we don't hang out together like we used to," he said. "You know, stuff changes."

"Yeah, I know," I said. He'd seen the announcement on TV. We talked about Nixon, Monty Python, and Mrs. Heller.

"Maybe," I said, "she ought to be impeached." John said he liked that idea. We're doing an OK job, I thought, of acting smart but normal.

"How come you never eat the crust of your bread?" John asked.

"Sometimes I eat it," I lied, and then ate some of it, so that I hadn't lied.

"It's just sort of weird not to eat crust."

I held up my peanut butter sandwich and pointed to the partly eaten edge.

"Yeah, OK," he said. "Did I tell you I got the new Flip Wilson record?"

"Yeah?"

I listened, bored, while he recited from it.

———

Through the thicket, strange growths
which touch me gently   or cut.
Down through the dark to the dark eyed lake
Black mirror of black sky

I've gotten it right, I thought. I feel pure and complete. My Bruce problems and all the shit at school don't matter. I'm not

317

self-conscious. The clouds have disappeared. The lake *is* a dark-eyed mirror. Idea, image, metaphor: all *balanced*. The feeling of fullness, a comfortable room in the mind, a room filled with light. A room so filled with light it will soon burst. That's *process*. It will lead me on to the next poem.

———

Karl had come and gone. I hadn't seen Anna much that week; it had gone well, she told me afterward, in her office. They had laughed a lot and he'd been amazed by her new work. There was other good news. Anna had been asked if she wanted to show the drawings she'd made on one of her trips with Abbott in the community college's lobby gallery. She wanted to accompany them with texts explaining their mythological meaning. "I'm going to have to be careful with the wording. I don't want to go *too* far into it," she said.

Some of the myths were about sex. Others dealt with the end of the world and the white man's role in it.

"They're sort of conservative over there," she added, in a light voice. She seemed to be making fun of herself. Or of the idea she could shock people.

"You don't want to freak anybody out," I said, slightly more seriously.

"That's right. And I'm going to have to be careful about the grammar. You know those academics."

I smiled. Neither Anna nor I were strong on grammar. Jack Osborne had cautioned her about this.

Karl, she continued, was going to spend another five weeks in Colorado and then return to Phoenix. They hadn't gone to the hypnotist. Anna was waking at five every morning and writing; she'd never had this kind of clarity. "I'm in the transmission mode," she said. "You know what I mean?"

"I think I do."

"I think you do, too," she said. "It's fucking grand, isn't it?" Anna sipped her tea, explaining further. "Before I was trying to make up meaning in my work. You know *that* was ridiculous." She laughed and I smiled. "I'm just a vehicle," she continued. "I'm *allowing* that. It's much more primitive."

"I know," I said. We sat quietly. She began to speak again. "Karl fixed the truck," she added. "It seems it had transmission trouble, too."

I laughed. She added that Nicola was going to have to move out of the house she'd been renting. She might move in with Anna; this would help with the rent.

———

Don Juan told Carlos that if he could see his hands in his dreams he would enter the dream. I heard some footsteps in the hall. The kitchen door opened. I stopped reading and took a sip of water. The Soleri bells clanged in the wind. My doubts were overcome by my desire to know more.

Dreaming is real when one has succeeded in bringing everything into focus. Then there is no difference between what you do when you sleep and what you do when you are not sleeping.

———

Mrs. Binder assigned Dan Baltz and Jeff Tucker and me to the same science project. Dan said he was glad we were in the same group; he said I was all right.

We walked to the library to get books on NASA. Tucker sang:

My name is Carlito
I work making fritos
I make five dollars a day
I visit my Lucy
She gives me some pussy
And takes my five dollars away.

The school was quiet except for some distant traffic and us. A small feeling of liberation—not being in class. No one (except for John) had mentioned Dad's announcement. I thought about seeing my hands in my dreams. They started talking about Heather Morel; I felt like an imposter. "Thinking about her gives me a hard-on," Dan said. Like a spotlight, the phrase transformed him.

"On ditch day," Tucker responded, "after Big Surf, I'm gonna screw Cheryl McCrae. Got to third base at Schaeffer's. I would have fucked her but you know what happened."

I didn't. I tried to act indifferent, walking several steps behind, like a shadow following a cloud.

"But after Big Surf," Tucker continued, "I'm gonna screw her all night long."

"Whaddaya say, Grosfeld?" Baltz asked, friendly and inclusive.

"I want to screw and ball her," I said.

It's frustrating not understanding things, I thought. I want understanding. But in order to have understanding I have to stop looking for it. I'm so impatient, I said to myself, sitting, later that afternoon, beneath the cottonwood tree in the dry wash. If I can learn to get beyond desire, then suffering will end. I *know* this will take time. But I'm sick of my *self*.

I squinted into a paradox as if it were the sun, which hovered above west Phoenix, above the houses, the palm trees, the few apartment buildings, and the power lines. Wasn't my desiring not to desire itself a form of desire? However much I tried, I could not see how I could stop desiring not to desire.

9

He explained that every human being had two sides . . . one was called the tonal and the other the nagual.

"The tonal is the organizer of the world," he proceeded. "Everything we know and do as men is the work of the tonal."

"If the tonal is everything we know about ourselves and our world, what then, is the nagual?"

"The nagual is the part of us which we do not deal with at all."

"I beg your pardon?"

"At the time of birth, and for awhile after, we are all nagual. We sense, then, that in order to function we need a counterpart to what we have."

—

My father spoke at a church on the West Side. Jason and I sat in the third row, trying to count the audience. "Fifty," Jason said. I thought there might be more but each time I came close to finishing my count I got distracted; Jason would make a joke or ask me a question or someone would move around or I would have a thought.

If a third of the people in the audience became involved, I calculated, if they held coffees or put up signs in their yards, then that would lay the groundwork. Then when the TV commercials started, there would be enough momentum to put Dad over the top.

A candidate for governor spoke angrily about the CIA's secret wars. I liked his speech, and people applauded excitedly, but this was the third time he'd run—everyone knew he couldn't win.

A woman with her hair in a bun, who was running for

superintendent of education, talked about standards. The tonal, I thought.

Dad got applause when he got up. "I'd like to second what my friend Marilyn said about standards," he began. "But I want to talk about standards not just for our kids, but for our leaders. We need men *and* women in government our kids can look up to."

People won't get the reference to Scanlon, I thought. Dad looked young in the church light. I noticed, in the shadows of his face, a luminous tone. The Italians, Anna had told me, sometimes used green underpainting for shadows.

Dad pointed toward Jason and me. "My sons are here with me." People turned slightly and smiled; I pretended to look attentively at Dad. "I want to promise them—and you—if I get to Washington, I will always make them proud." His voice, slightly awkward when he began, grew more resonant. But who cares about interest rates? He should talk about the suffering farmworkers. But that wasn't how you got elected.

We drove home through the darkness on Dunlap. Hills and silence. Dad doesn't feel the night's mystery, I thought; he doesn't feel its vastness. To the north the mountains merged with the sky. Somewhere, geodesic domes. The Milky Way: a galaxy, and other galaxies beyond it, thousands, millions, then other universes. And black holes. Jason, Dad, and I: tiny dust specks, bits of matter. But the universe exists in our minds. We went past Central Avenue and the Vista Corporation tower. Some lights and lots of big dark spaces. Gas stations. Full of power.

That night, after my shower, I stood in front of the bathroom mirror. Connie had been in: the carefully folded towels, the blue toilet water. I wiped the steam off the mirror. Don

Juan said a sorcerer could kill someone a thousand miles away. You could kill a person on the other side of the world by having a *thought* about them.

When will I have to think about my own death seriously? Maybe, I thought, in ten or twenty years. I can still put it off: an exam I won't get until the end of class. Time to acquire *understanding*. Don Juan says death is an adviser. I looked quickly behind my left shoulder, three times. An interesting thing to say, *death is an adviser,* but sort of useless. I probably have a lot of my opinions because they *sound* interesting—so I don't really *have* them. Dust motes, floating around.

I'm fooling myself believing I'll have time to prepare for death later. I shuddered, wiped away the steam, and switched off the light. Tonal Mark, in the dark. I turned the light back on and washed my hands. Every time I do this I kill more beings than there are people in France. Unavoidable dilemma for a Buddhist: living involves taking lives. Why there's the doctrine of inoffensiveness: *Try not to slaughter more beings than necessary. Be careful when walking through the woods.* My zit: not a sentient being. The Buddhists inherited the doctrine of inoffensiveness from the Jains. Perhaps I'm more Jain than Buddhist. How many Jains are left in the world? And how do you get in touch with them? . . . Jane Patterson, I laughed silently. Poor Lady Jane Grey, queen for six days— her story had made Sharon and me cry. There are three billion people on the planet. And I want to say that I'm a Jain. Another instance of my pride.

I switched the light off and on, off and on, studying the way it felt to disappear.

When I was seven, I'd shown Nanna my poem about a kumquat tree. I'd written it at the Desert Palm, where I'd spent the night with her and Posha. I was thinking about Peter, Paul & Mary's song: *Lemon tree very pretty.* But there weren't any lemon trees at the Desert Palm: kumquats, behind the white walls where the snapdragons grew.

I wished Nanna had liked my mother. When they'd first met, Mom had told me, she thought she did. She'd taken Mom to lunch at the Plaza. Mom had been reading Camus; they'd talked about him; Mom had been nervous, but Nanna tried to make her feel comfortable. When Mom went back to Wisconsin, Nanna wrote a very gracious letter. "The last one like *that* I ever got from her," Mom had said. When she returned to New York, when Nanna realized things were serious between her and Dad, she turned cold. It wasn't always obvious. "She could be so nice one day but then the next," Mom would say, and then shake her head. "I really do think it came down to money. *I* didn't have any. That embarrassed her. I don't think she could admit it to herself. She probably thought your father was going to marry one of those Dalton girls. *I* went to Benson High. That always seemed hypocritical to me. But what did I know? I was from Omaha. I thought socialists were supposed to be poor. Not from families that owned half of Queens. But you know," she'd add, "maybe that's not fair. She wouldn't have liked anyone your father married. She couldn't let go. Even when he grew up she threw birthday parties for him— which seemed a *little odd* to me. And I always thought it was my fault. If I just wore the right dress. Or said the right thing about a book. Then she'd approve of me."

After Sharon had been born things got worse. Mom wanted to breast-feed Sharon. Nanna didn't think this was hygienic. She hired a nurse for Sharon without asking Mom. "I thought I was going insane," Mom had told me. "I didn't understand how families like your father's worked. But," Mom would add (as if sensing she'd perhaps gone too far) "boy, did she love you."

One time at the farm Nanna walked into the living room; Mom held a copy of *To the Lighthouse*. "You're reading *that*?" Nanna commented. Not long after, Grandpa Vogel died, and Grandma Vogel died a few months later. Dad was worried about Mom, and then he got an offer, through an old school-mate, to join a firm in the West.

There were parts of Nanna I hadn't known. But they were just *parts,* I thought, looking in the mirror. She worried my mother didn't feed me enough. Oatmeal, with cream, brown sugar, and honey. I know Nanna favored people. Her unfairness should bother me; it doesn't. Only the unfairness that hurts *me* seems real. I think it's unfair to praise Schaeffer for his rugby goals but not to praise me for my grades. I'll never be good in sports and popular like Baltz. But I am *special,* I whispered to myself, as Nanna, my mother, and Anna had.

The light in the bathroom changes; sometimes stronger, then dimmer. Uncaused—a ripple in still water, perception's shifting inner light. Still the tonal—but the nagual's here, somewhere. Underneath. Microscopic stuff floats in front of the wall; light has textures. Anna, Nanna, Mom, and I are special. I don't mean better than other people. Yes, I do. Three billion souls in the world and Mark thinks he's special. But it *is* fair for me to get praise for being smart. Mrs. Heller thinks it's so great that Schaeffer scores lots of goals against the Cholla Bulls—that doesn't make the world a better place. You make yourself smart; you aren't born that way.

You are *so* egotistical, Mark. Pathetic. I put my fingers on the steam-covered mirror and traced a saguaro and the symbol of the Tao. I made a swastika, which I quickly wiped away. I retraced the day: "Why do you leave school early?" Baltz had asked that afternoon. I changed the topic, pretending not to have heard. I turned in my report for English on the myth of Icarus. I argued with Bruce. And then we made up—sort of. At dinner, Dad had complained that the *Journal-Observer* never used his name; he was going to call Jack McCarthy, although he knew it wouldn't do any good. He just wanted to see how Jack would respond. Sharon looked bored; she made a face (maybe); then they argued about whether or not she had. Dad told Mom he would probably have to ask Posha for a loan to air the commercial.

I made a face in the mirror. I want to move to Washington; how beautiful to walk among the white buildings, the cherry trees. In the spring they'll blossom; I'll sit by the river and do sumi paintings. I traced the Capitol on the mirror. I'm still so caught in this *stuff,* the tonal-consciousness steam; if I only could get beyond it. . . . Jason knocked on the door. "Would you hurry up?"

Before I fell asleep I studied my palm. If I saw my hand in my dream then I would be in the dream. I took a last sip of water from my plastic cup. Lilly slept quietly in the corner of her cage. I turned off the light.

For a while the thoughts chased each other like spirits in a dark wood; different voices, distinguishable, indistinguishable, melding together, separating, slowly slowing down. I listened to them, knowing I was not yet asleep, knowing that as long as I knew this I would not be.

I found myself looking at myself. Somehow I had shot up to the ceiling; now I hovered in the corner of the room; I was sort of sure of this. I looked down for a few seconds. It would be something I could tell Anna.

The next day I reported that I might have had an out-of-body experience.

"Shit," Anna said quietly.

The campaign, I felt, was going slowly; I'd thought that after the Phoenix Club incident things might take off. They hadn't. Dad drafted position papers on the important issues: the economy, crime, water rights. He didn't want to be caught unprepared. Each paper had ten points. Mom suggested he could have a theme a week. Mrs. Hanson, on her own, rewrote the fact sheet about Scanlon and mailed it to the teachers. A new poll showed that although Dad hadn't come up much, Scanlon had moved down. There were a lot of undecideds. Scanlon visited all the Mormon churches. He denounced the Trilateral Commission. Dad chose the campaign colors: orange and brown, like our furniture.

We were all sitting in the living room.

"What are you watching?" Dad asked, coming in from the study.

Dr. Welby felt his patient's neck.

"A very good show," Mom said.

"What's it about?" he asked.

"I'll explain during the commercial," she said.

He stood on the steps.

"Come in and sit down," she said.

"I think I'm going to finish this position paper," he said, "since no one wants to tell me what's going on."

"Honey, if you come in in the middle . . ."

Dr. Welby gave his diagnosis. They had to operate right away.

Dad turned to open the study door, but then didn't. He looked down on us from on top of the steps. He's the *candidate*, I thought. Maybe we've done this to him. They wheeled the patient down the hall. A commercial came on.

"Honey," Mom asked, "why don't you come in and sit down?"

———

I sipped my water and put my hand beneath the blanket and began to touch myself. It was like rubbing sticks in the woods, hoping to make fire. Or visiting the petting zoo; it felt good at the same time that it felt like something I *should* be doing, the way sometimes I knew I might not pet the animals if no one were watching. My mind wandered; I kept petting. Schaeffer, after the rugby game, with Cheryl McCrae. Or Baltz with Cheryl McCrae. In bed? In their parents' room? In the desert? At Big Surf? I don't know exactly what I want to happen; doesn't matter. Bruce and the prostitute. Bruce's blue jeans; Elton John's blue jeans, the crocodile rock. *Blue jean baby, Heather Morel, seamstress for the band.* Horseback riding, Catherine the Great. "Her tits," Baltz said, "melons, I'm tellin' you." "When she saw my meat the first time," Schaeffer said, "she was scared. Like she was gonna pass out. But, you know, now she can't get enough of it. . . ." The Germans, in the backyard, in Poland. *"Jawohl, Herr Kommandant,"* the boys said, to Oberführer Funk, in his tall black boots. And then the dogs were dead.

Heather's legs wide apart, on the beach, Baltz and Schaeffer above her.

If I turn the light on someone might see.

A sort of light and fullness and then a little quivering. Oh. Was this it? Was my life completely different now? I'd thought it was going to be a very new feeling, but it was only sort of new. Maybe this wasn't really it—maybe the feeling would grow. But there was something on my fingers. My children. I slowly reached over, turning on the bedside light, pulling away the mountain. I touched the pearly liquid on my little penis and lifted my finger to my nose. Raw eggplant. Oh well, I thought, now what?

No one in the house knew. Would they be able to tell, somehow, the next morning? Mom would look at me and know. Or maybe she thought this had already happened. All the souls on my finger; I'm responsible for their being, these thousands of beings who are going to die. There isn't any way to keep them alive; too late, I thought, gently dropping a Kleenex into the wastebasket.

———

The *Journal-Observer* ran an editorial:

Holier Than Thou?

Recently, a candidate in the Fifth District sent out a "fact sheet" that questioned Jim Scanlon's integrity. We're sorry to see things come to this. We do have to wonder whether the standards this candidate refers to shouldn't be applied across the board. Why hasn't this moral exemplar disclosed all his financial holdings? We don't know, for instance, if any of his stands on development issues could have been taken because he stood to profit.

330

The editorial wasn't signed but Dad was sure Jack McCarthy had written it. "What a coward," Mom said, angrily, at break- fast. "Can he get away with that?"

"Sure," Dad said. "Freedom of the press to say any damn irresponsible thing they want and not be held accountable. We didn't even *send out* that damn fact sheet. Jane Hanson did. And I'll tell you what really bugs me about that editorial: they don't even say my name."

It's so unfair, I thought.

"Ridiculous," I said.

"How are you going to respond?" Sharon asked gently.

"Sometimes, Sharon, the best thing to do when you're attacked is to ignore it."

"Do you think we *can* ignore it?" Mom asked.

"I don't think it's any of their damn business, frankly. We made a general disclosure. It's a matter of privacy."

Privacy. Nixon. The Grosfelds have an unlisted number. Be *open*. Something is happening but you don't know what it is. Do you? Why do you leave early on Friday afternoons? I ran my tongue along the back of my throat, scratching silently. Something, I thought, I can do *inside* my body, where no one will notice. Rhythmically, subtly; there can be a pattern to it.

The editorial didn't seem to do much damage. Dad had a long talk with Mrs. Hanson about the fact sheet. She agreed in the future she wouldn't do anything without Dad's authorization. Alger Johnson held a press conference. He read some of the quotes from the fact sheet and announced that he, too, was entering the race. "One candidate," he said, "doesn't care about life. Another claims to. But his personal life and his voting record tell another story. His hypocrisy is an even greater sin."

Even though Johnson was insane, his candidacy, I told myself, could definitely hurt Scanlon. Rouse told Dad he shouldn't worry about his poll numbers. It was still too early. Most people, he said, weren't paying attention. There were more precinct meetings, more church dinners. Barbecues, coffees, radio interviews. After practicing several nights, Dad spoke in Spanish at a school in South Phoenix. It wasn't in his district but it made the news. The phone rang often. "Grand Central Station," Mom said with pleasure.

I didn't let it get in the way of my epic poem. Which still didn't have a title. I'd thought of calling the whole thing "The Path," but now I'd realized that would just be one of the sections—a very long section. I still didn't know if I would have enough vision to see how all the different images and meanings connected. The poet's consciousness had to be (at least while writing) empty, perfect, *complete*. Emptiness *was* fullness, to the Buddhists. Not easy. But you had to have it, or you would always suffer. Most people just gave up and lived in suffering. The poem was getting pretty long.

Dad let me take his old Royal typewriter and keep it in my room. He'd decided to invest in an electric. This helped me get a lot more done.

"If we weren't so close, it wouldn't matter," Mom said one afternoon in the kitchen. Clothes tumbled in the hallway dryer. "The attacks, the pressure. I think it's *especially* hard on our family *because* we're so close."

The refrigerator hummed like a mind. On the counter, next to a bag of flour, a book of Gold Bond Stamps, which I was supposed to fill. "Most families *aren't*," she continued, softly, insistently. "It's a very special thing."

I felt like a figure caught in her dream; a warmly lit space, an anxious, hazy dome. If I moved too suddenly, I might rupture it.

I sat still. Maybe she's right, I thought, playing with a pretzel-shaped napkin ring. I nodded reassuringly. Don Juan would have said this was all the tonal. Which guarded the nagual. The nagual: my original self, the self at birth, that part of me I could sometimes sense, which had nothing to do with any of this. But even thinking this was part of the tonal.

Light crossed the kitchen table. I ate a sunflower seed. "But you know," Mom continued, "in spite of that, it is exciting." Mom, as much as me, had a nagual side. Sometimes I almost thought I heard, or sensed, the whispering of her nagual. But her tonal, her vulnerable tonal, protected it.

Outside the window, Sparky jumped at a bird. "She never gives up, does she?" Mom remarked.

The dryer buzzer went off; I sat while Mom unloaded the laundry. She brought the basket in: a pile for each of us. She began to fold. "I know *you* were the most reluctant about the campaign," she said. "But you seem to be getting excited, too," she continued, hesitantly. "Am I right?"

"I guess so." I *did* like the excitement; folding brochures, putting signs in yards, listening to Dad talk to Rouse about voter turnout and "Save the Babies" Johnson. Still, I wished it could be *more* exciting. I looked at the kitchen walls. There's *energy*, I thought, in the whiteness. The white refrigerator. The white oven. My white underwear.

"Yours?"

Seeing a stain, I nodded. Does Mom know I'm in *puberty*?

I put a shirt on top of my underwear, casually. She knows it's happened, or is about to. It must disgust her; it isn't supposed to; she's supposed to want this—something would be wrong if she didn't.

Jerk off, jack off, boner: ugly words. Mom knows them. We could *almost* talk about this. But there's a curtain in the air between us. We both want to pull it aside, we both want to leave it; we both know we both feel this way. Mom and I haven't given up on the idea of complete truthfulness; we don't know *why* we should. Maybe this curtain is *natural:* that just means we can't explain it or don't understand it. A tightness in our throats: the words we need are almost there, but then they slip away.

Maybe she doesn't think about it this way. Is the sadness I feel sometimes in the room hers or mine? If hers, from where? Does anybody know? Sadnesses beneath sadnesses. I shifted in my chair. Mom noticed a jelly smear on the edge of the counter, beneath the wandering Jew; she wiped it with a dishrag. "Where's Connie when I need her?" she asked. "I have to go pick up those brochures. *Oy vey.* Always a gazillion things to do."

———

Sometimes in my room working on my poem, I *knew* I was beginning to see into words in a new way. They'd become luminous. Writing could be a way of *seeing.* I checked to see if my poem was as long as "The Waste Land." It wasn't—yet. I could publish it along with "The Sun Library" and "Another Time" and other early works. Even if they weren't perfect, people would understand I'd written them when I wasn't fully developed: Allen Ginsberg had included his early poems in *Howl*.

———

I listened to the radio. Baltz, Heather, Schaeffer: they were the young Americans. Behind the bridge he laid her down.

———

We were busy. Dad spoke to the Elks Club and the VFW. Scanlon, in spite of all his big talk, wasn't even a veteran: Dad was, and so, he told them, they ought to support him. He talked about veterans' hospitals. They don't want to hear *this*, I thought. They want to hear about *war*. Jason and I sat in the back at a table by ourselves, eating biscuits and mashed potatoes. Dad doesn't fit in here, I thought, watching the old men looking at him. I worried that someone would ask what he'd done in the army, that they'd find out he had sat behind a desk at Fort Benning. But when Dad was done he got a lot of applause. The next week the vice mayor introduced Dad at the rodeo and it ended up on TV. He spoke to a rally at ASU; he shook hands with the workers at the Honeywell plant entering for the morning shift.

But then things slowed down. There were some coffees, Mrs. Hanson arranged some events with the teachers, and we handed out brochures at the mall, but that was about it. Life was going back to normal; this was disappointing—like leaving a movie theater's exciting darkness for the parking lot's ordinary light.

Dad took the opportunity to finish his position papers and talk to potential contributors. The phone didn't ring much more than usual. Sometimes late at night Mrs. Goldman would call. Mom would get out of bed to talk to her. Once, on a Saturday night, she got dressed and drove over to see her. They stayed up for hours talking.

The next morning Mom said Mrs. Goldman would be OK. But she was worried about her, alone in that big house. Dad said that maybe Mrs. Goldman needed to move on.

"And where is she supposed to move on to?" Mom asked dryly.

"I just worry she's exhausting you."

"I'm not exhausted," Mom said, getting up to get toast, as if to show she wasn't. Her figure reflected in the window; her face softened, and she rubbed Dad's shoulders briefly. "Now don't you worry about me."

Later, after breakfast, while we cleaned the air conditioner filters, Dad said, as if in explanation, that he worried Mom sometimes got overly involved. "She identifies with people," he said, "and then gets taken advantage of."

Jeff, a boy from the youth group, began to call for Sharon.

"I'm gonna get this in the other room," she'd say. I'd hold the receiver, waiting until she picked up the other line.

"How're you doin'?" Jeff would say.

"I think we've got a wiretapper," Sharon would answer. "The older plumber."

I'd hang up. Jason would say, "Come on, let's go listen at the door."

"OK, Gordon."

"OK, Howard."

One evening, Sharon picked up the phone, expecting Jeff. "It's for you," she said, as if a call for me were a regular event.

I wondered if she thought it was weird that most of my few calls came from a teacher. Sharon had met Anna and said she was strange; I'd asked what was wrong with strangeness.

"I'll take it in the other room," I said.

I picked up the phone by my parents' bed. A call from Anna had once been a rare event, but now that Karl was away she called more frequently. Anna told me how glad she was to have the house to herself. She had finished the texts for the show at the community college and was thinking of arranging some of the stones she'd gathered near the canyon in front of the drawings. She wasn't sure they would let her do this. She described the poem she was working on. "I was on the wrong path before," she said. She had misinterpreted a dream. "Now I realize . . . it wasn't about where I should go. It was about where I've been. That was staring me in the face all along. I didn't want to face it but now I know what it means. I've always had a fear of aloneness and I've ended up in relationships I shouldn't have been in."

It was dark outside. I sank into my parents' bed. I heard my father typing in the next room, and in the room beyond, my mother and sister talking during a commercial. I felt far away. At first I'd been in two worlds at once, but as the conversation had continued, the one I'd come from had faded. When I'd picked up the phone, I'd been determined to participate equally, and had at first, but then my conversation with Anna had floated further and further from everything I knew.

"I've realized how male Karl's ideas about art are. He told me every picture had to have a central composition. But I've been looking at O'Keeffe!"

In my corduroys, curled like a seahorse, I listened to the palm fronds hitting the window in the wind. "I don't see why they have to have a central composition," I said, feeling one step behind her. The moon rose above Great-Aunt Sylvia's rocking chair.

She told me how O'Keeffe had had to move to New Mexico. She's repeating herself, I thought; it was sort of weird. "There I go, I'm probably boring you again."

"No, no," I replied. And I wasn't bored. I was an underwater diver, traveling through seas, light-filled at one moment, then, in an instant, overrun with strange, dense growths. After a while I grew shriveled, dazed, and tired.

I heard my mother and sister laughing.

Walking down the hall after getting off the phone, I rose rapidly through the changing pressure of the ocean's zones, returning to the air. Shaken and waterlogged, I tried to seem composed.

"How's Anna?" Mom asked, a little cheerful, a little tense. She wants to know, I thought, not about Anna, but about Anna and me. And Anna and Karl.

"She's fine." I thought of the further things I might say if I could slow down time.

Sharon told me I'd missed a good show.

———

I listened to the radio. *Rebel, rebel. . . . You want more and you want it fast.* Bruce.

———

I watched my father watch my brother clean the pool.

"Jason," Dad said, "if I can give you a little advice."

He waited.

"*Can* I give you a little advice?" he repeated, as if unheard.

Jason nodded, continuing to drag the net across the water.

"If you start at the deep end and then move toward the shallow end, it will be much more efficient than the way you're doing it. And if you tilt the handle like *so* you won't miss so much."

"OK," said Jason.

"A little more," Dad said. "Tilt it a little more."

Jason tilted it.

"Just a little more."

———

My long poem had a section about Nanna's farm. A list of images: the leafy tunnel, the red dirt road, and the fireflies in the evening near the cornfield. When you read it, I thought, you felt you were there. The poem also had a section about the mountain at Vail, some recurring tarot imagery, and a part about Egypt, written in the voice of Osiris. It would be difficult, I told myself, to find the secret fibers of the poem. But by discovering them, I was not only completing the poem, but myself. The promise of completeness, of finally being done, hovered like a mist of light above distant gentle mountains. Poetry could be a spiritual path. You could use art to get beyond art. As Thomas Merton had done. I had to work patiently, quietly, secretly, hard. Perhaps my hopes for this poem were *somewhat* high. Time would tell. But I had decided at last on a title. Because there was bird imagery throughout: "The Year of Dead Birds."

———

I stood in Anna's office doorway; Richard and Ian sat on the couch, talking about girls. I heard Bruce's voice in the art room. The day before he'd suggested we go together to Anna's show at the community college.

"Your friend's here," Ian said bitingly.

"I know," I said, half-ruefully.

"Are you talking about me?" Bruce demanded, coming in.

"No," Ian replied.

"I guess I'm just a romantic," Richard said. I wondered what being a romantic meant and whether I was one. This was all the tonal.

"You should have seen him when Paula Swanson was in here," Bruce said. "He was standing up in his pants." I looked covertly at Richard's striped pants but saw nothing.

"You little faggot," Ian said to Bruce.

"Oh, fuck you," Bruce said. "I've got better fucking things to do than hanging out here." He returned to the art room and his bowls.

"I've got better fucking things to do," Ian repeated, mockingly. In the next room something slammed.

"The thing I can't get over," Richard said, lost in his musings, "is that they want it just as much as we do." I shifted my position in the doorway.

"You're finally figuring that out," Ian replied.

From the next room Carly Simon blared. Bruce sang along.

"Turn that shit down!" Richard yelled.

"Make me!"

"Oh, Christ," Richard said.

Anna came in from the patio. "Bruce," she said. He turned it partway down.

"I've had it with him," said Ian.

———

"How's the rabbi?" Bruce said when he saw me later.

"Bruce, please."

"Sorry. How's Confucius?"

"Can you just be *nice?*"

"Mark, I've got news for you. Life isn't nice. You want me to be *fake*. You don't care how I'm feeling."

"Bruce, I don't want you to be *fake*. How can you say I don't care how you're feeling?" Maybe, I thought, he's right. Maybe I don't care enough. I don't know, I thought, how to have this conversation.

"Oh why don't you just go hang out with Richard and those other fucking hippies?"

During social studies, Bruce showed me his notebook. He'd written in purple felt tip: "Mark wants to lick your pussy." He quickly passed it to Martha. She looked up for a moment in weak disgust. He's so stupid, I thought, restless and ashamed. Bruce must be a test.

"Go to hell," I whispered.

"Go to hell," he replied, mimicking me.

"Shut up."

"But you do like her. You said you did. It's just the truth. You don't like the truth."

I moved a few inches away from him and looked out the window at the white buildings, the eye-gray sky, the eye-green acacia.

"I'm really sick of him, too," I said to Richard.

"I think we can teach him a lesson," Richard said cheerily,

picking up Bruce's Carly Simon album. Ian picked up a needle from a jar of ceramic tools and began to scratch the vinyl. Richard handed me the cover, which I crayoned over wildly. Richard told Ian the job wasn't done. They took the album to the paper cutter.

I'm a piece of shit.

———

I sat, the next afternoon, in the backyard. I hadn't wanted to start meditating until the gardeners left. It was quiet except for Sparky and the birds, caw-cawing in the grapefruit trees; how sad and lovely, I thought. The birds' sound was the same as in Connecticut, the sad caw-caw I'd heard so often walking past the barn. Time and space didn't matter. The birds in "The Waste Land" said "tereu, tereu." Ours, "caw, caw." *Shantih: the peace which passeth understanding. Shantih, shantih.* Sparky came and licked me and then lay down. The air smelled of dust and rotting grapefruit and grass. Birds swooped through the darkening sky. Emptiness in Buddhism wasn't nothingness; it was limitlessness! A plane headed toward Sky Harbor, a distant silver mark between the clouds. Nirvana wasn't an object *in* consciousness; it *was* consciousness. The plane became smaller; the sky darker. Buddhist emptiness was really fullness.

It was the illusion of self that stood in the way of this fullness. My task was not to get rid of the self but to understand it had never existed in the first place. *I* had never existed.

The Smith boys shouted in the yard next door; I tried not to think about them.

Is there Buddha nature in a dog?
Chao-chou answered, "Wu!"

I wasn't sure what mantra I should use. Om seemed too obvious. I made up different sounds. Un. Wu. Fa. Do. Nur. I tried repeating them to myself, but then I went back to om.

For a while, a sort of quiet. I still had my thoughts, but they slowed. The quiet deepened. It took time to get used to this—like putting your toes in the ocean.

Dad opened the backdoor but didn't see me. He let Sparky in. I tried not to think about Stan Rouse, the poll results, or Anna's reception at the college. But after a few minutes the thoughts developed momentum. A single pebble rolling down a mountain could start an avalanche. I wasn't going to Anna's reception; we had to film the commercial. Why hadn't I just left the room when they started to destroy the album? *It's not such a big deal, Mark.* A sin I'll have to live with forever. But Bruce *did* provoke me. That's a justification. Hypocrite-shit.

I knew I had to let these thoughts float off. They floated off, they floated back. The birds on the phone wires launched into the air and flew around, but then they, too, returned. Om. Om. Om. For a little while I achieved silence, but it wasn't like the silence I'd read about in books. Thin and dullish: there must be a *deeper* silence beneath it. These are thoughts; thoughts about silence that keep me from silence.

For a few moments it deepened. But then the thoughts, the stuff beneath the thoughts, not words even, kept coming back. I can't stop thinking because I keep thinking about not thinking. I keep thinking about not thinking. I keep thinking about not thinking.

The wet grass beneath my corduroys. The sad sound of the mourning doves, the pinkness of the mountains. Why can't I experience them directly? Thoughts flit birdlike between the world and me.

The I stuff is still there. It disappears in one corner, reappears in another. Like mopping: you back up into a place you can't clean without getting the rest of the floor dirty again. Sometimes I think the *I* is gone but then I realize it's I who has had this thought.

The shadow keeps appearing. I sense it. I try to dust off the mirror but can't. Huineng, the rice pounder, showed: no mirror. I should try to get along with Bruce. I want to read *The Secret of the Golden Flower*. What's a tampon, exactly?

And what is it that stops thinking? Castaneda says the will—the will I do not yet have.

The sun went down. I sat. The air was fragrant with grass, weeds, chlorine, mud. The pool hoses splashed unpredictably. It will happen like that, I thought: suddenly. I won't *make* it happen. The pool became a darker blue; the light faded on the mountain. I went inside.

Mom and Sharon sat together, watching TV, eating Wheat Thins. Mom was asking Sharon about Jeff, the boy from youth group; he'd asked her to go ice-skating. Sharon was nervous; she didn't know how to ice-skate, but Mom told her Jeff was probably just as nervous. The evening news came on. The committee had subpoenaed the tapes. I hovered in the hallway, around the corner from the living room, wanting, sort of, to join them. Why am I so paralyzed? Who controls the controller? There's no little man inside the little man. . . . I moved my toes in my sneakers. I headed to my room.

What in me makes decisions?

—

I lay in bed. Something troubled me, like the feeling around my tailbone when I rode my bike too long. I decided to reread a passage from the night before. In it, don Juan explained the will. He told Carlos it came from the umbilical region and gave you extraordinary power. But this was too vague for Carlos. He didn't think he'd be able to really use it.

Don Juan told him he was wrong. *"The will,"* he said, *"develops in the warrior in spite of every opposition of the reason."*

I concentrated on the place below my navel. I sort of felt *something*—a kind of warmth. I'd been sure to check the end of *Journey to Ixtlan*. It *did* turn out I'd remembered it wrong: Carlos had *seen* but hadn't kept his appointment with the *ally*. So he hadn't really stopped the world; he'd just come very close. But it still seemed wrong that he could continue to take notes and write books after *seeing*. His inner dialog should have ceased. Maybe Castaneda was a liar. I looked at *Tales of Power*. Nonfiction. Bookstores decided that, not Castaneda. And why would someone go to so much trouble? That didn't make a whole lot of sense either. The books were *so* detailed. If they were a lie, they were such a big lie, which meant they probably weren't. Plus, if the books were made up, it would mean *so many* people were wrong. *The New York Times*. And Anna. I looked at the quotations on the back cover and listened to Lilly going round in her wheel, feeling troubled and wondering still: *hadn't* he had his vision?

Baltz and Heather, together at Big Surf. Bruce in Las Vegas. Schaeffer and Heather. The waves crashing in the dark night. Pounding up and down . . .

—

Anna called to tell me her show had been reviewed in the community college's paper. "I was trashed," she said happily.

"That sucks," I said, disturbed. I thought of saying something about Dad's feelings about the press but decided against it. Then I thought of reminding her of O'Keeffe's experience with the critics.

"He said I'd just borrowed from the *Book of the Hopi*. Can you believe that? I haven't even *read* the *Book of the Hopi*."

"You know it all on your own," I sympathized.

"I'm not upset," she said. "I realize that criticism is his form of expression. It's his thing."

I decided not to mention O'Keeffe.

—

The Year of Dead Birds (XV)

We have gone beyond the houses.
>*Dead oranges lie on the ground, rotting.*
>*They do not   touch surfaces. In their silence they cannot hear*
the planes in the sky or
>*the screaming in the air.*

>*Afternoons vanish like silent nurses down corridors.*
>*No knowledge of the shattered glass*
>*Or the magician's old gray mask.*
>*They do not hear the screaming in the air.*

—

Mr. Nachmann thought Dad needed to hire a scheduler. He

didn't think Dad should be spending his time talking to teachers and other people who were going to support him anyway.

"Frankly," Mom said, "I think he wants your father to be everywhere at once." Some of the events he wanted Dad to go to were, Mom thought, pretty stupid. Dad thought it was more important to rest and prepare for his major appearances. One time Mr. Nachmann arranged for Dad to talk to the Desert Cove Seniors' club; Dad did, but not many people came.

"A couple of them fell asleep while I was talking," he reported wryly.

———

I kept thinking about what I'd done to Bruce's album. If only I could undo it. It had happened so quickly. (Bruce still didn't know I'd been in on it.) Like being a murderer, I thought, who's gotten away. *I'm sorry but the governor is out now.*

Time passed. I tried to be friends with Bruce. This worked for a while. Sometimes I thought things could go back to the way they'd been. We ditched track together. Sitting on a rock in the wash, beneath the cottonwood, Bruce talked about horses. And people. "Baltz wants people to think he's nice," Bruce said. "But he's just choosing his personality. I don't know if that's bad. But you've got to recognize it."

Exactly, I thought. For someone who can be stupid, I told myself, Bruce can be really smart. How good it feels to be with someone who sees the world the way you do—it makes the world feel *solid.* The same way you feel when you read special passages in special books. Most of the time, nobody looks at the world the way you do. Which means maybe the world *isn't* the way you think it is. Which means maybe you're crazy. But when you find someone who at least *sometimes* sees things the same way, then you want them to see things the same way all the time. When they don't, you start feeling crazy again. So you get mad at them. I kicked some pebbles with my Keds. I wish the world felt solid all the time, not just at moments.

One day, Bruce told me he was getting ready to show me his poem.

"Sometimes," I said, "it's good to just go ahead and finish things and get them out." I thought this would be a good thing to say. I wanted to sound like Anna, I wanted to *help* Bruce, but once I'd said it, I knew it was wrong. I sound like Dad, I thought. But Bruce just ignored it. We discussed the latest episode of *Kung Fu*. And my father's campaign.

"Isn't it sort of conceited to run for Congress?" Bruce asked.

"No," I replied, trying not to be mad.

"Most politicians are crooks."

"Not *all*," I said. "Muskie wasn't."

"*Most* are," Bruce insisted. "You should watch the news."

"OK. Maybe *most*," I said.

Bruce still talked, sometimes, about doing coke. I read *The Prophet*. Things were OK. Sometimes Bruce hung out with the crater-faced boy and Debra, the girl who did speed. I was glad to be left alone. But, I thought, if *I* want to be alone—if I want to talk to Anna, for instance—then he gets angry. Which isn't fair.

Sometimes I felt like his prisoner. He punishes me, I thought, if I move away from him *even just a little*.

One day Bruce saw me with Martha. "Mark loves Martha. Why don't you get married? Mark 'n Martha, sittin' in a tree,

f-u-c-k-i-n-g. You can lick her twat all day and have baby
Jewish walruses."

"Would you bug off, Bruce?"

"Would you bug off?" he parroted.

This is so boring, I thought. But he wouldn't ignore me.
Sometimes he'd grab me in the hall and deface my notebook.
Sometimes he'd follow me and push me. I don't want to feel
sorry for myself, I thought; it's indulgent. I tried to think about
it this way, at least when Bruce was around.

*It is of no use to be sad and complain and feel justified in doing
so, believing that someone is always doing something to us. Nobody
is doing anything to anybody, much less to a warrior.*

Maybe, I thought, "warrior" is a metaphor. But don Juan
always reprimands Carlos for thinking things are metaphors
when they're *true.* My friendship with Bruce has been based on
the same *indulgence* Carlos is always caught up in. I've needed
him because I'm afraid to be alone. A warrior can't fear that.

Bruce stopped spending his time on ceramics. He stopped
taunting me in the corridor. He pretended not to see me. I'd
hoped that since I wasn't with him all the time I would now
start to make friends with other people. Sometimes I hung out
with Richard. Sometimes John Friedman and I sat together at
lunch. But often, still, I was alone. It was worse for Bruce.
Heather enjoyed having confrontations with him, which he sort
of seemed to enjoy, too. But other than that no one in our class
talked to him. Bruce, I thought, in spite of his faults, was still
probably preferable to John. One day John came into Anna's
office while Richard and I were there. After he left, Richard
remarked, shaking his head, "That kid is so straight." My

instincts were right. John *was* boring. At least Bruce had a soul. We had another reconciliation.

"I've been really shitty to you," Bruce said. "I don't know what's been happening to me. I can't explain it myself."

"I've been kind of shitty, too."

"No you haven't Mark. You haven't done anything."

Sitting with Anna and Richard on the patio, I thought about what school would be like next year if Dad lost. I had to be prepared. Richard and Ian would be gone. There'd still be Bruce, Drew, and Anna. But I hardly ever talked to Drew outside of the *Amethyst* meetings. Maybe I could start to get to know him better. Maybe someone new would show up. Bruce, Drew, and someone new. Bruce, Drew, and someone new. A mulberry leaf fell.

Bruce, Drew, and someone new.

There was some clay dust on Anna's white cotton dress. She read a statement Karl had written for a brochure. He'd come back down to Phoenix to work on some new commissions. The brochure would show his welded sculptures in the yards of wealthy homes throughout the valley.

Karl had written, "My inspiration comes from the forms of the land itself."

"Funny," Anna said, adopting a lightly sarcastic tone I'd sometimes heard on TV, holding the pictures that were to accompany the brochure at different angles. "I'm not sure *I* see it."

"I don't know much about art," Richard said, and they laughed.

———

A KPAK reporter went out to California and tried to interview Althea Scanlon but she closed her car door in his face.

——

Perhaps, I thought, I'm too skeptical. I lay in bed reading *Tales of Power*. Don Juan tried to explain the concept of the double to Carlos. But Carlos's reason kept getting in the way.

"All of us luminous beings have a double. All of us! A warrior learns to be aware of it, that's all."

"Why am I so afraid of it, don Juan?"

"Because you think that the double is what the world says, a double, or another you. . . . The double is the self."

——

Simon and Garfunkel stood in front of the Brooklyn Bridge at sunset; James Taylor looked pensive; I'd taken down the Banana Splits. Light passed through the empty wine bottles on the ledge. Lilly slept. I sipped my Dr. Pepper and looked at "The Year of Dead Birds."

> *Now there are two of us*
> *Wandering through the empty and dry land.*
> *Somewhere, caves.*
> *We can not know who waits for us in darkness*
> *Hermit or the Hierophant?*

It had come together so easily. I hoped it wasn't *too* derivative of "The Waste Land." I couldn't use the hanged man; that was

Eliot's! Would people understand the Hierophant? Maybe if he reappeared in the "The Suburbs" section . . . It was tempting to take shortcuts, but the connections had to be *real*. One knows, I thought, when something *comes* to you (once you've emptied yourself). You are, then, outside of time. Relief, at last, from the sorrow and confusion of the world.

I am moving beyond. Nanna set me on a path.

Outside, Sparky barked. *Suburb* became a weird word when you repeated it to yourself. *Suburb, suburb, suburb*. Eliot, who'd lived in England, described the desert and its waterless rocks. The images were like Castaneda's.

The sun came through the shutters; shadow bars crossed me in the beanbag chair.

———

We drove to Casa Grande; all the candidates were speaking in the hotel ballroom. The week before, Dad had been interviewed by the Tempe paper and cut the ribbon at the opening of a new mall. He went back to the Honeywell plant at closing time and many of the workers remembered him. "Give 'em hell," one said. Mr. Nachmann said the Porters were about to make a big contribution. The polls showed Alger Johnson had begun to hurt Scanlon.

"Anyone want to play 'Twenty Questions'?" Dad asked.

"Sure," Mom said.

"I've got one," Dad said.

"Animal, vegetable, or mineral?" Mom asked.

I stared out the window. My family was still my family. I'd hoped the campaign would change us, washing over us like the wave on *Hawaii Five-O*. But we were just the same.

"Is it alive?"

A trailer park, a Stuckey's, far-off copper mines. Electrical towers: watching gods.

"Was he European?"

As long as you feel that you are the most important thing in the world you cannot really appreciate the world around you. I looked out through the dusty window at the mountains. Somewhere there were caves and gulches through which don Juan could have wandered.

"Was it King Canute?" Sharon asked.

"How'd you get that so quickly?" Dad asked. Sharon went next. The sky slowly darkened, and somewhere near another trailer park I knew: Rosa Luxemburg.

Sharon's hurt, I thought; I got it too quickly. But she'll get me back. Someday, I thought, I'll go on *Jeopardy!* and make a lot of money. "Twenty Questions" is stupid—just a way of showing we're smarter than each other. And different. Or of *making* ourselves different. Illusion, maya: we decide to like this or that so we can be separate and have *selves*. The horizon turned orangey-pink. Existence by contrast: should I choose Arjuna or Don Genaro? They won't be able to guess either one.

Windshield dust, the turnoff sign for Florence and the prison. None of them know, I thought, about my epic poem. Years from now it will be the only thing that matters, the only thing about this time that is remembered. But they can't know. It's not their fault. I must be patient for now.

"I don't have one," I said.

Jason did Ernie Banks; Dad got it quickly, and after awhile we gave up on the game. Dad turned on KPAK.

"Who do you think Deep Throat is?" he asked.

Mom said Martha Mitchell, but Dad said she wouldn't have known enough. Bruce knew all about *Deep Throat*. Her vagina, he'd told me, was in the wrong place. "No one has a big enough dick," he'd explained, "except Jon Holmes."

If you could read my mind . . . what a tale my thoughts could tell. I'd be in major trouble. *The force that through the green fuse* . . . power lines. *Oh honey you turn me on, I'm a radio. . . .*

The farther from Phoenix, the fainter KPAK's signal. Jason joked about Jim Wynne, the drunken candidate for mine inspector, and his slogan, "Win with Wynne." We all laughed.

"When they're done with Watergate," Dad commented, "maybe we can start some investigations into some old scandals. Like Hull-gate."

How *weird* this would all sound, I thought, if someone heard it. But no one ever will. And I'll never be able to explain it. Maybe *all* families are this weird. Maybe you just never find out.

"I don't think that was a *crime*," Sharon said, almost patiently, almost amused.

"We don't know that it wasn't," Dad said, "until there's a full investigation. And, in case nobody was bright enough to figure it out, I was joking."

"We know, Dear," Mom said comfortingly.

I thought of some good ideas for "Twenty Questions." But, I told myself, it's too late now. I saw horses in the distance and thought of Catherine the Great. On the dim crackling radio, Senator Buckley urged Nixon to resign.

On the way into the hotel, Jason and I did silly walks.

"What *are* they doing?" Dad asked.

"It's Monty Python," Sharon explained. "The Ministry of Silly Walks."

"Oh."

We sat at a table with the Nachmanns, Mrs. Hanson, and Reverend Stephens. Across the ballroom: Cheryl McCrae. Her dad worked for Valley Bank, which somehow explained her presence. She waved. "Mark's got a friend," Mom said. Tom Bond, the candidate for governor, spoke first; Jack Murphy, who was running for Senate, followed. Then Sam Cruz, the candidate for attorney general. Dad didn't like Cruz; he hadn't wanted to go in with Dad on the telethon. Cruz had never been involved in politics before, but he was well-known; his family owned a chain of stores in Tucson and he'd appeared for years in their TV ads. When Dad went on, halfway through, we cheered loudly. Mom looked at him; that's *love,* I thought. I can't look in: a house with the shades drawn. Dad pointed to us; we stood up; he thanked us; he said we were the reason he was in this.

The next day I wrote about the drive home. The earth-moving machines parked by the highway in the darkness. Slumbering yellow beasts. I described Casa Grande, and wrote about a Ferris wheel at night. The images connected. Words were a world of their own—in which anything was possible.

10

Nixon sweated on TV; Jaworski wanted more tapes. He was closing in! Give me an I, I said to myself, in the shower. Give me an M. Give me a P. I want the *new day* to come. Things didn't need to be the way they'd always been. During my next session with Dr. Kurtz I told him I was *thinking* about quitting.

Scanlon ran a commercial: A cowboy saying Dad was more concerned about birds than jobs. An old woman was interviewed in front of a hot dog stand saying, "sounds like a birdbrain to me."

I read my book on Buddhism. There were philosophers in the West who had reached conclusions quite similar to the Buddha's. Hume had understood that there were nothing but thought processes; the ego wasn't real. Bishop Berkeley believed in *mind-only*. These philosophers, the book explained, had used rational thought to arrive at conclusions the Buddhists had reached through direct experience two thousand years earlier.

—

Anna gave me an envelope of new poems. She had also given them to Richard, but she didn't want to show the poems to everyone. I began to read them, sitting on the grass in the shadow of the science building.

The desert ceremony
beneath the thorny tree

was that
a wedding?

The canyon
beckons.

Later I went to her office to discuss the poems. She wasn't there. Bruce sat in her chair. Drew was on the couch, in his black turtleneck, smoking a cigarette and thumbing absent-mindedly through Anna's copy of *Portrait of a Marriage*. Bruce asked Drew if he was a fag.

"No," Drew said, "I like girls."

"So you're AC/DC?"

"No," Drew answered, with a high-pitched laugh, "why do you want to know so much?"

"Are you a virgin?" Bruce insisted.

"No," Drew said, "I've done it several times."

———

I came home and went to my room. I opened Lilly's cage; she lay still. I touched her, but she didn't move. No, I pleaded silently, make it not true. I ran my finger along her white fur. I wasn't ever going to hear her going round in her wheel again. Poor Lilly, I thought, exhausted, as I lay down on my bed to cry. She had died alone in my room, while I'd probably been thinking about something stupid. I watched the shadow patterns move. I got up and held her for a while, but then I put her down. I wouldn't try to save her the way I'd tried with Rose. It's awful, I thought, that people don't care about animals. I dried my eyes and lay back on my bed wondering whether I had more crying left in me. I listened to the house sounds. It's wrong of me, I thought, to *want* to cry more. There's nothing spontaneous left in me. I'm awful, but the world is more awful. I looked at Lilly again and cried again. My grief is real, I thought, comforted by the clearness I felt with this thought.

I went into the hallway. Weird to stand there, next to the thermostat, knowing I alone knew she was gone. I walked to the kitchen and stood at the threshold; Mom was stirring a pot. She looked at me. "Mark?"

"Lilly," I said. She put down the wooden spoon and came quickly; she hugged me. That evening Dad and Jason and Sharon told me they were sorry. The next day I buried Lilly in a shoe box beneath one of the olive trees, wrapping the box in masking tape to preserve Lilly from the earth for at least a little while.

———

But the sadness, then, is, perhaps, a river
  flowing through the dry land
    the haunted land
      (riverbanks glint with forgotten trash)
      the water, dark and gleaming, knowing
      yet not knowing
  moves past dead trees
    while here, only
the Magician (old gray voice—I have known you for so long)
                      watches.

———

Another morning in the desert. Sharon had the front page, Jason the sports section, Dad the local news. I was done with the comics but no one was ready to trade.

"How'd it go last night?" I asked. Dad had spoken to the Optimist Club.

"I'm optimistic about the Optimists," he replied.

"Har-har," said Jason.

"Har-har yourself," said Dad.

It's all so inadequate: Dad's talk, Jason's, the smell of burnt muffins, the jam on my plate, the pinks and blues on the mountains behind the window behind Sharon, the halo of light around her frizzy hair, her poncho—all these falsely concrete things. They aren't intense, I thought; this isn't poetry. It doesn't feel vivid or real. Mom and Dad and the plastic table mats; empty space: light and body and thing filled. We sit at the table, I thought, with our napkin rings, surrounded, sort of, by each other's souls. Maybe Mom's trying to figure out how to be Mom, Dad how to be Dad, and Sharon, and Jason . . . and we're pretending that we *know*, pretending we're not pretending to be Mom, Jason, Sharon, me, and Dad.

"Did you give your standards speech?" I asked.

"I think it's a pretty good speech," Dad replied, humorously, defensively.

Today he was going to review the footage Rouse had filmed (although there still wasn't enough money to air it). And there were other problems. Mr. Nachmann had used a nonunion printer for the brochures. Now, although Dad opposed right-to-work, the unions were threatening not to endorse him. "They're becoming a royal pain," he said. "It's extortion." They wanted him to reprint all the brochures or issue an apology. Mr. Nachmann still hadn't been able to get the contribution from the Porters. But some things were going well. The volunteer operation was a success. Mrs. Sklar, it turned out, knew a group of older women who came and made phone calls every afternoon.

"Are you really going to put sugar on *that*?" Dad asked. I poured it on my Quisp.

"He needs to put on weight," Sharon said.

Dad shook his head.

"It's better than cyclamates," Sharon added.

I looked out the window at Sparky lying on the patio. Behind her, behind the pool, beyond a patch of weeds, the pet cemetery, where Lilly rotted now. Her flesh becoming mud. In the dark earth, worms. I looked around the table; this would happen to all of us. After you die, darkness forever, infinity of days when you are not there. Mom Dad Sharon Jason I— unable to talk to each other in the darkness. Our mouths full of earth. We must try now, before it's too late, it is urgent, we *must*, we all know this, but it's something you can't say, and then it's too late. . . . The world was here forever before, it will be here forever after: deserts, mountains, sunny days, cars. But not us. Jason will be the last to go, he may not be able to remember this moment even if he tries, as he circles the earth in a spaceship, in a tin can, in the year 2121, or as he sits in a rocking chair, somewhere in the future, watching some waves against some shore, crashing—this moment will be as distant as a fading star. Right now worms eat Lilly.

Try to be friends with Bruce. Life is short.

Jason asked Dad if the unions were a big problem. "Teamsters gonna break your legs?" he joked, and we laughed. Everyone said Jason had started to come out of his shell during the last year; he'd made friends in Little League and played the piano at school on talent night. He'd said he might want to learn saxophone—his friend Tim played it; Dad said he'd get his old one out of storage. And he'd become friends with Mrs. Sklar, who was also musical. She said he was a very mature young man.

I knew Tim shoplifted. The sun lit my brother from behind. Tim called him Racin' Jason. Dad said, "I don't think the unions have anywhere else to turn." Jason nodded thoughtfully.

———

Bruce came up beside me on the pathway. We passed the cacti with the bright orange flowers; he could tell I was sad. I wasn't sure I wanted to tell him about Lilly. But I did. At first he was sympathetic; in New Jersey his horse had died; he'd cried and cried. But then, as if to assert the equal—or greater—importance of his own life, he added, "You did everything you could. After all, Mark, you do realize she *was* just a mouse."

I *knew* this. He didn't need to tell me. And, I thought, a mouse had consciousness and did not want to die. Only my mother really seems to care. I had hoped, I told myself, that Bruce would understand me—but it's all hopeless. Someday I'll find a friend who will. It just isn't time. I shouldn't indulge in self-pity. Make yourself *inaccessible*, don Juan says: don't hide, just don't let things affect you. I know Bruce can't help being the way he is.

The days passed at Loloma. One morning Cheryl and Heather were caught drinking beer in the wash. We beat the Cholla Bulls. *I am good to people who are good. I am also good to people who are not good. . . . I have faith in people who are faithful. I also have faith in people who are not faithful.* One day Bruce asked if I was going to move if my father won. "You and your Mom could stay here and your Dad could move," he suggested.

Anna told me she and Karl were planning a trip together. They might go to Hawaii or Mexico. She had a friend with a boat.

—

I breathed in and out, I went up and down, my tailbone sore on the bicycle seat. Lilly has *many* incarnations to pass through, I thought, as I went past houses, tan and blue. The Buddhists measure time in aeons. Her next life will be determined by her karma. How retarded. But, *in a way,* it makes sense. Cause and effect, understood deeply: the same. Like a math concept. They're differentiated by *time*—an illusion. Maybe the election's results are already determined. What is reborn, I wondered, pedaling beneath the peeling eucalyptus, if the self is an illusion?

I was out of breath, my mind was out of breath, there was out-of-breathness. *A bundle of attributes* is reborn, I remembered. The attributes seek the appropriate body. Some boys raced past, sleek legs pumping quickly, voices shouting something . . . at me? The voices disappeared in the heat; I noticed a dead bird along the bank of the ditch. I stopped my bike, put the kickstand down, and stood in the sunlight next to a chain-link fence, and looked at the brown water.

—

"You know Mrs. Voigt doesn't like me," Bruce said.

"That's not true," I said, irritably. You always *demand* that I be on your side. But you weren't there for me for Lilly. And I know Anna likes you. It's just you never clean up.

"How do *you* know?" he demanded. "She likes you."

We walked in silence through the white stucco archway; on the grass, in the light, some kids tried cartwheels. "Bruce," I said, thinking of the bodhisattvas and repeating a phrase I'd heard, "I need some personal space."

"Oh, you are just so *sensitive*," he said. "You are just so important."

"Bruce . . ."

"Oh, fuck you!" He stomped away.

———

The next morning, wanting to make up for the day before, I tried to be friendly. Bruce put his arm around me and said it was OK. We sat together at lunch but didn't have too much to say. I soon felt impatient but tried not to show it.

Bruce and I sat together at a table; we were friends; he looked deeply into my eyes, nodding sympathetically. There were mountains but I wasn't sure where we were, the Alps or San Francisco. They're the mountains of Saint Francis, someone explained, not Bruce, but maybe him.

I woke. How good it had felt to be his friend again. It had seemed so real; it was our falling out that felt dreamlike. It had all been a mistake; things *could* go back to the way they'd been: it would be as if he'd been away. I pictured us beneath the mulberry tree; I would tell him all the unreasonable things this new friend of mine had done. How odd, I thought: wanting to talk about Bruce to Bruce.

I got out of bed. From now on I'll try to make everything different; I'll be good. But, I thought, opening my dresser, *he* has to act differently first. I put on my underwear. I'm only being the way I'm being because he's the way he is. I couldn't remember where the dream had taken place, just its white feeling. Why couldn't things be the way they'd been when we'd talked under the mulberry? Sometimes you turned on the TV expecting to see a show but the schedule had been changed and it seemed odd the show was gone. I put on my socks. It was really Bruce's fault.

"So why are you trying to avoid me?" Bruce asked. "Oh, come on, like I don't know!" We sat in science, beneath a mobile of colored Styrofoam planets. "I know you think you're *so* superior," he continued, mocking me.

"Stop it."

"Stop what, Mr. Monk? Mr. Ching-Chow Bow-Wow. Mr. Me So Spiritual. Mr. I'm-the-new-Rod McKuen."

This is really boring. I just want to go home. Where I can work on my poem.

Home. Poem. Home.

"Bruce," I said, "oh, please. Come on."

His black eyes glistened like rocks on the beach, wet from the ocean. *"Oh, come on,"* he said, mincingly.

"Shut up," Schaeffer said, defending me—I wasn't sure why. "Leave him alone."

"Don't mind *him*," said McKnight, his eyes pointing at Bruce. "He's just a big fucking queer."

"He's the one who goes to a *psychiatrist*," Bruce said.

Everyone knows. My life is over. My mouth was dry. I pedaled past the olive trees. O haunted trees, o swirling sky; van Gogh shot himself; I know why. I hate you, Bruce.

This is just the *tonal*.

———

Later that afternoon, as dusk was coming on, I sat with my Strathmore sketch pad on my lap, next to the compost heap. I'd told Anna about the thin, wavering lines I'd seen in the corner of the backyard. "Draw them," she'd said. I was trying to find them again, trying not to think about what had happened.

I heard the patio door open; speaking sort of loudly, my father and Mr. Nachmann stepped outside. Mr. Nachmann saw me and pointed. Then they spoke quietly.

I wish Mr. Nachmann hadn't seen me with my sketch pad. Why had he pointed? What will I say if he asks what I'm drawing? I hadn't put any lines down yet. Because I hadn't *found* them. I shouldn't be concerned with what other people think, I thought, looking for the lines—if I see them, I told myself, I might be beginning, in some way, to *see*. But it's stupid to think *that's* going to happen. Bruce is right. I *am* egotistical. But still, sometimes, I seem so close. No one knows.

I wasn't able to see the lines. Because I hadn't stopped the world. In order to stop the world I had to forget everything I'd been told about what the world was like.

Everything. Dad and Mr. Nachmann went inside.

Maybe the lines I'd seen before were a natural phenomenon. Caused by the heat. Maybe I couldn't find them because it wasn't hot enough. I saw some faint squiggles by the compost.

I picked up my pad but then, hearing the sound of a mourning dove, sad and lovely, I put it down.

The sun, setting behind the olive trees, sent thousands of rays through the grass and dirt and weed-filled yard. The yard was made of rays. I watched the sky turn a darker blue; tree shadows moved toward me. Sparky yelped at a bird. It was all beautiful, sad, and lovely. Don Juan is right, I thought. I live in a most mysterious world and, like everyone else, I'm a most mysterious being, and yet I'm no more important than a beetle.

———

I don't know how I will get through this day, I thought, putting my bike in the rack; I must end my attachment to self. Mrs. Heller waved at me. *Mind-only.* Help me, Buddha. Help, help me, Buddha. Get him out . . . I *HATE* you Bruce. *All is ill, all illusion.* Get rid of the self.

But no one mentioned what Bruce had said about the psychiatrist. Maybe, I thought, no one believes him.

11

Sharon and I stood in front of the tropical-fish store at Tower Mall handing out brochures. "Here you go," we'd say, attempting to sound as excited as possible. Sometimes we tried, "Here's yours." The brochure read: "A family man who will work hard for Arizona. He has positive ideas. He has standards."

Lately Dad had been frustrated with everyone. Mrs. Hanson continued to do things without checking. Mr. Nachmann, who *still* hadn't admitted his mistake about the brochures, criticized Dad for not attacking Scanlon aggressively enough on his morals. Talking about standards was, he said, too vague. Mr. Nachmann had also criticized Dad for canceling several events that Mr. Nachmann had planned. Mom didn't agree about attacking Scanlon, but she *was* worried about the canceled appearances. Dad was spending a lot of time in his study, working on his speeches, practicing Spanish. Sharon had speculated that he wasn't over Nanna's death; he'd never mourned, she said.

"If everyone would just stop telling him what to do," Mom had said, impatiently, that morning. "Go here. Go there. Spend money on this. Spend money on that. I'm sorry," she'd continued, her tone swerving quickly, as if to avoid something in the road—and once her tone had changed it seemed impossible that it had been the way it had just a moment before— "I'm sorry to jump on *you,* Mark. If there's anything you could do to cheer him up. Maybe try to talk to him. I know that would mean a lot."

In the mall, across from us, wearing a sandwich board covered with fetus photographs, Alger Johnson paced back and forth in front of the luggage store. Most people avoided him. I wondered, secretly, for a moment, if he was right; maybe fetuses *were* babies. If it's wrong to kill cows, it also has to be wrong to kill babies. Bruce says Beth Rawley went to California to get an abortion. He says Jeff Cooper got her pregnant. Or maybe, he says, it was Richard. Bruce is full of shit. Thank God he can't follow me to Washington.

There was a rumor Heather might be suspended; she'd been caught drinking again. In third grade she'd written poetry, too, but that was a long time ago. People walked by in the mall. If they didn't know what our brochures were for they might not throw them away; they might take them back to their cars and one of the forty-seven reasons might somehow make something turn in their minds; causality, if you believed in it, was mysterious. If this happened enough times, out in the Tower Mall parking lot, Dad could win.

Everything *might* already be determined. By karma or atoms—either way, why make an effort to change things? But if everything is predetermined, it's already determined whether or not I make an effort. And my thinking about this has been determined. My thoughts *right now* have been. I don't want to think like this.

An old man took a pamphlet, looked at it, dropped it on the floor. *The world is ruled by letting things take their course.* It was good to have low expectations. Should I pick up the brochure? Did I have a choice? Sharon had said that unless Dad could raise more money he didn't have a chance. I'd been frustrated: her bad attitude could affect Dad's attitude. He'll stop trying, I thought. Maybe he already has. And I don't care.

Then I thought of Washington. The white buildings, the pink blossoms, the sumi paintings I would do. It will be so beautiful there. Next year Richard will be in Berkeley. Leslie and Ian will be gone. There's nothing I can do about Bruce. Maybe I should think about switching to Pueblo, the public high school. There won't be much left for me at Loloma without the *Amethyst*.

If I go to Pueblo, I might be lonely. There won't be anyone like Anna. But there'll be other people. A process: learning to overcome *fear*. And, after all, my external environment doesn't matter. I can make do wherever I am. I'll soon be done with "The Year of Dead Birds." My masterpiece! It isn't *quite* there yet, but soon will be. I will transcend. And once the poem comes out I will probably, gradually, start becoming famous. Bullshit, Mark. But still, after the poem is done, it will be time to move on.

Sharon asked if I wanted to take a break. We sat down at Orange Julius.

"You know what I've been thinking?" she asked, her braces glinting.

"What?"

She leaned forward, looking at me intently. "I think the reason Dad got into this was to prove something to Posha. And to Nanna. Now he's afraid he won't be able to. That's why he's having a tough time."

"That's hard," I said, trying to sound knowing. The important people Dad knows, I thought, aren't as important as those Posha knew: Roosevelt, Dag Hammarskjöld, Felix Frankfurter. Behind Sharon, hot dogs turned, beneath glass, on skewers, turned and went round, rotating and orbiting like long planets. And the people Nanna had known: Bruno Bettelheim and McGovern. Posha was going to publish her diaries. He'd sent us the manuscript and I'd begun to read it. In the early ones, she'd written about how clever Dad had been as a teenager, how he'd cheated at cards, making everybody laugh. The night he went to his first dance. He'd taken a girl from Dalton. And, when he was little, how he'd looked in his sailor suit. He'd made friends with their doorman, who took him to cartoons at the Trans-Lux. It had been weird to read about this; was he, now, the same person? He'd told Nanna lots of stories about the doorman; some of them, she knew, he'd just made up. He loved to play with his Lionel trains, when he could—he'd had asthma. He had to have adrenalin shots; they kept a steam kettle by the bed. At night Nanna would come to fill it. Or, when she was out, the German governess would.

We all want our lives to be as interesting as Nanna's and Posha's, I thought. They won't be. We have so many advantages but we'll never be like them. Everything about us is just *less*. Nanna was friends with McGovern, Mom and Dad are friends with the Nachmanns, I'm stuck with Douggy Dale: downhill all the way.

I sipped my Orange Julius in the mall light. Some teenagers came and sat behind us and started making jokes about the hot dogs. I hoped they wouldn't see our brochures. I turned my head very slightly to look at them, not far enough so they could tell; they'll think I'm watching people passing in the mall.

"We should get going," Sharon said.

I slurped thoughtfully. We threw our cups in the overflowing trash. Orange Julius Rosenberg. Sharon stopped to give a brochure to the teenagers; I hurried on ahead. The purses and scarves in the windows and the lights from the stores squiggled on the mall's floor: reflections of colored sails on a gray lake. The election's outcome could be determined by invisible forces which have nothing to do with this tonal, illusory world.

In the parking lot, the surging light. Swirling, ecstatic. Textures of dry air.

———

Later I listened, in my room, to Jethro Tull. When the album was over I read the newest section of "The Year of Dead Birds":

XXI (air)

Above the carport; a swirling.
Voices lead to the hedge. Where, now, the magician?
Past the cobwebbed garbage cans, I notice a dead bird.
     Webs everywhere!
          Too familiar, this gray air I swallow.
(waving at the postman passing by).
               Now I barely hear the voices in the hedges.
I put my ear on the gravel. There's laughter;
                    it's a dark maze.
Mirrors, small drops of bloodlight on the leaves.
          They come from the always changing air
     where Ethiopian horses galloping, through the trembling
maze, turn into horned creatures.

(I am not the only mutant)

The sky, a laboratory.
But whose? Who are they, these creatures?
The essence of leaves.

It's not working, I told myself. I *still* haven't brought together the concept of the mind as an endless series of mirrors and the idea of consciousness as a maze leading in on itself. And I want to get in the image of looking at myself in the dressing room at Norwich's. But where? Anna's probably going to think *blood-light* is too dramatic. Go deeper, I told myself, but felt tired. I put the poem back in the manila folder I'd taken from Dad's study, on which I'd crossed out *Rotarians: Speech on Infla-tion/Second Draft* and written: *The Year of Dead Birds.*

———

From Anna's office, I borrowed *Labyrinths,* a New Directions paperback. At home I read one of the essays, "A New Refuta-tion of Time":

Chuang Tzu dreamt that he was a butterfly and during that dream he was not Chuang Tzu, but a butterfly. . . . In China the dream of Chuang Tzu is proverbial; let us imagine that of its almost infinite readers, one dreams that he is a butterfly and then dreams that he is Chuang Tzu. Let us imagine that, by a not impossible stroke of chance, this dream reproduces point for point the master's. Once this identity is postulated, it is fitting to ask: Are not these moments which coincide one and the same?

If all that exists is mind, there are nothing but moments of perception. If two moments are the same, it doesn't matter that one took place thousands of years ago. If I imagine myself to be in another place, if I feel and see the same things I felt then, am I not there? Lilly's cage lay empty. I don't see any faults in the argument. There's really no such thing as time.

———

Mom seemed less worried about Dad. We drove, one evening, to Rosita's Mexican Restaurant; Dad said we should go there because the owner was a big supporter of the Democrats. The waiter wore a sombrero. I ordered the chile relleno platter. Jason took a long time deciding what to have. I watched him, wondering whether his decision was already determined.

"Stand not upon the order of ordering," Dad joked, "but order." Jason finally did, and I tried to picture the chain of events that had led to chimichangas. Maybe someone had said something during school. Or in a past life . . .

"Look who's here," Mom said quietly. I turned toward the back of the room. The McCarthys sat at a table in the corner.

It was odd that the McCarthys had been to our house, swum in our pool. Their sons had jumped from our diving board. I could remember, dimly, further back, playing in their sandbox. There was a clambake, once, at their house. I wondered how they talked about us.

Each family was a universe. One universe assumed the other universes were the same but there wasn't really any way to know. White lights grouped together in the dark—they only looked similar from far away.

Mr. McCarthy came over to our table.

"How're you doing, Jack?" Dad asked politely, getting up.

"Taking a night off from the trail?" Mr. McCarthy replied. Dad introduced us as if we hadn't met. We nodded. They spoke in friendly tones; they laughed. Mr. McCarthy went back to his table. Mom changed her drink order from an iced tea to a margarita.

—

I walked to Anna's room and found her there alone.

"You weren't at that talk," I said. There had been an optional assembly. The speaker, an assistant to Paolo Soleri, was trying to recruit volunteers.

Anna shook her head. "Oh, no, I couldn't."

"It was interesting," I said, a little uncertainly. "The models were cool."

"Well," Anna said.

I looked at her expectantly.

"Come with me," she said. "Walk with me to the parking lot."

Students waved to Anna while I described the domes and arcs that would one day house a hundred thousand people, including many artists and craftsmen, somewhere north of Cordes Junction.

Anna said, "I'll tell you something I wouldn't tell everyone." Her expression was unusually serious. We'd come to the parking lot; my social studies book and *Tales of Power* were tucked under my arm.

I looked at her, wondering. We reached the truck, with its bumper sticker: "Think Trout." She opened the door; I climbed in.

"You know they'll never be able to build up there," she said casually.

I looked at her. "The land is cursed. Abbott told me. All the Hopis know it. They just never talked to them."

I tried to gather the courage to bring up the topic that had been, for weeks, on my mind. But I didn't need to. "How are you liking that?" Anna asked, touching my copy of *Tales of Power*.

"I don't know," I said. Outside the window Mr. Ramsay, getting into his Buick, waved. "It sort of makes me skeptical," I said.

Anna's face was a question. I continued. "I just thought after *Journey to Ixtlan*—after you have a vision like that—I don't know, I guess it's weird he would write another book."

I fingered the ceramic fragments that lay on the shadowed depression of Anna's dashboard. "I didn't think about that," she said. The light came out from behind a cloud and passed through the truck's dusty window, illuminating Anna's long hair like the light on the grass on the rolling hills just north of the cursed junction.

"I guess that never bothered me," she continued. "But then you're more left-brain than I am."

She meant, I thought, to compliment me by saying I was analytical. But I just felt different. Exiled. I wanted to discuss how I felt about the campaign but decided against it; Anna was beyond that sort of thing. I touched the seat belt twice as Dan Baltz walked past, his arm around Heather Morel. He knocked on the truck. Anna smiled and waved. My eyes followed Dan as he disappeared down the hill toward the dead-grass field.

"Well I guess I'll get over it," I said. I wanted to believe in *Tales of Power,* to please Anna, but wasn't sure I could.

"I think you will," she said. I smiled in agreement. "I have something else I want to tell you," she continued. I thought she had already revealed her secret. The darkness had passed from her face. "Karl and I have decided to split up."

I didn't know what to say. I was surprised, but then it seemed I had known this would happen. I don't care, I thought, what happens with Anna and Karl. As long as she doesn't move.

"I'm sorry." How inadequate.

"It's all right. It wouldn't have been good to continue. It was always really *his* trip, you know." She shook her cigarette ash outside the truck window.

"When did you decide?"

"That girl had been calling and hanging up."

"The life-drawing model?"

"Yes. I didn't tell you. I wasn't sure it was her at first. Then my Dad was over one day and picked up the phone. She started talking, she thought he was Karl. He'd promised it was over. It wasn't my decision."

"You saw this on its way," I said, remembering her poem.

"That's right," she said. "You knew." She tousled my hair. "You are . . . I've never met anyone like you. You're exceptional. Those guys, Richard and Ian, you know how blown away they were by you? Someday you're going to do amazing things, Mark. I shouldn't say that. . . . Give me a hug. You won't ever forget your old teacher, will you?"

Glorious, embarrassed, ashamed, loved, I reached across the front seat; she hugged me. Crows flew past the power lines. The parking lot was full of light.

12

Alhambra. Cottonwood. Maryvale.

The names, I thought, had a kind of music. I wasn't disappointed that Alhambra was like every other precinct, with its palm trees and barbed wire. Walking the cracked sidewalks, *Alhambra* kept recurring in my head, making it *feel* different. Sharon was with me; Mrs. Sklar had dropped us off near the Dairy Queen. Sharon took one side of the street, I took the other. We walked up the cement paths past the shrubs and mailboxes to the houses. I hoped, when I rang the doorbells, no one my age would answer. There would be silence, or shuffling, or sometimes a shout: "Who is it?" Sometimes an older woman would invite me in for a glass of water or a coke; I'd politely decline. I was relieved when no one was home. I skipped the houses where the pickup trucks had "America: Love it or Leave it" stickers. On the sidewalk, I avoided the cracks in the cement. It's stupid, I thought, to think they're bad luck. But once the idea had occurred I couldn't dismiss it. It isn't *inconceivable,* I thought, that the way I walk matters; if the world is consciousness-only, and that thought is in consciousness, then . . . step on a crack, break your mother's . . .

I *tried* to take three steps on each section of sidewalk. Sometimes the last step had to be quite small in order not to cross into the next section. Sometimes I made the *first* step very small so the last wouldn't have to be. Once I became aware of this pattern, I couldn't *not* be aware of it. I wasn't sure if five steps would be OK. Three, then three, then five, then five, then three: a poetic form. Some sections of "The Year of Dead Birds" had a formal structure. There was a rhythm to the way the formal parts interacted with the free

verse; I'd had to feel my way into it. A journey in consciousness takes great discipline, I told myself. Without it the poem
won't come to you. You'll just continue living in this dumb,
illusory world. Only the artist achieves wholeness. Anna
knows this.

A white van passed. People say living is an art. Life is in the
mind, I thought. Your mind should be art—rhythms and
beautiful patterns.

A plastic ball lay on a lawn. Even with my sunglasses, I
scrunched my face against the light. Everything was quiet. It
was hot and I was running low on brochures. When no one
was home I stuck the brochure beneath the doormat and continued down the sidewalk. Sharon's side of the street had
more shade: gray-green trees, blue-green trees. People
changed; you couldn't see it happening. It happened somewhere else, somewhere invisible. What did this afternoon look
like to her? Did the trees have the same colors? Clearer?
Fuzzier? What was in her reality? How did she mumble to
herself? What song bits kept repeating? Weird that not
knowing this was something you lived with, always. I looked
at Sharon walking down the sidewalk, lost in her whatever,
different from my whatever. I didn't know what questions I
could ask to find out about this, just as she would never know
what the right questions would be to ask me. We were
together all the time; still, we didn't know.

I'd tried to write about Sharon in "The Year of Dead
Birds." I hadn't used her name; I'd called her Ophelia; I'd
described her moods and her frizzy hair. But it hadn't worked.
It was still just her from the outside.

The outsides of houses—white and pink and gray. Some
parts of the poem, like the Osiris section, were entirely in

iambic pentameter. Iambic pentameter was difficult, but so was free verse. Behind a wire fence, a dog barked at me. I began to make a sentence about the dog. Beneath the empty sky, a dog . . . Once I start to make the sentence, I thought, once I use the word *dog,* I'm not seeing the real dog anymore. The word *dog* stands between me and that which is barking. The word *barking* stands between me and what I hear. What I hear in the dry hot air. I looked back for a moment at the dog. Once I name it, once I use a symbol, my mind only sees the symbol. Symbols have their beauty. But one has to learn to see without them. That which is barking. That which is . . .

I now know the meaning of "The Year of Dead Birds." At last, the real meaning. I have to remember it.

A car passed. The sun showered down; an old man mowed a lawn. A VW Bug was parked on the parched grass. I clutched the meaning; a young woman answering her doorbell asked if I wanted a toke.

"No, thank you, but . . ."

She laughed, slamming the screen door.

A swing precinct. I felt nervous and powerful; I wanted to get home.

Shrubs shimmered; crows crossed the vast Alhambra sky.

———

"What do I do," the monk asked, "if I meet the Buddha on the road?"

"Kill him," the master replied.

———

The phone was for me; I made my way down the hall to my parents' room. Anna asked how I was. I began to tell her about "The Year of Dead Birds," how I was reconciling the mirror symbolism and the stuff about the maze and working *some* of the tarot imagery back in. I wasn't sure how this sounded—I wanted to tell her my new understanding of the poem: how it was about going *beyond* words. But would she want me to? Maybe it's better not to talk about this. It should stay in the dark; in silence. *The Tao that can be named* . . . I shifted my position on the bed. "I think I understand where it's all heading now," I tried, hoping this sounded modest and humorous. "I *think*."

"Oh, I *know*," she said.

I continued, uncertain of my direction, wanting more praise—and fearing it. "I have this new feeling about words. Like they're glowing, like in this whole new way. You know, the words are things. It's weird."

All wrong: *like; you know*. I knew what Posha would say.

"I hope you'll read some of it at the next meeting," she said. "I can tell: you've arrived at an important place."

"Hmm. Maybe I'll read it," I answered coyly, doodling on the pad by the phone. There are things, I thought, I never share with Anna. What it's like in our house: the shadows, the force fields, the stuff that isn't ever said, or isn't *really*, the feelings that never go away. And the way we're always so conscious of each other, of how we're *relating to each other*, the way we're always thinking about what the other person is thinking or feeling, the million thoughts in the room at any moment, I thought, laying on the bed; the way everything we do or say sort of floats on top of this *awful, unending, consciousness.* Everything that's actually said is unimportant when we know

there's this *sea of awareness* beneath it, this light- and snake-
filled sea. Sometimes I have to go to my room to keep from
drowning in everyone's consciousness of everyone's consciousness. I don't know if it's always been like this; I don't know if
it's like this *now,* I thought, for Sharon and Jason and Mom and
Dad. Maybe it's just me.

Perhaps the whole world's like this. Perhaps not. I don't
know how I could ever describe this to Anna, Whatever I say
will sound left-brained.

"What's going on with you?" I asked.

Anna told me she wasn't writing any long poems but was
reading one: "A" by Zukofsky. He'd begun it in the twenties;
he was still working on it. "I hope yours isn't going to be that
long," she said.

"Don't worry."

"I would have had to spend the rest of my life reading it,"
she joked.

"Is Zukofsky ever going to get to 'B'?" I joked back.

Anna said she didn't think so. The lights were dimmed. On
the dresser, ashtrays and campaign pamphlets and photographs
of my parents, grandparents, Jason, Sharon, me. Mom thinks
we can know each other through pictures. A sad lie—her anxious, warmly lit dream. But other families: Bruce's stepfather,
the belt. Maybe her idea of closeness is a dream, but a dream
that makes itself true. Maybe we need the pictures. Without
them, the void, the dark atom-wind coming from the desert.

There's nothing wrong, I thought, with the photographs.
While Anna told me about John Cage I looked at a picture of
myself. Three years ago on the farm. Who am I becoming?

I could hear the house sounds. Near me, on the floor,
Dad's shoe-shining machine with its two fluffy, bullet-shaped

ends. Mom's bathrobe, draped on her Aunt Sylvia's rocking chair. The moon shone through the curtains. I lay curled on the bed, in my shorts and "Hang Ten" T-shirt, listening to Anna. Cage, she said, based his compositions on the *I Ching*.

No one understands how different from my family I've become. The author of "The Year of Dead Birds." I looked at Nanna's picture. I've made the right choices, I thought. My family looked at me from the dresser. I think I'm better than other people, when in reality I'm someone who only thinks about himself. Nanna, Posha, and Dad: they made the world better. They did things for other people. The farmworkers. I wish I could be as I was in the photograph—innocent—but I can't, and it's my fault.

Palm fronds blew against the window.

Oh, just be.

Anna was talking about the Black Mountain School. I've heard this before, I thought. Still, I tried to pay attention. The poets and artists had worked together. They'd farmed the land and done spontaneous drawings. But they weren't good businessmen so the school went broke. Next to the wastebasket, by the dresser, the white cardboard sheets that came with Dad's new shirts. He used to give them to me to crayon on when I was sick and had to stay in bed. In one of the pictures, taken when he was a boy, Dad lay with the covers pulled up, making a funny face. It was, I guessed, when he'd had asthma. Nanna had worried so much about him then. What had happened to that love? Where was it now? Had it gone out somewhere into the deep blue night? He'd been in bed for a month. He'd written stories. Nanna would stay up all night, sitting with him while he gasped for breath. Posha was afraid she was pampering him. They fought over this. Doors slammed; Posha shouted at both of them.

Posha hired a student from Columbia. He went with Dad to Central Park where they would throw a ball.

"They weren't too strong on discipline," Anna said. "A lot of the teachers were refugees from Germany. So they'd seen where *that* led. Oh, listen to me," Anna said, "dominating the conversation again. We've hardly talked about you."

"No, no," I said, "you're not dominating." Weird, I thought, how she'd gone on about the Black Mountain School, about the *I Ching,* about her dreams, how she'd sort of rambled; weird, also, I thought, guiltily, how she was always on the verge of something. Each time *this* seemed to be it—as if she didn't remember the other verges. And it was odd that she hadn't mentioned Karl. I wasn't sure if *I* should. I thought quickly. "How's Nicola?"

"She's moving out," Anna said.

"Why?" I inquired, surprised.

"She said I was a witch."

"But you are a witch," I joked uncertainly. "She should have known *that.*"

"No, no, she meant I was a bad witch."

My father said he needed to use the phone.

My room was quiet. I read *Tales of Power.*

"I've been trying to live in accordance with your suggestions," I said. "I may not be the best, but I'm the best of myself."

"You must push yourself beyond your limits, all the time."

"But that would be insane, don Juan . . ."

"There are lots of things that you do now which would have seemed insane to you ten years ago. . . . Your total success in

changing yourself is only a matter of time. You know enough of the warrior's way to act accordingly, but your old habits and routines stand in your way."

"Do you think that writing is one of the old habits I should change?" I asked. "Should I destroy my new manuscript?"

He did not answer. He stood up and turned to look at the edge of the chaparral.

I should destroy "The Year of Dead Birds." But I'm too weak. Maybe my Castaneda doubts are just part of my attachment to my self, the self that has written "The Year of Dead Birds." I don't need to destroy the poem. The poem is only an *object*. The real goal is to gradually get rid of the self. A process. I read on.

"You had an appointment with knowledge," he said, pointing with a movement of his chin to the dark edge of the desert chaparral. "I took you there because I caught a glimpse of knowledge prowling around the house earlier. You might say that knowledge knew that you were coming and was waiting for you."

I put the book down and listened. I can't hear knowledge, I thought, just the air conditioner. But then I heard another sound. I got up and went out the backdoor. Sparky was asleep; she got up and licked my leg. The clouds and the stars reflected in the pool.

A hose broke the surface; birds sang in the warm darkness. Then silence. Sparky walked over toward the garbage cans; I followed, sensing she sensed something. I heard a noise and looked through the gate. A figure in a hood. The irrigation man. He turned the water on and walked to the next house. Water slowly flowed into the yard. I laughed silently. A joke, a Zen joke. Still, it was a sign. The birds sang again; the yard began to turn into a marsh and I felt full of power. It was clear, in the darkness, I would learn to *see*. Once I did, I wondered, how would I look back on this place? As if I were looking across time, I looked across the yard at the house where my family slept. Everything that bothers me will soon be unimportant. All my suffering *will* soon end. The suffering that came because I had to be with boys. The suffering that came (I thought for a second) because they made me *be* a boy. When that was so unnecessary. All my trials. Will soon be over. The humiliation, the sadness. Nanna had started me on a path, or I'd been on that path, without knowing it, even before I wrote the kumquat poem that night at the Desert Palm. And then Anna. My guide. My *ally*. Perhaps now I'll move beyond her. Or we'll move beyond together. Finishing "The Year of Dead Birds" will take me beyond language.

What will that place be like? Will emptiness be blissful? I felt ready to burst. *Katmandu,* Cat Stevens sang, *I'll soon be seeing you.* I don't know *where*, but I'll move on—it may be soon, it may not be for a while—but that's OK, too. Sparky's plastic bone began to float on the water. I love my family. I'll miss them; I'll miss everything when I'm gone: the barbecue, the pool, the clothesline. I'll probably miss weeding and shoveling manure, I thought, as I went back in through the kitchen door and walked to my room. I wanted to look at a passage I remembered from *Journey to Ixtlan*.

———

"The thing is," Dad said, "to time it right. Then you hit all the lights without having to stop." He was on his way to speak at the community college. He talked about the money they'd raised the night before at a party McGrath had thrown. Mr. Goldman had shown up unexpectedly; he'd written a big check. Mom had been polite to him. They'd raised more money than Dad had expected. "I really think there may be some momentum now."

No, there isn't, I thought.

"The Democrats' problem has always been they don't vote. If we can turn that around in some of those South Phoenix precincts. Two years ago it wasn't even fifty percent. Rouse says . . . "

Blahblurblah. I've heard all this. Numbers. I'm not interested and I won't pay attention. The cars were spots of moving light, the Granada Apartments were light—the asphalt, the edges of the trees; the world, made of different areas of barely distinguishable light, quivered. Through the delta of the sun's rays, I saw the Frontier Bank's glittering fountain—and a hitchhiker.

"It's too bad, Mark, what's happened to this country." The anti-hitching speech. "It didn't used to be so dangerous," he continued. When he'd gone across the country with Dick Epstein. They'd started out hitchhiking. Down the eastern seaboard. I'm bored, I thought. Knives of light. They'd met all kinds of characters. In Florida they bought an ancient Ford.

"A real clunker," he said. "It kept breaking down." One night he and Dick slept in a field. The sky was filled with a million stars. In the morning they'd woken to a plane taking off over their heads. "Dick was always getting us into scrapes like that," he laughed softly.

"There was this bar outside Tampa . . ."

I tried to picture my father, in a Tampa bar, hitchhiking, sleeping in a field. I should think of something to ask, I told myself.

"He was arguing with these rednecks. We almost got arrested. *That's* an experience I'm glad I never had. Spending a night in a southern jail."

"What made you decide to go on that trip?" My question felt formal and a moment late.

"I wanted to see the country. I'd grown up so sheltered. After the army I didn't know *what* I wanted to do. I didn't feel like going to college. I didn't want to just follow in Posha's footsteps. He thought I didn't have direction. He always thought he knew what I should do. Boy, I sure resented that. I never really knew how to deal with him until I met your mother. I sure hope you'll be able to find a woman like her." His voice grew quiet. "You know Mark, I've sometimes put myself first a bit too much. I probably don't always let her know enough how much I appreciate her."

The sun lowered; shadows lengthened. We pulled into Dr. Kurtz's parking lot.

My final session. Had he ever helped me? I wondered. Maybe, in some hidden, unnameable way. Birds chirped. *Mind-only.* Dr. Kurtz told me I could come back anytime I needed. And sometime, in the future, I should drop him a line, let him know what I was up to. He liked me; I was an interesting young man. He was proud. He wanted to know how things turned out.

Sitting in the reception area waiting for my mother, leafing through magazines I would, I told myself, no longer get to read, I felt nostalgic for Dr. Kurtz. I've said farewell, I thought, wondering if I would see a psychiatrist in Washington. How different that office would be. I saw my mother through the glass doors. We walked quietly down the driveway to the car. There were copper clouds behind the phone poles.

At home I looked at the passage I'd read the night before:

"In order to be a sorcerer a man must be passionate. A passionate man has earthly belongings and things dear to him. . . . Genaro left his passion in Ixtlan: his home, his people, all the things he cared for. And now he wanders around in his feelings; and sometimes, as he says, he almost reaches Ixtlan."

I was ready to sleep; I put the book down.

V
IXTLAN

1

I rode my bike home from school. "The Year of Dead Birds" was now thirty pages long! The images were *almost* resolved: the magician, the leafy tunnel, the mirrors, the willow tree. And the voice that spoke in the canyon. I still needed to work on the "Passages" section. I was getting ready to send a draft to Posha. He probably won't understand it, I thought, but that's OK. A mockingbird chirped in the blazing air. Beautiful. It's wonderful and painful to feel so much beauty, I thought, riding past the eucalyptus trees. Ecstatic; I'm bursting, I can't wait to finish the poem.

When I got home, Mom said, "I've got to ask you a favor. Remember Connie's sister?"

I nodded; I knew Connie had a sister.

"She was in an accident."

"Oh, no. Is she OK?"

"I think she'll be all right," Mom said distractedly. "But her boys are here. Connie has to take care of them until she's better. I think they're pretty bored. It would be nice if you could play with them. They're outside. I don't know why—it's so hot. But they didn't want to watch TV."

"OK," I said, "that's fine." I looked out the kitchen window. The boys, a few years younger than me, sat on the concrete doing nothing. Why did I have to be with them? Would their Mom die? Unreal: she could be dying while they sat in the sunlit yard.

"I'll go out in a minute," I said, and walked to the back of the house. I'll work on the poem later, I thought. I'll just have to remember the way the images connect. How can I even be thinking about my poem now, while their mother . . . I went into Jason's room and found his Hot Wheels. I went out the backdoor, with the Hot Wheels. I'll get through this; I'll be a bodhisattva. They don't want to be here any more than I. Do they live in South Phoenix? What do they think of our pool?

I wondered if I should bring out some other toys. What does Mom mean, I asked myself, when she says "play" with them? What's "playing"? Does she *assume* kids automatically know how to "play" with each other? Does she think *I* know?

"Hi. I'm Mark," I said, politely.

"I'm Greg."

"I'm Tom."

"I'm sorry about your Mom."

"That's OK."

I didn't know if I should ask more. I couldn't tell if they were upset. How easily an accident could happen; to me, to Mom, it was just luck . . . or was it? Maybe I'm watched over.

"I've got some stuff. If you want to play with it we could. Or we could do something else if you want." How prepared the words sounded. Was this how Mom thought you talked if you were a kid? But I couldn't be angry with her. What if she were in an accident? What if . . .

"These are OK."

I wasn't sure if Tom or Greg had spoken. I could see, through one window, my mother in the kitchen, and, through the other, Connie, in the dining room, polishing silver. Would they ask, "Why does our aunt work for your mom?" I wished I could pretend I was just visiting, too. I wished I could go into my room and work on "The Year of Dead Birds."

Nanna's poem about the Scottsboro Boys . . . If we're so liberal, why doesn't Mom come out on the patio and play with Connie? I'm full of shit, it's so hot, I am whoever I am in their eyes. A hypocrite like Mom and Dad.

"This is the Jaguar," I said, in my Jason-Baltz voice. "It's cool and it goes *real* fast."

"That's the Cougar, not the Jaguar," one of them responded, calmly.

But I was sure it was the Jaguar. Jason had said so.

"This one's the Jaguar," the other said.

"That's the Mustang," his brother said.

"Cougar beats the Mustang." They started racing the cars, off the patio, onto the grass.

Weird to sit on the concrete watching them a few feet away. I tried to think about other stuff. In a month school would end. Then, next fall, I would join Sharon at Pueblo. Mom had wondered whether I really wanted to do this; after all, we might move soon. But I knew it was what I had to do. I could always talk to Anna on the phone. I was ready for new things.

They don't want to be with me. Weird that their bodies are there and mine is here. I want to go inside but I don't know what I'd say to Mom. Why is my neck so tight? I don't know where to be. Sit in a different place? Will the energy be different a few feet over here, a few feet over there? There is no place of power; all places: the same.

It was almost one hundred degrees. Nothing, I thought, is going to happen. I began to swallow. I swallowed three times. Then I felt better. I looked at my mother in the kitchen's shadows. I got up, thinking maybe I should go sit next to them on the grass. I stood for a moment, awkwardly, and then sat down a little closer to the flower bed and looked at the white patio. I should be able to transcend my surroundings by using my mind. I focused on the patio. After a while I began to sense the energy in the concrete. The patio grew vibrant; and then, for a while, the fibers in my body felt connected to the fibers in the air. I am a conduit, I thought; I am in the transmission mode. I can feel the textures of the atmosphere. The citrus leaves shone.

I looked at the boys beyond the hedge. Younger than me. Bigger muscles. Sparky slept—too hot to go after birds. My neck began to twitch; I jerked my head back slightly, to the left. I hope they don't see me doing this. I can control it; I can be calm. I swallowed three times and was calmer. I started to be aware of the movements of my body and of deciding about each movement; aware of deciding when to breathe, when not to. To not move a muscle was a decision, too.

I looked at the ranunculus and zinnias in the flower bed. The whole universe is in your backyard. Ginsberg and Kerouac went down to the river; they saw a sunflower, a gray sunflower. Allen had a vision; when did the flower forget it was a flower? Have Mom's zinnias forgotten? Lights and shadows shifted in the hedge. I tried to remember how the images connected in my poem; if only, I thought, I could *see*. But my world is still upheld by reason. I stared at some squiggly lines in the shadows beneath the hedge. There were lines, there was something else—I didn't know what. Flies buzzed. I followed their movements; maybe they weren't *just* flies. Perhaps the hopelessness I'd been feeling: the darkness before the dawn. I concentrated on the place where the hedge's shadow and mine overlapped, noticing all the different colors and movements. I felt a slight, strange sensation on my skin. I could still hear Connie's nephews on the other side of the hedge, along with the buzzing flies, but both sounds slowly began to grow more distant.

I have left the *tonal*. I'm no longer attached to it. These thoughts still felt like part of the tonal. I let them go; they went. I am powerful, calm: an ocean. Perhaps this is what it's like. I've waited for this so long; now it's happening. I have emptied my self; I am learning to *not-do*. Maybe I'm beginning to *see*.

Then that feeling went away; the tension returned; the twitch. Stop twitching, I told myself, not quite sure what was happening. Control it. Don't be so tense. That thought starts to twitch. Thinking about the twitch is a twitch. Thinking about the twitch is a twitch.

A gust of calm; I'll be OK. I looked again at the hedge and wondered if I'd been on the edge of seeing. Could I use this experience in my poem? I shouldn't make art out of everything; that stood in the way of seeing. I looked at the boys, past the hedge-edge, playing with the cars. I thought about the images in my poem. If I use enough *will* I can be in the places I imagine. My grandmother's farm, her stone house. Since there is consciousness only, if I feel I am somewhere, I *am* there, in the way that matters—in my mind. In a way this is more real than actually being there. You feel things more purely later, more intensely.

The dream of the butterfly.

I shut my eyes, imagining the mountain at camp. I was there: needles brushed my face, I felt the power in the dark woods; branches like boys' limbs. I touched the Queen Anne's lace.

But I'm not there. I'm on the patio. Calm fades; I've left no-mind and gone back to mind. I have to return to *I*-lessness, the blank mirror, the pure land of consciousness, of poetry, of vision.

I have to return.

I tried to remember the images I had used to get there. Nanna's stone house. The mountain at camp. The Gunderson Ranch.

The boys played behind the hedge.

Yes, I am calm and at peace and empty and there is no *I* and there is power and light and I see the lines; I'm a conduit. In the brightness things blur and dissolve.

How good to be calmly aware of the movements and lines in the shadows in the flower bed and in the hedge.

But now I am not calm, I'm not clear, maybe I still am, but I can feel the shadow. Returning?

There is no mirror, no *I* to be tense, only consciousness; all the rest is illusion. One must have the will to *see* this.

It's not a question of *my* having the will since it isn't mine anyway. Try again: Nanna's stone house. The mountain. The Gunderson Ranch. The images are fainter now; I don't know why. Am I in the light too much? Still, it works. I am there, for a second. Calm, no-mind.

The boys played with the cars on the grass in the light, beyond the zinnias.

Calmness, no-mind; lines in the hedges; fluorescent fibers; white lines in the patio. Yes, I have done it, it is complete. I've had a vision; sort of. *I'm sick of all this shit.* No, I am calm; stay calm. There's the shadow again; don't look at it. If I don't look at the shadow it's not there—it's only something in consciousness anyway, I *make* it. Maya, illusion.

So don't fucking look at it. Don't think it.

But I think it. Or it is thought. The tension is returning, worse this time. I don't know why this is happening, or if I have the will to stop it. Is my will out there somewhere in the brightness? I swallowed three times, trying to calm myself. I jerked my neck, three times. But that isn't enough any longer, I thought. I'm way beyond that. My twitches have to be abstract. I have to do them in my mind. Something merciless grasped my spine and traveled from my body to my head. Where, unwatched, there was infinite space to bloom.

I am going down a slide and can't stop. I am the slide; I feel the cold metal surface. Whoosh—no control. Light glints on metal. Going down, again and again . . . thrilling in a way. Nanna's stone house, covered with ivy. Yes, got it; check that one off. The mountain, Yes, got it, check. The Gunderson Ranch; check; maybe not check. Calm for a second, then gone. And the other thing is back. The tension before was only a shadow of *this.* Nanna's stone house, the mountain, the Gunderson ranch. That's it. But is it? The words are emptier and emptier; the calm isn't real. Use the will, make it real. Consciousness, illusion, can suddenly crack—as in Zen! It's so bright. I don't know what's happening. I have to do it again. Nanna's stone house. The ranch. The mountain. Oh, I have done it wrong. I have to do it again.

I *should* be able to control myself, to stop. But where is the *I* who will stop it? I look inside for the *I;* it isn't there. I keep looking but only find gray shadows. No little man inside; no *I* at the wheel. Thought-gusts. Who controls the controller?

I have to do it again, I thought. Will this continue? Can I stop *it*? I can't feel anything. If I could feel something, then I could stop.

Feel something.

But instead of feelings there are numbers, like birds. Their flight makes a gray film.

I had stopped the world. Or *I* had stopped. I saw the house and the trees and the boys beyond the hedge, beyond the zinnias, and the sky; but there was something between me and these things. A gray, enclosing film.

Will this be what it's like from now on? I wondered. Maybe *it* would go on for a few more minutes, or the rest of the afternoon, but I would be OK the next day.

My mother's voice: "You boys must be getting hot. Do you want to come in and have some lemonade?" I wasn't able to respond; I had to first finish the series of image-thoughts. I didn't want Mom to know what was happening; I had to be OK before I went inside. But I couldn't just keep sitting there. After a few minutes I got up.

———

I hoped the next morning *it* would be gone, but it wasn't. I thought maybe *it* would last for a few days and then pass. But it didn't. Life went on; I did things; I went to school. I talked, but less. Sometimes I went with Dad to campaign events. I clowned around with Jason when, one afternoon in early May,

Rouse filmed us, in the backyard, talking about Dad for the commercial. Which was costing more than expected.

A few weeks passed. We had the final meeting of the *Amethyst*.

"When I heard, I thought, 'I'm on that list,'" Anna said, leaning back against her couch. Three teachers had been laid off, including Mr. Lewis. Mrs. Heller had wanted to fire more, but some of the parents, including my father, had intervened, and Anna's job had been saved. "Criminal," Dad had commented, "firing teachers so she can build her Aqua-center." It had all happened so quickly no one could quite believe it.

"I'm glad I'm getting out of that place," Richard said.

"It's turning into a prison," Anna commented. "Frank said he was almost glad he was fired." We sat on the floor in Anna's living room. She had made a ceramic mosaic and divided it into pieces; we each got one. When we were reunited, someday in the future, we would put them together.

I petted Basho. Animals, I thought, can see through you; animals know. Anna talked about the book Don had given her on the kabbalah. She had never known much about Judaism, but now she was studying its magical tradition. She had started work again on the book about her father. Jack Osborne had suggested she send part of it to Duncan; she had, and he'd written back with suggestions. It might take a long time to finish but she wasn't concerned.

Richard said he was considering not writing anymore. He needed more life experience: George Oppen had been silent for many years. Maybe, I thought, Richard is right. Maybe I should give up poetry until more things have happened to me. Is it wrong, I wondered, to want to continue writing? I hadn't been able to for the last few weeks, but whenever *this* stopped I'd maybe start again. If *this* ever stopped. If I didn't write, what would I do? Who would I be? Richard said he wanted to do construction work over the summer. I tried to picture myself, in the heat, doing construction. It was weird, I thought, to want to have a life just so you could write about it. Wouldn't that be a false life? Couldn't you just write?

The Gunderson Ranch. The creosote.

Ian was planning to spend a few weeks in LA; he wasn't sure what would happen after that. Leslie was going to live on a commune in Bisbee. She read some short poems; Richard and Ian read longer ones; I didn't hear what they read. I wanted to calm myself. I'd brought "The Year of Dead Birds."

"Mark," Anna said, "you're just sitting there with that manila envelope."

"Oh, I don't know."

"Don't be a tease," Anna said, smiling. "Read."

> *Then the magician asks:*
> *What is left*
> *When the symbols drop? Falling like autumn leaves?*
> *What lies underneath?*
> *The lies are gone, perhaps.*

> *The beast's voice echoes*
> *In the canyon.*

When I finished, Richard said, hesitantly, "It's cool. Like it *sounds* cool. But I don't get what it means."

The aspen trees at Vail, the chalet light; the hotel ballroom in Casa Grande and the patterns on the carpet; the feeling of talking with Sharon in the kitchen, sometimes, late at night. The light in the chalet at Vail . . . try again . . . the light coming through the trees . . . think about it, *feel* it. Then picture and feel the next image . . . is that the right one? *Even though we ain't got money;* Colorado light. Oh, God, start again.

"I don't know if it matters," Anna said, smiling at me approvingly. It was silent. Outside, her dad worked on the truck. It's awful, I thought, that you can fake it. The words I'd read meant nothing.

Dear Diary: The world is only in the mind and I guess that's exactly what the problem is.

On the last day of school everyone was friendly. We signed each other's yearbooks. Baltz wrote: "It's hard to imagine you're really leaving this place. You're a cool guy. Loloma isn't going to be the same without you and all your wiseass comments."

There was a graduation dance at the Camelback Inn. The palm trees were lit up; they were beautiful against the night sky. Douggy and I sat out by the pool. John Friedman talked to me for a while. Bruce didn't come; I wondered where he was. I knew this party was only the beginning of the evening. There would be others, later, that I wouldn't go to, out in the desert; everyone would get high and screw. I looked at the moving light reflections in the pool. Mrs. Binder came over on her crutches; she told me she hoped I would come back and visit from time to time.

"Whenever I look at that beautiful piece of stained glass, I think of you and Bruce. That was such a lovely thought." For a moment I regretted I was leaving.

How long is a moment? How long does it take to have a feeling, a thought? Where in the mind-fuzz does it begin or end?

———

I rode my bike along the canal through the warm shadows falling on the olive-strewn gravel. I had cleaned out my locker that afternoon; in the evening, I was going down to headquarters to stuff envelopes. Dad, I told myself, believes in direct mail; Stan Rouse says it's a waste of time. But it gives people something to do. That's important: giving people something to do. So they don't know there's *nothing* to do.

A feeling came to me, enclosed in a memory. If I can bring back the feeling three times, then I'll be in the world—I'll be in balance with it. Remember Nanna's farm. The turned earth, the fuzz on the cucumbers, the flaking picket fence; recall the *precise* feeling that goes with those images. If I can find it three times, if I can hold it all in my mind, I'll be all right. The first time comes easily. The second takes some work: I have to repeat the words again and again until I get the feeling. Farm, picket fence, cucumber. Picket fence, farm, cucumber. Farm, cucumber, picket fence. OK to vary the order? I rode through the eucalyptus shade. The third time's the most difficult. So much rests on it: the fading possibility of return. After a while, I've got the feeling of the light on the cucumbers, *and* Nanna's farm, *and* the picket fence. Or I'm content that I've come close enough.

But then I'm not sure. Maybe if I ignore the doubt it will go away. There's a figure following me. I know I will have to turn around to see if it's there. To see if I've finished the series of thoughts, the image-feelings. But by turning, by looking, I'll make the figure be there. Maybe I *will* be able to resist; but it makes me so anxious to not know whether I'll turn around. The only way to not be anxious *is* to turn around. I know I shouldn't; I shouldn't give in to the doubt. I shouldn't look. Then I'll have to do the series again. But eventually I will have to turn around— or the doubt will keep following me.

I could smell the eucalyptus in the air. I probably haven't gotten the image-feelings *quite* right. If I try again, maybe I can do it. Maybe I can reach *completion*. I know this won't happen; I'll never stop. The day, an endless bright glare. The figure is right behind me; eventually I will have to turn and look; I know this will happen; the more often it has, the more certain I am that it will again. That I will again. Look. I turn and look.

(It was something like that.)

Then I have to do it again. Three becomes one. The next three: six, then nine. If I reach nine I'll be all right. But nine is much *more* difficult. It's hard to get feelings out of words that many times.

Nanna's farm, the cucumber's fuzz, the light on the fence. When the images are clear you're really there. Nanna's farm, the cucumbers

Sometimes I'd convince myself the series was done, and then I'd be able to stop, or to stop *it*. I didn't know what the difference was (or there was no way to know). The moments when I stopped felt blanketlike. They happened, mostly, when I was alone. It was harder when people were around. I know, I thought, how to choose what to do or what to say. But I don't know how to choose what to think, I thought.

I had hoped it would end before summer. But it hadn't. Now I hoped it would end before fall. We campaigned. Sharon and I handed out leaflets at the mall. Connie had a coffee; we went to her condo for the first time. The hallways smelled of bacon. There were two dozen people, mostly women; I guessed they were from her church. Her sister wore a neck brace because of the whiplash she'd gotten in her accident. I was glad Connie's nephews hadn't come. Everyone was well dressed; I wasn't. Dad gave a short talk (as he always did at coffees) and then chatted comfortably with the women. Jason and I sat on Connie's flowery green sofa.

Dad challenged Scanlon to a debate and the women applauded. "Any time, any place," Dad said. "What are you hiding from, Congressman?" He had even issued a joint press release with Alger "Save the Babies" Johnson, demanding a debate. Johnson had said that Dad, although he was wrong about killing babies, was a moral individual. Dad had even thought of holding a debate with him, with an empty chair for Scanlon; Mr. Nachmann didn't think this was a good idea. Jason said Dad should put a dummy on the stage and debate it. "You could get a ventriloquist to do Scanlon." Jason had a lot of ideas. One day he and Mrs. Sklar went to a speech Scanlon was giving. "Why won't you debate Nat Grosfeld?" Mrs. Sklar had asked during the Q and A.

I noticed, on one of Connie's shelves, the book on reincarnation. Through the window I saw, next to the parking lot, a small pool. Shining, a dime in the sun.

The Gunderson Ranch, the creosote, the green, leafy tunnel on the way to Nanna's house.

I'd completed the series, done all the feeling-image-thoughts. But how could I be *sure* I'd had these thoughts? That's only what I think now, I thought. There's no way to be certain that it's what I thought a few seconds ago. I'm not *sure* yesterday happened, let alone a few seconds ago. Might be a trick of the mind, I thought, sitting on Connie's sofa. The only thing I can be sure of is what's in my mind in the *Immediate Now*. The other stuff, the memory of the feeling-image-thoughts, that's just residue, shadow residue. Jason took a brownie from a plate held by Connie's sister. A picture of Kennedy on the wall. The only way to be *really* sure I've done a thought, I thought, is to fully remember the thought, the Gunderson Ranch, the creosote—but if I remember the thought, I thought, if I fully remember having it so that I *know* I've had it, then I'll be having it again, which means I'll be having the image-thought a fourth time, when I'm supposed to have it three times, and so I'll be ruining the sequence.

Maybe I don't *have* to. Maybe I *did* get it right before—but I'm not sure. OK. Here I go again. It feels good to go again; a fresh start. A tiny bit of optimism. I will really finish this time. The Gunderson Ranch. The creosote. Connie's sister, in her neck brace, in front of me, holding the plate of brownies. Smiling, I took one—something always interferes. I need to be in a silent place, I thought, so I can get done with the thoughts. The creosote. The coffee ended and we walked out, in the scorching sun, to the car. . . .

Hello my name is Harry Cemetery. If you're good you go to heaven if you're bad you go to Hello . . .

It wasn't supposed to be like this. The journey I'd been on had been so long, I'd read so many books, and I'd thought satori was near; I'd had such a head start, and now *this*, for no reason, when I'd come so close. The poem had almost been complete. I'd wanted to be perfect, but I'd failed to destroy the self. Year of Dead Birdshit, Mark.

———

Rouse decided not to use the footage of us talking about Dad. Dad liked it but it made the film too long. Instead, there was a brief shot of us climbing Squaw Peak, and then another in which we stood, holding rackets, on a tennis court. Then Dad, in his office, talked about the importance of family.

Dad still thought Mr. Nachmann wasn't doing enough to raise money. "He wants me to make all the phone calls," Dad complained. "That's what he's supposed to do." The crowds at most events were small; Rouse said we shouldn't worry—it was the middle of the summer. Dad began, again, to cancel appearances. He spent a lot of time in his room, working on his speeches and practicing his Spanish.

"Soy un hombre de familia. Trabajaré para Ustedes si votan por mi."

Little Willy. The ocean, at night, in San Diego, the waves crashing. The light on the floor at Anna's. Little Willy, shimmyshuffling across the soccer field.

In July we went to a parade in Payson, in the mountains. The air was cool. A small crowd—and all the candidates. Bond for governor. Murphy for Senate. Cruz for attorney general. Wynne for mine inspector. Dad thought he should be third in the parade, after Murphy and Bond, but instead he was fourth, after Cruz. Dad thought Congress was more important than attorney general, but attorney general was statewide. Still, he seemed in a better mood. We rode in a pickup with balloons tied to the side. A few got loose and floated off. Sharon and Mom held a sign: *Scanlon: When's the debate?* I held it for a while, too. Dad waved to the people on the street; some of them held signs. I could smell the pine needles in the dusty air. The sky was immense; I wanted to stop counting. Later there was a barbecue at the fairgrounds. I stood next to Dad while he shook hands. Cruz stood a few feet away. He was taller than Dad, and darker, and had a bigger smile. All the cars had his bumper stickers; Jason said they probably put them on while no one was looking. "I'll have proof," he said, "if they put one on our car."

People don't know you're not there, I thought. It's weird. Mom doesn't know, Sharon doesn't, Jason doesn't. How are they to know that I'm not in time the way they are? I thought. It passes differently for me now. I just wait for it to end. Oh blahblurblah. It won't, ever.

Nanna had thought so much of me. *She'd loved me very much.* I'd come so close. I'd wanted to be like a blooming flower, unaware of its blooming. The poem was a flower, a blooming; now this . . . I've let everybody down.

Even if they don't know yet, they will soon. I don't know how to control how I think, I thought. A kind of fucking koan, I thought. There is no little man inside. *It* continued. All day: the orange blossom scent and the diving boys; Norwich's department store, the walkway there, in the afternoon; Cheryl McCrae. The boys diving plus the orange blossom's scent; the walkway at Norwich's, Cheryl

I asked him if his statements were a pronouncement that what he had called seeing was in effect a better way than merely looking at

things. He said that the eyes of man could perform both functions, but neither of them was better than the other.

I insisted that our argument could logically be stretched to saying that if things were supposed to be so equal why not also choose death?

"Many men of knowledge do that," he said. "One day they may simply disappear."

I told Mom I wanted to see Dr. Kurtz again.

"Are you OK?" she asked, concerned.

"I just think I need a sort of well-child checkup," I said.

"A well-child checkup," she repeated softly. "Yes, OK, a well-child checkup."

I explained the images, the counting, the series of feeling-thoughts. It felt good, at last, to be telling someone. He put out his cigarette and looked at me intently. "I want it to stop," I continued. "But it's like I'm trying to find the person who is supposed to do the stopping but then its like there's just a mirror looking into the mirror."

I had to do some images while I spoke, but I continued. I wasn't sure he was following me.

"I mean I know I should just stop. But it isn't that easy. I mean to have willpower. There's supposed to be an *I* in control but I don't really understand how *that's* supposed to work." I tried to sound humorous, confiding. "I mean, I look inside to find the *I* but then what's there? Maybe you need to use the illusion to stop the illusion. If I could just figure out what the trick is," I continued, my voice growing urgent and serious. I knew my time was almost up. "Since there isn't *a* self anyway—I know there's a way to do it, and I think I'm getting a little closer—I mean I feel a little closer today," I concluded hopefully, feeling, now that I was in his office, that perhaps things weren't so bad. I didn't want to exaggerate.

He nodded. "I *am* glad you came to see me, Mark. And I'm glad it's getting better. I will have to admit I don't entirely follow everything you're saying. Adolescence can be a time of great confusion. But I'm sure you'll be fine. You're such a bright kid. You know there's a book I think might be helpful to you. It's called *How to Be Your Own Best Friend*. I'd like to give you a copy. How about that?"

"Sure."

The feeling I had in the backyard in the night under the stars, the power surging through me. The road to Casa Grande. *Hey, Mr. Tambourine Man, play a song for* . . . Start again. The yard at night, feel it, the birds singing, the power

Scanlon agreed to debate Dad at a local TV station with three reporters asking questions. They disagreed about who the reporters would be; Dad didn't want anyone from the *Journal-Observer*. Scanlon didn't want "Save the Babies" Johnson. Dad thought he should be there. He had the right to be—and he would help Dad. After several weeks they compromised: no *Journal-Observer*, no Right to Life candidate.

Johnson said Dad was a hypocrite.

———

There go the hypocrites dressed in black. *Go tell it on the mountain, to let my people go*. We'd sung that once, at a creative seder; the smell of mesquite burning in the desert. Joni Mitchell singing: *Trina wears her wampum beads*. Bruce, and the smell of mown grass. I will try to remember these things again, and this time I'll get them right. I tried. I had it right, I thought, for a second, a perilous second. Then I had to do it again

.

———

The debate was in a week. "You've got to take this opportunity, Nat," Mr. Nachmann said. "Get in there and deliver a knock-out punch. If you want people to fight for you, you've got to do a little more fighting yourself."

"He should keep his mouth shut," Mom commented. "It's pretty easy for all these people to give your father advice. Do this. Do that. But damn it, they're not the ones out on the frontline."

But, I thought, Mr. Nachmann's right. Dad isn't trying hard enough. It's a half-campaign, I half-thought.

I sat in the campaign office stuffing envelopes with Jason, Sharon, and Mrs. Sklar.

"I can't wait for this debate," said Mrs. Sklar. "I just know it's going to turn things around. Scanlon won't know what hit him. His positions are *so* indefensible."

"We've just got to put some vodka in his water when he gets on stage," Jason said.

"Yeah," said Sharon, playfully. "That's a plan."

"So, how are we going to put the secret plan into action?" Mrs. Sklar asked. "Did you see the latest poll? Your father came up two points."

My father, my father, my father.

"I'm ready for lunch," said Jason.

"So who wants to go to the sandwich shop?" Mrs. Sklar asked.

In front of me there's a pile of envelopes and a pile of

brochures and a list of registered voters; above me, a Phoenix precinct map. The ones we've canvassed have green dots. I have a dish of water and a little sponge for sealing envelopes. I have paper cuts. There's a bumper sticker above the water cooler; there's a squarish light. I can't be in the room anymore, I can't do my thoughts and be with people at the same time, but I can't not do my thoughts.

"I'll go get the sandwiches."

I walk out into the light. There are currents and forces and shadows and areas of brightness; I don't know if I should pay attention to them or not. And feelings—so many specific feelings. The feeling I had turning the corner behind Safeway on my bike when the sun came through the clouds a certain way. I have to remember that three times. I walk in the sunlight down the sidewalk. Once I'm done with the Safeway memory I have to remember the words to "Space Oddity," and the feeling that goes with "Space Oddity," the feeling that went with it, once, when I was in the art room with Bruce. For a moment, a whiff of Bruce—a blue-green color in my mind. Horses. Where is he? I can't be distracted. I have to retrieve the Bruce and "Space Oddity" feeling three times before I can rest. Three times—or five? I'm no longer sure. If I fuck up on three, I can go to five. It's never four. Well sometimes, but not often.

Sometimes the feeling-thoughts are sort of combinations. The feeling I have when, at the same time, or *nearly* the same time, in nearly simultaneous succession, I remember a song and a place. Neil Young: *See the lonely boy out on the weekend*—that plus the scent of pine needles in the air that I'd smelled walking around the cabin at camp. And a third thing, say, Anna's living room. Or maybe not that—maybe Schaeffer by the pool at the graduation party. No, not that, the smell of a meadow at dawn.

Which meadow? I'm trying to remember what it felt like the last time I remembered these things together; it's difficult to do the combinations. I *do* have the power to do this. But it's hard to get it right several times. I know I shouldn't be doing this. Sometimes I have to summon even more ineffable feelings that I can't connect to any memory.

_____ _____ _____. _____. _____ _____ _____.

Calm for a moment. The feeling-thought-whatever series slows, retreats. I can sort of think. I walk by the Laundromat; cars go by in the light. Where are the drivers going? From Phoenix to Scottsdale, Scottsdale to Mesa, Mesa to Phoenix. Who are they? Accountants and lawyers and brokers; I don't know what they do, they sell things, buy things, a few of them make things, but most don't. They talk, drive back and forth, get older. Flesh in steel on asphalt in motion. What do they tell themselves the point is? How can they stand all the light? There's nowhere to go. All a huge illusion. Beneath Phoenix, the flat, dry earth.

There's no one on the sidewalk. It's taking me a long time to get to the sandwich shop. I might as well be dead. I am; so unnecessary; my fault. I could just step out into the traffic; why not? Because someday there's a chance I might return—just a chance. It would be so easy to walk into the traffic.

The sprinklers in front of the dentist's office hissed; I walked in the shadow of the Berge Ford billboard; a paper bag lay on a grass patch. Kick it or not? Predestined? Not kicking: an action too. Around me, rectangles, beige and tan and white and silver, rectangles and squares, light gray-green and silver, flat or shimmering, plain and still. I walk very slowly, then I stop; sometimes I just have to stand still and try to recall. I'm a shadow on the sidewalk; what would people think if they walked by and saw me, standing motionless? What would I tell them? Were there other people in the world like me—how many? I left the bill-board's shadow. The dentist's sprinklers grazed the sidewalk.

____ ____ ____. ___. ____ ___ ___.

People don't know that it's possible to not to be in their world. They don't realize another world exists. I am, I thought, one of the few who knows. A gasoline puddle shone in the road. The only noise: traffic. Although I can't tell who my companions are, I thought, I know they exist, the ones who will gradually be left behind, who'll end up in corners. People will think we're vague. We'll slip out of the world. I'll die, like the rest of us, without anyone knowing what has happened. _____ _____ _____. The thing I'm most afraid of: dying trying to finish a series of thoughts.

"Two tuna fish, a turkey on rye, a grilled cheese, three large Pepsis, and one Sprite."

A gray-yellow light in the sky.

I don't know what it's like for any of the others who are like me. Their minds must be strange in ways I can't imagine. No one could imagine the way mine has become strange. Though they don't know I'm gone, I thought, I miss Mom, Anna . . . Bruce. Awful—there are holes in the world and most people don't know—but it can't be explained. I don't *think* it can be. Gasoline fumes, sunlight. I wish I were mad. If I were mad I'd be a torrential river—out of control, not in. I'd say strange things; I'd be dangerous. People would notice. *It* wouldn't be inexplicable. My mind would be filled with weird images. Birds and rats. I'd hallucinate, like Aqualung, and then I'd describe these hallucinations; people would understand. It would be colorful and interesting.

Cars pass me. Perhaps *this* exists alongside madness, I thought, an old, parallel road next to the highway, which most don't even see, which isn't on the map, which has never been described.

_____ _____ _____ . _____ . _____ _____ _____ .

It's my fault. I used to have such promise. My poem and vichyssoise; the pathway, lined with olive trees, in back of the temple; Bruce, Schaeffer, Baltz. I can't quite get it.

I have to do it again.

I opened the office door. Sharon went through the sandwiches. "I didn't want turkey, Doofus," she said. "I told you tuna."

"He probably got distracted," Mrs. Sklar said, smiling. "I bet there was a cute girl at the sandwich shop."

"No," I said.

Rouse sits in back of us, next to Mr. Nachmann. Mrs. Sklar is next to Mom.

"Congressman, your priority if reelected?"

"I'll continue to preserve our liberty from the international communist threat. Now I know my good friend Nat is a well-meaning man—I'm not questioning that. But being well-meaning isn't going to be enough to protect our freedom. Eternal vigilance, it was once said, is the price of freedom. But my opponent—he's a member of the ACLU! Now maybe he doesn't know the ACLU defends communists. Did you know that, Nat?"

"They defend everyone's rights," Dad said, gravely, shaking his head, pointing his finger. "Yours, too."

"I say 'no thanks' to that. I don't need the help of an

organization that wants to subvert our way of life. I notice you didn't answer the question. Here's another one. Did you know your friend César Chavez is a *known* communist sympathizer? Just where do you draw the line?"

"I came here tonight to discuss the issues that matter to real people. Issues that matter to the family that's trying to make ends meet. Let's talk about my economic plan."

"He came off as a lunatic, *I* thought," Mom said, later, in the parking lot. "You were great, honey."

Mr. Nachmann shook his head.

Time stretches blurrily. It gets hotter. Things will be better in the fall.

The mountain in back of the Nachmann's at night plus Cat Stevens: *Catch Bull at Four* in the dark living room, plus the color blue; Elton John: *I remember when rock was young, me and Suzy,* being on the hill at camp and the number five, and something about Schaeffer, his Jim Morrison hair, and a white color somehow infusing those images; the hallway at Connie's condominium, that plus the number seven, plus the drive to the airport.

Maybe that will do. Maybe that's the third feeling, I thought. The third feeling-thought. It's so confusing. I can't be *certain*. I just want to be certain; I am certain, no I'm not. If you think you're going to think a thought, you might as well think it, I thought—you're *already* thinking it by thinking you're going to think it.

The mountain in back of the Nachmanns' . . .

Nixon resigned in August. Soon after, Scanlon began a barrage of commercials. The documentary was finished, but there still wasn't enough money to air it more than a few times. Most of the unions' financial support was going to Cruz; this was Mr. Nachmann's fault, Dad said; it was because of the stupid mistake he'd made with the brochures.

Dad began to make more speeches in South Phoenix; Reverend Stephens set them up. He and Mrs. Hanson worked on a get-out-the-vote plan. Alger Johnson appeared at several Scanlon events.

"You're a baby-killer!" he would shout; then he'd be dragged away.

He and Dad both came up, a little, in the polls. The Porters made a contribution, it wasn't as much as Dad had hoped for, but then Ted Ortiz, who owned Rosita's Mexican restaurant, donated thirty thousand dollars, which no one had expected.

"I guess he appreciates all the chimichangas we've eaten there," Dad said. Posha then decided to loan Dad another ten thousand dollars, which meant the documentary could be shown several extra times.

Mondale came out for a fund-raiser. Scanlon called him an ultraliberal extremist. The birdbrain commercial aired again and again.

One day in the car on the way to a speech, Dad said, "You seem a little quiet, Mark. Is everything OK?"

"Yeah," I said, my nose against the window, "everything's OK."

I thought I might expand "The Year of Dead Birds" to include a section on Nixon's resignation. I tried to write it but nothing came. I can put words on paper, I thought, but I know they're false.

In September I started at Pueblo. It had walkways lined with olive trees and I was left alone. The teachers didn't know me so they didn't expect anything. I ate lunch by myself in back of the library. Ford had pardoned Nixon and Dad thought this might help the Democrats. Even the *Journal-Observer* questioned the decision. Bond pulled ahead in the race for governor. Dad hadn't moved much in the polls since September. But the crowds at some of his speeches grew larger, and Mrs. Hanson said the get-out-the-vote plan was going well. Althea Scanlon, who hadn't been seen for months, began to appear with her husband. She didn't say anything, but she smiled.

"I think they've got her drugged," Jason commented.

Even though it wasn't in our district, we went to a parade in Chandler.

The Gunderson Ranch; the ocean's crashing waves in San Diego at night; Bruce on his bike plus Neil Young: *See the lonely boy,* in the hazy oleander light, plus _____ _____ _____;

Dad spent election day shaking hands outside a polling place downtown at Watkins School. That night everyone came to headquarters. Mrs. Sklar, Mrs. Hanson, the Nachmanns, Connie, Lloyd, Beth Fineman. There were thirty people and several pizzas and everyone was quiet when the first returns came in: Scanlon way ahead.

"We don't know where those votes are from," cautioned Mrs. Hanson. But then Dad's numbers began to improve. And "Save the Babies" was doing better than anyone expected. I ought to be able to feel *this* moment, I thought. Sharon and

Beth Fineman started jumping up and down when, at ten-thirty, Dad moved ahead. Jason jumped up and down, too. Mom gripped Dad's hand.

If I start *counting,* we're going to lose, I thought, as I snuck out the backdoor into the darkness. Walking through the parking lot, I heard the traffic whoosh. My mind was sort of clear *just* at the moment when he moved ahead. I don't *know* if I caused the votes, but I *might* have. It felt as if I had. Listen to your feelings. I traced my fingers along the cool, dusty surfaces of the cars. If your mind is in balance with the world, I thought, the world will be in balance. Empty yourself, the way of the Tao, all things will come to you, we'll win, the universe is in your mind, the precincts in Peoria. This *might* be true so I must stop *it;* maybe *it* doesn't matter but maybe it does. The dining room at Le Chemin, white napkins like white mountains, the grapefruit through the window; *Major Tom to ground control*—so what is the third feeling? But the pressure is too great now. I can't stop *it* so Dad will lose: my punishment for thinking I'm so important, for thinking that what I think matters, for doing this stupid shit. Buddha-God: I *promise* I'll stop if you let Dad win. I sort of stopped. It was quiet. I could faintly hear the noise from the office; I'd wandered over to a Dumpster at the edge of the parking lot. A dog barked. The scent of gasoline, of creosote. I'm calm so he will win. The silence outside, the big flat silence, the noise within: equal, sort of—Bruce and Major Tom—stop, don't go into it, but maybe you already have—Bruce and Major Tom—I can't stop *it,* I thought; I'm breaking my promise to Buddha-God. I guess I have to go in.

———

Something was happening. More people had shown up. I wondered if anyone had noticed I'd been gone. There were more pizzas from Papago Pizza, and Mom and Dad were shaking people's hands.

"Hush," Mom said, pointing to the TV.

"The real surprise tonight," said the newscaster, "is in the Fifth District, where a surprisingly close contest is taking shape."

Everyone clapped. Jason hooted.

"We're still not sure where those numbers are from," Mr. Nachmann warned.

Around eleven-thirty, Scanlon pulled ahead. He led by only a few hundred votes at first, but then that number grew, and people began to go home, and we ran out of pizza. Mom wondered whether she should try to order more; she wasn't sure there was anyplace still open. Some more precincts from South Phoenix reported, and Dad was again within a thousand votes, and the newsman commented that we might not know the results until morning, but then Scanlon's margin started slowly to increase, and around one-thirty Dad told Mrs. Sklar and the few others who were still there that it really was time to go home.

2

"It's such a vindication for your father," Mom commented one afternoon not long after the election. We stood, drying dishes, in the kitchen. "He's really proven something. You know I worried whether he could handle losing. But the fact that it was so close . . . I guess that makes it sort of a *moral* victory," she said, as if to persuade herself. "He seems to be doing *fine*."

"*I* think so," I said.

From the living room, I could hear Jason changing channels.

"I was concerned," she continued, "that since it *was* so close he'd think he should have done *just* a little more. But he's convinced he did everything he realistically possibly could. I think that's true."

"I agree," I said, and then added helpfully, "that profile really seemed to boost his spirits."

"You know, I think you're right."

The profile had appeared in *The New York Times* a few days after the election:

"One of the most unexpectedly tight races nationwide turned out to be in Arizona's Fifth District. Democratic challenger Nat Grosfeld came within three percentage points of unseating incumbent Jack Scanlon. Grosfeld, whose bid was helped by a challenge from Right to Life candidate Alger Johnson, is now being talked about as a possible contender in the upcoming '76 Senate race. "He showed how Democrats are going to have to run if they want to compete in states like Arizona," commented Jack McCarthy, editorial page editor of the Valley Journal-Observer. *"He was outspent almost two to one, and got off to a very slow start. But he used his money effectively, saving his firepower for the end, and stayed away from some of the left-wing environmental issues with*

which he's been associated in the past. The Republicans are saying this is a one-time fluke. But they might want to watch out. The demographics out here are changing."

"Of course," Mom added dryly, handing me a spatula, "it doesn't hurt to know someone at the *Times*." The article had been written by the son of an old friend of Posha's. "You know," she continued, "I'm not *sure* where all this leaves us as a family. It's something we'll have to figure out together. I'll tell you," she mused, more intimately, "I'm not sure your father realizes—and I don't want to say this to him—in some ways I'm glad we lost. I *saw* what politics can do to you. He was quite depressed there for awhile."

I nodded.

"One thing that's come out of this," she continued, trying on a more upbeat, half-combative voice, "is I don't think *I'm* quite as naive as I used to be."

You weren't naive, I thought, wiping some flour from the counter. I wonder if she believes what she's saying. I don't know how her world works. Her tone, shifts so unpredictably, so suddenly sometimes. How does it all connect?

"I always thought of politics," she continued, "idealistically. But now I've seen it up close. All that petty squabbling. The worst thing was realizing there were people who'd encouraged your father to run who never believed he had a chance. They had to get *someone* to run against Scanlon. They made a lot of promises. But then they didn't come through."

"He showed them," I said, through my thoughts.

"He certainly did. Still, it's depressing when you find out people are like that."

"The Nachmanns?"

"No," she said. "I'm not saying they weren't also *used* in that way. By DelBlanco. He was the one who really pushed your father to run. Him—and some of those other power brokers. You know they really built up his ego. I think men are often vulnerable to that. Then they let him down."

Dusk was falling, outside, on the mountains. My parents and the Nachmanns had hardly spoken during the last weeks before the election. "You know he wanted your father to go after Scanlon personally," Mom had explained, a few days ago. "But he wouldn't. He didn't want them making false accusations."

"About Nanna?" I'd guessed.

"Yes. Largely that. About the Rosenbergs. And other people she knew. Stuff."

"Did Scanlon know all that?" I'd asked.

"He could have. Maybe not. Posha was quite worried. Your father didn't think it was worth the risk."

I nodded, now, listening to her. "I'm not sure," she said, "what will happen with the Nachmanns. I don't know if that friendship can ever be the same."

"What's that mean for Beth Shalom?"

"I'm not sure anyone has the energy for it."

I nodded. It takes so much energy, I thought, to keep talking—and to get done what has to get done in my head. To keep track of where I am in the image-series—*and* talk. Weird the way *it* continues at the same time that *things* continue. The refrigerator, the sunlight, Mom, me. Weird I can carry on a conversation; the words come out of my mouth the same as always, only with, I guess, a little less energy. It takes so much to do what I have to do, to be sure which number I'm at—but still the words come, and the world continues. Everything is different, everything the same, the sunlight on the blue kitchen table and the white refrigerator.

The dark woods on the mountain at camp. The branches. I have to capture the feeling.

We were quiet a moment. In the living room, Jason kept changing the channel. I could smell, through the thoughts, Mom's scent, an apple scent, her bath oil or perfume. "I'm glad," Mom said, "he decided not to go for a recount. When I hear your sister talking about two years from now, the Senate—I know he's tempted. But I think there are more important things than winning elections. And writing books. And all the things I've thought were important because your father's family thinks they are."

"I know."

"Well, we don't have to decide about that Senate race now," she said. "You know what I think? I think I want to start living for the moment. Not to be always planning. And you know, in a way, I'd like to start doing something more for myself."

"At Jewish Family and Children's Services?"

If only, I thought, I could stop *it* at least while I'm with her. But wanting that just makes it worse. The dark woods at camp. I want to care about what she's feeling. The dark woods at camp. The dark . . . I want to love *people;* but I don't, not really. The dark woods; Anna's living room in the afternoon; the tea, the silverfish, the fire; the white stucco walls at Norwich's;

"Possibly. Possibly not. Maybe I should try finishing that article for *Ms.*"

The tea, the silverfish.

"Or maybe something *totally* new. What do you think? You always have good suggestions."

She's sharing with me, I thought, and I'm not taking advantage of it. All I want is to be here, in the kitchen, while the words are spoken. To not have to pretend. Terrifying how easy it is to pretend. To perform undetected all day. And then the next. I'm good at this—excellent. There's no way she could know. All I want is to return to the room where I'm standing, in the light, with my mother. If I can't, I want to be able to hope that someday I'll return to some room, any room. For a few minutes before I die. That will be enough.

"And what about you?" she asked. She seemed to be trying to find me. Though I stood next to her in the white, lit room. "The last few months must have been hard. Starting a new school, not knowing if you're going to stay."

"No," I said vaguely. "It's been OK."

"I think it could be awfully disorienting," she tried again.

"I guess I'm coping." My voice pushed her away. Surfaces hummed in the kitchen light. I hoped, a little, that she would see through me. I want to go back to the world for *more* than a moment. I know I won't have a life, but maybe I won't miss out on everything. Perhaps someday I'll awaken.

"Sometimes I think *you're* better at coping with things than *I* am," she mused, handing me a pot. The aluminum gleamed. The drying towel was damp. "Are you still feeling it was the right choice to go to Pueblo?"

Maybe there are things she wants to tell me, too. It doesn't matter, I thought, where I am. At my new school, no one tormented or spoke to me. One boy followed me, sometimes, imitating the way I walked. It's better, I thought, to be where no one knows me.

"Oh, yeah," I said. "I guess so." It's not a great distance: the present is right here; it would be like stepping to the other side of the patio door. But I can't. A matter of will; I need the will to stop myself. But where in the shadowy cavernous space of my self or whatever will I find that?

I want to be outside the numbers. The only way out of the numbers is through the numbers. I know this isn't so, but what other way is there?

"Sometimes," she said, "it's hard to know if you've done the right thing."

She senses something's wrong, I thought. Maybe she feels she shouldn't push too hard. She's supposed to respect my boundaries. I'm a teenager.

"Yeah," I said.

Maybe we *are* together and *are* communicating, I thought, even *while* this is happening. Maybe you can be close to someone even if you're not there, even if you aren't *present in the moment*. Maybe when you look back later you'll see you somehow were together. Somewhere beneath the counting.

"Why don't you go see how your father is doing?" Mom suggested. "He's trying to finish those thank-you letters. Ask him if he needs anything."

A crumpled mulberry leaf in the light. Houses in San Francisco: picture them. Water in the canal; *ripple in still water*, coolness. The leaf, the pink and white houses, the muddy canal water

"Do you need anything?"

Dad was sitting in a patio chair, in his tennis shirt, writing. The hair on his arms: a golden halo, sort of. Sparky at his feet. "No," he said, looking up, "that's all right. But thanks, Mark."

Sparky ran after a bird. The pool hoses broke the surface. Through the window, in the kitchen, I saw Mom doing dishes, alone.

"Here's another letter saying I ought to ask for a recount. Jeez. It's really flattering," he said, smiling. "So many people have wanted me to do that."

"Isn't it kind of late now?" I asked.

"You're right. I'm not reconsidering. Although," he confided, "I know your sister wants me to. Funny—I don't think I understood at *all* how important this was to her. You know sometimes," he continued, "you've got to let things go. You probably didn't realize this, Mark, but I think I went through a little midlife crisis last summer, when I really understood I probably didn't have a chance. I felt disappointed in a lot of people. Myself more than anyone. But then I guess I realized: the things you think are important aren't always the *truly* important things. Once I stopped worrying so much about winning and started saying what *I* wanted, I started to enjoy it a little. If I did it again . . . but your mother's been through enough. And there are things *I'd* like to be doing besides fighting losing battles. I want to be able to spend more time with all of you. Play more tennis. Maybe start a vegetable garden."

How much to disbelieve? Maybe he *is* different. Maybe he's not like me. What's anyone like? There's no way to know and then you die. You spend your whole life thinking *maybe* you're starting to understand people and *maybe* you're finding out who they really are, thinking you're beginning to understand how things work. Collecting little moments of truth. Pebbles on the beach. You think you're getting somewhere even though you know, really, that you aren't.

And then you die.

"Look," he said, an expression of contentment arriving on his face like the light on Squaw Peak. He pointed toward the birds in the sky. "You know I sometimes think it's just fascinating to watch the way they fly."

I didn't know what to say. "I guess I'm going back in."

"You know, Mark," he added, as I turned to leave, "I just want to say: I've been noticing how much more self-confident you've seemed lately."

The crumpled mulberry leaf in the light. _____ ____ _____.
_____ ____ _____.

"He doesn't need anything," I said to Mom.

"Thanks, Mark," she said. She was in the middle of a conversation with Jason. I wasn't sure what to do. Maybe, I thought, I'll go and look at my poem. Maybe I can *try* to work on it.

Outside of me things happened. Jason became popular. His team won in Little League and he went on his first date. Jewish Family and Children's Services offered Mom a paying position. She decided to accept. She finished "Notes of a Candidate's Wife" and it was published in *Ms.* Mrs. Goldman got better. Baltz was in a dirt bike accident; it was in the paper. Connie quit; she'd been hired as a receptionist in a chiropractor's office. Richard went to Berkeley; Ian to the community college. I heard that Bruce had been thrown out of school. He was going to be sent to a military academy, somewhere in the East. Anna told me Nicola had become involved with some Edgar Cayce enthusiasts. Through them, she'd met a publisher in New York who was interested in her novel. Sharon and Beth

Fineman started to smoke a lot of pot. Occasionally they asked me to join them. One time Dad caught them; nothing much happened. People continued to talk to my father about running for Senate. Spring came and Saigon fell. I was left alone, mostly, at school. My parents forgave Rabbi Horowitz. He'd sent them a note after the election. "Nathaniel—even though we've had our disagreements, you are, like your father, a genuine man of principle." Mrs. Sklar told Mom she'd seen Horowitz at the mall with Mrs. Goldman; they might, she thought, be dating. Mrs. Sklar was upset. Mom wasn't.

There were days when I thought I might be able to stop counting. Days when *it* subsided a little.

Nanna's barn, the light on the cucumbers, their fuzz, the white picket fence. The white picket fence, the fuzz. The light in back of Safeway plus Aqualung. The road to Casa Grande. The word *Colorado*. One two three, one two three, one two three. The birds in the azure air. The birds in the azure air. The

Long ago I'd had a dream. We were at the Desert Palm. Mom had been inside, talking to Mrs. Sklar. A boy had stood across from me—we were separated by a green stoplight. The light turned red. The boy turned into Frankenstein.

I sat, late one afternoon, in my room. Mrs. Weinberg was coming for dinner. There's half an hour left, I thought, as I shifted in my beanbag chair, trying to get my position right. Several days before I'd gathered the courage to call Anna. I told her I would come to visit some day after school. I was always afraid now, when I spoke to her, that she'd see through me.

Anna had told me how well life was going for her. Duncan wanted to include one of her poems in an anthology he was editing; he'd said she should visit him sometime. She might go to San Francisco over the summer. And she'd met a rancher. She had dreamt about this last spring. She didn't know yet if it would work out between them, but it felt right. If it did work, she'd leave the school. She was ready.

I remembered her telling me, a year before, the dream about the rancher. I am not, I thought, at all like her. She asked if I was writing. Just some really short things, I'd told her. She knows, I thought, that I'm not the same.

The boy with the headband on the hill at camp, Neil Young, birdsong.

The light in back of Safeway.

The Gunderson Ranch; the creosote . . .

I sank into the beanbag chair. The sun was going behind the mountain but its light still came through the shutters. I felt myself sink; the Styrofoam beans rearranged themselves beneath me. I tried to rearrange my thoughts; or they tried to rearrange themselves. Perhaps I could quiet myself, in the time before dinner—just a little.

From the floor I picked up the manila folder with my poems. I had written a few during the last several months. They *looked* like poems; the words were placed in a certain way, but they were, I knew, just words on paper.

Nanna and Anna had had such hope for me. I'd thought that through them, through my poem, through all I'd done to cleanse the mirror, to realize that there was no mirror, that I might reach satori. I'd come so far for someone so young.

The Gunderson Ranch. The creosote . . .

I couldn't get the feeling.

I got up and paced around my room. But it didn't matter where I stood. *It* still continued. I'll never get it right, I thought. I have to do it again.

I lay on my bed. I did the series—and, for a moment, calmed myself. This time the feeling of completion lasted a little longer than usual. Breathing slowly, I felt a kind of peace, a gray, warm something. I didn't know where it had come from. Perhaps this will continue for a while, I thought, watching the light waves cross the wall. Perhaps *it* will ebb and flow and then someday be gone. Maybe, someday, I won't even remember it.

The ripples on the wall.

I felt the way I did when I would wake, sometimes, from a dream, uncertain where I was. I looked around my room, at Lilly's empty cage and the clothes piled on the floor. Don't start thinking, I thought, about whether you've done the thoughts. I looked at my bookshelf. *The Chronicles of Narnia. Howl.* The *Tao Te Ching. A Separate Reality.*

I lay there; I thought of getting up. But doing something might disrupt the calm. Could I do something *and* keep the calm? Lying still, thinking about whether or not to move—that was risky, too. I rose cautiously and returned to the beanbag chair. I opened the manila folder and read the letter Posha had sent in response to "The Year of Dead Birds." *"It is important, Mark,"* he wrote, *"to remember that the purpose of art is communication. All of this may mean a lot to you. But you must find a way to make things clear to other people."*

I put the folder in my dresser drawer, next to my underwear, my piggy bank, and Nanna's leaves. Outside I heard Jason and one of his friends splashing in the pool. The gardeners mowed

the lawn. I didn't know if the calm would last. Ten, fifteen minutes to dinner. ____ ____ ____. ____ ____ ____.

Sparky barked; Mrs. Weinberg's car pulled up the driveway. The
doorbell would be ringing soon.

ACKNOWLEDGMENTS

No part of this book gives me as much pleasure as the chance to thank:

For their belief and their insightful criticism from the day I started this book, Cliff Chase and Lynne Tillman. For their faith and for years of patient encouragement and careful readings, Neil Goldberg and Steve Lin. For their generosity, friendship, criticism, and hard work, Michael Ashley, Lauren Cerand, Allen Frame, Lia Gangitano, Hilary Harp, Oliver Herring, Chris Hiebert, Elisabeth Kley, Peter Krashes, Eve Levy, Rose Marie Morse, Carrie Moyer, Joanne Pasila, Elizabeth Schambelan, Ira Silverberg, Ed Stein, John Tevis, and Don Weise. For their love and support, Jonathan Herbert, Laura, and Lucinda.

This book and so much else would not have been possible without Linda Bryant. I can't express how grateful I am to her.

I would also like to thank the MacDowell Colony, the Virginia Center for the Creative Arts, the New York Foundation for the Arts, and the Corporation of Yaddo for their support of my work.

ABOUT THE AUTHOR

Robert Marshall, a writer and visual artist, lives in New York City. His work has appeared in *Blithe House Quarterly* and in the anthologies *Fresh Men 2, Afterwords,* and *Queer 13,* and his artwork has been exhibited widely throughout the United States, Europe, and South America. He is the recipient of a 2005 New York Foundation for the Arts fellowship.